She'd been waiting for him, concerned about him, but when he finally called, he gave her even more to worry about…

Everyone was assembled in the communications room of the headquarters. The men were playfully insulting each other while waiting for Duncan to arrive. Iron Angel got increasingly irritated as time ticked by. She could be downstairs drinking with Little Al, softening the serrated edges of her PTSD, listening to Little Al's sage advice.

Her cell phone rang.

She frowned at the Caller ID. Duncan was late for the meeting—the meeting he called. The meeting was supposed to have started at three—over an hour ago. *This better be good.*

She took a deep breath and answered the call. "Where have you been? I've been worried about you."

"I'm sorry, *chica*, something came up."

Her blood froze in her veins. Wishing she hadn't downed so many shots with Little Al that afternoon, she looked up at Jason, Kearney, and Gunther across the communications room. They were in the middle of some kind of joking, male bonding thing with Joe-Sam.

Eyes pinned on the unsuspecting men, she said, "Did you just call me *chica*?"

The joking stopped. All heads turned toward her. No one blinked. No one moved. No one breathed. *Chica* or *chico* used early in a conversation was code for making a call under duress. Joe-Sam remained seated, but the other three men crowded around her.

Joan Bowman and Duncan are fugitives, but trouble doesn't seem to have any problem finding them...

Joan, Duncan, and Kearney race across the country, barely avoiding capture by the Constitution Defense Legion Task Force. They settle down in the Phoenix area to begin new lives with new identities, unaware that a group of discontented Mexican-Americans called *La Espada*, The Sword, led by an ex-con, Tito Orrozco, has a bone to pick with them because Joan killed Tito's brother while defending a crippled woman during an attack by *La Espada*. Duncan's response to the attack is to form a militia, but his attempts to right the wrongs around him clash with Joan's efforts to keep her life on an even keel as she struggles with PTSD. When traitors within their group lead them all into a trap, everything falls apart and Joan and Duncan are left fighting for their very lives—and each other.

KUDOS for *Hottest Places in Hell*

In *Hottest Places in Hell* by Janet McClintock, Joan Bowman is back with Duncan and Kearney. Now fugitives from justice after the arrest of most of the Constitution Defense League, they can't seem to stay out of trouble. They happen to be in the wrong place at the wrong time and Joan kills the brother of terrorist while protecting an invalid woman. Now the terrorists are after her and everyone close to her. As action-packed thrillers go, this one's a doozy. Like the first book in the series, this one is fast-paced, full of surprises and will hold your interest from beginning to end. ~ *Taylor Jones, Reviewer*

Hottest Places in Hell by Janet McClintock is the second book in the Iron Angel series. We're reunited with Joan, Duncan, and Kearney, this time on the run from the law and a terrorist organization Joan pissed off when she killed the brother of the leader during a home invasion attack, where Joan was protecting a woman confined to a wheelchair. Now the terrorist leader wants revenge and that means that Joan and her compatriots have to die. But Joan isn't easy to kill, although sometimes she wonders if it's worth the fight trying to stay alive. Like the first book in the series, *Worst of All Evils*, *Hottest Places in Hell* is a bonafide page-turner which fast-paced action and plenty of twists and turns in the plot. Make sure you have some time to spend before you start reading because once you pick it up, you won't be able to put it down. ~ *Regan Murphy, Reviewer*

ACKNOWLEDGEMENTS

Many thanks to the current and past members of the Critique Group North, who molded me into the writer I am today. Likewise, many thanks to Frances McClintock, Susan Sofayov, and Nancy Hammer who were my beta readers. And of course, I must thank my great editor, Faith, who gently instructs while she perfects my writing.

Kimberly Walla's medical expertise was invaluable in helping me create realistic injuries.

And again I must thank my boss, The Rev. Canon James Shoucair for giving me time off to attend my critique group meeting each month, and who has supported my writing efforts since the beginning of my writing journey.

HOTTEST PLACES IN HELL

JANET MCCLINTOCK

A Black Opal Books Publication

GENRE: THRILLER/SUSPENSE

HOTTEST PLACES IN HELL
Copyright © 2015 by Janet McClintock
Cover Design by Jackson Cover Designs
All cover art copyright © 2015
All Rights Reserved
Print ISBN: 978-1-626943-19-3

First Publication: AUGUST 2015

Published by Black Opal Books **http://www.blackopalbooks.com**

HOTTEST PLACES IN HELL

PROLOGUE

Two months, one week, three days was all that remained of Tito Orrozco's sentence.

The raised voices of the corrections officers announced the imminent clang of a closing metal door at the far end of the cell block, but Tito's stare didn't falter from a map of Arizona on the wall opposite his bunk. He pictured himself on the cutting edge of history.

While he languished in prison, a group had sprung up, *La Espada*, The Sword, a coalition of violent street gangs and underling drug lords. Sensing a weakness in the American government, they decided it was time to reclaim the land of Arizona, New Mexico, part of Texas, and Southern California for Mexico. While the administration in Washington was distracted with dissent among its citizens, the Southwest United States was ripe for the picking.

La Espada had the fighters, the fervor, and the money. It was the perfect storm. They were getting stronger as the imperialistic Americanos were getting weaker. It was time. It was *his* time.

And his hometown gang, *Las Cobras*, would be *el punte de La Espada*, the point of The Sword. *Las Cobras* would spearhead the fight because his gang members were the best fighters. He had trained them himself. They had the fire in their stomachs. They would lead the way.

He smiled and crossed the short distance between his bunk and the wall to touch the place on the map where his war would begin. With a short nod of his head, Tito smiled and tapped his index finger on the map at a bowl-shaped area twenty-two miles north of the Mexican-American border. It was surrounded by the Tohono Indian Reservation on the West, the Ironwood National Forest on the northeast, and the Saguaro National Forest to the east. This dusty patch of ground would become the corridor for future incursions.

Yes, this is the spot, he thought as he crossed his arms and nodded at the map.

His gang had researched the land and told him it was the Pennington Ranch owned by a gringo named Jake Pennington. Tito circled his finger over the bowl-shaped area then tapped the map again. This was the spot where this historic war would begin, and Pennington and his crippled wife would be the first casualties.

Movement at his cell door brought him out of his self-congratulatory, silent monologue. A dark-skinned man hovered there, his face and neck glistening with nervous sweat. He licked his lips, as if unsure about entering the cell uninvited. Tito glowered at the interloper—this inmate was not an associate. He was merely a go-between, a runner, nothing more.

The man hesitantly reached into Tito's cell and whispered in a heavy Mexican accent, "Samir sent this message. It is set. When you get out, call this number and ask for Rashid." The man pressed a small folded piece of paper into Tito's hand. "Tell him the code words, 'the lantern is lit,' and he will know it is you. He wants to be a part of this war you talk about." The man's eyes darted left and right when the buzzer sounded, indicating lights out in two minutes. He repeated the code and disappeared into the shuffle of men heading toward their cells.

Two months, one week, three days. That's all that stood between Tito and his rightful place as Latin America's newest revolutionary leader.

౭౩౭౩

Two miles east of the spot on the map where Tito had tapped, on the western border of Ironwood National Forest,

Joan Bowman knelt and tucked the end of the strap through the slide to secure her sleeping bag that looked like a dusty Tootsie Roll. She looked over at Duncan who sat on the sandy ground poring over a dog-eared map.

After the prison break, he could have disappeared off the task force's radar, but he didn't go on the run until she joined him. He had been her mentor, her champion, and, at times, her savior. Only toward the end did their relationship change from professional to intimate. A few months of sporadic, lusty sex ended when the Legion fell apart—because of her. Now they were fugitives—former Constitution Defense Legion fighters running from the CDL Task Force. Duncan rose above the betrayal and saved her from going to prison. Went on the run with her. Chose her for his partner.

The sleeping bag forgotten at her feet, she eyed the man whose freckle-faced, fresh look of the boy next door now had a hard set to his jaw and war-carved creases around his eyes—a battle-hardened soldier. He must have felt her looking at him because he turned his head and pinned his hard-stare on her. She didn't flinch under the scrutiny. Then, as if a ray of sunlight burst through heavy gray clouds, he smiled and her stomach flipped.

"You want to come and look at the map—just in case we get separated in the dark," he said.

Joan pulled the strap tight, walked the short distance, and knelt on one knee by his side. As he pointed to landmarks to use as visual guides, she tightened the band that held her long brunette hair in a low ponytail.

Hoping the authorities had followed their trail to Mexico, they had dropped hints they were headed south for Cabo San Lucas. Instead, they headed north across the Sonora Desert for the United States. While the task force searched for them in Mexico, they were heading north to Laguna, Arizona to meet up with Kearney, another Legion fugitive. He would provide them with false identification and handguns.

Duncan folded the map and stood up, signaling it was time to move out. As they fastened their bedrolls to their rucksacks, a pickup truck appeared at the end of two ruts that were barely a road. Its spotlight found them, pushing back the dusk, freezing them in the light beam while dust and mosquitoes danced around them. It was too late to run. All they could do was wait for an opportunity to escape.

A man got out of the truck and, with a slow, western drawl asked them what they were doing on his land. When Duncan told him they were hikers who were lost, the rancher lowered his rifle.

"Sorry for the rude greeting. Illegals cross my land, leaving their trash behind, and cutting my fences. Don't mind 'em coming and trying to make a life for themselves, but they're just so doggone destructive." He studied the gaunt faces of the two people standing in the wash of his headlights and felt the tension they were trying so hard to hide. His eyes narrowed.

Joan braced herself to fight. Every nerve ending screamed he knew who they were.

He held out his hand. "I'm Jake Pennington. I bet you two could use a shower and some good home cooking."

"The hottest places in hell are reserved for those who, when faced with a moral dilemma, do nothing."
~ *Mis-cited as Dante by John F. Kennedy in a speech in Berlin 1963*

CHAPTER 1

Three months later:

The serenity of the desert conveyed a sense of ease Joan hadn't felt for over a year. The ranch, far from prying eyes, was the perfect daytime retreat. In town, a momentary lapse in vigilance or a slip of the tongue, and federal agents would descend on her with overwhelming force. They considered her armed and dangerous. Joan snorted. She hadn't strapped iron in months.

She smiled at Miss Abigail, who cooed to Dolly, her white-and-tan Maltese/Poodle mix in the adjoining family room. Multiple sclerosis had robbed Abigail Pennington of her mobility, but she was the undisputed lady of the house. Although unable to walk without assistance, she ran the house with an iron hand, yet was gentle and generous. They were both trapped by circumstances they could no longer control.

Miss Abigail smiled up at Joan as she spun her motorized wheelchair a quarter turn and whizzed by, heading for the master bedroom at the far end of the Spanish Mission-style ranch house. Padding along behind her down the terra cotta tiled hallway, Joan wondered how Miss Abigail kept it together.

"I think I'll take a nap," Abigail said over her shoulder. "But don't let me sleep too long."

Joan helped Miss Abigail onto the bed and covered her with a rose-colored afghan. "I'll wake you in a couple hours, okay?"

"Angel, don't forget to close the kitchen door and the windows. It'll get hot when the sun comes around."

"Yes, ma'am," Joan said as she arranged the pillows behind Miss Abigail's head. When she had introduced herself to the Penningtons, she had not yet obtained a fake ID so, when asked her name, she had simply said, "Angel." It was a nod to her street name, Iron Angel.

Miss Abigail commanded great respect, not only from Joan, but from the surrounding community as well. Not commanded in the sense of direct orders, but by virtue of the stately strength and dignity with which she faced down her disease—complainin' didn't change her fate. Complainin' didn't get things done.

The phone on the nightstand next to the bed rang.

"Would you get that? Tell whoever it is I'll call them back. I'm feeling sleepy." Sometimes strength had its limitations.

Joan casually picked up the receiver.

Before she could say anything, Jake Pennington started talking. "Are you okay?"

"Yes, why?" She turned to face away from Miss Abigail.

He was talking fast and sharp, different from his usual slow, western manner. "We've been shot up by some crazy, wild-eyed...I don't know...some of them looked like Mexicans. Both my boys are down." He coughed then continued, "I've been hit, too."

"Where are you? I'll come out to—"

"No. There's no time. They took our trucks and are headed toward the house. Get Abigail in your car and get outta there!"

Joan put her hand on the back of her neck. A knot wrenched her gut. "Mr. Pennington, I drove my motorcycle today."

Without missing a beat, he said, "The spare key to the gun cabinet is on a hook under the kitchen sink, toward the back, on the left side. You've shot a gun before, right?"

"Yes, in Iraq, but I don't—"

"Then put on your war paint, darlin', 'cos trouble is headed your way. There's eight, maybe ten of them." The line went dead.

"Was that my Jake?" Miss Abigail was wide awake and leaning on one elbow. Her usually smooth forehead held uncharacteristic furrows.

"Yes. It's probably nothing." Joan helped Miss Abigail to a seated position. "But I think I should put you in the bathtub, you know, for your protection." Slowly and gently she pulled Miss Abigail's legs over the side of the bed—the purposeful actions in direct contrast to her racing mind. *Damn that Iron Angel bad karma.*

"In the bath tub? Protection from what? Angel, what is going on?"

"You trust me, right?" Joan helped Miss Abigail to her feet, put her strong muscular arm across the older woman's back, and half-carried her to the master bath. A lifetime of weight lifting, martial arts, and calisthenics was paying off.

"Yes, of course, but—"

"No 'buts.' This is what Mr. Pennington would want you to do."

Joan helped Miss Abigail into the vintage cast-iron soaking tub. Her methodic movements and soothing tone belied the adrenaline coursing through her arteries. She raced to the bedroom to get a pillow to support Miss Abigail's neck. With her head pounding and hands shaking, she turned toward the bathroom door and stopped.

A movement caught her eye. Dolly looked out from under the bed, her dog senses told her something scary was going on. Joan snatched her collar and received a nip in return then hurried to the bathroom with the pillow and the snarling dog in her arms. Dolly calmed a little in her mistress' arms, but, not sure where the danger was, she watched Joan's every move, one lip curled in warning.

Miss Abigail saw Joan's shaking hands and she gently covered them with her weak ones. Joan looked at her hands, then into the stately woman's eyes for the first time since the phone call. What she saw there was strength more powerful than anything she could ever muster.

"I know you can handle any situation," Miss Abigail said. "I told Jake that very thing the first time I met you. Stay calm. Stay alert. Everything'll be okay." She squeezed Joan's hands as best she could and nodded. Joan reflexively nodded back.

Giving Joan's hands a slight push, Miss Abigail added, "Now go and do whatever it is you have to do."

Joan raced down the long hallway to the kitchen. She dropped to her knees, yanked open the cabinet door, and made a frenzied search with her hand under the sink. *How can I be in the middle of nowhere and trouble still finds me?*

The key wasn't there. A deep, shaky inhalation slowed her heart rate and settled her mind—a little. With her cheek pressed against the panel above the cabinet, she tried again, reaching past the cleansers and sponges. Her fingers felt the cool metal of the key and grabbed it. With key in hand, she hurried into Mr. Pennington's office to unlock gun cabinet. She speed dialed Duncan.

"Talk to me," he said.

Her breath caught in her throat at the sound of his voice. "If I ever needed your help before, baby, I need it now." She cradled the phone between her shoulder and her ear. The 9 mm semi-automatic caught her eye. She snatched two loaded magazines from the drawer at the base of the cabinet.

"What's up?"

After slapping one magazine into the butt of the 9 mm with the palm of her hand, she put the other magazine into the back pocket of her jeans. "Mr. Pennington and his sons have been shot, and whoever shot them is headed for the house. I'm alone with Miss Abigail, and—"

"I'm at least fifteen minutes away."

After pulling the slide of the 9 mm back to chamber one round, she tucked the gun in the waistband at the small of her back. "Then at least come to claim my body." *Shotgun next. This is a beauty. Mr. P knows his guns,* she thought while loading double-aught buck cartridges into the chamber.

"Don't talk like that," Duncan said. "I'm as good as there. Soon, baby."

"Soon." She disconnected the phone and dropped it to the floor.

❧❧❧

Duncan grabbed his 9 mm and some extra magazines. Stuffing a box of shells into his medic bag, he raced out the back door and into his truck—thirty seconds, tops. Another two seconds and the truck's tires were spinning in the gravel driveway, pinging dirt and small stones against the rundown shed in the back yard.

The truck fishtailed when its tires hit the pavement, but he kept it going forward.

Sheer determination kept the truck on the road as he hit speeds up to sixty miles per hour on the canyon curves. Once on the flat, straight road he dialed his best friend. He and Kearney had been friends since the time they met in a jungle in Nicaragua.

Duncan had been a mercenary and medical support for his team. Kearney had been CIA.

"Hey, Kearney, meet me at the Pennington ranch. You know where that is?"

"Yeah, why? What's up?"

"Joan called. She needs help."

"Shit, man. What trouble has found her this time?"

"I guess some guys shot up Mr. Pennington and his sons and they're headed for the house. She's alone with Miss Abigail."

"I'm not going. She can get herself out of this jam. You can do what you want, but count me out."

"She saved your ass that time—" Duncan checked his side view mirror and swerved around a slower moving car.

"Yeah, and she also broke my arm and a couple ribs, too. And my jaw has never been right since she broke that. No. I don't owe her anything. Let her go, man. She's nothing but trouble."

"You tortured her for nothing."

"We've been over that, Duncan."

"For *nothing.*"

"It was *business.*"

"I need you for back up."

"Don't pull that shit on me—"

"And what about Mrs. Pennington? She's in a wheelchair for God's sake."

"Damn you, Duncan, I'm coming, but when are you ever going to learn that Joan is bad news? It's never going to change. You know that, right?"

"Roger that." Duncan dropped the phone onto the passenger seat, adjusted his ball cap over his curly reddish-brown hair, and stepped on the gas. He had only been to the ranch one time before. It had taken fifteen minutes when he was traveling at seventy miles per hour. If he could maintain ninety-five miles per hour, how long would it take? He tried to do the calculation in his head. *If a train leaves Chicago heading east, and another leaves New York...*he frowned. High school math word problems had always been hard for him. He decided to keep his concentration on the road. It had to be a good eight minutes, at least—if he didn't end up in a ditch.

ℰ❧ℰ❧

Joan spied a leather-embossed gun case and opened it. *Wow!* With great reverence, she slid her finger down the highly polished chrome barrel engraved with swirling lines and roses. *This must be an anniversary edition.* A glance at the bore brought a brief smile to her face—.45 cal. There was one magazine for the .45, so she grabbed it and a box of shells and hoped Mr. Pennington wouldn't mind her firing a valuable collectable.

Something about the weight of the guns in her hands calmed her. Her surroundings became surreal as her military training and experience took over. Cover and exposure, funnel of death, and wide open spaces. Sight, hearing, touch became one. Each creak in the floor, the ticking mantle clock, and outside sounds were sharp and riveting. Even the lemon-scented furniture polish was intensified.

She took a deep breath to slow her thundering heart. As she wiped her shaking, clammy hands on the front of her jeans, Miss Abigail's words came back to her. "Stay calm. Stay alert. Everything'll be okay."

Joan inhaled through her nose and exhaled through her mouth two more times.

The faint sound of vehicles approaching from the west—the kitchen side of the house—caught her attention. *Good. The appliances are metal and thick. Good for slowing bullets.* Crouching low, with a gun in each hand and one in the small of her back, she headed to the kitchen. While she waited for Mr. Pennington's attackers to get within range, she loaded the magazine for the .45. Adrenaline made her fumble the first couple rounds into place, but with concentrated deep breathing, loading the magazine became easier and more accurate with each round.

As each round slid into place in the magazine, a quiet life under the radar with Duncan slipped a little farther from her grasp. It was all she wanted, and now...*Well, so much for that.* She slapped the loaded magazine into the handgun and laid it across her lap.

Her breath control slipped and her breathing became heavy, almost gasping. *Control your breathing.* She tried to remember other pointers Kearney had given her. His marksmanship training had produced a shooter with pinpoint accuracy, but targets were different from people. Head leaning against the cabinet door at her back, she twisted her brunette ponytail around her finger in rhythm to her silent chant, *You can do this. You can do this. You can do this.*

She rolled her head to the right as the sound of the approaching vehicles got louder. She got to her knees to shove the .45 into her front waistband. Feeling the heft of the .45, she again admired the etchings. Her thoughts drifted to Duncan and she hoped he would make it before it was too late. She wanted to see him one last time. *This might be the end of the road, but these jerks, whoever they are, are going to know they've been in a fight. If I'm going down, I'm going down hot.*

Tires crunched in the gravel driveway.

Crouching, using the counter for cover, she headed for the kitchen door. Iron Angel stood up in the doorway and, without thinking about it, pumped the shotgun and fired. Another quick pump. Another quick shot and the kitchen became a hellhole. She dove for cover behind the dishwasher. Glass sprayed across the floor as rounds from automatic rifles flew past her head at supersonic speed. *Phfft—phfft—phfft*—over and over, whipping over her head and through the wall into the formal living room. She could hear lamps shattering somewhere out of sight.

There was movement in the kitchen door. Quick pump, another shot—too quick to brace the butt of the gun properly. The recoil slammed the shotgun hard against her shoulder, knocking her flat on her back. She grimaced from the pain, but before the man hit the floor, another was right behind him. Another pump, another shot, this time braced properly. As he fell on top of the first man through the door, she saw the blood splatter on the wall behind him. *Don't think about that. Think about what you're doing. Stay focused. Keep moving.*

The kitchen was too big to defend. She dropped the shotgun, pulled the handguns from her waistband, and raced for the hallway.

In her peripheral vision, she saw movement behind the beveled glass in the front door. Shooting simultaneously with the 9 mm toward the front door and the .45 through the kitchen door, she raced to the relative safety of the hallway and ducked into Mr. Pennington's office. Two more down. Maybe. Things were happening too fast. *That's six. Two, maybe four, left.* Unsure how many shots had been fired, she ejected the magazine out of the 9 mm and put the full one in.

Time passed, no telling how much—could have been one minute, could have been three. Voices came from the hallway. She knew Spanish, but some of the words weren't familiar. Too much slang…and something else she couldn't put her finger on. A figure appeared in the doorway. Popping up from behind Mr. Pennington's massive mahogany desk, she fired two shots. He went down but she didn't have time to celebrate. Bullets sprayed through the window behind her. The green-shaded desk lamp exploded into a million pieces as she dropped and flattened herself against the floor.

Once again, the *phfft—phfft—phfft*—whizzed over her head as the shooter emptied his magazine. When the shooting stopped, she saw the feet of two men inching into the room— mere shadows through the space at the base of the desk.

Twisting onto her side, she placed the .45 on the floor in

front of her. Gripping the 9 mm with both hands, she shot seven times through the desk. The eighth time, it locked open—empty. She dropped it and picked up the .45.

She peered over the top of the desk. No one there. *Where'd they go?* Crouching low, using the desk for cover, she moved to the right and around the corner of the desk. A hand holding an AK-47 poked around the edge of the doorjamb. She buried her nose in the glass covered carpet. The gunman blindly sprayed the room with bullets. When the shooting stopped, she got to her knees, the .45 aimed at the doorway. A head poked around the corner. She fired. The man fell backward out of sight.

Brushing glass fragments from her clothes, she moved toward the door, trying to avoid making crunching sounds on the broken glass. She flattened herself against the wall and peeked around the doorjamb. The hallway was empty. A quick check for the outside shooter. He was in the open struggling with his jammed weapon. She took aim and shot him in the chest. Pulled the trigger again. He flew back three feet and did not get up. Her .45 empty, she dropped it. No time to reload the magazine.

Empty-hand combat was her specialty anyway. Proficient in three martial arts, empty-hand fighting was her first choice when feasible—or necessary. Necessity ruled the moment.

The hallway was eerily quiet, or maybe the ringing in her ears made it seem that way. The haze of burnt gunpowder filled the air and tickled her nose. With small, tentative steps, she sidled along the wall toward the kitchen and family room.

Dolly started snarling and barking furiously. Iron Angel spun around to squint down the hallway behind her, all her senses now fixated toward the rear of the house. Without looking at it, she grabbed an M16 from an intruder sprawled in the hallway—he wasn't going to need it anymore–and tiptoed toward the angry dog sounds. In a crouch, M16 at the ready, she slinked toward the door to the master bedroom. When she reached the door, she stopped to peek around the doorjamb.

A man was making his way across the master bedroom checking every nook and cranny, not much more than a foot from the bathroom door—and Miss Abigail. Joan raised the

M16, pulled the trigger. Nothing. A quick look at the dust cover. Open—empty. She silently chastised herself for not checking the rifle when she picked it up.

She grabbed the end of the rifle barrel. Heat be damned. Nothing was more important than protecting Miss Abigail from this intruder. She stole up behind the man, brought the hand holding the barrel across her chest and, in a hooking motion, brought the rifle around and slammed it against his throat. At the same time, her left hand moved forward, and to the right, and grabbed the stock. With a cross-grip and knee in the back, there was no escape. Dead within seconds of the rifle strike to the throat, he was limp and heavy, but she kept pulling, until she heard a familiar voice.

"To your right!" Before she could step, she heard a gunshot and felt a sting on the outside of her left thigh. She released her grip on the rifle and stepped to her right. Another shot, and she turned to see another intruder drop to the floor. Behind him stood Duncan.

His wide shoulders and strong, thick waist were a wonderful sight. Smiling into his worried eyes, she touched her thigh. When she pulled her fingers away, they were bloody. She twisted to find the entrance wound to plug it with her index finger.

When she looked up, the smile had disappeared from her face. "I killed all these men."

He smiled. "I can see that."

"I never killed anybody before—"

"I know. Your specialty is making them *wish* they were dead." His smile faded. "Hey, hey, hey." Each "hey" became progressively softer and drawn out.

With a hopping-step over the pool of blood from the man he had just shot, he approached Joan. He cupped her face in his hands. "You did the right thing. It was them or you. Good thing you had the skills you have, or this could have been worse."

"I know, but still—"

"You. Had. No. Choice." He pulled her into him and rested his chin on the side of her head. "It's gonna be all right. The first time is the worst. I'll help you work through it."

Joan nodded and pulled away from him to twist and find the exit wound on the front of her thigh. Without looking up, she said, "Hundreds of rounds flew around me and through some miraculous quirk of fate, they all missed. The only bullet that hit me came from *your* gun." Finding the exit wound, she plugged it with her thumb.

"I told you to move to the right. I shot low the first time to be safe."

"I know. I'm just saying—"

"Maybe these guys weren't very good shots."

She looked up at him with a half-smile. "I don't know about that. They managed to hit every lamp in the house."

Duncan laughed out loud.

The smile faded from her face. "Duncan?" The realization that the ordeal was over made her body grow heavy, and, as the adrenaline dump diminished, a warm sense of relief filled her in waves.

He saw it coming before she was aware of it. He grabbed her arms. "Why don't you sit down?"

Duncan's voice seemed far away. In the encroaching darkness, her own voice sounded weak and barely audible. "Can you take over now? Everything's—I don't feel so good." Her knees buckled, and Duncan carefully sat her on the floor, her back braced against the heirloom bureau.

"Take some deep breaths." He gently bent her knees. "Put your head on your knees. Where'd you learn to plug bullet holes like that?"

The deep breaths got oxygen moving through her system and cleared her head. Not a lot, but enough to fend off the darkening at the edge of her vision. "I read it in a news story somewhere." Her voice was weak and breathy.

Kearney appeared in the doorway, holstering his weapon. "Is she dead?"

Duncan turned his head toward Kearney's voice, but didn't turn all the way around. "As much as you'd like that—no. It's only a flesh wound. Go get my medic bag out of my truck. Hey, Kearney," Duncan said.

Kearney stuck his head around the doorjamb.

"Make sure no more of these bastards are still alive."

Kearney smiled his big toothy grin and disappeared.

Duncan turned back to Joan. "You gonna be okay?"

She nodded.

"I'll go check on Miss Abigail."

He found Miss Abigail unharmed in the tub where Joan had left her. He lifted her out of the tub as if she were a cotton ball. Joan watched as he fussed over Miss Abigail, settling her in her wheelchair, assuring her everything was going to be okay, and promising her he'd check on her husband and sons.

Kearney returned with Duncan's medic bag and knelt next to Joan.

She looked up at him. "I'm really not up for your bullshit right now."

But he was staring at Duncan as if he had never really seen him before. "You two are like twin panthers. Strong and agile and—deadly."

To break the awkward moment, she said, "Thank God you taught me how to shoot with my left hand. You should have seen me. A gun in each hand firing away. Just like in the movies."

"You were lucky, that's all." He turned his attention to her. "I can see what he sees in you. You're Duncan in a hot chick's body."

She leaned her head against the bureau behind her and rolled it toward Kearney. "You're more screwed up than I thought. You think a woman with a bullet hole in her leg is hot?"

"No...I mean...you know what I mean." Camouflage legs appeared at his side. A panther. He stood up, eye to eye with his best, and only, friend.

"Call 911. Use Joan's phone," Duncan said. He looked down at Joan, "Where's your phone?"

"I...uh—" She rubbed the back of her hand against her forehead, trying to get her scattered thoughts to stop dilly-dallying around her still-foggy head. "In the office. On the floor."

Kearney disappeared down the hallway.

"We're going to check on Jake Pennington and his sons. I'll patch you up to hold you over until the ambulance comes." Gauze appeared out of the medic bag and, in seconds, Joan's leg was bandaged.

"Don't leave me to deal with the cops," she pleaded. "I can't do it."

"Yes, you can. Just tell them the truth. It may not seem like it, but you did a good thing—saving Miss Abigail." He tucked a stray strand of hair behind her ear. "Remember, you're the victim here." He leaned in until his lips were next to her ear. "The local cops don't know who we are. Identifying fugitives is a slow process. This isn't TV, okay?"

She barely heard him. She was squinting toward the doorway with the corners of her mouth turned down. "Kearney said I was just lucky."

Duncan hooked his curled index finger under her chin and raised her face. "Hey, baby, don't let him bother you. He's a misogynist. Nothing a woman does will ever earn a compliment from him."

"I know, but I'm good, right?"

"Yes, you are." Duncan gave her a quick kiss on her forehead. "You'll be fine."

And he was gone.

CHAPTER 2

The deputy checked the name on Joan's fake license. "So, uh, Lisa, is this your current address?"

The deputy sensed an immediate, invisible tension in the room. His eyes snapped up, first to Joan, then to Miss Abigail. He squinted through the familiar stillness. It was a sixth sense he'd developed over the past several years in law enforcement. It was like walking into a room where there was an odd smell. You stopped, sniffed, and hesitated as you tried to put your finger on it.

He zeroed in on Miss Abigail. Joan held her breath, hoping Miss Abigail would play along—that she was as mentally sharp as she seemed.

Lisa Brown was Joan's fake identity, and she only used it when a license had to be produced, when an identity had to be established. Everyone knew her as Joan or Iron Angel or, in the case of the Penningtons, just Angel.

The pucker factor kicked in, her heartbeat picked up speed and her mouth went dry. *Keep bluffing. Maybe the paramedics will come before he realizes who I am.* Fighting the urge to bolt from the room, she kept her gaze riveted on the deputy.

Until the coroner released the bodies that blocked the door and the homicide detectives completed their assessment of the scene, Miss Abigail was stuck in the bedroom in her wheelchair. If Joan left, Miss Abigail would have to look at the blood and bodies alone. Staying and facing the deputy was Joan's only option. She took a deep breath to calm her nerves, and remained seated on the armless, padded chair opposite the entrance to the room.

Blood had pooled on the pale green, cushy carpet leaving a burgundy wet patch, the edges of which were already turning brown. It had stopped spreading, which was creepier than when the pool was growing. The room suddenly seemed crowded with the two bodies, Miss Abigail, the deputy, Joan, and the specter of Lisa Brown. A wave of nausea rolled through her stomach.

She pushed the bile back down her throat and answered the deputy. "No. I currently live at 3088 West Thirty-First Street."

The deputy moved his squinting gaze from Miss Abigail to Joan. He wrote in his notebook a second before looking down at it. Not sure if that was a bona fide address, Joan had to maintain her composure until the paramedics came and whisked her away from the suspicion—and the bodies. She studied the deputy, trying to forget about her sticky situation.

He was a short, young man, early thirties, with hair cut close to his head. He wore his sunglasses on the back of his neck, ear pieces hooked on his ears. She wondered whether he had eyes on his neck. A wisecrack would have calmed her nerves, but she reminded herself to give the deputy the information he asked for, nothing else. He had been on the force too long not to notice subtle cues from body language, eye movement, no movement. The throbbing in her leg intensified. Where were those paramedics?

The corners of the deputy's eyes tensed. He looked back and forth between Miss Abigail and Joan. *He knows. He knows something's up.*

"How long have you lived there?" he finally asked.

"Several months."

"What's several months?"

"Four." Joan pretended to count on her fingers, "No, five. Five the end of this month."

He made another note. He offered the license in his hand to Joan, but when she grasped it, he didn't let go. He stared into her eyes. "Make sure you get an Arizona license right away."

She didn't flinch. They lingered there, she sitting on the silly armless chair looking up into his eyes, the deputy looking down into hers until another man appeared at the door. The one extra person seemed to suck the oxygen out of the room. Joan's breathing became heavy and a bead of sweat formed at her hairline.

The newcomer had brown, shiny skin and a barrel chest. Gray tinged the hairline of his thick, black hair. He was dressed casually in a faded Grateful Dead tee shirt and knee-length khaki shorts. Knees locked, shoulders squared, his eyes swept the room, rested briefly on the deputy, a little longer on Joan. Nodding in deference to Miss Abigail, he finished the sweep. He was definitely no lookey-loo. The deputy released the license and turned toward the newcomer. When Joan wiped the sweat from her forehead, she noticed her fingers shaking. *Get a hold of yourself. If he suspected something, you'd be in handcuffs by now.*

The deputy turned his back on Joan and took a step toward the newcomer. "So what's your take on this?"

"I recognize most of these guys. They're known *La Espada* members. The others—"

"I thought *La Espada* was peaceful," the deputy said. "That it's *MECha* that's the militant arm of the group."

"Lately the line between the two has become blurred. *La Espada, MECha*, it's all the same nowadays. This one here—" He pointed at the man Joan had strangled. "—is Tito Orrozco's brother."

"Tito Orrozco?" the deputy asked then blew a low whistle. "I heard Tito just got out of prison."

"Yeah, a week, ten days ago. This is not going to make him a happy man."

The deputy hooked his thumbs in his utility belt and nodded his head in agreement. He gave Joan a long, hard stare over his shoulder then returned his attention to the newcomer.

Two paramedics appeared at the door to the bedroom. The deputy nodded toward Joan. Undaunted by the scene in the bedroom, they stepped over the bodies, avoiding the sticky, brown pools of blood.

As the Hispanic-looking EMT put a blood pressure cuff on her arm, Joan answered his questions about basic information.

The larger, African-American man knelt at her feet. "Gunshot?" His voice was soft, but confident. He already had scissors in his hand.

She nodded. The man sliced her jeans, starting at the ankle and up the outside of the leg past the holes the bullets made on their way through the material.

The denim gave a slight pull where the blood had started to clot. She flinched.

"That hurt?" the paramedic asked.

"Well, I've been shot. So—"

The big, almost-square, ragged scar on the top of her thigh was about to be exposed. It would lead to questions she didn't want to answer. The scar was a reminder of an hour bound to a chair at Kearney's mercy. One hour that she would rather not talk about.

The paramedic finished cutting her pant leg, pulled back the material to expose the thigh and sure enough, there was the long look at the scar followed by the predictable knitted brow.

Then, right on cue, the expected question, "That's a nasty scar. How'd you get that?"

"I had tattoos removed." And there was that piercing look. It was the story she had settled on to explain away the ugly skin on her chest, thighs and abdomen.

He fingered it as if it were raw flesh. "I never saw any tattoo removal that looked like *this*."

"I went to a quack. I guess it's true what they say—you get what you pay for."

The paramedic shook his head and set about cleaning and bandaging, using tons more gauze than Duncan had used. A Special Ops medic was more judicious with supplies. When you were in the middle of nowhere without imminent support, you only had what you carried in with you and efficiency of use was paramount.

Eying the paramedic putting the finishing touches on the bandage, the man with the Grateful Dead tee shirt turned to Joan. "So you're the person who did all this?"

She looked up and nodded.

"That's some mean shootin'. Ten guys, one woman."

"I grew up around guns," she said. "My father was a

hunter. He took me target shooting with him." She smiled. "Father-daughter time."

Her father had been a hunter, true enough, but they had only gone target shooting a couple times. But it was hour-after-grueling-hour on the range built on a remote piece of property owned by the Constitution Defense Legion that had saved her. Becoming familiar with every gun in Kearney's collection. Firing from every position imaginable, stationary, on the move, in the dark. Training that had thankfully kicked in when she needed it. *That* was what had enabled her to survive this onslaught.

But that was something she couldn't exactly share with law enforcement.

She swallowed and took a shaky, deep breath. "But it didn't prepare me for shooting a *person*." At least that part was true.

The newcomer nodded, as if to empathize with her. "I have a pretty good idea how this went down. Do you feel up to telling me your version?"

With a shaking voice, Joan recounted the events of the morning. In time, her voice evened out. The man in the Grateful Dead tee shirt groomed his moustache with the inside of his index finger and thumb. He listened intently, watching her eyes, her gestures. Assessing the tone of her voice. He interrupted her story twice, only to clarify a couple small details. Fingers motioned for her to continue then returned to stroking the mustache.

The man produced a billfold with a badge and pulled out a business card. "Call me if you think of anything else. Anything at all."

He handed the card to Joan. The card read Detective William Ramos, Supervisor, Gang Crimes Unit, Phoenix PD. The logo for the police department was in the upper left hand corner. Several phone numbers skittered across the bottom. It joined the forgotten .45 shells in her front pocket.

"I told you all I know." Joan winced as she shifted in her seat partly because her leg ached from her hip to her ankle, partly out of nervousness.

"When your mind settles down and you aren't in pain anymore, sometimes an event clears up and you may remember details you don't recall right now."

"Okay, but I don't think there's anything else."

"That's understandable, but if you think of anything, no matter how small, call me. There might be some small detail that doesn't mean anything to you, but will be important to the investigation."

"Of course, officer, I want to help however I can."

"Detective," he corrected her.

"What?"

"It's 'detective.' I'm Detective Ramos."

"Oh, sorry, Detective Ramos."

He walked across the room to talk with another man in civilian clothes. She assumed it was his partner.

As the paramedics helped her to her feet, the deputy looked at Joan with that stern penetrating look all cops developed.

Must be something they learn at the academy—Stern Looks 101. Joan bit her tongue.

"Make sure you take care of that license," he said.

At that admonishment, Detective Ramos turned, looked at Joan, then turned back to his conversation.

A firm voice penetrated the low hum of voices. "Can Lisa help me one more time before you take her to the hospital?"

Joan let out a quiet breath. She had to hand it to Miss Abigail, though physically handicapped, her mind was sharp.

"I can get you whatever you need, Mrs. Pennington," the deputy said.

"I have to use the bathroom," Miss Abigail stated with a sharpness that warned against crossing her.

The deputy raised his eyebrows and looked at the paramedic, who nodded back. Looking at Joan, the deputy used a sideways nod to indicate for her to help Miss Abigail.

Joan limped after Miss Abigail as she followed her to the bathroom. The pain in her leg made her light-headed and bile crept up the back of her throat, but she made it into the bathroom and closed the door behind her. Miss Abigail turned on the cold water in the sink surrounded by colorful, Spanish tiles. She soaked a face cloth, wrung it out and handed it to Joan.

"Here, put this on your forehead. You look a bit peek-ed."

After the color had returned to her face Miss Abigail motioned Joan toward her. "When your leg is healed," Miss Abigail said in a voice just above a whisper, "you'll have to tell me why you have two different names in addition to the one I know you by."

Their eyes locked. Joan leaned in, resting her hands on the armrests of the wheelchair. She looked over her shoulder. The door was closed. The water was running. No way the guys in the bedroom would hear anything. "Miss Abigail, I never wanted to lie to you. I—"

"Oh, shush," Miss Abigail said patting one of Joan's hands. "You saved my life. I'll never forget that and neither will Jake. I'm just curious, that's all." After a brief pause, she added, "Besides, a little mystery never hurt anybody."

Joan smiled. Miss Abigail was the real angel in the room.

"Now flush the toilet, Angel. I have to make arrangements for a place to stay tonight."

⋄⋄⋄

Tito Orrozco slammed his fist on the coffee table in the basement of his mother's house. Upon release from prison, he had moved back in with his family and immediately taken over the basement for his gang's clubhouse.

The police had left a little over an hour ago after informing his mother, his sister, and himself that his brother was dead. Did they know anything about what his brother was into? No? Any other information that would be helpful to the investigation? No? Sorry for your loss. Good-bye.

Although the detectives had wanted to take Tito downtown for further questioning, his mother's hysterical pleadings convinced them to wait until after the funeral. It bought him some much-needed time.

He called a meeting of *Las Cobras* and now sat on a beat-up plaid couch at the far end of the basement. His second-in-command sat on his right. Some of the other men sat on wooden chairs, others stood around, hands in the front pockets of their faded jeans. Their expressions ranged from sadness to anger to fear of Tito's reaction to his brother's death.

They all wore gray-and-black haskies—the colors of their movement. The name, haskie, was derived from the combination of the words 'hoodie' and 'mask.' Haskies took the place of hoodies as the identity-hiding fad of choice for criminals, especially in the southwestern United States where hoodies could be too hot. They were one-piece items made of fine netting with a high percentage of spandex. Worn around their necks, the back could be pulled up and over the head for a hood. The front could be pulled up like a mask. Available in a wide variety of colors, patterns, or pictures, haskies in gray-and-black camouflage pattern were favored by *Las Cobras*. When the front was pulled up like a mask, the Mexican flag covered their lower face.

A large green, white, and red Mexican flag hung behind a makeshift bar on the left side of the room. Across the room from the bar was an old, red Formica table with chrome trim and legs—furniture that looked like it came from his grandmother's house. Neatly tucked under it were two chairs with red vinyl seats and two others covered with yellow vinyl. Dusty boxes were stacked under the stairs that led to the main living area.

He started to rant. "I sent ten guys to do a job that should have taken only five. Only that crippled lady was supposed to be in the house. And the cops are telling me they are all dead? That my brother is dead?" He yanked the camouflage-colored haskie from around his neck and threw it. It landed in the middle of the maple coffee table.

"And our 'friends,' who were supposed to be so battle-hardened, they died, too. Who was in that house? Superman?" Tito stood up and rubbed his hand over his shaved head. Short and muscular, he was the unchallenged leader of the group. The words 'Brown Pride' peeked out of the neckline of his white wife-beater shirt. He had two teardrops tattooed under his right eye, indicating he had killed two people.

No one moved.

"Find out who was in that house," Tito added as he side-stepped to the left to get around the coffee table and headed for the bar. Knees and shoulders moved to make room for him to

pass. The room was too quiet. He had to do something to ener-
gize his men. Revenge was sweeter when it was hot.

Upon reaching the bar, he turned to face his posse. "I want
whoever killed my brother dead."

He grabbed a bottle of whiskey and splashed some into a
smudged shot glass. A small puddle formed from the liquor
that didn't make it into the glass. He downed the shot.

"*Puño*, I know one of the names," someone said from the
back of the group.

Tito glared at the newest member of the group who dared to
use a name that indicated familiarity. *Puño*, was short for *Puño
de hierro*, or Iron Fist.

Confident in his knowledge, the newbie stood his ground.
"Lisa Brown," he said as if he had made a great revelation in
the science of physics.

"A woman killed all my men?" Wiping his lips with the
back of his hand, Tito challenged him, "How do you know
that?"

"I have a cousin in the police department."

Tito walked over to the new member. Roughly pushing the
back of the man's head, then putting his arm around the man's
shoulder, he said to the group, "See? This is how we get things
done."

"But, Tito, there's a small problem," the new member said.

"What's that?"

"The address she gave the police is bogus, and there are six
Lisa Browns in the phonebook. It may take a while to find
which Lisa Brown it is."

"I don't see a problem." Tito looked around the room.
"Does anybody else see a problem?" The room was silent. He
continued, "Kill *all* the Lisa Browns. When we succeed in re-
claiming this land for Mexico, we will exterminate all the
white people anyway." He smiled when enunciating the next
two words, "Eth—nic cleans—ing." He paused for emphasis
before continuing. "There will be six less Anglos for us to take
care of later, right?" He took a long pull from the whiskey bottle.

"This is *our* land," Tito continued. "Stolen by the white

man from the Mexican people. They have no right to be here."
The liquor sloshed in the bottle as he gestured to emphasize his
point. "White people do not have a right to life on *our* land,
right?" Everyone around him nodded their heads and murmured sounds of support. He raised the bottle in salute. "*Viva
La Espada! Viva el Mexico!*" He handed the bottle to the closest man, who took a drink and passed it on to the others in the
room.

"You and you." Tito pointed to two longtime members of
Las Cobras. "Take care of it."

They affirmed his order by raising their chins in a quick
upward nod.

Tito walked over and plopped down on the sofa. He picked
up the haskie he had discarded minutes before and put it on his
head like a watch cap, taking great care with the creases and
placement. It was so far down on his forehead, he had to tilt
his head back to see. He crossed his arms over his chest and
nodded.

CHAPTER 3

Duncan tugged on the shade and let it go. "Get up!" The shade flapped as it recoiled and kept rotating around the central rod. "You have a visitor."

As light filtered through the sheer curtains into the bedroom, Joan stirred under the sheets and coverlet. In one tug, he yanked the covers so they landed in a heap on the floor at his feet.

"Who?" she croaked.

Too much sleep and too much tequila for far too many days in a row left her throat parched. She smacked her lips and grimaced. Something must have crawled into her mouth and died.

"Doesn't matter," Duncan said. He moved to the side of the bed closest to where she had curled up in a fetal position, hands tucked under her cheek, ready to go back to sleep. His voice had a sharp edge when he continued, "Get your lazy ass up. For almost a week now you've managed to get up to start another night of drinking, but you can't get up for a visitor?"

Without opening her eyes, she felt the heat of his displeasure radiating toward her like the sun's rays on her back at the beach. But bed was the only place she could tolerate. Darkness, quiet, and drunken numbness had become her best friends. They surrounded her like a shroud of protection from the memories of the home invasion at the Pennington Ranch—the blank eyes of the men she had killed, the pools of blood, the fear of being recognized as a fugitive.

The alcohol dulled her senses, muffling sounds and blurring the deliria that stalked her. Without the alcohol deadening her body, the sound of gunshots would make her jump and she'd realize that they were only sounds of horror escaping from her memory. Visions of the splattered blood on the kitchen wall made her stop in her tracks because they blocked her vision, and she searched the house for the source of the raw meat smell of fresh blood.

As if the vivid delusions weren't enough, something was gone from her life—not innocence but something like that. The memory of the men she killed filled her head, making it hard to focus on anything else. The sedative effects of alcohol anesthetized her to the serrated, cutting edge of death. In the fuzzy world of intoxication, she was able to feel normal again, although normal had become something elusive, undefinable, different. Besides, the energy needed to maintain a conversation, act civil toward others, even eat, was difficult to muster with the nine tenacious ghosts of the men she had killed whispering in her head, taunting, and judging her.

And then there were the three Lisa Browns. Innocent of any wrongdoing, they died simply because of her—because their names and her fake identification were the same. Joan pressed her lips into a thin line, rubbed her fingers against her eyelids, and silently ridiculed her street name, *Iron Angel*. She shook her head. *You are one serious screw up.*

She knew if she didn't move soon, Duncan's foul mood would follow her all day, creating a wall between them. It was Duncan's support and understanding she needed the most. She knew that as well as the creases on the palm of her hand, but she couldn't seem to act in a way that would bring him closer to her. Running her fingers through her hair to get it off her face, she smacked her lips again. The sun shot bullets of sand into her eyes as she tried to see the clock on the table next to the bed.

"You have a visitor," Duncan said through clenched teeth.

She swung her legs over the side of the bed. Moving to an upright position sent bolts of pain across her head from temple to temple. She braced her elbows on her knees, cupped her head, and moaned. "I don't want to see anybody," she said to the dusty floor between her feet.

Duncan sat on the bed beside her and took a deep breath. "Look, baby, it's done. You can't change what happened at the ranch." He tucked a strand of hair behind her left ear. She tilted her head toward the gentle, soothing touch. His finger rested behind her ear, then brushed down her jawline. "If you can't find a way to get over it, you have to find a way to get past it and move on with your life—our life."

"I never wanted to ever kill anybody, you know, outside the Sandbox," Joan said. She pressed the back of one hand against her chin to stave off the quiver that threatened.

"I know."

She swallowed and gritted her teeth. "*Ever.*"

"I know."

She frowned at Duncan's insistence that she was not responsible for the men's deaths, but she had pulled the trigger. It was them or her, but she killed one man with her hands, up close and personal. But he would have killed Miss Abigail. For every action there was a "but," *but* it wasn't enough to allow her to clear her conscience. Round and round it went. They had been over this many times—sometimes sober, sometimes drunk.

Neither way seemed to work any better.

She pressed her lips together and rubbed her leg that ached when she moved it—another reason to stay in bed forever, if that was what it would take to get her sanity back.

"Look, Joan," Duncan said. "Some days are going to be harder than others. In time, there'll be more good days than bad days, and before you know it, bad days will be a thing of the past. We'll take it one day at a time, okay?"

She peeked under the gauze on her thigh. "You're just talking bullshit to get me out of bed."

"You have a visitor. Suck it up and get through it."

Getting no response from Joan, Duncan hesitated before continuing. "When most people say 'I know how you feel,' they don't. But, I *do* know how you feel. I've been where you are now. Believe me, it's normal to feel bad when you kill another human being—even bad guys. I know things look dark now, but you have to get up and go through the motions of everyday living. Doing day-to-day activities will bring you to a place where you start to feel normal again."

There was that word again. Normal. Normal for who? Normal like it was? A new kind of normal? If she allowed things to go back to normal, whichever version assumed prominence, would that disrespect the lives she took. These men had been someone's son, or father, or lover. And the Lisa Browns. She was no less guilty for their deaths. They, too, had loved ones who were devastated by their absence. Devastated by her actions.

Duncan gently kneaded her neck and shoulders. "You have to start talking about your feelings, or the ghosts of the dead will never go away. You have to light a candle to get rid of the darkness."

The words spilled out of her mouth before she could stop them. "But I like the darkness."

Duncan jumped up and reached for her clothes from the night before, piled up on the floor where she had left them. It was a sideways, one-step reach, grabbing the whole pile in one big hand. Still leaning over, he flung them at her in an underhand swoop.

"That's it! I'm done talking. Get up and get dressed. It's rude to keep a visitor waiting."

When she looked up, all she saw was the door slamming behind him. The clothes at her feet reeked of stale alcohol and something else. Perspiration and unwashed body, she surmised. She shrugged and replaced the shorts and tee shirt she slept in with the musky, smelly clothes she had worn every day for the past five days. What did she owe somebody who dropped in unannounced?

Wobbling down the short hallway, using the walls to keep her balance, Joan looked up and saw Duncan twist his torso through the doorway to the living room. He had been talking to whoever was in there. Whoever had come to make her day more miserable—as if that were possible.

The view from the doorway showed Jason sitting directly across the room from the entrance to the living room, arms crossed, looking at her with his expressionless, dark brown eyes. She looked back at him, not sure what to make of the situation. Same black hair slicked back into a low ponytail. The same chin hair and small dot of hair under his bottom lip—womb broom, he liked to call it—tattoos, piercings. Nothing new. A former member of the Constitution Defense Legion, Jason had found Duncan via a Facebook page he had put up, under the code name Charles Darnell Lutz, to attract former CDL members. But he had arrived in Phoenix two months ago, maybe more. Jason was a regular, not a visitor. Joan blinked, stumped.

Jason nodded across the room and to her right. Jason's girlfriend, Flora was handing someone a glass of sweet tea. Jason and Flora met the second day Jason was in town and hadn't been apart since. Flora was a short, chubby, third-generation biker chick with long black hair. A blue streak was dyed from the hairline above her left eye to the tip of her hair that brushed her waist. Heavy makeup, black nail polish. Goth. Not really Goth. Goth-light. Tattoos, piercings. She was Jason's girlfriend. No doubt about that. But she was a regular, too.

The remaining tequila in Joan's brain slowed her thought processes. It was difficult to focus. The headache was a mean distraction and was intensified by the light that stung her eyes. But it crashed into her head who the visitor was.

"You were supposed to be back at work three days ago," Miss Abigail said as she moved her wheelchair forward to get a better look at Joan. Ice cubes tinkled as she steadied the glass on the arm of the wheelchair.

Joan didn't want Miss Abigail to see her in this unkempt, bleary-eyed, washed-up way. She backed up, but bumped into Duncan, who was blocking the doorway and any chance of escape.

His lowered voice came from behind her, so close she could feel his breath. "Miss Abigail came all this way to see you. Aren't you going to talk to her?"

After a glance over her shoulder at him, she went to Miss Abigail's side and knelt next to the wheelchair. She winced at the increased pounding in her head.

"Get back, girl," Miss Abigail said. It was loud, and unmistakably an order. Joan didn't move, confused as to what she could have done wrong. "Get back," Miss Abigail repeated wrinkling her nose. "You stink!"

Looking over her right shoulder, Joan saw Duncan cover his mouth to hide a smirk. She looked over her left shoulder at Jason. Same thing. She moved back and sat on the edge of the coffee table.

"You didn't show up for work, so I came to find out what your major malfunction is." College educated, a dignified member of the ladies community, the use of slang was especially funny when used by Miss Abigail. Joan smiled. Before she could answer, Miss Abigail continued. "I can see now what your problem is. You're feeling sorry for yourself. Oh, boo-hoo. Poor little Miss Angel. And that's another thing we have to straighten out. How many names can one girl have?"

Joan snapped her head to look at Duncan. He gave her a short nod. She guessed it meant it was okay to confide in Miss Abigail.

"About my names—" Joan started.

"Pooh about your name. We'll get to that."

Miss Abigail took a sip of the sweet tea. It was a slow, nerve-wracking move. Hands shaking under the weight, one wrong move and it would spill down the front of the beautiful, yellow, silk blouse she wore for the visit. Joan waited patiently, ready to leap to her aid.

"Very well made, Mr. Kearney," Miss Abigail said. "You must be from the South."

Joan spun around in her seat on the coffee table. Kearney was sitting on the recliner. When she entered the room, he would have been to her left. She hadn't looked that way. Her attention, cloudy as it was, had been only within the triangle of Jason, Flora, and Miss Abigail. She was losing her edge.

Miss Abigail nodded approval past Joan toward Kearney. "He's a nice man."

Kearney smiled his big, toothy grin, hands raised, palms up as if to say, "Am I great or what?"

Joan looked back at Miss Abigail and forced her answer through her teeth. "At times." She wasted no kindness on Kearney. There was bad blood between them, and nothing had happened in the past several months to change that.

The sweet tea safely back on the arm of the wheelchair, Miss Abigail continued, "I understand that you are going through a hard time. It's going to be up and down, good and bad, happy and sad. But moping around all day, and drinking God knows how much liquor all night, is not the way to get over it. Isn't that right, Duncan?"

Duncan was leaning on the doorjamb with his arms crossed, a serious look on his face. "Yes, ma'am. That's what I've been telling her."

Miss Abigail addressed Joan. "Girl, this wonderful, smart man has told you what I just told you?"

"Yes, but—"

"And you didn't listen to him? Instead, I had to drag myself out of the house and make that long ride over here to tell you the same thing?"

Unsure how to respond, Joan sat with her mouth open.

"They say you have to hit bottom before you can start working your way back to rights," Miss Abigail said. "Well, girl, *I say* this is the bottom-est you are going to get. You will be at work at seven sharp tomorrow morning. No excuses. Hear me?"

"Yes, ma'am."

"Now who's going to drive me home? It took so long for Angel to come and greet me, now I'm tired and it's time to go."

Kearney, Jason, and Flora stood up. Duncan pushed himself off the doorjamb. Miss Abigail spun the wheelchair and whirred through the dining room toward the back door.

Before going through the doorway, she looked over her shoulder. "Well, Miss Lady of the House, aren't you going to see me out?"

Duncan put his fingertips in the small of Joan's back and guided her after Miss Abigail.

They still hadn't discussed her names.

ⱭⱭⱭ

After everyone left, Joan remained on the small back porch

leaning against the bare wood of the roof support. In dire need of paint for many years, it felt rough against her left temple. If only the pounding headache would stop. A white mug filled with black coffee appeared next to a hand offering two pills. She looked up into Duncan's face.

"Naproxen for you headache," he said.

"I never heard Miss Abigail speak so harshly," Joan said as she picked the pills out of his hand.

"She's a sweet, gentle lady, but she knows how to dish out tough love. It got your attention, didn't it?"

Joan nodded. After washing down the pills with the hot, dark liquid, she saw the thoughtful look on his face and asked, "What are you thinking about?"

"I think *La Espada* is trouble. Big trouble."

"But it doesn't have anything to do with us, right?"

"Three Lisa Browns have been killed in the last three days. What do you think?"

"That's just a coincidence," Joan said.

It was a bold-faced lie. She winced and rubbed her forehead. She and Duncan had an honesty pact. They didn't have to tell each other everything, but what they said to each other had to be the truth. Her feet were wet already, might as well jump into the murky waters. "It doesn't have anything to do with the incident at the Pennington ranch."

Gently grabbing her shoulders, Duncan said, "Admit it. It isn't a coincidence. What is your gut telling you?"

"It's juiced. Blotto."

"No, it's not. Your instincts are as sharp as ever, and they are screaming through the alcohol haze. That's why you've been drinking so much, to drown them out. Your instincts are the best I've ever seen. What are they telling you?"

She swayed as she shifted her weight back and forth between her feet. She studied the indentation below the Adam's apple in Duncan's throat. She knew the answer, had known it the second she heard about the first Lisa Brown's death. But admitting it, saying it out loud, would damn her to being just as responsible for their deaths as she was for the deaths of the nine intruders at the ranch a week and a half ago.

"Talk to me, *nena*."

The endearment brought her eyes up to his. He only used it when they made love, but that hadn't been so often lately.

"Say it," he said softly.

Several seconds passed before she spoke. "It's no coincidence. *La Espada* has somehow learned my alias. They're seeking revenge."

After thoughtfully placing the mug on the railing, she wrapped her arms around his waist.

He pulled her against him. "It's a *fake* name. They won't find you. But this is something bigger. Bigger than us. I can feel it. Can't you?"

She pressed her head against his chest. "Don't do this. Don't make this something bigger than it is." She looked up at him. "Put your inner soldier to sleep."

His eyes twinkled, the corners creased. "My *inner soldier?*"

She frowned. This conversation was going down a dark and deadly path. Trouble loomed at the end, and yet he found humor in her words.

"My *inner soldier* is telling me this is bigger than you and me. My inner soldier says these *La Espada* guys are itching for a fight. Their warped minds want this land for Mexico, and they've started their fight for it."

It became clear to her, like the sun emerging from behind a cloud. This was about him. It was always about him—him and his fighting to save the world. "I don't see it. It's just them against us. And you don't think they'll find us. So..." She let her voice trail off.

"Washington is weak. To *La Espada*, this is their chance and they're taking it."

"This isn't our land. We're from Pennsylvania. Let the Arizonans fight for their land." She sighed. "I just don't see it being our fight."

"Or won't." He saw the darkness come over her eyes and crushed her in his embrace.

"Maybe you're right," she said, her voice muffled by his chest. "But it still doesn't make it *our* fight."

"If not us, who?"

"The police for one. Local Arizonans for another. The national guard trains for this kind of thing. Let them earn their pay."

"Washington has made it clear they aren't interested. The states are hamstrung with high debt." He added with a half-smile, "Like it or not, it's us, or there'll only be forty-seven-point-five states in the future."

She overlooked his attempt at humor. "You don't know that."

"One thing I do know is I need you in this with me."

"If I don't support you, you won't go ahead with this?" she asked, knowing nothing she said or did would stop him once his mind was set.

He rocked her in his arms. "Come on, baby, I need to know you support me. I can't do this without you."

She pulled away and leaned against the porch railing. Thoughts of the stress and paranoia at the end of her time in the Constitution Defense Legion raised her heart rate. She hadn't realized it at the time, but joining the underground resistance group destined her to a life on the run or in jail. She was a fugitive. Once a fugitive, always a fugitive. All the more reason to stay under the radar. Starting up another militant group was not under the radar. It was stepping into a spotlight. Unaware that she was rubbing the backs of her hands that had been broken during the final interrogation by the Legion leadership, she continued, "I don't know if I can go through this again. I'll have to think about it." After a pause, she added, "You joined the Legion without me, and you did just fine."

"I was a different person then."

So was I, she thought as she turned her back on Duncan and reached for the door to the kitchen.

CHAPTER 4

Jake Pennington closed the door after the last person arrived. The response to his open invitation was far greater than he had imagined. His refurbished, expansive living room that overlooked the foothills was packed, leaving many people standing. A few joined his younger son on the hearth. His eldest son sat in the overstuffed chair to the right of the hearth. Not fully recovered from his gunshot wounds, it was a strain for him to be there, but he wouldn't hear of missing it.

Jake knew the majority of the people in the room, having grown up with them and attending high school together. There were some old timers, too. He had been a wild high school football star. At one time or another, each of the older men caught him up to no good and had lovingly corrected him and straightened him out. The rest were newcomers to the city, who had moved to Phoenix to seek their fortunes in a clean, safe environment. Occupations ranged from ranchers and large business owners to Mrs. Chung, who owned a deli in Glendale, and Patti, a beautician at Abigail's favorite beauty shop. The common thread they shared was fear for the futures of their businesses.

After making sure everyone was comfortable, he glanced over at his wife sitting in her wheelchair in the doorway between the formal living room and the kitchen. She gave him a smile of encouragement. He knew he could always count on Abigail to be his support system. Behind Abigail stood his daughter with her arms crossed. Away at college during the attack on the ranch, she didn't have the emotional attachment to the invasion that he and his sons did. But Pennington blood coursed through her veins, and in time the tight-lipped frown would turn into support. He'd stake the ranch on it.

With one last look around the room, Jake called for everyone's attention. Eyes of ranchers, businessmen, and locals who were concerned about the rise in violence turned to look at him. Lou Gomez, owner of the next ranch over, nodded support.

Jake didn't waste any time getting to the point. He started by summing up what he felt were everyone's fears. No one disagreed with any of his points. Some added a few of their own concerns. Without asking directly, Jake could tell who the supporters were, and who was there out of curiosity. Body language told him several were on the fence—they wanted to help out, but weren't sure what they could do. Jake was not worried about them. They'd find their footing and come through.

A united front was called for, and they agreed to work through their state and federal representatives. At a future meeting, he would invite local law enforcement so those who were interested could set up block watches, although out in the rural areas, a "block watch" would take on a whole new meaning. There'd be roving guards in pickup trucks with massive firepower.

This preliminary meeting was called merely to send up a trial balloon. Jake thought better of bringing up the support they would receive from Duncan and his group. Until he was absolutely sure who was supportive and who was not, it was better to conceal the identities of the militia members. Only he, his sons, and Abigail knew who they were. His daughter wouldn't even know until he was sure of her full and undisputable support.

The members of the militia had put their lives on the line for his family, and now were putting their lives on the line for the community. Betraying their trust would go against every ounce of life in his body.

Time sped by and the meeting finally broke up at ten-thirty. As people were talking quietly among themselves and generally heading toward the door, Jake motioned for Lou Gomez to hang back. Lou nodded and finished his conversation with the real estate broker on his right.

When the house was finally empty and his daughter was starting to clean up, Jake indicated for his neighbor to follow him to his office. Once inside, Lou smiled at the offer of some rare and well-aged Scotch whiskey and sat in one of the leather chairs facing the desk. The bullet holes from the home invasion did not go unnoticed.

After handing Lou the glass of scotch, Jake closed the door to his office and sat in the chair next to Lou. Their families had owned and worked the adjacent ranches for generations. They grew up together and played high school football side by side. They watched each other's kids grow into well-adjusted, hardworking adults, shared the joys of ranching, and helped each other when ranching was more of a struggle than a joy.

It was time to bring Lou Gomez into the loop.

℮∽℮∽

Just as Duncan had promised, good days started to nudge out the bad. But Joan was tired—tired of being on the run, tired of a dead-end job, tired of Duncan's fixation on *La Espada*, and tired of a house full of people.

With the Pennington's daughter home from college, Joan was given the summer off, so Flora wrangled a job for her at Colors, the hangout of the Demon Brotherhood Motorcycle Club. When Flora's parents died in a motorcycle accident, she moved in with her grandmother, but was raised with thirty-two moms and dads. The motorcycle club was her family, Colors her home, so it was easy to get Joan the job as the short-order cook.

It wasn't a challenging job. Bikers ate simple food that was easy to prepare. They would come into the bar in groups and there would be a flurry of action at the grill, then it would drop off to nothing.

She only worked the supper rush, which meant only five or six hours, four days a week, but she was paid in cash at the end of each shift—no paper trail, no questions, no cops.

One of Flora's "dads" was Red Dog, a skinny, red-haired member of the Brotherhood, who'd latched onto the group of former Legion members. Everyone liked him well enough. The biggest problem with him was Rosemary, the girlfriend he brought with him. Joan thought of her as the *too*-girl. She was too talkative, too loud, wore too much make-up, her nails were too flashy, her hair too brassy, and she wore too few clothes that covered her too large breasts that were just…too…fake. But what got under Joan's skin was the way Rosemary always had her arm around Red Dog but her eyes on Duncan.

Maybe if Joan was less tired, she could sort it out, but she was expending every ounce of energy she had to keep herself from spinning out of control. It was like sand in an hour glass. There was only so much sand, and when it fell to the bottom globe, it was gone, used up. When the finite energy was gone, she had no more energy for self-control. She settled into a routine she could handle of working, taking care of herself, and taking care of Duncan. She had enough energy for that. There wasn't enough energy for anything else, and that included Rosemary.

Joan always took a shower when she arrived home from work to wash away the smell of charred hamburgers and onions and the grease that clung to her skin, and tonight was no exception. Freshly washed and moisturized, she gave Duncan a quick kiss on the head as he sat at the dining room table playing cards with Jason, Kearney, and Red Dog. She noticed Rosemary's absence at the table and her thoughts turned to the pleasure of getting off her aching feet.

She rolled her shoulders and sighed as she walked through the wide archway to the comfortably decorated living room. The TV was on, which gave the room a soft, flickering glow. The house Duncan and she shared was a small ranch, located off a winding road that skirted one of the many canyons north of the city limits of Phoenix. It was situated in such a way that the long gravel drive funneled visitors to the back door that led to the kitchen. The front door, into the living room, was unnoticed and unused.

She gave a wave of hello to Flora who was sitting on an over-stuffed leather chair, watching TV. Joan turned toward the cushy leather sofa, and stopped short. The blood surged to her face. Rosemary was lying in her spot. Rosemary knew the routine. She had been there often enough—too often for Joan's liking.

In as pleasant a tone as she could muster she said, "C'mon, get up. I want to lie down."

"I was here first."

"I always lay on the couch when I get home from work. You know that."

"Not tonight. Everybody doesn't have to jump when you talk."

Everything went white. Rosemary's impertinence fueled a slow burning ember of resentment.

Blinded by rage, Joan yelled, "Get the fuck up!"

Flora half raised herself out of her chair and looked anxiously at Jason and Duncan in the dining room.

"Sit over there," Rosemary said, making a dismissive gesture toward a recliner at the end of the couch.

Who the hell does she think she is? She's acting like this is her *house. Her house—*

Joan repeated the thought to herself as she looked over her left shoulder at Duncan with a glare that would have stopped a tractor trailer in its tracks. He was watching her with a scowl on his face. He had been impatient and sharp-tongued with her lately, especially where Rosemary was concerned. *Why would he be so concerned about Rosemary? Unless...*

She saw that the dumb bastard had no idea what Rosemary lying on the couch had to do with him. Sitting erect and frowning at her, he placed both hands on the edge of the table as if he were about to get up.

Joan looked back at Rosemary. *There's only one thing that would make her think she is above me in the pecking order in* this *house.* The thought released a blast of anger that had been bubbling behind a very thin filter.

"Why you no good piece of shit," Joan said through clenched teeth as she grabbed Rosemary by the waistband of her low-hung shorts and by the shirt between her breasts.

Too late, Rosemary saw the wild, primal look in Iron Angel's eyes, before she picked up Rosemary and propelled her across the room, sending her crashing against the TV stand and sliding to the floor. Like a wild predator focused on her hapless prey, Iron Angel stalked Rosemary, who was in a heap on the floor moaning and holding the back of her head.

Iron Angel didn't see Duncan fly into the living room or Red Dog race past him to Rosemary. Duncan grabbed Iron Angel, yelling something at her, but she had tunnel vision. And at the end of that tunnel was Rosemary. Voices were muffled and far away. Slowly Duncan's voice became clearer, and the rest of the room came into focus. He was telling her to settle down. Relaxing enough to get Duncan to let her go, she stood eye to eye with him in the center of the room, fists clenched, trying to control her breathing.

Meanwhile Red Dog had helped Rosemary to her feet. She was poisoning the air with her 'poor little me attacked by the crazy woman' act. Duncan put his index finger up as a warning to Iron Angel, then turned to examine Rosemary's head. As soon as his hands parted her hair to check the wound, she shot a smug look at Iron Angel.

Iron Angel dove for Rosemary's throat.

Duncan reacted quickly, accidentally hitting Iron Angel's nose with his elbow. He peeled back her fingers that were clamped around the woman's neck like steel cables. When the last finger was pulled off, he grabbed her by the shoulders and backed her up across the living room toward the doorway to the dining room. He pushed her hard against the doorjamb. She couldn't see or hear him clearly through her anger, but the growl in his voice told her she had stepped over the line. He nodded his chin to someone behind her before turning back to see if Rosemary needed any medical attention.

Joan stood motionless, unsure of what had just happened, eyes watering, a dull humming sound filling her ears. She felt something warm on her upper lip. She touched her index finger under her nose. When she looked at it, it was covered with blood.

An arm covered in a tattoo sleeve reached across her and gently tugged on her shoulder to encourage her to go into the dining room. She allowed Jason to back her up a few steps.

With every step backward, she felt a chasm widening between her and Duncan. He was so in control. But even on her best days, she was simply circling the rim. How much longer would he put up with this and stay with her?

And had she just attacked a defenseless woman? She had never assaulted a woman before, or anyone for that matter— even Kearney escaped the pain she would have loved to inflict on him. The memory of the two cops in Cleveland came back—living proof that she couldn't say she had never used her skills and training except in the case of self-defense. Who was she becoming?

The adrenaline dump faded and she was left muddled and drained. It drained like water from a toilet, circling, circling, then gone. Her head swam. She dropped her arms to her sides and groaned.

She relaxed as Jason leaned in toward her, talking in soft, soothing tones, slowly moving her toward a chair. He was the youngest in their group, but he was the least volatile, as well as the most methodical, detail-conscious, and at this moment, mature beyond his years. Once a marine, always a marine.

Medical complaints and insults aimed at Joan came from the living room. Rosemary was bemoaning that Joan was out of control, and something should be done before someone really got hurt. It worked its magic. Joan watched helplessly as Red Dog helped Duncan tend to Rosemary on the far end of the living room.

Jason guided Joan into a dining room chair and put a hand on her shoulder. Kearney, convinced Duncan had calmed down, joined them and knelt next to Joan. Flora appeared with a frozen bag of corn.

"Go away, Kearney," Joan said as she pressed the bag of frozen corn to her nose. "I'm not in the mood for your freakin' bullshit right now."

"We need to talk about what's going on with you," Kearney said.

"Butt out."

"I helped Duncan through his PTSD and I can help you, too, if you'll let me," he continued anyway. "I'm not going to lecture you, but I do want to say one thing. Rosemary wants Duncan. I think we can all agree on that."

"Thank you for your support—" The moisture in her eyes was from more than the accidental blow to her nose.

"Sarcasm aside, Rosemary wants a man of her own. She knows Red Dog isn't going to leave his wife for her, and so she set her sights on Duncan. She doesn't understand the bond you two have and how it plays out. That lack of understanding, combined with sensing weakness in you, gives her the confidence to go after him. She doesn't know what you are capable of." He looked up at Rosemary in the living room. "Well, maybe she does now. But you have to get a hold of yourself and be strong."

"He's right," Jason added. "You're a freakin' roller coaster ride. It's painful to watch. You were *always* strong and steady and in control before…things got shitty."

"And how do I do that? How can I be strong when I can't sleep? I have no drive and—" She sighed and her shoulders hunched forward. She leaned her elbow on the table and put her head in her hands. "I don't have the energy to deal with this anymore." She swallowed a sob and slowly shook her head. She couldn't cry in front of these battle-hardened men. "I hate myself the way I am. I know I'm out of control sometimes, but I can't seem to stop myself."

"Did you know Duncan made a vow to do whatever it might take to make sure you don't do time?" Kearney asked. "He would throw himself in front of a speeding police car, if it meant you got away. That's why he got so angry when you hurt Rosemary. If she presses charges, you'll end up in jail. All his protection, his attention to detail his…love for nothing. I don't think you understand what it takes for a guy like Duncan to love that much. He just doesn't *like* you right now."

"Doesn't like me?" It was weak and almost inaudible. Salty tears built up and stung her lower eyelids.

Jason shot a grave look at Kearney. "What Kearney means is Duncan *likes* you." He pushed Kearney aside and leaned toward her with one elbow on the table, other hand on the back of her chair. He looked into her eyes. "He just doesn't like the wishy-washy way you're acting. He misses the woman you used to be." After glancing at Kearney, he continued, "We all do."

Flora reached out to him and he moved back to stand next to her.

"I miss that person, too," Joan agreed, voice weak and low. She used the back of her hand to wipe away a tear before it slid down her cheek.

Kearney put his hand on her shoulder and braced himself for her rejection, but he had to say it, "Be strong, Iron Angel. You didn't get the nickname by being weak and out of control. You are good, and you are strong."

"I'm not that person anymore."

"Yes, you are." He leaned in. She could smell the alcohol on his breath. "Yes. You. Are. You never stopped being that person. I know it doesn't seem like that now, but take my word for it, you are that person. You *are* Iron Angel, but you're going to have to reach down deep inside and find the old you and drag it out—kicking and screaming, if necessary."

Her weak, fleeting smile encouraged him to continue.

"Sometimes you have to play the game."

"I don't play games. What you see is what you get."

"That's it exactly," Jason piped in.

Kearney looked at Jason with shrugged shoulders, hands palms up.

"You know how they say," Jason continued, "'if when you feel sad, you force yourself to smile anyway, your mood improves?' Well, what Kearney is getting at is this—when you're feeling weak, you put on the *appearance* of being strong, and what people perceive is what they'll believe."

"I don't believe in that bullshit."

"You don't have to believe it," Kearney said. "You just have to make everyone else believe it. You said you didn't like who you've become, right? Well, *act* the way you want to be and you will *be* what you want to be, if only in other people's eyes. You will respond to the way they see you, and they'll respond to your response, and so on."

He knitted his brow, not sure if what he said made any sense, and looked at Jason. Jason shrugged.

"Play the game," Joan whispered under her breath, glancing over at Rosemary and the attention she was getting. "Play the game," she repeated with more emphasis. Meeting Kearney's gaze with a slight tilt of her head, she finished her thought. "So all I have to do is *pretend* to be strong, and—" She looked down at her open hands. "—everyone will *think* I'm strong." Her voice took on an unexpected edge. "And if I play the game long enough, I won't have to play the game anymore because—" She curled her fingers into fists. "I *will be* strong?"

"Yeah, something like that," Kearney said. "Give it a try. What do you have to lose?"

They all looked up at the sound of raised voices coming from the living room. Red Dog was telling Duncan to get his girlfriend under control. To his credit, and Rosemary's dismay, Duncan was defending Joan.

"That son of a bitch, Duncan, needs to get his head screwed on straight," Flora groused. "How can he even touch that piece of shit tramp without burning the skin off his hands to get her filth off his skin? And Red Dog—telling him to get *you* under control. He's running around with that cold-blooded, manipulative lizard when he has a great wife at home. He's a worthless, sub-species of a human, if I ever saw one."

"Flora, honey, why don't you tell us what you really think?" Jason joked as he gave her a playful squeeze.

Joan laughed, winced, then they all laughed.

Red Dog and Rosemary passed through the dining room on their way to the back door, glaring at Joan on the way past.

Strengthened by Kearney and Jason's pep talk, Joan said, "You want Duncan to get *me* under control? You better work on your messed up girlfriend. She's heading for a—"

Duncan interrupted, "Knock it off!"

Emboldened by Duncan's rebuke Red Dog retorted, "Why you insolent—" He squared off with Joan, but Jason and Kearney stepped forward to confront him.

Kearney poked him in the chest. "Hey. Watch your step. She's right. Your chick is way out of line here." With his thumb pointing over his shoulder at Joan, he continued, "This is *her* home," then added, poking Red Dog in the chest, "so *you* better get *your chippie* under control."

"Knock it off, all of you," Duncan interjected to exert some control over the situation before it exploded again. "Red Dog and Rosemary are leaving. It's over. Let's all calm down."

Jason and Kearney glared at Red Dog who glared back. Red Dog backed off first. The power of Duncan's rebuke of Iron Angel was fading and the other former Legion members were closing ranks around her. Red Dog grabbed Rosemary and yanked her toward the kitchen. The back door slammed.

"Why don't you go and lie down on the couch and relax, my angel. I'll get you a tequila and Coke," Duncan offered as a sign of peace.

"Go to hell," Joan said, standing slowly to test the stability of her legs. Kearney's and Jason's words came back to her. With a glance at Kearney then Jason, her tenseness disappeared. A broad smile came on her face. "Thank you, but I'm fine. I can take care of myself."

Grabbing the bag of frozen corn, she calmly walked to the couch, flopped down, and put her head on the armrest. With the bag of frozen corn on her nose, she picked up the remote and started changing channels.

Duncan looked to the others with a questioning look on his face.

"Too little, too late, buddy," Kearney said.

Before he could ask for an explanation, Flora offered, "Why don't we play some poker or something?"

After a couple rounds, Flora checked on Joan. By that time, Joan had fallen asleep, hand dangling off the edge of the sofa, remote on the floor. Flora gently placed Joan's hand on her waist. After placing the remote on the coffee table, she returned to the dining room and whispered, "She's sleeping."

Duncan looked longingly at Joan and started to go to her. Jason stopped him and shook his head. After a long, thoughtful look, Duncan sat down and picked up the cards in front of him. He rearranged the cards in the newly dealt hand and got his head into the game.

CHAPTER 5

It had seemed right to Special Agent Woyzeck. The tip had all the hallmarks of the Constitution Defense Legion. Two men and a woman, armed to the teeth, but quiet and unassuming. Even the descriptions had been close—not real close, but close enough. From his office in the Pittsburgh Fusion Center, the tip had seemed too good to be true, and he had jumped on the first flight out of Pittsburgh International Airport to Little Rock. *Well, you know what they say about something seeming too good to be true—*

"Agent Woyzeck," the SWAT Team leader broke into his thoughts, "we're ready to button this up. Did you get everything you needed from the target location?"

"What?" Agent Woyzeck snapped out of his retrospection. "Oh, yes, I'll be downtown in a few to question the male." His fugitives were not here, possibly never were. As it turned out, one of the men in the house had an outstanding warrant and was taken into custody for that. Maybe he would know something about any Legion members in the area. It was a long shot, but all the short shots had been picked clean long ago.

Once lean and muscular, Agent Woyzeck lumbered to his rental car to head downtown. A spare tire had formed around his waist from all the late night pastries and fast food gobbled down during the hectic first three months of the manhunt. Losing the extra weight now was not on the top of his To-Do List. When this was over, he'd find the time to hit the gym again.

As he stood leaning on the doorframe of his car and eyeballing the house the SWAT team had just raided, he rubbed his angular jaw and thought through his case. Duncan and Joan were together. That was a given. Back in his office he had a pile of store surveillance tapes all the way across the country from central Pennsylvania—grainy photos of Duncan getting gas, Joan buying fast food—always two steps ahead of the CDL Task Force.

Duncan had to have sucked Joan back into his ill-conceived, soldier-for-hire, irrational underworld. Surely, sometime during the last five months, she could have escaped. No, she was with him willingly.

And Joan really stuck in his craw. The state's evidence she had given had been right on the money, and the resulting dragnet had nabbed eighty-one of the known one hundred eighteen operatives in the Constitution Defense Legion. Of the thirty-seven that were not caught in the dragnet, twelve remained at large. It was only a matter of time, and their cases would be closed out as well. No, it wasn't the information she had given, it was that he had worked hard to make a great deal for her. And how had she repaid him? By getting caught up in the same old shit.

If that was not enough to get under his skin, Joan had been nabbed out from under his nose by ten men dressed in black, who remained unidentified to this day. Dragged by her hair out of his car by a man with a black ponytail, while he and another agent sat helplessly, MAC-10s pointed in their faces. Heavily shackled, Joan had been unable to save herself. Her screams and pleas for help still rang in his ears and haunted his dreams.

It was still a mystery, to this day, why he and the other agent were not executed while they sat defenselessly in the car. Maybe it was because they were federal officers. Maybe these men were the last few human beings in the Legion. It didn't really matter why he and the other agent were allowed to live. He used the time he was given industriously. The first two weeks after Joan's abduction from his car, he had worked relentlessly and virtually without sleep to find her. As day after day passed, the likelihood of recovering her alive faded, but he did not give up.

Eventually, surveillance tapes surfaced with sightings of her—alive—with Duncan.

He had to find her. She was the first priority, the key. After all, as the well-worn saying went: *if you find the woman, you'll find the man.*

As Agent Woyzeck slid into the front seat of his Altima rental car, he hoped the perp they had downtown would know something. Anything. This was his last viable lead, and so far, it had not proved to be so viable.

ɛ⁄ɔɛ⁄ɔ

In her dream, Joan had three ligatures around her neck. All she could see was the ceiling where it met the wall. And the knife in Kearney's hand. He asked her a question she didn't quite understand then peeled off a swath of skin from her thigh. She tried to scream but there was something over her mouth. She couldn't make out what he was saying. He peeled off a swath of skin from her abdomen. She screamed for Duncan...

ɛ⁄ɔɛ⁄ɔ

Duncan had slept on the chair in the living room where Joan had fallen asleep on the couch. When he heard her scream his name, muffled by a pillow, he crossed the room in a flash and knelt on one knee beside the couch. "Joan. Wake up. You're having a nightmare."

Still not fully awake, she moaned, "The pain. Duncan, give me something for the pain." She sat up and grabbed his arm in a death grip. Still in a hazy half-awake, half-asleep world, she looked around the room with unfocused darting eyes. "Where am I? Where's Kearney?"

"You had a bad dream. We're in our living room."

"It was the same dream. With Kearney..." She rubbed her thighs and stomach. "The pain feels so real."

"Yes, I know. Dreams seem very real sometimes." He rubbed her arms to calm her. "What was it you said the first time you were in my bed and I woke up from a nightmare?"

With several last strokes of her thighs and abdomen, she said through a yawn, "Sometimes the past won't stay there."

"I wish I could find a way to keep it there for you. Better yet, erase it from your memory altogether." He coaxed her to turn toward him with his fingers behind her elbows. "Come, let me hold you."

She turned to face him, placing her feet on the floor on either side of his knees. "I don't know what got into me last night. But Rosemary—ooh, she just chinks my chain—"

"Don't let her get to you. She's just a screwed up bitch."

"But she has her eyes on you."

"Don't let her bother you. I'm not going anywhere." He added playfully, "Like it or not, you are stuck with me."

Joan frowned. "I just have to ask, have you ever done anything to encourage Rosemary?"

"No."

"Anything. Anything at all."

"No. Nothing."

"But you've thought of it?"

"Of course, look at her." He saw the deepened frown on her face and quickly added, "But thinking isn't doing."

"Thinking leads to doing." She poked him in the chest with her index finger. "Do something about this or I'll take care of it."

"This isn't like you. I didn't think jealousy was part of your DNA."

"Me either, but take care of this or I will."

Duncan sat back on his heels. "What do you mean by you'll 'take care of it'?"

Joan shrugged. "We've been under a lot of pressure lately."

"I can handle it," Duncan said. "You have PTSD—"

Joan opened her mouth to interrupt, but Duncan put a finger to her lips. It silenced her denial. Post-Traumatic Stress Disorder. She didn't have that. She just had some memories to deal with, that was all. Once they learned their place in her past, and she gained some perspective, everything would be back to normal and she could finally have a quiet life with Duncan.

Under the radar, low profile, unseen by prying eyes. It was not PTSD.

"You feel out of control. I get that." He rubbed the side of her thighs. "Vibrant, unpleasant memories are triggered by sights, actions, even insignificant words, and they send you into a tailspin. I get that, too. I've been there—actually I'm still there because once you have PTSD, you always have PTSD."

A half-smile made a brief appearance then fell from Joan's face. "A—I don't have PTSD, and B—I've been to Iraq and back. It'll take more than an event where I was the victim to take me down."

"That's good to hear. Because the thought of decades of a living with a highly-trained woman with pinpoint accuracy with dozens of weapons *and* PTSD is *not* an appealing prospect at all."

"Decades?" Joan was stunned.

This man wasn't going anywhere. In spite of all her outbursts and weakness and pushing-and-pulling in their relationship, he was planning on staying by her side. Maybe just having Duncan in her life would lick this thing called PTSD, if she had it at all.

He leaned forward placing his forearms next to her thighs and looked up into her face. "Decades. I will gladly spend the rest of my life with you, if it means you would always be with me. I am determined to bring back that joy of life you had in the beginning. It was my saving grace, and I want to see it again."

"My joy of life?"

"Remember when we met, I was closed down and unconnected to what went on around me? Well, it was the joy I saw in your face that made me realize what was missing from my life. It was the very quality—"

"—that I lack now."

"Yes, that you lack now, that brought me out of my shell. It's precious to me and I *will* see it again in you. I will, or I'll die trying."

Joan swelled with confidence and love, but before she could answer, they heard someone walking through the kitchen. They reached for their guns, and, as one, they pointed them at the doorway with parallel arms.

Gunther walked into the room and, without flinching at having two guns pointed at him, said, "Well, look at this. Isn't this cozy?"

Being on the run hadn't changed Gunther at all. For a man in his sixties he was still spry and wiry, and still formidable looking with his buzz-cut salt-and-pepper hair. He had a slight under bite that hardened his jaw and gave him an intensity that did not belie his temperament. Bushy, gray eyebrows gave his eyes the look of a bird of prey.

"Didn't you ever hear of knocking?" Duncan said as he holstered his gun.

Gunther was the best fighter Duncan knew. He had no qualms about killing everybody and letting Satan claim his soul. But he was also an expert at silent assassinations. You never knew when someone like him might come in handy. Another piece of the fledgling militia plinked into place.

Gunther held his hands open and in front of him. "Didn't you ever hear of locking your doors?"

Resting her revolver on her thigh, Joan whispered in Duncan's ear, "What's he doing here?"

"What do you mean? I thought you liked working with Gunther."

He could feel the calm he had brought to her drain away. He leaned back and looked into her eyes. She had told him about the incident when she worked on Gunther's truck hijacking team. Could that be it? Duncan got up to shake hands with his old friend.

Gun still in her hand, Joan slowly got to her feet, trying to avoid cringing from the headache that simple movement had initiated. Duncan pulled her into him to steady her and to indicate to Gunther her place in his life.

"So St. Joan, I see you two are together. Why the last time we worked together, you—"

"I go by Iron Angel now," Joan interrupted. "And I don't want to relive the night I was part of your truck hi-jacking team."

He had killed a man in cold blood just to see her reaction. He was one cold-hearted bastard. He squinted in his usual thoughtful way with the familiar nod of his head and cleared his throat. "I knew you two would get together. I knew that if it wasn't happening that night—back then—it was inevitable. You are two buckets of water from the same friggin' well."

"I'll make some coffee." She looked at Duncan. "Can I talk to you in the kitchen?"

"Sure." On his way past Gunther, Duncan said to him, "Make yourself at home."

In the kitchen, Joan spun around. The throbbing in her head increased, but it didn't take the edge off her voice. "What's Gunther doing here?"

"Can you put the gun away?"

Joan hesitated. The hard stare in Duncan's eyes telegraphed that he wasn't going to back down. She put the revolver in the small of her back, tilted her head, and raised her eyebrows.

"If we form a militia, he's here to be a part of that."

"And you have no qualms about him being here after that attempt to kill me?"

"So that's why you're acting so strange. Shit, Joan, I thought that died with the Legion." Duncan rubbed her arms. "I told you it wasn't him. It was just a carjacking."

"It was him. You're right he wasn't the one with the gun, but he was the driver."

"You're not sure of that. You said yourself you only got a glimpse of the driver."

"I know what I saw. It was Gunther."

"What can I say to convince you that he wasn't sent to kill you?"

"I only know what I saw," Joan reiterated as she turned away from him to start making coffee. "Go spend some time with your *friend*."

Duncan grabbed her wrist. She turned and pointedly looked at his grasp on her wrist then glared into his eyes.

"I'm going to sort this out once and for all," he said as Joan yanked her wrist out of his grasp.

He returned to the dining room to find Gunther feigning interest in a painting on the wall.

Pulling the gun from the small of her back, Joan took two steps and leaned her left shoulder on the ancient rooster-themed wallpaper on the kitchen wall, just inside the doorway to the dining room. With the gun against her thigh, she slowed her breathing and listened.

"Everything okay with the old lady?" Gunther asked.

"She still harbors ill will about the attempt on her life."

Gunther jumped in to explain. "I told Kempton it was a waste of an excellent asset. All she needed was some time off. But it was his decision. He was the boss." Gunther squinted at the frown on Duncan's face and continued, "You did know there was a kill order on Joan, right?"

Joan thumbed back the hammer to cock the gun.

"No. You just told me." After a pause, Duncan said, "Something isn't right. Why would he have sent you to kill her if Kearney was ordered to interrogate her later that evening?"

"Funny thing, that—"

From where she stood, Joan could see the side of Duncan's face. She saw his jaw tighten and the blood rush to his face.

Gunther must have noticed it too, because he put up a hand and took a step back. "Not funny—more like interesting. I didn't get the order directly from Kempton. There was a mis-communication. We were only supposed to pick her up and deliver her to Kearney for him to interrogate her—and kill her, if that became necessary. As it turns out, you wound up deliv-ering her to Kearney yourself."

"Watch it, Gunther, that's my girlfriend you're being so flippant about." Duncan squared his shoulders and leaned for-ward. Gunther took another step back. Closing the gap, Dun-can continued, "It's a new day, and I'm the leader now. If any-one has a problem with her, or anyone else in the group for that matter, they come to me, and *I'll* decide what's going to be done about it. Got that?"

"Whoa, buddy. You don't have anything to worry about. I'm not here to close on a contract. That kill order expired the second the cuffs clinked shut on Kempton's wrists. That's his-tory. That's a bale of hay thrown into a paddock of hungry horses."

"Yeah? That better be the case."

"She's a warrior at heart, and you know me, I eat the hell out of that shit. Believe me, Duncan, I did not want to follow through on that order."

Duncan took another step toward Gunther. "Yeah? Well, you better hope nothing happens to her, because if it does, I'm going to hold you personally responsible. Got it?"

"Yes, sir."

"And another thing. *You* are going to tell her what you just told me. She has enough shit going on in her head without worrying about you trying to kill her."

"You know me, Duncan—"

"Do I? I'm not so sure."

CHAPTER 6

Gunther had turned out to be what he said he was—just another member of Duncan's militia. But that didn't quiet the ghosts in Joan's head. She hadn't heard a ghost gunshot—a sound no one else heard—in a couple months. But now her nerves were on edge and she wasn't sure if what she sensed was real or another manifestation of her PTSD.

She pulled her brand new Colt .45 from the holster in the small of her back and laid it in front of the row of bottles on the sideboard they used as a makeshift bar. The half-empty bottle of tequila caught her eye. She grabbed it and unscrewed the cap. Questions swirled around her mind.

It had been dark and, with only headlights in her rearview mirror, it had been hard to tell for sure, but her instincts told her she had been followed. It had to be *La Espada*. How did they find her? She had only worked at Colors for a little over a month. As short-order cook, she had very little opportunity to interact with the patrons. Besides, bikers were a secretive, close-knit group. Even if they knew something, they wouldn't tell anybody.

The tequila stung her throat as she took a long pull directly from the bottle. Wiping her lips with the index finger of her left hand, Joan thought through the circuitous trip home. She had taken steps to shake the tail—if there had been one. She raised the bottle to her lips, but hesitated before drinking. Her instincts had never been wrong before. Could she still trust them? Should she tell Duncan? She took the pull from the bottle. At least, the familiar taste of the tequila told her *something* was still right with the world.

Gunther, who had settled in well with the group, was the first to notice Joan's unusual behavior. He tapped the table to get Duncan's attention then pointed past him toward Joan. Duncan glanced over his shoulder and, in one movement, he was by her side.

"Whoa, save some for me," Duncan said putting his hand on the bottle. "Bad day?"

Joan shrugged.

"Something rattled you," Duncan said. She shook her head and reached for the bottle. He held it fast to the sideboard. "Talk to me."

"It's nothing." If Duncan knew she thought she had been tailed, when no one knew who she was or how to find her, he would worry about her. She was sure of it. She couldn't tell him.

"*Nothing* made you drink straight from the bottle?"

"It's nothing, really. I'm okay now."

"No, you're not." Duncan pressed his lips together and studied her face. Finally, he continued, "It's not like you to beat around the bush. Pick up two shot glasses, we'll go someplace where we can talk in private."

"I want to take a shower, that's all." Not sure if something actually happened or if her imagination was running wild, Joan cursed her PTSD. Some days up. Some days down. And some days her self-confidence faltered. She wanted to keep it to herself, at least until she could sort it out. No sense in getting everyone excited over a possibility.

Without raising his voice, Duncan quietly commanded, "Pick up the friggin' glasses."

"Really, I just want to—"

Duncan answered in a lowered voice that was not quite a growl, "It was not a suggestion, and I'm not going to say it again."

Joan snatched up two shot glasses.

"Look, baby, I can see you're off your stride tonight." He rubbed her upper arms to relax her as much as himself. "I'm not doing this to be mean. I'm just trying to help you stay on an even keel.

She looked straight into Duncan's eyes. "Are we going somewhere?"

"Well, at least you haven't lost your sarcasm," he muttered as he gently wrapped his muscular arm around her shoulders and guided her through the dining room toward the kitchen. She offered no resistance until Duncan grabbed the knob on the kitchen door to the porch. She pulled back with all her strength.

Duncan pinned her with his gaze. "What the hell? C'mon, let's go outside where we can talk in private."

Joan squirmed out of his embrace. "No." Squirming was so out of character for her. He was right. She was off her stride. Way off.

Duncan stood stone-faced, looking at her, the bottle of tequila dangling from his right hand. She could see he was trying to make a decision. He turned and leaned his back against the kitchen counter. "We don't have to go outside, my angel. We can stay right here." Raising the bottle of tequila, he said, "Let's make a toast."

Joan mechanically put the glasses on the counter and watched as Duncan filled each one, set down the bottle, picked up both shot glasses, and handed one to her.

"Live free or die," he said quietly, raising his glass. He didn't remove his gaze from hers.

After a brief pause, Joan responded in the same quietness, "Death is not the worst of all evils."

They chugged the shots and placed their empty glasses on the counter. As was Duncan's habit, he refilled the glasses right away. Instead of picking them up, he pulled Joan into his arms and hugged her, pressing his cheek on the side of her head.

"You've been doing so well lately. What happened?"

Joan ignored the question. Instead, she let his strength support her. His embrace allowed her to relinquish her need to be strong—if only for a moment. Duncan's toughness could be her toughness, his fortitude, her fortitude.

She relaxed in his arms. Just as she relaxed, he tensed up. She felt a presence in the room.

Without looking up, Duncan said, "Go away, Rosemary."

"I just wanted to get a beer for Red Dog."

"Not now you don't."

"But—"

Duncan raised his head and yelled into the other room, "Red Dog, get your woman out of the kitchen or I'll send her back to you in pieces."

Red Dog called Rosemary back into the dining room. Joan heard a loud exhale and could feel Rosemary staring at the back of her head.

The gentle, intimate moment lost, Duncan leaned back to look into Joan's eyes. He took both her hands into his large ones and kissed them softly. "Now, tell me what's going on."

"You're going to think I'm going crazy."

Duncan smiled. "I already think you're going crazy."

Joan smiled back. The smile was brief, and, as her eyes dropped to his sternum, she felt a deep heaviness in her gut.

He bent his knees slightly to lower himself so his eyes were level with hers. Tilting his chin down, he said, "Seriously, just tell me and let me be the judge."

Joan met Duncan's gaze, and, after a big inhale and a quick look over her shoulder, she answered him, "When I left the bar, I thought I was being followed." She said the words quickly, as if the words tumbling all over each other would make them sound rational. Duncan's hesitation, the unblinking stare, made Joan's heart drop. *I knew it. He thinks I've gone off the tracks with this one.* But relief washed over her at his next words.

"Kearney, come here a sec," he yelled to be heard in the next room.

Kearney's head appeared around the door.

"Joan thinks she might have been followed. Do a recon of the area."

Seconds later Kearney, Jason, and Gunther headed through the kitchen to the outside door, the metallic sounds of sliding bolts on their semi-automatics and checking the magazines accompanied them.

Red Dog was right on their heels. Duncan stopped him saying, "Red Dog, you stay here—just in case."

Red Dog was a newcomer to the group. It was better if he stayed in the house where Duncan could keep an eye on him.

"Got it," was all he said and he started looking out each of the windows to check the surrounding yard.

Joan moved away from Duncan and leaned on the counter where it made an L. He picked up the filled shot glasses, handed one to her, and they threw back the shots. Silence surrounded them as the familiar numbness from the alcohol flowed through her in waves, deadening her extremities, hushing the thoughts in her head. She fingered the empty shot glass, arms crossed, chin to chest.

After gently taking the glass out of Joan's hand, he reached up to touch her face. She tilted her head to accept his gesture.

He broke the silence. "I'm more determined than ever to see this through until you are the woman I met and fell in love with."

Before Joan could respond, Jason, Kearney, and Gunther returned from their recon. "It's clear now. Nothing out of place."

"So, I'm crazy, then." The words were out of her mouth before she could stop them.

"We didn't say that—" Kearney started, but was cut off when Duncan shook his head and indicated for them to leave him and Joan alone. They quickly left the kitchen.

"Don't doubt yourself," Duncan said.

"How do you do it?" Joan asked.

"Do what?

"Deal with the anxiety of being a fugitive? Don't you get a knot in your gut when you hear a police siren?"

"Look, my angel, when they come for us—if they come for us—they won't come with their sirens blaring. They consider us armed and dangerous, so they'll come quietly, with overwhelming force, in the middle of the night, when we're least expecting them."

"Great, thanks. I don't have enough trouble sleeping." Her bedroom was already buzzing with nine aggressive ghosts and the specters of the murdered Lisa Browns. Gunshots rang in her ears. The smell of burnt gun powder filled her nostrils. Splattered blood blinded her. And now, she had to worry about a SWAT team breaking their way into the room.

"Don't worry about it." He drew her back into his arms. "When they come, they come. They have the ultimate power, and they'll have the element of surprise."

"I don't care how much force they come with," Joan said, "I won't go without a fight."

Duncan cupped her face in both his hands. "No, you won't. You'll give up and do whatever they say. If you fight, they'll kill you, and I couldn't stand the thought of that. When they come, make the best deal you can—"

"What about 'live free or die?'"

"That refers to fighting for a cause. A SWAT team in our bedroom at three in the morning is not a cause. It's..." Duncan hesitated, as if searching for the right words. The corners of his mouth turned down. "...the end."

Joan hugged Duncan with all the strength she had. She couldn't bear to think about the end. She had to reserve what little strength she could muster to simply keep her day-to-day life on an even keel. She barely had enough when the routine stayed the same, but one extra stressor, one unnecessary comment, one unwanted problem, and it slipped into shit. Thinking about the logical end to their life together was that one extra thing. There just wasn't enough sand left in the hour glass.

Duncan continued, his lips pressed against the side of Joan's head, "Just pay attention to the details and stay off their radar as long as possible. It's all we can do to buy some time. In the meantime, we just live every moment to the fullest."

After several minutes of holding Duncan tightly, Joan eased her grip. The questions had stopped churning around in her mind, and Kearney's "playing the game" idea popped into her head. She was goal-oriented by nature and, with something to do, she could put this incident behind her, focus her erratic thoughts on strategy. Shaking off the tension, she started to relax. It didn't matter to her if the relaxation was the result of Duncan's comforting presence or the tequila or—the new task at hand.

The darkness had passed. She wasn't exactly happy, but she felt renewed.

"Are you hungry?" she asked.

"I could eat, but you aren't my servant."

"I know, but it's an honor to do 'wifely' things for you."

Duncan squeezed Joan. She playfully exaggerated being crushed by squeaking out, "How about quesadillas? I think we have everything I need for them."

"Sounds good to me." He kissed her lightly on the lips. "Thanks, my angel."

Joan walked with him to the dining room door and asked the others if they wanted quesadillas and a chorus of yeses all around. Joan turned to Rosemary. "You want to give me a hand?"

Duncan spun around to Joan. "What are you doing?"

"I've gotten off on the wrong foot with Rosemary. Maybe I just need to get to know her better."

Duncan shook his head and muttered, "It never ends with you."

Joan smiled in spite of the frown on his face.

"No funny stuff," he ordered.

"No. It'll be okay."

Duncan pointed his finger at her for emphasis. "No rough stuff."

"It will be okay," she said emphasizing each world, then turned to Rosemary with a smile. "Come on, Rosemary. I won't hurt you."

"Need any more help?" Flora offered.

"Rosemary and I will get this." Joan gave Rosemary a smile and a friendly "come on" wave.

Rosemary gave Red Dog a pleading look. Red Dog looked up at Duncan, who gave him a nod and indicated for Rosemary to go.

Red Dog reluctantly assured her it was okay and watched as the two women disappeared into the kitchen.

Rosemary stood in the kitchen in an uneasy silence as Joan juggled leftover chicken, a jar of salsa, cheese, and tortillas and kicked the refrigerator door shut. "The can of refried beans is on the middle shelf of the pantry, could you get that for me?"

When Rosemary appeared beside Joan with the refried beans, she asked about a can opener. Joan stopped what she was doing, pointed to the gadgets drawer, and said, "Rosemary, we got off to a bad start, and I never really gave you a chance. I want you to know that I'll make an effort to change that."

Rosemary looked over her shoulder toward the dining room. "I'm not sure we have much in common."

Joan smiled inwardly. It was obvious Rosemary wanted to escape and get away from her. "We have Duncan in common," Joan said flatly.

"Duncan? I don't know...there's nothing..." Rosemary backed up. "What do you mean?"

"I see how you look at him."

"I don't look at him any special way. I don't want Duncan. Red Dog is my man."

Joan turned to light the burner under the griddle. Leaning over to adjust the flame, she said, "I'm not blind and I'm not stupid." The flame set at the perfect intensity, Joan stood up and turned to face Rosemary. "Just watch yourself and everything will be good between us. Okay?"

Rosemary nodded and fumbled to open the can of refried beans.

While cooking up the dinner, in an attempt to ease Rosemary's nervousness, Joan asked her what her interests were, what she liked to do when she wasn't with Red Dog, and engaged in light conversation, including where she got her nails and hair done. At the end, she suggested they should have lunch together some time. Rosemary agreed, but the hesitation in her voice told Joan she was just appeasing her—probably just to get out of the kitchen without injury.

Joan smiled to herself. *This is going to be easy.*

When Joan and Rosemary appeared in the living room, Duncan smiled. "Well, I see you both came out alive."

"And at times I even had a knife in my hand," Joan said, returning his smile as she set his plate down in front of him. Rosemary was already giving Red Dog and Gunther their plates. Moving to the left, Joan handed Jason his plate. She walked around to the end of the table opposite Duncan to set down some carrots with a bowl of hummus while Rosemary handed Kearney and Flora their plates.

Kearney took one look at the bowl of hummus and said, "What the hell is that?"

"Eat your vegetables," Joan replied, giving him a playful smack across his head.

Pleased at the pleasant interaction between Joan and his friend, Duncan smiled and started eating.

A catchy contemporary Latin tune came on the stereo and Joan started dancing to it. She locked eyes with Duncan and danced around the table toward him. His eyes never left her, his half-eaten quesadilla forgotten on his plate. Watching Duncan's reaction to Joan, Rosemary crossed her arms and plopped back in her chair. His obvious delight in Joan as she danced toward him brought blood to Rosemary's face. As if putting her petulance side, she turned in her seat and put her arms around Red Dog in an overly solicitous display of interest.

Gunther turned his gaze from Rosemary and nudged Jason. He pointed to Joan and Duncan and said, "When those two lock onto each other the whole rest of the world fades away, doesn't it?"

Jason picked up a piece of carrot and dunked it into the hummus. He made a circle in the air with it. "Us around the table, at this moment, we're no longer in their universe." He popped the carrot in his mouth.

"That could be a bad thing in the middle of a mission," Gunther said.

"Uh-uh." Jason shook his head and picked up his can of beer. "They're all about the mission. No worry there."

He stopped mid-gulp when Duncan stood up from his chair.

Duncan put his right arm around Joan's waist and said, "What do you think you're doing?"

Joan smiled and said with a lilt in her voice, "Dancing."

"Dancing? So, you like to dance?"

Joan nodded.

He placed her left hand on his shoulder, gently lifted her right hand, and took a dancing posture. "Let's just see what kind of dancer you are." He stepped off dancing the merengue.

With her eyes wide and her mouth open, Joan followed his lead. She had never thought of Duncan as a dancer. Sure, they had done the Texas Two-Step once, years ago. But *Latin* dancing? She flirtatiously leaned her head at a slight angle. "I never knew your hips could move like that!"

He smiled and leaned in. "Yes, you did." When he saw the color come to her cheeks, he chuckled. "I made the rough-and-tumble Iron Angel blush."

"No, you didn't," she replied, suddenly self-conscious.

He pulled her in close. They finished the dance and remained in their embrace after the music ended.

Gunther nudged Jason again. "I never realized she could be so sexy. I've only seen her as tough. She is, without a doubt, *the* toughest woman I know."

Jason looked across the table at Kearney. "Unbreakable. Right, Kearney?"

Kearney had just put the last of his quesadilla in his mouth and he answered without swallowing. "Screw you." He slid his chair back with a thrust and stomped out of the room.

Gunther watched Kearney leave the room. He squinted and leaned forward on the table to address Jason. "What was that all about?"

"You don't know?" Jason looked over each shoulder as if he was about to tell a secret.

Before he could say anything a loud thump came at the back door. Followed by the sound of breaking glass.

CHAPTER 7

Duncan pulled his semi-automatic gun from his holster and pushed Joan aside, but she was already diving for the Colt .45 she had left on the sideboard. While Jason and Gunther, guns cocked and ready, rushed to either side of the large dining room window to check out the yard, Red Dog put Rosemary in a safe position on the floor.

The Colt tight against her thigh, Joan quickly surveyed the room, frowning at Rosemary huddled on the floor in a corner of the dining room. Looking across the room, Joan saw that Flora's face reflected her own disdain. They locked eyes and shook their heads together, reading each other's thoughts: *Worthless bitch.* Joan turned her attention back toward the kitchen and the source of the noise.

Behind Duncan and to his right, Joan gently touched his waist to let him know she was there. He moved her farther to his right, away from the doorway, and looked around the corner into the hallway just as there was a final crash and the intruders were in the house. He ducked back into the dining room. "Four. Wait till they're all in before firing."

The intruders flew through the kitchen and into the dining room. Gunfire erupted on all sides, filling the small house with the acrid smell of burnt gunpowder. Spent rounds hit the floor with metallic tings. From the surprised look on the faces of the intruders, it was obvious that a houseful of fully-armed occupants had not been part of their plan.

One of the invaders yelled a command in Spanish and they

all retreated toward their car blindly firing behind them.

Iron Angel and Duncan flew after them with Jason and Flora on their heels. One of Duncan's bullets hit one of the men in the back of the head and he dropped to the kitchen floor. As Duncan knelt to check the body, Iron Angel and Jason slid past him and fired at the three remaining invaders from the back porch, hitting them several times. The driver slumped over the steering wheel. Panic-stricken and bleeding heavily, the two remaining attackers ran around the car to pull the driver out so they could escape. Jason fired on them, and they collapsed to the ground. Iron Angel and Jason inched forward, guns raised, eyes down their barrels at the downed men.

Absorbed in their movement toward the invaders, they were unaware that Duncan had turned his attention to the activity outside and quietly slipped past the screen door to the porch. Head on a swivel, eyes down the barrel of his gun, Duncan scanned the dark, sparsely wooded area surrounding the backyard. Gunther took up a position on the porch to Duncan's left and scanned the shrubs and beat up old shed in the backyard.

One of the attackers staggered to his feet. With a knife in his hand, he made a feeble stab at Iron Angel. Duncan moved his gun to shoot him but, before he could aim and fire, she grabbed the attacker's hand, bent his arm, and stabbed the man in the abdomen with his own knife. After disarming him, Iron Angel slipped behind him and slit his throat. Blood squirted out of the severed artery, spraying her on the side of the face. While the man was still gurgling and reflexively trying to breathe, she swept him to the ground. He stopped moving. After wiping the blood from her face with the back of her arm, she stood looking down at the man at her feet, unaware of Jason approaching her.

"Angel," he said.

She heard him, but didn't answer. Thoughts bounced around in her head, never falling into a rational sequence. Her mind was dark, cold, numb. She had seen the blood drain from a man struggling to breathe and the life drain from his eyes. One thought coalesced. *Ten.*

Jason repeated her name clapping his hands inches from her face. "Iron Angel."

She turned her head and looked at him with wild, unblinking eyes.

He reflexively took a step back. When she had wiped at the blood from her face, rather than getting rid of the blood, she had only smeared it. Along with her wide, unfocused eyes, it gave her an eerie, primitive, war paint appearance. She returned her attention to the man at her feet.

Jason tried again to get her attention. "Hey, let's try to find out who these guys are and why they picked us to attack."

The adrenaline draining from her head, Iron Angel's mind settled down to the task at hand. She wiped her face again and, as she knelt down by the body at her feet, she said, "I hate the smell of blood." She looked at her fingers where the once slippery blood was drying and becoming sticky. *I hate the feel of blood.* She rifled through the pockets of the man in front of her. *Why can't I stop myself before I draw blood?*

☙❧☙❧

Back on the porch, Duncan watched the scene unfold. He was a hands-off leader. Everything in the yard was under control—no need to get involved. He holstered his gun and crossed his arms over his chest.

"That's quite a girlfriend you got there," Gunther said.

Duncan nodded slowly in agreement. The two men fell into a comfortable silence as they stood side by side, watching Iron Angel and Jason working the scene. Duncan finally broke the silence. "What have you been teaching her?"

"I didn't have much to teach her. She has had some seriously extreme training by some seriously deadly teachers," Gunther replied, slowly unwrapping a piece of gum. "Well, I guess we have the other person for our Special Actions Team." He popped the gum in his mouth and started chewing.

"I don't think that's a good idea," Duncan responded. "She's on the edge. Special Actions requires self-control and patience, and she's in short supply of those attributes these days."

"I hate to be the one to break this to you, my friend, but she is *way* past the edge. I'd venture to say she's in free fall. No, make that a downward spiral. She might be able to pull out of this." Gunther chewed the gum thoughtfully for several seconds before continuing, "I can get her to buckle down."

Duncan snorted. "Good luck with that."

Kearney's head appeared between the two men. "Good luck with what?"

Duncan frowned at his friend, "Where were you during all this?"

"Taking a shit. A man can't even take a shit in peace around here. So, who needs good luck with what?"

Gunther saw Duncan's jaw clench, and decided to change the subject. "What's going on between you and Rosemary?"

"Why? What have you heard?" Duncan replied.

He glanced over his shoulder at Kearney who was looking at him with a shit-eating grin. Duncan's glance slid over to Gunther.

"I didn't have to hear anything. The look on her face when you and Joan were locked onto each other was all I needed."

"What look was that?"

"Contempt. Jealousy. I don't know, but it wasn't a happy face. So, are you bangin' her?"

"No, but Joan thinks it's only a matter of time. Mentally, she's a mess, but her instincts are still sharp as hell."

Gunther couldn't let it go. "So, you *are* going to—"

"No! God, no. Joan's giving me enough shit and I haven't done anything. But you have to admit, Rosemary is tantalizing." Duncan thought for a moment while he rubbed the side of his face with the back of his fingers. "Just the fact that Rosemary has made it clear that she's interested in me causes Joan heartburn. Something has to be done about Rosemary. She's nothing but trouble."

"So, let me get this straight," Gunther said, "Joan just *knows* you're going to cheat on her and—"

"She said she'll know when it happens—like a damn Jedi warrior, she'll feel a ripple in the freakin' force and..." Duncan's voice trailed off.

Iron Angel picked up the guy she had just killed, grabbing him under the arms, to help Jason carry him to the trunk of the car. His head fell backward, revealing the gash across his neck.

Gunther stopped chewing his gum. "That is one helluva scary-ass woman to have you by the short ones."

"Yeah," Duncan snorted. After a moment he added drolly, "I got her right where I want her."

Gunther winced. Kearney gave a loud snort to cover the word "Bullshit."

At the sound of Kearney's snort, Jason looked up in annoyance and yelled across the yard, "We could use some help out here."

Kearney turned and went into the kitchen to fetch the dead guy that still lay on the kitchen floor.

"We'll bring the other one out to you," Gunther yelled back. He turned to help Kearney, but before leaving Duncan's side, he clamped his hand on his friend's shoulder. "You better start doing all the cooking and learn to sleep with one eye open," he said quietly

"That's what she told me—not in so many words."

Gunther looked over his shoulder at Iron Angel. "I'm anxious to work with her again. Like you, she's quick to react. Without fear. Forward moving on the attack, stopping only to make a quick assessment. And as you said, she has great instincts. Iron Angel is *my* kind of warrior." After another couple seconds watching her work with Jason, he added, "Like I said before: that's quite a girlfriend you got there." He removed his hand from Duncan's shoulder and pointed a finger at him, "One eye—"

"Roger that," Duncan said twisting his torso to watch Gunther disappear through the back door.

His attention was brought back to the yard when Iron Angel called to him, "Hey, Duncan. Come here, you have *got* to see *this*!" She was holding a book in her left hand.

CHAPTER 8

The loud music vibrated the table in the dark, crowded nightclub. Tito Orrozco sat upright, his left elbow leaning on the table, his right arm around his girlfriend who had a bored, vacant look on her face. When he left his *novia* to go to prison, he had been the center of her world. She had been lively in conversation and passionate in bed. She was all he thought of on the inside—smelling the soft scent of her shampoo, feeling her softness in his arms, having a family with her. But she was different now. She no longer had passion for him and less for his cause. The world changed in one year, six months, twenty-three days.

He spotted one of his crew as he shouldered his way through the dense gathering of chic Latinos. When he spotted Tito, he raised his chin in greeting and slid into a chair opposite Tito and his girlfriend. He ordered a drink and looked around at the women on the dance floor and the young men working their lines on the beautiful women seated at the bar. Everyone looked like they were having a good time, but he was not here to play.

The newcomer leaned across the table and said in a voice just loud enough to be heard above the music, "No one has seen them. It's like they vanished into thin air."

"What about the car?" Tito asked.

The newcomer shook his head to indicate that was gone, too.

Tito pulled his arm from around his girlfriend and leaned

forward on both elbows. "So'thing's not right. They go to hit the house of a Lisa Brown, and they do not come back?" Making a sucking sound, as if he had something stuck between his front teeth, he leaned back in his chair and shook his head. He licked his bottom lip and rubbed his front teeth against it. "This has to be the same bitch from the Pennington Ranch. Who the hell is she, this super woman?"

"I asked around," the newcomer said. "She didn't call the police. Whatever happened there, she took care of it herself. Four guys, one woman. That's a lot of cleanup to do by herself. Even for a super woman."

"I think the same thing. There has to be others, but who? How many?"

Loud music filled the pause in the conversation. Tito leaned forward in his chair when his girlfriend got up to go to *el baño* to freshen up. He wistfully watched her ass as she walked over to a couple of her friends, who had been drinking at the bar. They all got up and went together to the back of the club. The open space left behind by his *novia's* friends revealed a brunette in a short black skirt topped by a shiny blue, backless blouse. Seated near the center of the bar, she was leaning forward on the stool talking with the bartender. Before sitting back on her seat, she glanced over her shoulder at him. Tito nodded to her and flashed his best tough guy smile. She turned away.

The member of his crew leaned across the table and said, "Do you want to hit the house again? Send more guys this time?"

"No," Tito said as he smiled at the woman in the shiny blue blouse, who was flirting with him again, showing him a little more thigh. Thoughts of what he would do with her sent a wave of excitement through him. Of course, it would have to be after he dumped his girlfriend.

Without taking his eyes off the woman at the bar, who was now openly flirting, he said, "They will expect that." He reluctantly turned his attention from the beautiful woman to the fellow gang member across the table from him. "We need to find out more about this super woman and her friends. Put the pressure on her. Capture this bitch and *'esplain'* to her that she is *not* Superwoman. She will pay for the killing of my brother— if I have to do it myself."

Tito stood up, indicating the meeting was over. He headed toward the bar.

CHAPTER 9

Joan and Kearney had turned back on their twice-a-week desert run, but they were still two miles from the trailhead. Joan's green camouflage pants were stuck to her thighs. The sweat trickling between her shoulder blades was making an already foul mood worse. Kearney's comments were especially prickly this morning. The heat, the sweat, and the ache in her left leg were not helping her deal with him today.

Duncan had suggested to her that quitting her mind-numbing job at the biker bar to spend more time training would be good for her. He told her flipping burgers was not challenging enough to keep her focused and stable. Joan was inclined to agree. The home invasion—in *their* home—made her realize that she needed to be on top of her game. Trouble could descend on them at any time. After three weeks of intensive training, Joan realized it had been a good decision. Exercising had always been a stabilizing factor in her life, and it was comforting to know it still was.

"Gunny said that we can't touch each other," Kearney said. "So what if you twist your ankle. Can I touch you then? You know, to help you back to the car."

Gunther was in charge of overseeing their training, and he knew sending Joan and Kearney into the harsh desert environment could fuel the ill will between them. Fearing for Kearney's safety, Gunther had warned them against touching each other.

He had wrested a special promise from Joan to refrain from

hurting Kearney. A promise she was regretting on this day—one of her bad days.

"Do me a favor." Joan didn't look at him. Instead, she kept her eyes on the trail three feet ahead of them. She knew he was looking at her with that toothy grin. "If I twist my ankle, just shoot me and put me out of my misery. Death has to be better than struggling in this heat with your bullshit."

"It would be my pleasure." Kearney barely grazed Joan's shoulder with his hand in the shape of a gun. She shot him a withering look and slowed to a walk to ease the dull ache in her thigh. It was getting stronger every day, but the muscles were stiffening and she didn't want to overdo the exercise and slow down its recovery.

"Get away from me," she said, picking up the pace once again to put distance between them.

Kearney stopped, putting a hand in the air. "Shhh."

"Don't *you* shush *me*," Joan said. If pissing her off was his goal, he was succeeding.

"No, really, hear that?" Kearney said.

Joan stood still and listened. "No. Now stop with the jokes. No wait. I hear it now. It's voices."

"I think it's coming from over there," Kearney whispered, pointing to a ravine to their right, where a small stand of trees struggled to survive in the small canyon. "Let's go check it out."

Shoulders slumped and head flopped back, Joan groaned and dropped her arms in submission. Bidding adieu to the idea of getting to the trailhead—and the air conditioned car—she headed toward the voices. They crouched and stealthily followed a game trail that wound between the scrub brush and continued to some boulders at the edge of the ravine. Kearney stopped and peeked between two boulders to catch a glimpse of the action below them. She snuck past him to look from the other side of the opening. In unison, they dropped to the ground. Leaning their backs against the hot rocks, they discussed what they had seen.

Five dark-skinned men held captive two members of the Demon Brotherhood. One of the bikers was lying on the ground with his mouth, hands, and ankles duct taped. Another was on his knees. The duct tape had been removed from his mouth, but his hands were still taped in front of him. One of the captors was holding a gun to his head while another was pointing a gun at the biker on the ground. There was a third man leaning on the fender of the white van in feigned relaxation, ankles crossed, cleaning his nails with a knife. Two others were acting like patrolling guards.

"I count five," Kearney whispered. "They aren't Mexican. Middle Eastern is my guess."

"Yeah, that's what I thought, too," Joan whispered.

It was suddenly clear to her why she had not been able to understand the intruders at the Pennington Ranch. And it dovetailed with the Koran she had found in the car of the home invaders three weeks previously. Why hadn't she made that connection before?

"That's it," she said. "The intruders were speaking with an Arabic accent."

"We know that," Kearney said.

"What? How did you—no, not *our* home invasion, the invasion at the Pennington Ranch."

"What do you want to do?" he asked, trying to get her attention back on the task at hand.

"I want to get out of here. I've had enough of this shit for a lifetime," she said, hoping against all odds that Kearney would agree with her.

"We *have* to do something."

"No, we don't." She felt sorry for the captive bikers, but she was starting to get a handle on her PTSD. She didn't need any more apparitions haunting her thoughts.

"We can't leave them here," Kearney said. "If we don't do something, it will haunt us."

Joan leaned her head back on the rock and rolled it to face Kearney. "What's your plan?" She'd rather have the memory of dead unknown men haunt her than memories of bikers who had been good to her when she needed a job.

"What gun did you bring with you?" Kearney asked, pulling back the slide on his Sig Sauer to chamber a round.

The knot wrenching her stomach took Joan back to Iraq,

when she had always worried whether she had heard everything in the briefing properly—whether she had everything she
needed, enough ammo, food, water. The correct route. Attention to detail, bordering on obsessiveness, had kept her safe in
the desert of Iraq. Now her worst fears had materialized in the
Southwest American desert, except worse. She had Kearney
for a battle buddy. "I left it home today. I got tired of carrying
that extra dead weight around. But I have a knife."

"So, basically, you brought a knife to a gunfight."

Iron Angel rolled her eyes at the Kearney's corny comment. "Screw you," she said as she unsheathed her knife.
Holding it up, she admired it. "This isn't just any knife. This is
a Fairbairn-Sykes World War Two Commando knife."

"Will the knife stop a bullet?"

"Screw you."

"Can the knife cover the distance of a bullet?"

Knife in hand, Joan got to her feet in a crouch and snarled,
"Come here. The knife wants to explain to you the meaning of
'screw you.'"

She saw the look of surprise in Kearney's eyes an instant
before she was yanked backward to an upright position with an
arm around her throat and what felt like the barrel of a gun
against the right side of her head.

A voice behind her said, "Drop your weapons." As Iron
Angel dropped her knife, Kearney complied by bending to
gently place his Sig Sauer 9 mm on the ground. The move
fired up Iron Angel. Leave it to Kearney to care about the
well-being of his weapon when things were going south at
Mach Two.

As he straightened up, Kearney looked directly into Iron
Angel's eyes. Then, sliding his eyes up to the man behind her,
he added, "Take it from someone who learned the hard way,
buddy, she does *not* like having a gun put to her head."

"I am not your bud—"

Before her attacker could finish the sentence, Iron Angel
grabbed the barrel of the gun at her head with her left hand and
pushed it backward.

While she twisted the gun out of the attacker's hand, she
landed an upward elbow to his chin. Placing her left foot be-

hind his right, she followed up with a palm heel to the chin. The man reeled backward, flailing his arms before smashing the back of his head on the ground. Pulled to the ground with him, she used the momentum to end the fight by a well-placed knee in the solar plexus and a strike to the throat. She dug her fingers in and pulled. Blood spurted everywhere, drenching her in the man's gushing blood. He gurgled, struggling for breath, for a few seconds then lay still—his eyes looking skyward. Lifeless.

She put the back of her hand against her forehead and winced. *Eleven.*

"Oh, that's *nasty!*" Kearney whispered as he bent over and grabbed his stomach, fighting the urge to vomit.

Knee still in the dead man's torso, she wiped the blood from her face with her shirttail. "I bet those couple broken ribs and broken arm don't look so bad now, do they?" she said over her shoulder. There was a searing pain as she rubbed the blood from her cheekbone. "Ouch! Damn it! Why do I always get hit on the side of my face?! Now, I'm going to have *another* shiner."

With the blood wiped out of her eyes, she finally got a good look at the assailant's gun. It was unlike any gun she had ever seen before. It had a minimalistic stock and housing of a rifle, but a short barrel—half-handgun, half-rifle. "What in God's name is *this?*"

"Let me see," he said in a low voice, crouching and approaching her. "Holy shit. You know what this is? It's a Magpul FPG." Kearney tried to take it from her hands, but she held onto it. "This is a top of the line mini-submachine gun," he continued. "See this short barrel? It's for close-quarters battle. You know? Clearing buildings and shit like that. These are expe-e-ens-ive."

"So, this is a good gun?" she asked with a half-smile.

"Well, *yeah,* top shelf."

"Well," she said affecting her best hillbilly accent. "Looky here. I got myself a gun."

"If you fell into a pile of shit, you'd come out with a freakin' M1-A1 Tank."

"How does it work?" she asked, turning the rifle over in her hands.

"You had a Glock once, right?" She nodded. "All the exterior controls are the same as your Glock. But that's not all. Let me show you something."

She grudgingly let him have the weapon. Once in his hands, Kearney expertly folded the stock, and, with a few other folds, the gun no longer looked like a gun. It was square-shaped with a handle. It looked like it could be a battery or a flashlight. In one flick, it snapped out into the original configuration, ready to fire.

"Maybe I should use this," he said. "It might be too much gun for you."

"Give it back. It's mine now."

After a brief, spirited struggle, Kearney relinquished the FPG.

She smiled broadly. "We can't let this beauty go to waste." Jerking her chin toward the kidnappers, she added, "How do you want to take care of the situation down there?"

"Thought you'd never ask. I'll take out the one standing over the kneeling biker. You take out the one standing over the other one. Then shoot whoever you can."

"What about our six? If this scum-for-brains was doing a wide patrol, there are probably others."

"Then, after your first two shots, take our six. I'll take out the guys down there."

After her first two shots, she knelt and faced the other way. Head on a swivel, she took out two patrolling guards, one above them and one to her left. After several minutes that seemed like hours, the shooting stopped, and Kearney cautiously stood up. Iron Angel stood up slowly, keeping her gun pointed to the sides and to the back, always moving.

"I think we got 'em," he said.

Iron Angel was still on edge. "They couldn't have gone down that easy."

"We're good shots," he said, still looking down the barrel of his gun. "They didn't have a chance against us."

"*We*? Was that a compliment from Mr. Misogynist?"

"Hey, Joan—"

She didn't look at him. She was still on guard.

"Hey," he said again, putting a hand on her arm. When he had her attention, he continued, "That day, at the Pennington Ranch, when I said you were lucky, I didn't mean it. You did great. You did as well as Duncan or I would have done under the same circumstances."

She ignored the glow of self-esteem warming her gut. If she acknowledged it, she might jinx this moment. "Let's go check on the bikers."

Heads swiveling, guns at the ready, they edged toward the bottom of the ravine.

"Don't shoot. I'm coming out," a voice came from under the van.

Kearney and Iron Angel jumped back, training their guns on a scuffling sound under the engine block. When duct taped wrists appeared coming out from under the running board of the van, she slung the mini-submachine gun over her shoulder and helped him out. The other biker followed him.

"Damn, man, what the hell are you dudes doing out here?" one biker asked while she cut the duct tape off his wrists.

"Exercising," she answered.

"Exercising? In the desert? With guns?" he asked, rubbing his wrists where the duct tape had been removed. He noticed her blood-soaked shirt and asked, "You okay? Where'd you get hit?"

"This? This isn't my blood." She jerked her chin toward the rocks at the rim of the ravine above them. "It's from a sewer-rat who made the mistake of putting a gun to my head up there."

"Who are these guys?" Kearney asked. "What's their connection to the Brotherhood?"

"I don't know who they are. They kept asking us about someone named Lisa Brown."

Without any hesitation, Iron Angel asked, "Who's Lisa Brown?" In her peripheral vision she saw Kearney look at her, but she kept her gaze on the biker.

"That's just it. We don't know a Lisa Brown. Do you know her?" the biker asked.

"What made them think *you* know this Lisa Brown?" Kearney asked.

"That's just it. They wouldn't tell us that. They just wanted answers."

"Well, lucky for you we came along when we did," Iron Angel said.

Kearney flashed his teeth and bumped her shoulder with his. "Aren't you full of yourself?"

"I'm just stating facts. Can we jump a ride to the trail-head?" she asked the bikers. "This blood might raise some eyebrows with hikers on the trail."

"Are you kidding? We owe you way more than a ride!"

ᴇ⁄ᴐᴇ⁄ᴐ

Later that day, Duncan appeared in the doorway to the workout room in the basement of their house. It was low-ceilinged, dark, and musty. Tiny dust particles danced in the shaft of the filtered sunlight that spilled through two small windows—one on each side of the room. In the far corner hung three heavy bags of different weights, two duct taped from overuse. Along one wall, a wide array of knives, machetes, hatchets, and rubber training guns hung in a neatly positioned display.

Without decreasing the speed or intensity of her heavy-bag workout, Joan said, "What's up?"

Duncan leaned against the doorjamb, arms crossed. "Your name should be Rose." The workout stopped abruptly. She set her jaw and glared at him. He quickly added, "I'm just saying, it should be Rose, because you are beautiful to look at, but if you're mishandled you draw blood. That's all."

"I never took you to be poetic," she said, leaning over to grab a towel and wipe her face and neck. "I know you didn't come down here to compare me to a flower."

"We need to talk."

"About what?"

"You aren't responsible for other people's actions. You know that, right?"

"It's because of me people are getting hurt. I know that

much." She dropped the towel and resumed her workout, this time attacking two bags to simulate fighting multiple assailants.

"You want to talk about what happened today?" Duncan asked.

"Not really."

"You must have some feelings about it. Talk to me."

"Well, I'm racking up quite a body count."

"And..."

"And two Demon Brotherhood members almost got wasted because of *La Espada's* search for me." She put out a hand to stop the swing of one of the bags. The other bag gently bumped her in the back before stopping. "Maybe I should just put myself out there as bait and draw them out. Take care of this thing once and for all, before somebody else gets hurt because of me."

"You aren't responsible for their motivations or their actions."

She rubbed her knuckles. "You said that already."

"When *you* hurt somebody—"

"—or kill them."

His exasperation blew out his nostrils. "Or kill them," he acknowledged. "You never say 'they *made* me do this' or rationalize that someone else's actions motivated you to do it. You accept responsibility for your actions. Right?"

"I'm trained. I'm proficient in deadly arts. I live by a higher standard."

"Who told you that? Some high-minded, shit-for-brains monk? That's nonsense and you know it. Everybody is responsible for their *own* actions. That includes these *La Espada* guys."

She looked at the floor and pursed her lips in thought. With a half-smile, she said, "All my teachers were American."

Duncan dropped his chin to his chest and slapped his hand on his forehead. "That's not my point."

She watched as his hand slid down his face, fingers brushing across his lips before resting on his chin. *Damn he's sexy.*

He changed the subject. "We're not done talking about this,

but I have to talk to you about something else. I want to have your support for this militia. You have an uncanny ability to read people. A two-minute conversation and you—it's like you can read their minds. I need that input if I'm going to be an effective leader."

Oh, no, not this again. Picking at a sliver of loose skin from one of her knuckles, she said, "So, in effect, you're saying you're nothing without me?"

"Once again, not my point. I'm serious, Joan."

She took on a more thoughtful tone. "This is about Lisa Brown. *La Espada* is not planning some widespread takeover of the United States. There's no need for a militia."

"C'mon, Joan, use your head. This isn't about the takeover of the United States, just a portion of it. Being unconcerned and flippant will not make the problem go away."

"This is not about a problem for the United States. This is my problem."

"Okay, for the sake of argument," he conceded, "let's say it is your problem alone. A militia would be able to protect you."

Joan almost laughed in his face. The only militia members who came close—a distant close—to her self-defense abilities were Gunther and Jason. Though both were good in their own styles, their speed and fighting savvy left a lot to be desired. They didn't train often enough, or hard enough, to gain her respect.

In an effort to lighten the mood, she smiled. "You'll say anything to drag me into this group of yours, won't you?"

He smiled back.

"And you're not going to stop badgering me until I agree, are you?"

"Have you ever known me to give up? How long did I chase you before you finally gave in to me?"

Her smiled broadened. "That bumbling around was *chasing* me? No, *I* came to you."

He pulled her into him. "Yeah, after I chased you."

Self-conscious about her sweaty body against his clean clothes, she pushed away, but he tightened his hold on her. A silence fell between them.

As she slowly relaxed in his embrace, she asked, "Can I

support you without actually taking part in the militia?" She closed her eyes and groaned. Just like that, she had stepped out onto the ledge.

CHAPTER 10

The smell of stale beer filled his nostrils as Duncan walked the length of the bar at Colors, the clubhouse of the Demon Brotherhood Motorcycle Club. This initial meeting with the president of the Demon Brotherhood was important, and Duncan had to get his head into the game. But memories of the passionate lovemaking before he left the house hung with him. The aroma of Joan's shampoo lingered in his nose. The sound of her voice whispering his given name whirled around his head like a refreshing breeze that heralded approaching rain. It had been especially exhilarating and rough, just the way she knew he liked it. He pinched the front of his dark blue polo shirt and shook it to brush away the memory of her soft skin against his.

Wild Bill rose to greet Duncan. He wasn't tall—five foot nine or so—and stocky with a small beer belly, but Duncan had no illusions about his toughness. Bill looked like he was in his late-forties with shoulder length salt-and-pepper hair. Brown eyes looked out over cheeks that were rosy with broken blood vessels. A silver moustache fell into a sternum-brushing goatee that matched his hair.

Their hands met in a firm handshake. Their eyes locked. Unsure of what Wild Bill had to offer, but willing to get much needed support for his fledgling militia, Duncan decided to hear him out. It never hurt to listen.

As Duncan slid into the stool beside him, Wild Bill asked, "What'll you have?" and motioned to the bartender.

"Sam Adams." Duncan decided against hard liquor. The Brotherhood was throwing a party in honor of Joan and Kearney in two hours. It could be a long night.

"Boston Lager or Summer Ale?" the bartender asked.

Duncan knew this was Flora's grandmother, Ruby. There was no smile, no attempt at congeniality, not a glimmer of recognition. Just a matter-of-fact query with the gravelly voice of a heavy smoker and, Duncan guessed, a heavy drinker.

"Boston Lager." Duncan watched the seventy-something woman dispense the beer perfectly.

When the drinks arrived, he reached for his wallet, but Wild Bill waved him off. "We—" he said, gesturing to include Duncan, "—don't pay here."

Taking a sip from the frosty mug, Duncan silently congratulated Wild Bill. In one gesture, he received prestige and indebtedness at the same time. He turned on his stool to face Wild Bill. "Nice riding weather."

"Wondering why I'm holed up in here with you when I could be out on my Hog enjoying the sunshine?"

"Something like that," Duncan said, before taking another sip.

Wild Bill looked the length of the bar. Content that Ruby was busying herself at the far end, he got down to business. "What your guys did in the desert last week took balls." He hesitated. "Sorry, guy and girl."

Duncan smiled. "It's okay. She wouldn't mind being called a guy."

"Oh, one of those." The ice slushed in the glass as Wild Bill waved it at Ruby for a refill.

"No." Duncan laughed. "She's straight. Just tough."

"Straight? Are you sure?"

Duncan smiled at the memory of Joan's torrid lovemaking. "Positive."

"If your women are that tough, I can't wait to meet the guys. What's the name of your group?"

"The Counter-Insurgency Army," Duncan replied.

"The C-IA? That's good." A hearty chuckle escaped Wild Bill's throat. "That's real good. A thumb in the eye of the government." He took a sip of his drink and did a simultaneous cough and gulp. He looked up at Ruby, but she was busy cutting lemons.

"You okay?" Duncan asked.

"I think Ruby forgot the soda," Wild Bill answered.

"There's something you should know before you hook up with us," Duncan said, getting back to business.

"What's that?"

"We won't be fighting some partially-trained wannabes. They are financed and trained by Mussies."

"How do you know that?"

"We found a Koran in the car of the guys who invaded our house a month ago. One of the guys looked Middle Eastern. And it's no secret they've been building mosques in Mexico for decades, trying to convert a nation on our border—an unsecure, poorly patrolled border."

"Why do you think they're training the Mexicans and not just using Mexico as a staging area?"

"Think about it. They can get the Mexicans to fight the US for them. The Mexicans are all too happy to fight 'to reclaim the land that was stolen from Mexico by America,' or so their bullshit propaganda states. The Muslims get the Mexicans to fight their battle, take the lion's share of the casualties, then they take over. Voila! They have a foothold in North America at a relatively small cost."

"Nice theory. What makes you think it's feasible? Won't the government step in?"

"Oh, yeah, sure. Eventually. But the UN is talking about rules of engagement that are restrictive. Remember NATO and Libya several years ago?" After a thoughtful sip of beer, Duncan continued, "No drones. No helicopters. Limitations on satellite images. They're going to need unconventional help, if you know what I mean."

"Why you? What's your stake in this?"

"Let's just say it's what I do."

Wiping his moustache with the knuckle at the base of his index finger, Wild Bill thought for several seconds. "This is bigger and more dangerous than I thought. But it's an easy decision. Our code calls for us to lay down our lives for anyone who lays down his life for the Brotherhood. What do you need?"

"What can you do for us?"

What Wild Bill offered was security for certain situations where extra muscle was needed. Well-known in the area, they could act as a distraction or deal with the cops, if the C-IA needed it.

It was less than what Duncan expected, but he understood negotiations. After some back and forth, all the cards would be on the table. And until the militia's numbers increased, the extra muscle could come in handy. Running interference with the cops could prove valuable, but also a liability. Once the local law enforcement connected the two groups, they would drag the C-IA into every investigation of drug deals gone bad or stolen motorcycles. No, he wanted more.

What the C-IA needed was guns, ammo, and intel. Intelligence could mean the difference between losing well-trained members and obtaining a victory. And if intelligence was the brain, armament was the body. Without a strong, powerful body, ideas would fizzle into nothing. After all, Steven Hawking, though a brilliant physicist, would be useless in a firefight in an industrial complex that covered six city blocks. Duncan knew all too well it would be suicide if the body couldn't carry out a strategy formulated by the mind.

Wild Bill explained to Duncan that he had no problem sharing what information they could scare up, but armament was another story. The Brotherhood financed its operation via drugs and prostitution. He could obtain ghost guns–to be used once, then tossed—and would give the C-IA great deals on those, but Duncan was talking quantities that would send alarm bells to the feds. Avoiding the alarm bells was tricky business. What he *would* do was introduce Duncan to another motorcycle club that dealt in guns, but it was up to that club whether they wanted to transact business with the C-IA.

Satisfied that he'd gotten the best deal he could, Duncan finished his beer and motioned to Ruby for another one. The conversation turned to things other than business, and Duncan settled in to wait for the start of the party.

ɛ⌃ɔɛ⌃ɔ

Joan was late for the party, but, when she made her appearance, it was nothing less than spectacular.

She had driven her motorcycle and when she stepped through the door, she took off the helmet and shook loose her long, brown hair. Black, painted-on jeans showed off her muscular legs. A bright red top with thick, crossed straps revealed her muscular shoulders and arms, yet cleverly covered her scars. Others were turned off by her muscularity, but it was what Duncan loved about her. That, and her fearlessness. And her kindness toward the weak. And her passion. Her fortitude. Determination. Loyalty—Her. He. Loved. Her.

Earlier in the week, he had given her money, to go buy something nice for the party, and immediately regretted it. The last time he had asked her to wear something nice, the evening ended in torture, ensuring she could never again wear a mid-thigh skirt or expose her midriff. Looking at her now, if she had negative feelings about wearing something nice, she wasn't showing them.

Joan's day-to-day appearance was non-descript—not too short or too tall, not too thin or too plump, not too plain, not too pretty. She could become invisible or blend into any crowd. But this evening, there was a glow that lit up her features as if she were holding the only candle in a dark room.

One person started clapping, then others joined in until the whole room broke into applause. The bikers closest to Kearney and Joan patted them on the back and did elbow bumps. After the first clap, Duncan no longer heard anything. The whole of his consciousness was pinned on the beautiful woman standing at the far end of the bar. While tucking her hair behind her ear, Joan turned and said something to Kearney behind her hand. His heart plummeted. He should be the man standing next to this beauty—*his* beauty. Kearney pointed to the end of the bar where Duncan sat with Wild Bill, and she turned in his direction.

As Joan approached Wild Bill and Duncan, attention flowed behind her like the wake of a gracefully moving sailboat. Walking with a graceful, leonine confidence the length of the bar, she held Wild Bill's gaze with hers. Once again, Duncan felt like the odd man out, but when she was a few feet away, she switched her gaze to him. He felt as if his heart swelled and pressed against the inside of his rib cage. He swiveled on his stool just enough to pull her in between his legs.

"Stand over here like a rose between two thorns," Duncan said as he slowly spun on the stool and guided her to his left.

Unaware of Wild Bill eyeing them and stroking his long silver moustache, Duncan said quietly, "Did you want the attention of every man in the room?"

Joan put an arm on each side of Duncan's neck. "Did I get *your* attention?"

"Oh, *yes!*"

"In *that* case, I got what I wanted," she whispered.

The soft, smoky scent of her perfume wafted up Duncan's nose as he enfolded her in a hug that would have squeezed the air out of the lungs of any other woman.

Suddenly remembering they were not alone, Duncan ended the embrace. Joan curled in his arms and demurely looked at Wild Bill. As Duncan put his arm around her waist, he said, "Wild Bill, this is Iron Angel. Angel, this is Bill Torrence, the president of the Phoenix Chapter of the Demon Brotherhood."

Joan offered her hand to Wild Bill. "I've seen you here before, but we've never been formally introduced. I want to thank you for your hospitality. You didn't have to throw a party in Kearney's and my honor..."

As her words trailed off, Duncan saw the glimmer of interest in Wild Bill's eyes. Duncan leaned slightly forward to look at Joan's face, slid his eyes to glance at Wild Bill, then looked back at Joan.

The handshake lasted a little too long for Duncan's comfort, and he saw the questions swirling around Wild Bill's head about who this woman really was. Duncan poked a finger into her ribs. As he nuzzled her ear he whispered, "Stop playing with his head." After a light kiss on the neck, he suggested, "Why don't you go and have some fun while I finish some business with Bill?"

After a quick smile at Duncan, Joan turned to head back down the bar to where Jason and Flora were sitting. As she turned, she bumped into a short woman in her thirties with waist-length medium brown hair. There was a hint of freckles, suggesting, in her younger days, she would have looked like the innocent, sweet girl next door.

The woman hastily said, "Hi." Joan looked into her green eyes, maybe a little too long, but the woman continued without a beat. "I'm Dee Dee, Red Dog's old lady."

Joan briefly glanced over her shoulder at Duncan before replying, "I'm Iron Angel, Duncan's old—"

"Everybody knows who you are," Dee Dee interrupted. "Why don't you come and sit with us at our table over there?" She pointed to the other side of the room where Kearney was waving her over, his toothy grin boding nothing but mischief. As Dee Dee gave a gentle push in the direction of the table, Duncan pulled Joan back.

One corner of his mouth curled up, "Don't wander too far if you expect me to defend your honor." Seeing the confused look on her face he added, "You came unarmed."

With a wink over her shoulder, Joan said, "Who says I'm not armed?" Duncan watched her retreating figure. He had checked out her back and waist. A piece of paper couldn't be concealed under her jeans. *Where in hell—*

He took a long pull of the cool beer.

Nodding toward the table where Joan was pulling out a chair between Dee Dee and Kearney, Wild Bill asked, "Is that going to be okay?"

"No problem," Duncan said. "No matter how much she drinks, she'll keep her mouth shut about Red Dog and Rosemary."

"I hope so. Dee Dee can be worse than a swarm of bees," Wild Bill warned. "Speaking of Rosemary," he continued. "She's gone missing. You wouldn't know anything about that, would you?"

"Nope."

"Rosemary was a pain in the ass, and I can't say I'm not glad to see her gone, but Red Dog seemed to like her. Her disappearance could be a nuisance, if the cops get involved."

"Don't know a thing. As a matter of fact, this is the first I heard of it. How long?"

"A little over a week. Are you sure your girlfriend didn't have something to do with it?"

"Why do you say that?" As Duncan sipped his beer, he thought back and couldn't remember any indications from Joan that she had done anything out of the ordinary. But bluffing came easy to her, and Kearney's playing the game idea only added a new twist to that ability.

"I heard that Rosemary had a thing for you, and they got into blows over it."

"As far as I know, they were starting to get along. I think they met for lunch a week or so ago." Duncan jerked his chin toward the table across the room. "Maybe it was Dee Dee, if she's as dangerous as you say."

"A week or so ago," Wild Bill mused aloud. After a brief silence, he said with a half-smile, "You wouldn't tell me anyway, if you knew."

He was right. The last person Duncan would tell would be Wild Bill. "I would take care of it," Duncan said, before draining his mug of beer.

Wild Bill nodded and chugged the remainder of his JD and coke.

℘ↄ℘ↄ

Duncan spent the evening watching Joan partying with the bikers. It had been a long time since he had seen her relaxed and happy, so he let her have some fun. Hard times were ahead, and there wouldn't be much time for relaxation. But later that evening, he got engrossed in a conversation with Wild Bill and the Brotherhood's Vice-President and lost track of her. She was not in the bar. He and Gunther set out to find her.

They found Joan with Dee Dee in the litter-strewn alley behind Colors, sitting and swaying on Red Dog's shiny, black Harley Davidson. Joan was on the passenger seat, facing forward, and Dee Dee was sitting on the seat in front of the gas tank, facing Joan. With Joan's feet on the front foot pegs, and Dee Dee's feet on the passenger's pegs, their legs made an X on each side of the bike. A nearly empty rum bottle awkwardly swung about in Dee Dee's right hand as she gestured to emphasize a point. They each took a swig and talked for a few seconds. After a brief silence, Dee Dee slapped Joan's face. When no retribution came from Joan, Duncan knitted his brow. No one hit her without payback. No one.

Seeing Duncan's confusion, Gunther said, "They're trying to keep each other awake."

Duncan crossed his arms and rested his chin on his chest as he watched the women in their drunken ballet. "They seem to have hit it off right away tonight."

Gunther did a double-take. "This isn't the first time they met."

A heavy, sick feeling snaked through Duncan's stomach. "Yes, it is. Dee Dee introduced herself earlier."

"I don't know what they did earlier," Gunther said. "But I *know* they knew each other before tonight."

Duncan pushed Gunther to the side, away from the bikers standing nearby. "How do you know that?"

Gunther leaned in toward Duncan's shoulder to muffle his words. "One afternoon, I stopped by your house to see if you wanted to go to the gun show, and these two were in the living room drunk on their asses. They were drinking some kinda sweet green liquor out of a pitcher—Midori and coconut rum, or some shit like that. I drove Dee Dee home because she couldn't stand, much less drive."

"When was this?" Duncan asked.

Joan had cut way back on her drinking when she pumped up her training three weeks before. How could he have missed the hangover that would have followed a heavy drinking episode? Too much attention to the militia and too little to Joan— that's how.

"...I don't know," Gunther was saying, "...maybe a little over a week ago—sometime during the week before the incident in the desert."

Duncan narrowed his eyes and snapped his attention back to the two women.

As if on cue, they both fell asleep and leaned forward onto each other. They slowly slipped sideways to the ground.

Joan punched Dee Dee on the shoulder and slurred, "You pushed me off the bike!" Not getting any response, she pulled out a sheathed knife with alcohol-induced awkwardness.

Duncan lunged toward her. "Where the hell'd that knife come from?"

Gunther blocked him with his arm. "I'm on it," he said, taking two steps toward the women, ready to jump in if necessary. "Let's see what she does with it."

After slipping her hand between the hilt and the sheath, so she had a reverse grip on the knife, Joan laydown and put her head on Dee Dee's waist. She snuggled in to go to sleep, holding the knife at her sternum.

"Did you see that?" Gunther said, eyes and mouth open wide. "I knew it. Even on the verge of a drunken stupor, she has the presence of mind to prepare to defend herself. She is a natural-born warrior."

"Okay, rocket man," Duncan said, "if you can come down to Earth long enough, get the knife, and I'll wake up Sleeping Beauty."

The sudden grab on her arm woke Joan with a start. Instantly aware that she had her head on a body, she flew to her feet, but lost her balance and stumbled backward onto her butt. Using Duncan's arm for support, she staggered to her feet and stood leaning and swaying. With bleary eyes on Dee Dee, she slurred, "Is she—" Joan swallowed hard. "—is she dead?"

"No," Duncan said through his teeth. "She's drunk."

Joan looked up at Duncan and back at Dee Dee. "Good. I hate killing women, they're so…you know…" she slurred and wiggled her fingers, "…girlie." Her wiggling fingers caught her attention. "Hey, where's my knife?"

"Gunny has it."

Joan hiccupped. "Maybe Gunther should hold onto my knife for me."

"Good idea." With an arm tightly wrapped around Joan's shoulders, Duncan whisked her toward his truck. "Let's get you home."

"Hey, what about my bike?" Joan said, looking over her shoulder as he half-carried her down the dimly-lit alley.

"We'll get it tomorrow."

With Joan safely in the passenger seat, Duncan jogged around the truck. Sliding into the driver's seat, he asked, "What did you mean back there when you said you hate killing women? Have you ever killed a woman?"

Occupied with trying to get the retractor mechanism to release the seat belt, Joan didn't hear the question.

With a finger on Joan's chin Duncan turned her head toward him. "Joan, you said you hate killing women. Have you ever killed a woman?"

"I said what? Uh-oh, the truck is spinning."

While Duncan reached across her and pushed the button to put the window down, Joan pulled the seatbelt across her chest and struggled to hook it.

Snatching the seatbelt out of her hands, Duncan continued, "You said you don't like killing women. Joan, what have you done? Did you kill Rosemary? Tell me the truth. It won't leave this truck."

"I don't remember saying that," she said before she lurched away from him, opening the door just in time to vomit outside the truck.

Duncan shook his head and grabbed her waistband to keep her from falling out.

CHAPTER 11

The blistering noonday sun chased Joan to the cool sanctuary of Colors for a quick drink. Zipping into the parking lot on the side of the building without touching the brakes of her Honda motorcycle, she slid to a stop. Visions of lots of ice-cold water filled her head as she smoothly backed her bike between two Harleys. After hooking her helmet into the helmet lock, she headed toward the street side of the building.

It wasn't really the cool refuge that drew her to Colors. She was in avoidance mode. It had been easy to dodge Duncan's questions last night when she was hammered, but now, in the light of day, dodging the questions would not be so easy. She felt him circling her like a panther on the hunt, waiting to pounce at the first sign of weakness. It had unnerved her. She had bummed a ride to Colors to pick up her bike and promptly escaped to the open road.

Rosemary was gone. That should be the end of it, but Duncan would not to let it go. The woman was as much trouble out of the picture as she had been before she disappeared. It wasn't the anticipated questions or the specter of Rosemary that made Joan jump on her motorcycle and go for a long, hard ride. It was the way he scanned every crease, movement, and expression on her face, as if he was seeing her for the first time.

She pulled open the front door to Colors, and the cool air brought relief from the searing desert heat. As her eyes adjusted to the darkness, she noticed that nobody was behind the bar.

Guessing Ruby was off somewhere taking care of something else, Joan took the time to look around Colors in the light of day, or in what little light found its way into the space. Although the law that prohibited smoking in public places was over ten years old, the tobacco residue on the glass-block front windows cast a sickly, yellow glow over the sparse and miss-matched furnishings. A half-dozen bikers were scattered around the tables. Each in turn acknowledged her presence with a curt nod of their chin or a raised glass in salute, except one large, beefy biker sitting at a corner table. An unheeded television on a shelf in the corner closest to the door was showing a daytime talk show with several women cackling over some inane topic.

Joan headed toward a stool at the far corner where the hinged door to the area behind the bar was flipped up and lay against the wall. As she made herself comfortable on the stool, Ruby appeared on her right and, without any words exchanged, grabbed the bottle of José Cuervo Black. Joan stopped her and asked for a mug of ice water instead.

With raised eyebrows Ruby asked, "Rough night last night?"

"Something like that. Got anything for a headache?" Joan nodded her head toward one of the tables. "I don't remember seeing the big guy at the corner table before."

"He's been out of town for a while. Just got back."

Something about the inflection of the words "out of town" caught Joan's attention. "You mean jail?"

Ruby walked toward Joan, the ice tinkling in the glass. "Yeah and, unlike ninety percent of the inmates, he really was innocent. He took the fall for Wild Bill."

Joan snuck a peek over her shoulder at the big man with shoulder-length curly hair and a full beard. His stature dwarfed the table and chairs around him, giving him the appearance of a loving dad sitting at his daughter's play table with a toy tea set.

After placing the mug of ice water on a colorful cardboard coaster in front of Joan, Ruby placed two white tablets next to it before plopping down on a stool just inside the open passageway and picked up a cup of tea. Neither woman was big on small talk, so after a perfunctory comment on the weather, they fell into a comfortable silence.

While Ruby was in the back again, Joan helped herself to a refill of ice water. The old boards creaked under each footstep as she made her way halfway down the bar. The sound of the scoop in the ice, and the cubes tinkling into the mug were refreshing. As she finished filling the mug with water, a voice from across the room asked her to turn up the volume on the television. A brief hunt for the remote ensued and, once found, she pointed it at the TV. Bumper music for a Special Report filled the small space.

A yellow screen with red letters flashed the words, *Special Report*, and a faceless voice announced breaking news on the *La Espada* peace march that afternoon in downtown Phoenix.

When the camera cut to the anchor, she reported the demonstration, which had started out as a peaceful *La Espada* march, had turned into chaos and destruction. She went into a brief recap of *La Espada's* belief that much of the land in the southwestern United States had been stolen from Mexico during the Mexican-American War. A photo of a reporter appeared in the upper left-hand corner of the screen, and the anchor segued to his telephonic report of anarchists in black haskies throwing rocks and bottles at the police. With gunshots in the background, he described the volatility of the mob. They were throwing Molotov cocktails into stores while chanting "Viva Mexico!" and "Death to America."

The broadcast switched to a live aerial shot from Channel-2's SkyViews News. Flames shot from the roofs of several buildings. Buildings not yet on fire had people running around them like a colony of ants on an Oreo. A few blocks away, the streets were filled to overflowing with a surging throng of people marching, shaking their fists, and rocking cars in attempts to flip them. Flames licked the air from cars and dumpsters in the middle of rings of chanting protesters. While the chopper televised the corridor of devastation, the crawler at the bottom of the screen related the breaking news that *La Espada* was taking credit for the demonstration.

Overwhelmed, the police fell back to a safe, defendable position to regroup, clearly hoping the riot police and the national guard would arrive in time. The absence of municipal authority and discipline was like throwing gasoline on a fire. The mob took full advantage of the situation, which was deteriorating, as the news chopper recorded it live.

Every biker rushed the door to get their motorcycles and bring them inside to protect them from the mayhem headed their way. Joan jumped up to follow suit.

Avoiding Duncan's questions had triggered her Iron Angel bad karma. She was sure of it. Was there such a thing? If so, then once again, it had found her when she was relaxing and minding her own freakin' business. It was like living in the eye of a hurricane. Everything was calm and sunny as long as she stayed in the center. Wander away from the center and the one hundred mile an hour winds would overtake her, making things a whirling hell. Was she cursed to be in the wrong place at the wrong time, or blessed to be in the very place her skills were most needed? Either way, she didn't like it. Not liking it did not change the threat.

A biker exited the kitchen after barricading the back door and said, "Is your bike inside?"

Joan nodded.

"They're only five blocks away and the news is reporting that shots have been fired. We're preparing for a fight."

Shit! I'm stuck here with a five-shot .38 revolver. Joan slipped into the kitchen and pulled her cell phone out of her pocket.

"Talk to me." Duncan's familiar greeting triggered a flash of déja vu.

"Hi, it's me. I'm stuck at Colors."

"Are you okay?"

"So far. We've brought our bikes inside and the Brotherhood just barricaded all the doors."

"Something told me you'd be in the middle of this shit." The dry edge to his voice disappeared when he added, "We'll figure out a way to get to you, but the police have the north and west blocked off. *La Espada* has the south and east in flames. What's your metal?"

"My little Smith and Wesson .38."

"Hang in there, my angel. We'll get to you as soon as we can."

"Ruby just turned off the lights. Maybe the bar will look empty and they'll go right on by."

Duncan's silence said it all.

"I gotta go. It's getting loud outside."

"I'm afraid you're going to have a hectic few minutes. Come home to me, Iron Angel."

"Soon, baby." As she broke the connection, she choked back the lump in her throat.

Her life with Duncan was *not* going to end, not now, not at the hands of people whose first act on American soil was to thumb their noses at immigration laws—lawless people bent on mindless destruction. Duncan's unasked questions and the implication they carried seemed small and insignificant with the possibility of losing everything important to her. The next time Duncan asked about Rosemary, she would answer him. *The truth will set you free.* Hoping whoever said that knew what he was talking about, she took a deep breath and stuffed the phone into her back pocket. Instead of adrenaline, the calm warmth of catharsis flooded her system. Time to get to work.

The bar was not yet under attack, but she reflexively crouched as she exited the kitchen and scooted past the sink and taps to where Ruby leaned against the bar, the stock of a .20 gauge shotgun pressed against her shoulder. Joan glanced back at the kitchen door as two bikers slipped through it on their way to the tables. Her gaze followed them to the main room where other bikers had flipped some of the tables onto their edges. Those beat-up wooden tables wouldn't be protection from a bullet, but it was all they had at hand. It would at least provide *some* cover.

"What do you think, Ruby?"

Without moving the shotgun, Ruby glanced out of the corner of her left eye. In a voice that seemed deeper and more gravelly than usual, she said, "I think this is one fucked up situation."

"I meant do you think they'll pass us by? Do you think we have enough fire power to repel any attack on the clubhouse?"

This time Ruby did not move when she answered, "If I thought we'd be safe, I wouldn't be standing here with a shotgun aimed to blow off the head of any freakin' wetback that dares to come through that door."

Joan opened the cylinder of her revolver out of habit. It was loaded. It always was. Empty-hand fighting was her forte, but there was nothing like the feel of smooth, oiled metal to add to her confidence. With a flip of her wrist, the cylinder clicked back into place. She slid the revolver into its holster on her right hip.

"We have this covered out here," Ruby said. "Why don't you go check on Flora in the ladies' room. She ain't feelin' so good. Stay with her with that flimsy little thing you call a gun. You can be the last line of defense."

Joan headed to the ladies room at the back of the building in a cinder block addition built in the mid-to-late-sixties. After a short, ten-foot hallway it made a sharp right turn. The first door on the left was the men's room. Joan passed it and continued to the next door on the left. She opened the door to the ladies' room and froze. *What the hell?*

e⁄se⁄s

At the house, Duncan paced from the dining room to the living room, around the coffee table in the middle of the floor, and back to the dining room. With each pass, Kearney, who was sitting on the leather couch watching the television, would lift his feet off the coffee table to allow Duncan to go by. The unending-circuit was pumping up everyone else's stress levels. To create a distraction, Gunther opened his i-Pad and pulled up a map of Phoenix on the screen. Jason, Red Dog, and Dee Dee huddled around him, each in turn pointed at a spot on the monitor to suggest a route to the bar. A brief stop to look at the screen was added to Duncan's tour of the two rooms. So much for relief from the tension heightened by Duncan's relentless pacing.

The backs of Duncan's fingers brushed his day-old stubble as he mulled over the situation. There would be cops everywhere, and the national guard was mobilizing. His pacing stopped and the corners of his mouth turned downward. The former Legion members were fugitives, and if caught, they would go to prison for a very long time. He had to protect them, but they had to do something. One of their own was in a greasy situation. Sitting here in safety was not an option. Leaving one of them exposed to danger, and possibly arrest, was not an option. They *would* do something, but what?

The pacing resumed and his thoughts turned to Joan. His stomach twisted at the thought of his responsibility for the situation she was in. If he had just come out and asked what she knew about Rosemary's disappearance, she'd be here now, safe and secure. He should not have tried to play her. He had successfully played her once when she was on the fast track to the leadership of the Legion, but she was a different person now. Stronger. More Experienced. A player herself. When would he ever learn? Never play a player.

A heaviness came over his body that neck and shoulder rolls couldn't shake. Relaxation only came after he made his decision. He would not ask Joan about Rosemary's disappearance. Bottom line: he trusted her. She would tell him the truth when she was ready.

Jason intercepted Duncan's path to hand him a cup of hot, creamy coffee. Duncan stopped pacing to take a sip. He looked Jason over. Something was going on with him. Always calm and composed, Jason was uncharacteristically uneasy.

"You okay?" Duncan asked.

"Flora is at Colors. The only comfort I have is Iron Angel is there with her."

Duncan nodded, clapped Jason on the shoulder, and resumed pacing. He forced his thoughts back to strategy. For stealth, it would have to be a small group, but not too small. Who would go, who would stay behind to give updates from the news?

Thank God for the news helicopters spewing information as it happens. Lost in thought, he did not notice the hush that fell upon the house.

He stopped short. Everyone in the room was looking at him as if frozen in time. He gestured. "What?"

Jason broke the silence. "*La Espada* is four blocks from the bar and heading that way."

"They're reporting gunshots," Dee Dee added.

Duncan sprang into action. "Jason, Gunther, Red Dog, Dee Dee, you're with me. Kearney, you stay here and keep us updated on the situation. Let's get started loading extra magazines. We leave in five."

While the others loaded magazines, Duncan pulled Jason aside. "You are my tactics guy. I want you to take the lead on this."

"Flora's there today so I have to get to her. Besides, I wouldn't want anyone else to lead the operation to save the mother of my child."

"What? *What* child?"

"Flora's three months along." At Duncan's blank stare, he added, "Pregnant with our baby."

Duncan snapped out of it. He made a chopping action with his hand. "That's it. I'm leading the mission."

"Your woman is there as well," Jason said. "You aren't going to be any more clear-headed than me." He lowered his voice. "And I was the head of the special actions team for the Legion."

"I'm leading the team and that's final."

"This is what I was trained to do. I got this," Jason persisted.

"Are you guys done playing '*Quien es mas macho*'?" Gunther said. "Because time is not on our side."

Jason put his hand on Duncan's shoulder. "I can do this, boss. I *have* to do it."

Duncan thought through the choice. Jason was capable of thinking on his feet, and he was the tactics expert. Level-headed, detail-conscious, mission-oriented, he was the natural choice. But could he keep his mind focused on the mission if Flora was in danger?

Jason must have sensed Duncan's hesitation. "C'mon, D, you know I'm the right man for the job."

"Okay, but if I say you're done, you're done. I take over. I don't want any shit from you about it."

"Wouldn't have it any other way, boss."

With a quick nod to Jason, Duncan addressed the others. "Mount up. Let's fuck this chicken."

Dee Dee looked at Red Dog and mouthed, "Fuck this chicken?"

Red Dog just shrugged, picked up his bag of ammo, and threw it over his shoulder. While Dee Dee stuffed the remaining magazines into her purse and Red Dog adjusted the straps on his backpack, Duncan and Jason picked up the earbuds and transmitters. After some adjustments and a quick radio check, they were ready.

Duncan said, "Kearney, keep us informed of anything— *anything*—we need to know."

"Roger that," Kearney said, giving Duncan an elbow bump.

The small C-IA team headed out the door. It was their first mission under the banner of the infant group. It would test their mettle and voracity—and the effectiveness of Duncan's leadership.

వెనెవె

An abandoned factory stood like a decaying, battered dinosaur on the southeast perimeter of Phoenix. It virtually vibrated with a frenetic activity it hadn't seen in many years. Closed down in the late 'nineties, the building had been purchased by a Muslim businessman who subsequently offered it to Tito Orrozco to use as his headquarters. These new Muslim *compadres* had endless resources, which was what Tito needed to get this war started and sustained until his fellow countrymen took up the fight with him. History—Viet Nam, Lebanon, Somalia—taught him that the US government would give up when the American people felt the loss of life and treasure wasn't worth the struggle. *He* would not give up until he won back the land for Mexico.

Only two obstacles stood in his way. His Muslim benefactors wanted the same land he was fighting for and the 'superwoman' problem. He would take care of the Muslims when the time was right. They had the money, the manpower, and the training, but he, too, had manpower. And he had the fire in his belly and fortitude, the *razon de vivir* or reason to live, that the Muslims did not have. They were fighting for religion, but he was fighting for something greater—his homeland, Mexico. The resolution of the 'superwoman' problem was in the works. He knew who she was and where she was at this very moment. Victory was as good as his.

Out of respect for his mother and his sister, he headquartered his gang, *Las Cobras*, in this five-story hulk of a building. Unidentifiable, cannibalized equipment lurked in the corners throughout the building. Dirt and debris still covered the floors, but there was plenty of space for his growing army, as well as the supplies that were flowing in on a daily basis. The ground floor easily accommodated the swelling stockpile of ammo and food, and the office spaces along the far wall served as a makeshift barracks for his freedom fighters—*las guerrillas por la libertad.*

At the west end of the building, a stairwell provided access to the other four floors. With minor variations, the other floors were laid out the same. He'd replaced the broken windows and hardened the doors, which turned this building into a fortified headquarters. He chose the second floor for his base of operations.

"Useful idiots," Tito muttered to his second-in-command as he watched the same newscasts the C-IA was monitoring. "With the tiniest spark, they run through the streets destroying what the white man has created. They will keep the police and soldiers distracted so we can go forward with our real objective." He shook his head and chuckled as he turned to his communications tech who was manning the radios, monitors, and the phones. "Any word from the *las guerrillas* attacking the ranches?"

The communications operator turned in his seat to look at Tito. "*Sí, puño*, Alpha Team is still *en ruta* to the Pennington ranch. Five minutes out. Bravo Team is in place at the perimeter of the Gomez ranch and waiting for your command."

"Tell Bravo to go. Tell Alpha to attack in fifteen minutes. That will give plenty of time for the men of the Pennington ranch to rush to the Gomez ranch to help them. Then Alpha will attack a defenseless Pennington ranch. Let me know when the Pennington ranch is taken. We will break down everything here and move to the Pennington ranch. It will be our new base of operations. *Las Cobras* will stay here to defend our arsenal."

Tito smiled and chuckled as he walked toward the large map of Arizona on a board in the middle of the room. "*Compadres*," he said with a raised voice and with a wide sweep of his arm, "by sundown we will control a vast strip of land from the National Park along the southern border to within a few miles of the city limits of Tempe. We will have the land we need for training and launching attacks on the incompetent and unsuspecting white man."

Shouts of patriotism and support answered him. The talking allowed him to speak privately to the computer tech. He bent over and braced himself on the table that held the electronic equipment. "What about superwoman?"

The computer tech pulled the headset off his head and wrapped it around the back of his neck. He looked over his shoulder at Tito. "She is at that biker bar. We have three of our newest operatives leading the riot in that direction."

෫෨෫෨

The sight of Flora bunched up into a ball on the filthy floor and leaning against the wall stopped Joan in her tracks. She was holding her stomach and looked at Joan with a pained, scared look in her eyes. Streaks of mascara smeared a pathway to her jawline. Joan fell to her knees beside her.

Flora looked terrified. "I'm losing the baby."

"*What* baby?" The sight of Flora in obvious discomfort, and the news, paralyzed Joan's body, but her thoughts swung into a headlong sprint, *This can't be happening. A miscarriage? In the middle of a riot? And* what *baby?*

Flora started sobbing uncontrollably. Between sobs, she squeezed out the words, "I was three months—we were going to make the—announcement to everyone—tonight."

Joan pulled the distraught woman into her arms. "Sweetie, we'll get you to the hospital as soon as we can." Placing her cheek on the top of Flora's head, Joan rocked her for what seemed like a long time. It gave her time to think about what she should do.

"You're squishing me," Flora said, sniffling, an indication the bout of sobbing was coming to an end.

Joan loosened her hold. When Flora spoke, her voice was muffled by the wad of toilet paper she was using to blow her nose. "I'm scared, Iron Angel. I've never been afraid of anything before."

Joan ended the embrace and leaned back to look Flora in the eyes. "Me neither, but if there ever was a big gulp moment, this is it."

Flora grasped Joan. "Don't leave me!"

"Oh, sweetie, I'm not leaving you. Ruby asked me to look after you, and that's what I'm going to do." With a strong arm around Flora's shoulder, Joan stood up, easily lifted Flora to her feet, and guided her toward the sink. "Let's get you cleaned up as best we can."

Bent over with her arms crossed over her belly, Flora docilely followed Joan's guidance toward the chipped and rust-stained porcelain sink. Without warning, Flora bolted to one of the stalls and vomited into the bowl.

While holding Flora's hair, Joan fought the dread overtaking her. A heavy, burning lump formed in her stomach. *Damn, damn, damn! If she were being attacked, I'd know what to do. But* this *is way outside the scope of my training.* Joan squeezed her eyelids shut. *You're losing it, girl, get your shit together.*

Her army training kicked in. *When not sure of the exact course of action, do something. Move. Doing anything is better than doing nothing. Adjust fire midstream if you have to.* Joan started filling the sink with water.

Before the sink was full, the building shuddered. A small piece of plaster fell from the ceiling, followed by a spray of plaster dust.

"Stay here," Joan ordered. "I'll check it out."

CHAPTER 12

With her .38 revolver in front of her, Joan edged along the wall of the hallway. The harsh odor of smoke tickled her nose. With every step, the air got hotter. After a couple of seconds to gather her wits at the corner, she snuck a look around the bend in the hallway.

Her move was a quick out and back. The sight was as heart-stopping as it was inconceivable—something out of a horror flick. Her second look was longer with a full step into the corridor to the barroom. Where there once had been tables and chairs, sat a car on fire. Flames shot up from the windows of the car and across the ceiling. It rolled across the top of the once highly polished oak bar and licked its way up the supporting beams. Frozen in place, unable to take her eyes off the scene in front of her, Joan tried replacing her gun in its holster on her hip. It slipped past the holster three times before she pried her eyes from the inferno and looked down to find the opening.

Flames burned a hissing, scorching path toward the back of the room where it opened into the hallway where she stood. The heat was intense. Sweat broke out over every inch of her body.

The hot, dry air parched her mouth and throat. She fought the urge to cough. In minutes, the hallway where she was standing would be a fiery hell. As sweat dripped down the side of her face, she realized she had to gather up Flora and get out of there.

She backed away from the flames, but stopped when a man's voice pierced the smoke.

"Iron Angel, are you there? Is that you?"

Joan shielded her eyes and inched forward, searching for the source of the voice.

"A flaming car burst through the front wall and we beat feet to the alley, but when we got outside we realized you and Flora weren't there. We came back to get you."

"We're not going to leave you here," another voice yelled.

"We need help." Joan put up an arm to shield her face from the blistering heat and took another couple steps forward. Her left eye stung from sweat, and she wiped it on the sleeve of her tee shirt. The smoke was getting thicker and several hacking coughs dropped her to one knee. Before pulling the neckline of her tee shirt over her nose and mouth, she said, "Flora's in really bad shape."

"We're looking for the fire extinguishers. Don't worry. We'll get you guys out."

"I'll get Flora," Joan said.

If there was a response, she didn't hear it. She was already running back down the hallway.

On the way to the rear of the building, Joan looked for a rear exit. None. With the knot getting tighter in her stomach and her confidence fading, she checked the men's room. No window, just like the ladies' room. Muttered curses escaped her mouth, aimed at the builders who must have paid off the building inspector to overlook the fact that the building did not have a rear exit. She opened the door to the ladies' room and motioned to Flora to come to her, trying to relay urgency without instilling fear.

Bent over in pain, Flora struggled to her feet. Joan grabbed her arm. "Come on, honey, let's get you to a hospital. Stay low." With Flora under her protective arm, they raced down the hall in a crouch. "The guys are looking for fire extinguishers to make a path through the flames so we can get out," she continued.

The hallway seemed hotter than before, and smokier. Joan's eyes stung, and a cough caught in the back of her throat. She pulled her tee shirt over her nose and mouth and encouraged Flora to do the same. The fire had become a living, breathing entity, roaring and sucking the oxygen out of the small space. Popping sounds came from somewhere above them. Joan's stomach tightened into a heavy, coiling knot.

She shielded her eyes with her arm and yelled through the flames, "We're back."

"Hang on. We're doing what we can," someone shouted through the haze.

Flora moaned and her legs gave out from another powerful spasm. She crumpled to the floor.

"Hurry up. We have to get Flora out of here."

"Hang on, ladies. We'll piss on these flames if we have to." The sound of fire extinguishers pierced the smoke and briefly drowned out the roaring fire.

For a fleeting couple of seconds, the flames parted, offering a pathway to the other side. In one motion, Joan lifted Flora off the floor and shoved her through the opening. The biker on the other side grabbed Flora and ushered her away. The other biker finished the last of the carbon dioxide in his extinguisher and threw it aside.

"C'mon, Iron Angel, grab my hand. I'll pull you through."

Joan eyed the flames. They roared back at her. Bigger with each passing second. And hotter. They sizzled and popped on the ceiling above her head. The only way out was through the blaze in front of her. Sweat dripping from every pore, face flushed, she pushed herself forward only to drop back. Each rock back and forth only wasted precious time. But the heat was blistering. Going through the flames was unimaginable. The thought of getting burned was just…unthinkable.

"C'mon, grab my hand. Come through as fast as you can! Don't think. Just do it!"

"I can't. It's too hot." Panic filled her stomach, then scaled her spine to the base of her skull, and tightened her scalp. Time slowed. She marveled that the sweat rolling down her back had turned cold. She shivered. All the seemingly hopeless situations she had overcome in the past flashed through her mind. None compared to this. This was different. Fire couldn't be kicked, stabbed, shot, or manipulated. Overcoming the fire was the only action left to her. But how? Frozen with fear, one thought filled her consciousness. She had discovered the one thing in the world she was afraid of—sizzling, blistering, searing fire.

The loud male voice jolted her back to real time. "Close your eyes and barrel through. I'll catch you."

"I can't do it. I—I just can't." She looked in horror at the flames hissing and roaring above her head. Taunting her. Mocking her fear.

A coughing fit forced her from a crouch to one knee. A dark form flew through the flames and knocked her backward, slamming the back of her head against the floor. Through the smoke, unfolding his large frame, was the biggest biker she'd ever seen. She guessed he was at least six-foot-eight and weighed and two hundred-eighty-five pounds.

Rubbing the back of her head, she said, "I've just been tackled by Grisly-friggin'-Adams!"

The big biker put out a hand to help her to her feet. "I'm Little Al."

She stopped rubbing the back of her head and looked up at him. "If there's a *Big* Al, I can't wait to meet him."

"There *is* a Big Al, but we're going to have to get back through the flames for you to meet him." He grabbed her hand. "Ready?"

She pulled her hand away. "How did you get through there?"

"By the grace of God. You wouldn't come to me, so I came to you. Ready? I'm taking you back to the other side."

Joan pulled her arms in close to her chest to get them out of this crazy biker's reach. Her wide, unblinking eyes looked up at him then at the inferno between her and safety.

"Calm down. It's going to be okay. We're only a few feet from safety." His voice was as calm as his body was large. He leaned down and put his arm around her shoulder with his huge mitt of a hand in her armpit. Before he could get back through the flames, a beam fell in their path.

"I take that back," he said with an uncanny composure. "We're in a shitload of trouble. What's down that way?" He pointed down the hallway in the direction Joan had just come.

"Nothing. No door. No windows."

"Let's go." Bent over to keep his shoulder-length, brown curly hair away from the flaming ceiling, he headed down the hallway with her wrist buried in his left hand.

She thought of Duncan. Was he coming for her? How far away was he? As she entered the ladies' room behind Little Al, she said, "I can't die here, not today, not with some strange man."

Little Al was already at the sink with his back to her, splashing water onto handfuls of paper towels he had stuffed into the sink. He said over his shoulder, "I think you meant to say that with your inside voice."

"Sorry. I didn't mean you were strange in an odd way." Her voice was weak, distracted. Pinned to the door, her body clung to the only exit it knew, unconvinced it was no longer the escape route it had been for Flora.

Little Al grabbed all the towels out of the sink and handed them to her. "I know what you meant. Stuff these in the crack under the door."

When she was sure no smoke would make it beyond the door, she turned back to Little Al.

He snatched more towels from the sink and handed them to her. "Here, put these over your nose and mouth. Come over here. Get low. Sit under the sink."

"But it's overflowing." Brain cells were firing and misfiring. Nothing to fight, nowhere to flee to, her fight or flight reflex was only increasing her anxiety. Escape was the only reality her brain could accept, but escape was not a realistic option. Sheer willpower prevented her body from shutting down completely. Rule number one of any operation—have an exit strategy. Why had she never noticed there was no back door to Colors? Was she losing her edge?

She had always pictured the end as a blaze of glory. Joan pressed her lips together over the poor choice of words. *I thought I would at least go down fighting. But in my last minutes I'm going to be a quivering puddle of pink goo—make that smoldering black goo.*

Little Al's mellow voice brought her back to the current

desperate situation. "If there's a fire coming, wouldn't you want to be wet, or would you rather stand there and become a crispy critter?" He sat down and slid sideways to get his shoulder under the sink. He covered his huge face and beard with wet paper towels.

Joan scurried across the small room, knelt, and crawled under the sink. Her pucker factor was in overdrive from thoughts of what would happen next. Thoughts of never seeing Duncan again made her groan inwardly. Her eyes, wide and barely focused, jerked toward Little Al to see if she had groaned aloud. He reached out and pulled her farther under the sink.

"Don't worry, most people are unconscious from smoke inhalation before the flames get to them." His eyes assessed her. "I thought you were the unshakable, tough Iron Angel."

Eyes ready to pop out of her head, she looked at the giant next to her and struggled to swallow. "Even Superman had Kryptonite."

Little Al guided the wet paper towels in her hands to her face. In a low, serene voice, muffled by his own paper towels, he intoned, "Be merciful to me, O God, for in you, my soul takes refuge; in the shadow of your wings I will take refuge till the storms of destruction pass by. I cry out to you…"

યૢ૭

"Dee Dee, pull the van in behind that white car." Duncan pointed to a white sedan halfway up the block on the right. He partially turned to the others. "We'll walk in from here. There's no sense in getting our ride burned up."

"Blackbird, what's your twenty?" Kearney called out to Jason for a location report. Rather than revealing names over the radio, Duncan had established call signs. He gave himself Thunderbird, Kearney was Firebird, Jason, Blackbird.

Jason answered while stepping through the driver's side sliding door into the street, immediately checking to the rear in an arc left to right, high to low, hand on the grip of his 9 mm semi-automatic. "Firebird, this is Blackbird, we're at the designated start point, exiting the vehicle, and heading east. Do you copy?"

Gunther exited the other side of the van and checked in front of the group in the same manner as Jason. The others gathered on the sidewalk, waiting for the signal to proceed.

"I got you loud and clear," Kearney responded. "From the latest news update, the mob is moving east about ten blocks to your twelve. Cops have returned to the streets with national guard in tow. And from what little I can see, they are right on the heels of the mob."

"When was the last update?"

"Three minutes, maybe more. So keep your heads on the swivel."

"Roger that. Blackbird out," Jason signed off as he scanned the surrounding buildings one last time and stepped backward onto the curb to join the rest of the team.

Duncan assessed the team. Dee Dee didn't have the quiet confidence of a seasoned soldier, but she wasn't falling to pieces either. Red Dog was an Iraq War veteran. The first gunshot would test his mettle. Gunther was dependable under fire, almost cold. He'd need watching as did Jason, but for another reason. Jason was a former marine, calm, detail-conscious, collected, but he now had other things on his mind. Ignoring a pang of regret at leaving Kearney behind, Duncan put his game face on.

This was the team he chose. This was the team for this mission. With any luck, they would get to Colors, everyone would be okay, and he could head home with Joan. *Luck favors the prepared*. Well, scratch luck from the equation. Preparation had been swift and, in his estimation, incomplete.

"Gunther," Jason commanded, "you take point. I'm your cover man. Then, Dee Dee, then Duncan. Red Dog, you get our six."

As Red Dog swiftly moved to the rear of the group, Jason tapped Gunther on the shoulder and motioned for him to move out.

"Let's fuck this chicken," Dee Dee said as she turned to follow Jason.

Duncan's lips pressed into a thin line. *Jesus Christ, another Joan.* He loved how Joan could calm jangled nerves with a sarcastic, witty comment at the height of a tense situation. Under other circumstances, the sarcasm would be endearing. *Under other circumstances*. The thought got his head back into the game.

The smell of smoke, that had prickled their senses when they first got out of the van, seemed stronger now that they were on the move and heading toward the danger. They passed garbage-littered streets so unlike the normal cleanliness of Phoenix. Garbage cans were overturned, some still smoldering. As they continued on West Buckeye the damage got worse in degrees. At first, it was broken store windows, then looted stores, then burned out stores, and, finally, still-burning cars and dumpsters. When they reached the designated point to turn south, a group of young people ran down the middle of the street toward them. Their soot-streaked faces distorted from fear, they yelled something at Duncan and his team, who froze, poised for trouble. They relaxed when the rag-tag group raced past them, heading west away from the riot.

"What did they say?" Dee Dee asked.

"I don't know. 'Go back.' 'Run for your lives,' some shit like that." Duncan tapped Gunther on the shoulder. "Go."

Gunther turned right and headed south. As they continued along the chosen route, everything looked as they expected from the Google aerial map they'd studied before leaving the house. They crossed a short open space and jumped the expected fence into a residential area. So far, so good.

The streets were empty. The residents had either evacuated or barricaded themselves in their homes, presumably hoping danger would pass them by. Everyone stayed alert to any danger, but tension drained from their limbs like sands in an hourglass. Sweaty palms and hyper-alertness replaced knotted-up muscles. Breathing smoothed out.

They walked along in silence and turned onto the last leg of the trip that tracked along a wooden privacy fence. Smoke was sensed more than seen. Distant sirens and inaudible distant voices interrupted the eerie calm, reminding them there was chaos somewhere outside their bubble of safety. Staying in the short shadow of the fence, they inched past a small housing development.

An apartment complex loomed on their left when Jason's lowered voice broke the silence. "Anyone else feel it?"

"Yeah, man, my spidey-senses are going wild," Red Dog whispered.

He had been in the second Gulf War and was familiar with the sensation unique to soldiers that warned them about greasy situations. Call it a gut feeling, intuition, a sixth sense. Call it anything but brain chemistry playing a joke on the soldier, because every battle-tested soldier would attest to it. It saved many soldiers, and just as many soldiers wished they had listened to it.

"Keep your mouths shut and your eyes open," Jason whispered. "Gunther, check the far side of each building before we reach it."

Gunther nodded and jogged to increase the distance between him and the rest of the group. He passed the first building and flashed a thumbs up. After creeping past the second building, he turned to give another thumbs up, but froze. Something on the faces of Duncan and Jason told him something was wrong. He backed up toward the group to rejoin them.

"Say again, Firebird. You're breaking up." Jason and Duncan were pressing on their left earbuds, trying to drown out any outside noise so they could hear Kearney better.

More static. Duncan was now by Jason's side. "I think he said something about the bar being on fire. Is that what you heard?"

Jason didn't have to answer, his face said it all.

"Wait. Say again, Firebird." Duncan said, more firmly pressing the earbud in his ear.

"Breaking...heading...way," was all Jason and Duncan heard.

"Say again. You're breaking up." Nothing but static answered his command. Duncan turned to Jason. "Did you get that?"

Jason shook his head.

"Do you think he was saying that the mob has broken through the police lines and are heading our way?"

Jason shrugged.

Duncan pulled a monocular out of his right cargo pocket and, with the grace of a cat, leaped to the top of the wooden fence. He scanned the area.

"You thought to bring a mono? Good thinking," Jason said.

"That's why I'm the boss," Duncan replied without removing the mini-telescope from his eye. As he focused it, he continued, "Can't see very far because of the apartment buildings. I can see the roof of the bar."

The roof was smoldering. Announcing it would only give credibility to the fear that something happened to his angel. He sprang down to the ground and returned the monocular to the cargo pocket of his camouflage-patterned pants. "Colors is just past the park on the far side of these apartment buildings. Let's double-time it."

They jogged past the last two buildings and, just as they entered the small park, they heard someone yell, "Hey, Gringos, we're going to beat your lily-white asses."

The group spun around toward the voices. Duncan counted nine men in gang-colored haskies striding toward them. Their chins were raised and their chests puffed out. Their mouths slanted into sneers.

Gunshots would attract unwanted police attention. Outrunning them was not an option. Statistically, it was an exercise in futility to talk down anyone with a mob mentality. Burying the thought of how close they were to their objective—and Joan— Duncan faced the approaching men. The C-IA fighters closed ranks behind him.

CHAPTER 13

The fight was over as quickly as it had begun. Jason stood with his hands on his knees, trying to clear his head and get his breath back. Four feet to his right, Duncan wobbled, checking out the slashes on his torso. Gunther, chest thrust forward, sinewy arms slightly back, a blood-drenched knife in each hand, dared the retreating figures to come back.

Three attackers, supporting each other, disappeared around the white-washed stucco house at the end of the street. Five more lay on the ground in growing pools of blood.

"Everyone okay?" Duncan asked.

"Duncan!" Dee Dee's desperate tone prompted Jason and Duncan to spin around, guns raised and ready. Red Dog was in a heap on the ground. A dark-skinned Latino with a jutting chin below a dark green haskie held a knife to Dee Dee's throat.

"Give me all your guns," he sneered, "or I'll kill her right here."

"Wait," Duncan said, aiming at the middle of the man's forehead. "We can discuss—"

There was a muffled crack and, as the man with the knife fell to the ground with a bloody hole where his right eye used to be, Duncan leapt to his right swatting at his left ear as if a bee was buzzing around him. "*Jee*-sus, Jason," Duncan swore through his teeth, "another inch to the right and I'd be borrowing one of your friggin' earrings."

"He wasn't getting *my* gun," Jason said, holstering his weapon.

"A heads-up next time would be a good idea," Duncan replied, holding his hand out to help Dee Dee to her feet. He hesitated whether to tell her about the blowback blood sprayed across her face and pink flesh stuck in her hair. "You okay?"

"I think so." Her wobbly legs gave out and she dropped to her knees at the side of her husband. "Red! Red Dog, baby, wake up."

Duncan knelt by her side and started checking for injuries. "Did he get stabbed or hit with something?"

"That low-life bastard hit him over the head and knocked him out."

Moans and slight stirring prompted Dee Dee to renew her pleas for Red Dog to respond to her.

Jason tapped her on the shoulder. "Let Duncan take care of your old man. I'll clean you up. You can't go waltzing down the street with blood and brains in your hair." As Dee Dee reluctantly stood up, he asked, "Where's your bandana or shemagh?"

"Shemagh?"

"You know, those scarves the Arabs wear. Like this," he pointed to his brown and black shemagh around his neck.

"I never heard of a shemagh, and bandanas are so...yesterday."

Jason untied his cammo-patterned shemagh and started to wipe the blowback blood and flesh from the side of her head.

"They aren't a fashion statement. They're—" He stopped while he picked a particularly stubborn piece of flesh from her hair, "—one thing you never go on a mission without."

"I'll put that on my packing list for next time."

The clean-up complete, she knelt next to Red Dog, opposite Duncan.

"What do you need, boss?" Jason asked.

"More bandages to cover the gash in the back of Red Dog's head. Scalp injuries are always such bloody messes," Duncan said as he helped Red Dog sit upright until he could brace himself with his elbows on his knees. The foggy-headed biker cupped his head in both hands.

Jason ripped the earbuds out of his ears. Without thinking, he pulled his tee shirt over his head and started tearing the thin cotton into strips. He handed them to Dee Dee, who in turn handed them to Duncan. The third time she reached to take the cotton strips, she froze. Jason followed her stare to his chest where a muted brown and gray heart wrapped in thorns with one red drop of blood proclaimed his connection to the now-defunct Constitution Defense Legion. It was a symbol of his status as a fugitive. His gaze slid to her green eyes.

"I saw that tattoo on 'America's Most Wanted.'" She looked quickly at Duncan then back to Jason.

"No one can know, Dee Dee. Do you understand?" Jason said.

Duncan looked up at the uncharacteristically harsh tone and spied Jason's bare chest. He looked over at Dee Dee. "We'll answer any questions you have later, but right now we have to get your old man patched up and be on our way. Okay?"

"Okay."

Duncan's eyes pierced her. "No one can know who we are. Understand?"

"Yes, I understand. Besides, I always kinda knew you guys weren't regular joe-schmoes off the street. Iron Angel, she—"

"Yes, she's one of us." Duncan said.

"Well, that explains—" Her eyes snapped up to Gunther. He squinted at her. She dropped her eyes to her husband. "—a lot."

Duncan looked from Gunther to Dee Dee. As he tied off the last bandage, he wondered what he was missing. Silently batting the words away, he set his jaw, stood up, and easily pulled the injured biker to his feet. "You okay, buddy? Will you be able to keep up?"

"Don't worry about me. I've been hit harder."

Duncan nodded, clapped him on the back, winced, and pulled up his blood-soaked shirt to check his own wounds. A slash along the waist on the left side hid beneath a thick coating of blood. There was another, shallower slash across his ribs on the right.

They weren't deep, so Duncan pinched the edges together

and applied pressure with the black-and-white shemagh Gunther offered him.

"Colors is just on the other side of the park," Jason said as he covered his Legion tattoo by strategically wrapping his shemagh like a bandolier across his chest. "Stay close to the fence."

He motioned for Gunther to lead the group south toward Colors. When they scaled the fence that bordered Colors's back parking lot, their shoulders slumped. Beyond the cinderblock addition, three of the four stucco walls of the original part of the building stood as lonely sentinels to the past. Inside them was a smoldering pile of black Pick-Up-Sticks. Firemen stood guard, watching for any flare ups, and police were controlling the growing crowd of onlookers. Bikers stood in small groups.

"Dee Dee," Duncan said in a lowered voice, "take the guns and ammo and hide them somewhere. We can't let the cops catch us with this much fire power. They'll ask a lot of questions we don't need to be answering."

Heavy bags in hand, she headed toward the shed at the back of the parking lot.

Blackie, the Demon Brotherhood VP, approached the group with his mouth tight, eyes on the ground. "I'm sorry, man."

Duncan's heart stopped.

Blackie passed Duncan and grabbed Jason by both shoulders. "Flora lost the baby."

Jason pressed his hand against his mouth, but behind the swollen bruises, his eyes gave away his emotion.

"She's at St. Luke's Hospital. I'll take you there."

Jason nodded and let Blackie lead him away.

"What about Iron Angel?" Duncan called after them.

"Oh, I'm sorry, man. I should have told you. The paramedics are working on her in the front of the building. If you hurry, you might be able to catch her before they put her in the ambulance."

Duncan didn't hear any words after "paramedics." He was running full-speed to her and reached her side as the paramedics opened the ambulance doors. He choked back the tightness in his throat.

She rolled her head toward him and pulled the oxygen mask off her face, "Duncan, you came for me. Are you okay?"

He pressed his hands on his blood-stained shemagh. "Just a couple slashes. What about you?"

She reached out for him. "What happened to you?"

"We had to fight off some punks along the way," he said, kissing her sooty knuckles.

"I wish I could have been there to help you."

"Me, too. What about *you*?"

"Just smoke inhalation. I told them—" She stopped to cough then took a long inhale from the oxygen mask. "Tell them I don't have to go to the hospital." She coughed again. "I'm okay because I have you. You're as good as a doctor. Tell them, Duncan." The legs on the gurney folded as the paramedics slid it into the back of the ambulance.

"Don't worry I'll take care of the bill," he reassured her.

"How are you going—"

The doors closed. She was separated from Duncan again.

ℰ/ͻℰ/ͻ

Joan was alone, or as alone as anyone could be in a busy emergency room. The lines that fed the oxygen to the nose clip were rubbing her ears, and she absent-mindedly fussed with them, trying to find a comfortable placement. The *yeeks* of the nurses' shoes, as they hurried up and down the corridor, were comforting. There was a man, maybe two or three rooms away, who was moaning. A phone rang somewhere nearby. The nurse hadn't checked on her for a while and the hum of quiet voices lulled Joan into much needed sleep. Her lids closed then opened. They continued their rhythmic closing and opening until one time they remained closed, and her breathing evened out.

She was jolted awake when she heard a desperate, "Joan!"

She opened her eyes to see Jason with his shoulders squared and his hands balled up into fists. His fury filled the open doorway. He was always the calm and quiet member. The precise and careful person whose motto was "The details will kill you." Yet, he just spoke her given name in public.

"What happened?"

Jason spoke through clenched teeth. "Flora lost the baby." He worked his lips between his teeth to control his emotions. "My son."

"I know, I'm sorry, Jason," she said gently.

"The doctors said if she'd gotten here earlier they could have saved him."

Joan pushed with her hands and slid her hips back to sit upright. "I'm truly sorry. I tried to get her here as soon as I could, but the fire slowed us down."

He rushed toward her. "I don't blame you. It's *them*." Jason's red-rimmed, swollen eyes were hard as he jerked his head toward the unseen *them* out *there*.

She wanted to say something to calm him down, to disarm the combative desperation she felt radiating from him, but her warrior took over. "Those bastards. If we hadn't been pinned down at the bar—" she said through clenched teeth. "They killed your child."

"Fuckin'–A."

Before he had finished the third syllable, she yanked the oxygen clip from her nose, swung her legs over the side of the bed, and stood up. She got a whiff of the smoke from her clothes, and a rolling, deep cough racked her lungs. He put his arm around her waist to steady her.

The coughing finally stopped and she rasped out, "Where's Duncan?"

"He's here somewhere."

"We have to find him."

They took off down the hallway, dodging carts full of medical supplies, looking into each room until she found Duncan sitting on a gurney, tee shirt slung over his left shoulder. One gash was stitched closed. A young doctor was stitching up the slash over his left ribs.

She stuck her head out into the hallway. "Jason, he's here." She looked back into the tiny room. "Let's go, Duncan."

"Who's this?" the intern asked.

"My angel. How long till you're done?"

"Couple minutes," the intern said without looking up.

"Come on. We have to go."

"What's so important that it can't wait a couple minutes?" Duncan asked, keeping his eyes on the doctor's hands.

"I'm in."

He looked up. "In?"

"Yes, I'm in. Twenty-four square. To the hilt. Until the birds sing."

Duncan cocked his head and smiled. "'Until the birds sing?'"

She ignored his sarcasm. "Stop being a sissy. Put a butterfly thing on that cut and let's go."

The intern glanced up at her then up at Duncan. He went back to work.

Little Al appeared over Iron Angel's right shoulder. "What's up?"

"Duncan's being a pussy."

"Who's he?" Duncan asked, nodding his chin toward the giant behind her.

She nodded back over her right shoulder. "This is Little Al. He helped me survive the fire. Now, let's go."

Jason tugged her arm. "C'mon, let the doctor do his job."

Iron Angel glared at Duncan and impatiently jerked her head toward exit.

CHAPTER 14

In the cool, dark basement of their house, Iron Angel gave one last powerful low hook to the heavy bag. Working out had always cleared her head and filled her with her daily fix of endorphins, but her slow recovery from smoke inhalation had limited the intensity and duration of her workouts. Unable to immerse herself in strenuous activity, she couldn't clear her head of the events during the riot.

With her lips fiercely pressed together, she kicked the duct-taped bag as if it were the rioters who had caused so much havoc a few weeks before. The Penningtons had lost their two sons in the attack on their ranch, and their neighbor, Lou Gomez, had lost two ranch hands. Flora lost her baby. Duncan got stabbed. The Pennington ranch house was destroyed, as was Colors. All this destruction and where had she been? Cowering under a sink, afraid of fire. She clenched her teeth. Afraid? Her? She let loose a flurry of kicks and punches on the bag.

A coughing spasm stopped the workout and she hugged the taped-up bag for support. When the coughing stopped, she grabbed a bottle of water and chugged the cool, clear liquid to ease the tightening in her scratchy throat. Empty water bottle in hand, she stood mindlessly crushing it, wishing the world would go away, loathing the person she had become. Shrinking from phantoms. Quick to anger. Slow to recover from her injuries. Cowering. Weak. Afraid of fire.

She threw the crumpled plastic bottle against the wall.

Kearney's words of advice percolated through her brain: "Act strong, and people will respond to you as if you are strong."

Long inhales, jagged and forceful at first, slowly eased into a soothing, relaxing rhythm. After several shoulder rolls, she reached for the hand-carved mahogany box of throwing stars and knives—a gift from Master Yu. The motion of throwing the knives, pulling them out of the target and throwing them again, quieted her mind. With each toss of a star, anger transformed into determination.

At some indistinct point, the thoughts of the Pennington and Gomez families' tragedy slipped away. Jason's lost baby and Duncan's injuries fell into their rightful position within the grand scheme of things.

She prepared to toss a star, hesitated, and pressed her lips together. The Counter-Insurgency Army was not the Constitution Defense Legion. When things went bad with the Legion, she broke ranks and ran. Not this time. This time things would be different. She was different. *The hottest places in hell are reserved for those who, when faced with a moral dilemma, do nothing.* Joining the C-IA was do or die, come hell or high water.

La Espada didn't give her the option of waiting for another solution to present itself. They were hunting her down. Another innocent Lisa Brown was found in a dumpster, making it six. Six too many. They'd thrown down the gauntlet. She would pick it up and shove it up their collective ass. She was in. Do or die. Hell. Or. High. Water. She tossed five stars in quick succession.

As the morning sun rose in the sky, and the basement temperature warmed, she reverently wiped the knives and stars then tucked them into their respective places in the red felt lining. One of the knives needed to be sharpened, so she sheathed it. There was a whetstone in the gadget drawer in the kitchen.

As she ascended the stairs from the basement, she decided to check on the new communication guys before her shower. Duncan would not leave any of his fighters behind for communication coverage again, and he had put out a call for cyber/communications experts. Removing all the dining room furniture, he'd turned the room into a first rate communications center with state of the art computers, monitors, and radios on tables that wrapped around two walls in a big L-shape. Space was tight, but it was efficient and effective. Meals now consisted of balancing plates on knees or the arms of the couch. She'd lived through worse—at least they weren't sitting in the dirt of a foreign country eating cold food mixed with sand.

Duncan's call was answered quickly, but what they got was very different from what they'd expected. Little Al's sons, Joseph and Samuel, stepped forward with credentials that filled the bill. Joined at the hip, so to speak, there was rarely a need to address them individually, so they were called Joe-Sam. They were slender, young, effeminate identical twins. Nineteen-year-old, blond preppies, Iron Angel called them. Everyone thought they were proficient and highly qualified, but when she watched them, they nervously made typing errors, fumbled with the equipment, and spilled things.

With no apparent reason for wanting to get mixed up with a militia, they set off alarm bells for her. Duncan reminded her that she hadn't had any apparent reason for joining the Legion, and they deserved a chance to prove themselves. She acquiesced, but silently decided to keep a close eye on them.

She stopped in the middle of the kitchen and, in spite of the sunny warmth, shook off the chills going down her spine. She tucked the sheathed knife into her waistband and crept across the small kitchen. Someone was in the house, and it wasn't just Joe-Sam. She heard deep, accented voices coming from the dining room.

With her back pressed tightly against the wall between the two rooms, she silently told the ceiling, *We have* got *to move.* She inched one eye around the corner to the dining room where two men stood with their backs to her, facing Samuel...or Joseph. She scowled down the hallway, wondering where the other twin was. They were *always* together. Damn them. Now, when it was important for them to be together, one was missing. If he walked in on this, he might ruin her plan— whatever it was. Couldn't things go right, just once?

After another furtive glance down the hallway, she slowed

5l

her breathing and tried to hear what the men were saying. There were some words from one of the older men, then a voice with a lighter tone would answer. The exchange seemed firm and professional. Cops.

After one last deep breath to calm her nerves, she stepped around the corner and into the dining room. The tension on Samuel's face, or Joseph's, told her his gut said something wasn't right.

This is me being strong. "Hello, can I help you?"

The men spun around, surprised at a voice behind them. They wore jeans and polo shirts with the faint outline of a bulletproof vest. Their blazers fit as if they belonged to someone else. Her heart rate increased.

"We're from the Phoenix Gang Crimes Unit, and we have some questions for Lisa Brown. Is that you?"

"Show me some ID."

"We already showed it to this young man," the barrel-chested man on the right said.

Cops were always ready to show ID. And they identified any and every person in a house. A distant, faint alarm bell started to ring.

The twin shrugged. "They showed me some badges."

"Are you Lisa Brown?" the thinner man on the left asked.

She checked every line on their faces, the position of their hands, their posture. Her eyes narrowed. "Yes. What do you want to know?"

"We had a hard time finding you. How long have you lived here?" the thinner cop asked.

"A few months."

"How many people live here with you?"

"One other person."

Something in their eyes echoed in their voices. It suggested tension and winked at malice. Nothing in their conduct was similar to the casual, comforting conversation with Detective Ramos after the Pennington ranch invasion. No notebooks, no people skills.

Her heart quickened a little more.

"What's his name?"

Her pulse went into overdrive. "I didn't say it was a him. What's this about?"

"Miss Brown, you may be in danger. We would like you to come down to the headquarters with us to answer some questions so we can close the file."

The larger man reached behind him and when his hand reappeared, it held handcuffs.

All the saliva in her mouth disappeared. "Am I under arrest?"

Memories of her arrest in Cleveland filled her head. Tough fight. Long chase. Arrest. Jail. Her tongue stuck to the roof of her mouth and her throat tightened. As casually as she could, she moved her hands to her hips.

"You aren't under arrest," the thinner man said. "Don't let the handcuffs scare you. It's just standard procedure for transporting someone in the car. Please turn around." When she didn't move, he added, "We just want to clear up some details. Maybe there's something you can tell us to stop the attacks on local women with the name, Lisa Brown."

She squared her shoulders, slowed her breathing, readied herself. She looked into the eyes of the heavier man on her right. "You need to leave now. If you leave your business cards, I'll go downtown to answer questions later this afternoon."

Her gaze slid from one to the other, hoping it was true that a bulletproof vest would stop a bullet, but not a knife. She licked her lips and waited. The first to speak would not be the attacker.

The barrel-chested man spoke first.

She pulled the sheathed knife from her waistband, flicked it so the sheath flew into the bigger man's face, and slashed at the thinner man. He bent forward to hitch his hips out of the path of the blade. A left palm heel to his temple stunned him, but the bigger man was on her.

She got in an elbow strike to his torso before his big arms closed around her in a bear hug, pinning her arms to her sides. The thinner man approached. As he lashed out, she kicked at him, hitting him in the right thigh. A dull thunk filled her head as his blow, meant for her temple, hit her jaw instead. She spit the blood in her mouth at the thinner man and stabbed the right thigh of the man hugging her. His grip eased enough for her to step to the side, and she plunged the knife into the right side of his abdomen, but not before the thinner man got in a blow. Pain exploded from her left eye throughout her head.

The metallic sound of cocking a semi-automatic pistol froze everyone. Through her hazy, half-lit vision, she saw Joseph, or Samuel, pointing a gun at the thinner man. Joe-Sam had received only one hour of training and, in spite of shaking hands, the twin was standing his ground, coming to her aid.

The big man noticed the twin's shaking hands and pulled his gun. Iron Angel slashed out, slicing the tendons in his right forearm, then she sliced the tendons in the front crease of his elbow. With a wristlock, she swept him to the ground and stabbed him in the throat.

Before the big man hit the ground, the thinner man pulled his gun. The twin pulled the trigger, but nothing happened. Iron Angel dove for the thinner man. His shots went wide, missing the twin, hitting one of the monitors instead. She slashed randomly, taking several flailing blows from the thinner man before she got a grip on him and finished the fight with an upward thrust of the blade into his chest. The man slumped to the floor.

With her face and shirt soaked in blood, and blood dripping from her knife, she stepped toward the twin. She saw his legs get wobbly. "You have to click the safety off," she said before she grabbed him and broke his fall to the floor.

A few moments later, kneeling next to the unconscious twin, tapping the back of his hand, she heard a desperate cry from the doorway.

"What did you do to my brother?"

Joseph stood in the doorway holding bags from the local burger joint. Now that they were in the same room she could tell them apart. Joseph had darker eyebrows. Samuel's eyes were a grayer blue. He dropped the bags and rushed to his brother's side.

She stood up, mouth slack, and looked from the two bodies to the blood to Joseph and back to the bodies. "I just put my hand on his shoulder and he fainted. Why would you think I did something to him?"

"Kearney told us all about *you*," Joseph said over his shoulder.

"About—why—what did Kearney tell you?"

"He told us how blood thirsty you are and how one time you killed a guy just for leaving a ring from a glass on the table, and—"

"I never did those things." Iron Angel clenched her teeth. "That bastard. He'll pay for this." Her eyes widened with new insight. "So that's why you guys always screw up when I'm around. You're afraid of me. Hey, you guys don't have to be afraid of me. I like you. You're part of the team." She pinned her gaze on Joseph. "I could never hurt you guys. You're one of us."

Samuel was regaining consciousness, and she knelt down beside Joseph. He flinched at her touch.

"Joseph, I would never hurt you or your brother. Do you believe me?"

"You can tell us apart?"

She turned to Samuel. "*You* believe me, right?"

"Believe what? What happened?" Samuel asked. His eyes widened when he saw the blood spatter on his shirt, even more blood on Iron Angel's shirt, and two dead men.

He frantically scootched away on his buttocks, unable to get to his feet. "Who were those guys?"

"I don't know. They weren't cops. I surprised them when I walked into the room. No cop goes into a house and doesn't determine who's there. No notebooks. No people skills."

"I kinda thought so, but wasn't sure. How can you be sure?"

"They referred to the case as a file. And no cop will tolerate anyone not following his orders. When I refused to turn around so he could cuff me, he launched into an explanation, instead of demanding compliance. That's what sealed it for me. I don't know who these jerks are, but one thing I do know, they aren't cops."

Joe-Sam huddled together, amazed at her insight, but still wary of her assertion of solidarity.

She observed them, sensed their lingering fear of her, and stood up. "Damn it, Joe-Sam, I'm not mad at you. I won't hurt you. Ask Duncan when he gets back. He'll tell you that Kearney is lying to you."

Their shoulders relaxed but they remained huddled together.

"And you, tough guy," she said to Samuel. "You were going to shoot men who might or might not have been cops. What was that all about?"

"We don't like cops," Joe-Sam said in unison.

"One at a time."

Joseph took the lead. "Our dad did time for something Wild Bill did."

"Yeah," Samuel said. "And the cops knew he didn't do it. They knew they didn't have any evidence against Dad, but they arrested him anyway."

"And they beat him up while he was cuffed," Joseph added.

"And you thought *I* was dangerous," Iron Angel said as she wiped her knife on the pant leg of the thinner man.

"We only know what Kearney told us," they said in unison.

"But you have killed people, right?" Samuel asked.

She frowned. "I'll get stuff to clean up this mess. And…well, just promise me you won't believe *anything* that rat bastard, Kearney, tells you," she muttered on the way out of the room, "I'll never understand men and their practical jokes as some kind of male bonding ritual."

ဢၼ

They had just wrapped the second body along with the cleaning rags in black plastic when a knock came at the back door. Iron Angel's shoulders slumped, *Now what?*

Joe-Sam looked at each other. She looked at them. Another round of knocks. Joseph took off his tee shirt and offered it to her to replace her blood soaked shirt. After a brief hesitation about undressing in front of Joe-Sam, she hurriedly exchanged it for her bloodied one. Ignoring their shocked looks at the broad, cheese-grater scar on her abdomen, she wiped her hands and arms on a towel and dropped it to the floor. She put a finger to her lips and headed through the kitchen to the back door.

The face on the other side of the door was Hispanic. Dread slithered down her back. It could be a friend of the bodies in the dining room, playing it cool to see what happened to his *compadres*. But she didn't want to kill some lost soul asking for directions. She held the knife behind her thigh, stood so the base cabinets hid her blood-stained sweat pants, and inched the door open with her left hand.

"Hello, I'm Lou Gomez," the man said, but stopped when he saw the swelling, discolored bruises on her face, the broken blood vessels in her left eye, the knitted brow. He continued hesitantly, his statements sounding like questions, "I'm a friend of Jake Pennington? I have an appointment to talk with you about how I might be able to—help you?" His gaze fell to a missed smear of dried blood on her neck.

Unable to concentrate, suspicious of the timing, the name, the ethnicity, she asked, "What kind of help are you talking about?"

"Money, guns, ammo. You name it."

She fingered the grip on the knife. "Why would you think we need these things?"

A confused look spread across his face. "Maybe I have the wrong place. I'm looking for a woman named Angel."

"You have her. I ask again, why would you think—" Her head cleared and she remembered the conversation on the phone three days earlier. "Oh, yeah. *Lou Gomez.* I'm sorry, Mr. Gomez. I remember now." She looked straight at the man, her eyes hard and unblinking. "Look, Mr. Gomez, I'm in a shitty place right now. Can we make arrangements to meet at another time?"

"Sure, but if there's something I can help you with right now, I'm here for you."

The continued, unblinking stare of Iron Angel said "No," loud and clear.

Lou Gomez didn't flinch under her fixed gaze. "I'm on your side. I want to help."

His calloused hands holding a dusty, beat up Western hat caught her attention. His fingernails were clipped short and scrubbed clean. His scuffed work boots wiped and polished. *Why is a decent man like this getting involved with a group like us?* She searched his eyes for the answer. He stood his ground.

She looked away from the stranger, for the first time since she'd opened the door, and tossed the bloody knife into the sink. After wiping her hand on her sweat pants, she opened the door wider and offered her hand. "What are you driving?"

CHAPTER 15

While she paid her former employer a visit, Iron Angel watched Miss Abigail playfully feeding a treat to Dolly. Miss Abigail was more or less confined to a wheelchair, unable to do many common tasks for herself and dependent on others for the simplest of things.

Yet, she seemed happy and relaxed in the temporary residence, in spite of everything that had happened to her family. She took charge of the household and kept it running smoothly. Strong. In charge. Untainted by the past.

Iron Angel sat curled up in the corner of the sofa in the day room of the Penningtons' rented bungalow. When she stretched, she felt the tension fall away from her toned muscles.

Her early morning workout had left her feeling tight and strong. Ready to take on the world. However, she was unable to open a conversation with Miss Abigail, who was the most approachable woman she knew.

"Having a bad day today, Angel?"

It was her chance to open a conversation, but Angel dropped the ball. "Oh, I don't know. What makes you say that?"

"You only sit still when you're having a bad day." Miss Abigail gave Dolly a gentle push to encourage her to jump off her lap. "On your good days, you keep yourself busy."

"You know when I'm having a bad day?" Not wanting to disturb Miss Abigail or bother her with her problems, Iron Angel had hidden her ups and downs and masked her emotional roller coaster. Or thought she had.

"You wear your emotions on your sleeve. It's hard to miss."

"I'm sorry. I don't want to burden you with my problems. You have enough of your own with your sons gone and your husband injured and everything."

"I worry about you whether you want me to or not," Miss Abigail said. "Why don't you tell me what's making you so withdrawn today?"

"You wouldn't understand."

"I won't understand if you don't tell me. Explain to me what is bothering you, so I can understand, or at least try to."

"It's hard to describe."

Miss Abigail remained silent.

Iron Angel was grateful. She opened her mouth to speak a couple times, but nothing came out. Finally, she said, "It's like sand in an hour glass, only it isn't measuring time, it's measuring energy."

She traced the welting along the edge of the sofa cushion. "There's enough sand to get through a normal day. On a day without stress or demands or...a trigger...I can get through the day and feel good about myself."

Miss Abigail motored her wheelchair across the room so she was only a foot from Iron Angel. She leaned forward. "Go on."

"But if something happens that is outside the normal routine—well, as normal as it can be—it uses up the sand and I run out."

"Run out of what?"

"Energy. I don't have the energy to deal with what life throws at me. I feel like everything is out of control, and since I'm out of energy, I can't control myself."

"When have you been out of control?"

"I hurt Rosemary."

"I heard about that."

"You don't know the—" Iron Angel thought better about telling Miss Abigail everything. She changed tracks. "I killed two guys who came to the house pretending to be police officers."

"When?"

Iron Angel stood up, but was blocked by the wheel chair. "The other day. The day I had planned to meet with Lou Gomez about helping the militia."

Miss Abigail put a weak, thin hand on Iron Angel's arm and nodded for her to sit down. "What was their intention?"

She sat back down. "They wanted to handcuff me and take me downtown, but the only downtown I was going to see was the pointy end of a bullet, if you ask me."

"Was there any other way out of the situation?"

Iron Angel thought for a moment. "There are three instances when a person absolutely has to fight—when they tell you to lay face down, when they tell you to get into their vehicle, and when they want to restrain you."

"So then, you had to fight."

"Yes."

"And they were going to kill you."

"In my opinion, yes."

"But you struck first."

"I know what you're thinking. I killed them before they could kill me." Iron Angel folded her feet under her thighs and sank into the corner of the sofa. "All the people I've killed were gunning for me or someone I cared for. I consciously know that. When I think it through, I understand it and accept it. But *inside* I can't seem to comprehend it." She rubbed her forehead. "And the inner struggle to grasp the concept is exhausting."

"How many people have you killed?"

"I lost count." *At eleven.*

"Okay. How many did you hunt down and kill in cold blood?"

"None, but—"

"Have you thought of how many people you may have saved by killing these men?"

Iron Angel furrowed her brow. "What do you mean?"

Miss Abigail put a hand on Iron Angel's knee. "If these men tried to kill Jake and my boys and you and your friends, surely they must have killed before. And if they killed before, they most assuredly would kill again. Many times over." She pointed at Iron Angel. "You, girl, are a savior. A savior with a capital 'S.'"

"I don't know about that."

"Look at you, all strong and agile. Skilled in the martial arts and shooting. You have all the right physical capabilities, but can't think your way through this."

"It's complex and...hard."

Miss Abigail whirred her wheelchair closer to the window. "It seems hard now, but one day it'll surprise you how easy it is after you discover that one thing that will make it click in your mind."

"What is it that will make it click?"

A horn honked in the driveway.

"There's your wonderful man coming to pick you up," Miss Abigail said, pulling back the sheer curtain and looking out the window. "What do the two of you have planned for today?"

"Duncan says he has some real estate he wants to show me."

"Well, you two have a nice time together. And Angel," Miss Abigail said turning the wheelchair a quarter turn, "listen to him. He's a smart man."

Iron Angel smiled, pecked Miss Abigail on her cheek, and headed toward the door.

❦❦❦

Iron Angel stepped onto the sidewalk, shook out the front of her tee shirt to cool off, and looked up and down the desolate midday street. She frowned at Duncan as he came around the front of his truck. His return from his mystery trips usually filled her with a sense of ease, a sense of being complete, but this time he'd arrived with a larger wad of cash than previous times. She pursed her lips and watched him from behind her dark glasses.

"What do you think?" he asked, raising both hands toward

the unoccupied storefront to her right. "For our new headquarters."

"A store front. In the middle of a neighborhood. In town. Have you lost your mind?"

"We'll be hiding in plain sight. We'll share the building with the Demon Brotherhood."

She leaned back to examine the three-story brick building. "Now I know you've lost your mind."

The sun snuck around the edge of her sunglasses, and she cupped her right hand to block the glare. After a long look upward, she stepped to the left to look down the side of the building.

It was a corner property in a mixed commercial and residential neighborhood. Brick-faced, with two storefronts, it was dilapidated but not too old, nothing that couldn't be fixed. Both storefronts were empty with brown paper covering the windows. The store on the corner looked larger than the other one. Its entrance opened catty-corner to the street, making it visible to all three sides of the intersection. The second story provided a bit of overhang for...what? Protection from rain that was rare at best? She shook her head and turned to check out the surrounding buildings.

An apartment building stood across the wider street at the front of the building. There was an *Apartment for Rent* sign with a number handwritten across the bottom. The line of her mouth hardened as she looked at the balcony of the upstairs apartment. Unless the Brotherhood planned on planting their members in the apartments, it was too close for comfort. Too much of an opportunity for watchful eyes.

Diagonally across the intersection was another closed up building with windows broken out of the space above the former store. Not good. Anyone could be in there looking out. Across the side street, a two-story commercial building housed a bodega with fresh vegetables displayed on tables in front of the store windows. Above it was an apartment with an empty window box at each window.

"Think about it," Duncan was saying, "two store fronts. The larger one on the corner could be the Brotherhood's clubhouse, the other could be rented out for some income. The bottom floors will be a buffer between us and the street."

She slid her sunglasses down her nose and scowled at him.

"There are three apartments on the second floor and three more on the third floor. The Brotherhood could use the second floor apartments, and we'll take the third floor apartments. One for us, one for Kearney, and one for the headquarters. That'll make a two-floor buffer between us and the street."

She shook her head and squinted at him before pushing her sunglasses up the bridge of her nose. Before she could say anything, a white SUV pulled in behind Duncan's truck.

"Here's the real estate agent," Duncan said. "Reserve judgment until you see the inside, okay?"

She slowly nodded as she watched a young, well-dressed Hispanic man approach. Duncan made the introductions.

"I see you brought the decision-maker with you," he said to Duncan as he shook Iron Angel's hand.

"She's the boss," Duncan agreed.

She turned away, the sugary-sweet words grating on her foul mood. Lou Gomez had been there a couple days ago to help her ditch the two cop impersonators while Duncan was...who knew where? His absences, that she'd never questioned before, were becoming a problem for her.

"We're just waiting for one more from our group and the other investors," Duncan said.

The two men talked for a few minutes, discussing the exterior of the building until they heard the throaty rumble of Harley Davidson motorcycles, made deeper and louder as the sound echoed off the buildings lining the street.

Iron Angel watched from behind her shades as three motorcycles in turn made a small arc and backed up to the curb behind the SUV. They leaned their bikes onto the kickstands, stood up, and stretched. Wild Bill—gussied up in indigo, bootcut jeans and snakeskin boots, flanked by Blackie the club VP and another biker whose name she couldn't recall—swaggered toward Duncan and the real estate agent. They all shook hands and Duncan introduced the real estate agent. The showing of the property began unceremoniously without waiting for Jason to arrive.

She hung back, listening to the sales pitch of the agent and the comments of the men as they walked through the sad, battered building. Nothing about the building impressed her. Average size, mediocre condition, high security risk. Easy to like. Nothing to love.

Wild Bill called down the third floor hallway. "We're going to check out the basement. Ya'll coming?"

Duncan gently herded Iron Angel down the hallway toward the back stairs.

Her funk increased with every step toward the basement. This building was a borderline money pit. But when she reached the bottom step her jaw dropped. The room was well-lit and spacious. Unlike most cramped, dank basements, the ceilings were eight feet high, the walls painted white. It sang a love song to her.

"This could be used for—" Duncan began.

She smacked the back of her hand against his chest and stepped into the space. Her mind's eye saw the placement of heavy bags, the rack for training weapons, mats, and open space for martial arts training. She paced off the space. After measuring the width of the room, she glanced up to see Blackie smiling and looking past her. She twisted to see Duncan watching her with a broad smile on his face. She turned completely to face him.

"That's a pretty big grin. What are you smiling at?"

Duncan walked up to her and pulled her up against him. He nuzzled the side of her head. "*Joi de vivre*," he whispered. "If my life ended tomorrow, it would be complete."

"Don't talk like that."

"It's just an expression." He stepped back to look into her eyes. "I told you I wanted to bring back the joy of life I saw in you so long ago. I think today was a big step in that direction."

"I was just pacing off the space," she said. "So don't give yourself too much credit."

"Oh, okay. If you say so," he said, the smile playfully dropping from his face. "Then you won't be crushed when I tell you that you have to give up some of the space for weapons and ammo storage."

She looked over one shoulder then the other. "You can have a third."

"A third it is. So does this mean you're on board? Because I think Bill and his crew are happy with this place."

Iron Angel crashed back to reality. "So this is what that bundle of cash is for."

He winked at her and gave her a quick squeeze. "Want to be part of the wheeling and dealing?"

She shook her head.

"What do you think about the security of this place?"

"I don't want to step on Kearney's toes. He's head of security."

Thanks to the monetary assistance of the local ranchers, Kearney was out of town with Gunther and Red Dog, handling the first deal with their new arms provider. He wouldn't be back for another couple days.

"I value your opinion. You were the best security officer the Legion had."

She took a deep breath, pursed her lips, and launched into her security concerns. "Federal agents could set up surveillance diagonally across the street. And don't get me started about the balcony on the apartment building in front. This money pit is located on a corner, and that makes two sides we have to protect and defend. The garage in the back is good, but we'll have to build a breezeway between the garage and the back of the building so we can load or unload trucks unseen."

Duncan's expression caused her to hesitate before continuing.

"A tunnel would be even better..." Her voice trailed off at the slow smile emerging on Duncan's face. "What?"

"And here I thought you weren't paying attention during the tour."

"Do you want the rundown or not?"

Duncan nodded for her to continue. He wiped the smile off his face, but his eyes betrayed his interest and enjoyment.

She continued her assessment. "I like the buffer of two floors and a motorcycle club between us and the street. High ground and all that. Well-placed CCTV cameras and hardened doors could make it difficult to get to us. No surprises." She squinted and cocked her head a little.

He was losing the battle to hide his smile.

She continued a little slower, watching his face. "I think the headquarters should be in the back apartment. We, of course, should get the largest of the three, which, unfortunately, means we'll have the apartment along the side street...*What*?"

He kissed her lightly on the mouth. "You're as competent as you are beautiful." He looked past her and, before she could respond, said, "Blackie is signaling to me. Let the dealing begin." He crossed the room to join Blackie and the real estate agent.

She watched them until they disappeared up the stairs.

Planning the placement of training equipment absorbed her until she sensed she was no longer alone. When she looked around, Wild Bill was leaning on one of the supports, arms crossed, watching her.

"Aren't you part of the negotiating?" she asked.

He shook his head, pushed off the beam, and walked slowly toward her. "We're going to be neighbors. We'll be seeing a lot more of each other."

The hair stood up on her arms. "Yea, Duncan and I'll be living on the third floor." She didn't like the look in his eyes. Maybe the mention of Duncan's name would remind Wild Bill there already was a man in her life.

He reached out for her hand, but she was faster, and pulled it out of his reach. He stepped closer. "I saw the way you looked at me at the party a couple months ago."

She stiffened, but stood her ground. His spicy-scented aftershave assaulted her nostrils. "Don't get any ideas," she said, glaring a warning at him. "I was just playing with your head."

The words were barely out of her mouth before he snagged her right arm just above the wrist with his left hand.

She glared at him. "Take your hand off my arm, before I take it off your arm." Her voice came out almost as a growl.

He didn't get the hint, and she knuckle-punched him in the bicep. The muscle spasm made him release her wrist.

"Look, Bill, I know the C-IA and the Brotherhood are forming an alliance," she said in a low, firm voice. "And I don't want to do anything that will upset that." *And neither should you.* It was hard to stay calm. Her voice rose as she poked his chest with her finger. "But if you are *ever* alone with me, anywhere, any—"

There was movement in the doorway to the basement. She looked past him to see who it was. Before addressing the newcomer, she poked Wild Bill one more time and snarled, "Watch your step. Jason," she said in a lighter tone, as Wild Bill stepped back and eyed the unexpected arrival of a C-IA member. Waving her fingers to include Wild Bill, she continued, "We had a little misunderstanding, but we got it all straightened out. No biggie." She pinned her eyes on Wild Bill. "No need to tell Duncan. He has enough on his mind." She switched her gaze back to Jason. "Right?"

Glaring at the biker, Jason adjusted the holster at his waist and hooked his thumbs into his thick, black belt.

CHAPTER 16

It was moving day. Beginning before first light, the process had been long, arduous, and, at times, frustrating, but Iron Angel was driven to get the kitchen organized before calling it a day. But now with the light dwindling outside, she stood on a stepstool and contemplated the crumpled newspaper, empty boxes, and the counters stacked with dishes, pots, pans, and small appliances. They arrived in Phoenix less than a year ago with only two backpacks and the clothes on their backs. When did they accumulate so much stuff?

There were two entrances to the apartment—one into the kitchen, the other into the living room, but that one was the ideal location for the television. She frowned, that meant the most difficult room to keep orderly would be the first thing seen upon entering their home—again.

An ancient breakfast bar, the countertop in desperate need of replacement, was framed by cabinets above and opened to the spacious, combined dining and living room. Beyond that was a hallway to the bedroom and bathroom. The living room and the bedroom had large picture windows that let in a lot of daylight, but now, with sunset imminent, long shadows blanketed the jumble of boxes in the next room.

Out of the corner of her eye, she saw Duncan breeze past the kitchen door. The door slammed shut. She looked over her shoulder at Duncan casually leaning against the door with his arms crossed.

Wiping out the top shelf of one of the kitchen cabinets, she asked, "What are you looking at?" She had meant a kinder tone, but fatigue sliced off the softness.

"The most beautiful woman in my life."

"You're looking at my ass." She reached for a seldom-used appliance, put it on the shelf and reached for the baking pans.

"Yes, I am looking at the beautiful ass of the most beautiful woman in my life."

"May I point out, I'm the *only* woman in your life."

"That doesn't make you any less beautiful."

She searched for anything else that could go on the top shelf. "What do you want?" Again, too sharply.

"That's a loaded question." When she kept placing items on the shelf, he added, "Since the fire, you've been in a foul mood and contentious. What's going on?"

"Nothing. I'm not sleeping well. That's all."

"Speaking of contentious," he continued, "you need to resolve this thing with Kearney. You tiptoe around each other with the occasional friendly gesture. That's not going to cut it now that he's living directly across the hall. You'll be bumping into each other all the time, and I'd hate to see things get messy because you guys didn't come to some kind of understanding. You don't have to be bosom buddies, but you need to find some common ground."

"We're getting along."

Duncan snorted as he approached her. "Yeah, like a mongoose and a cobra." He traced the outline of the tattoo on the side of her calf. "I like the shorts. Not worried about showing your scars?"

"I waited till the guys left."

The militia numbers were gradually increasing, and the guys had thrown themselves into moving the headquarters, with special attention to their leader's possessions. Most of them were prior military, of one form or another, and their courtesy to her as the leader's girlfriend had impressed her. But not enough to bare the ugly scars on her legs in their presence.

"He's trying to make amends with you," Duncan said, getting back to the subject of her prickly relationship with

Kearney. "All I'm asking is for you to make an effort, too. Just talk to him. What's so hard about that?"

"He's a psychologist and an interrogator. He'll play his mind games, get into my head. He makes my skin crawl as it is. If he got into my head, it'd give me a chronic case of the mind-willies."

"Yeah. I see your point." Duncan snuck his fingers beyond the hem of her shorts. "No one wants the mind-willies."

She pushed him away and half-smiled. "You're not afraid the conversation will end with Kearney saying something that sets me off and I wind up killing him?"

"Good point, maybe I should have Gunther facilitate."

"A cold-blooded killer. Yeah, good choice," she grumbled, as she slapped his hands away again. "Now stop teasing. I have work to do." She reached for platters.

Handing the platters to her, Duncan asked, "Having second thoughts about joining the militia?"

"No second thoughts. I'm good."

"Great, because together, we're unbeatable."

Iron Angel stopped, but didn't turn around. She clenched her teeth. "*Unbeatable? Together?* You prick. How would you *even know*? When Kearney was sent to—" She used air quotes for the next word. "—'interrogate' me, I waited for you to give the sign to resist. *Together*, we could have taken out him and his two goons, and we wouldn't be having this conversation for the zillionth time."

"That was a long time ago."

"Not that long ago." She wiped the other two shelves with excessive vigor. "Not long enough. Not for me."

He hesitated then bravely continued, "Look, I was wrong. I made a mistake, okay? I misjudged the circumstances. I've tried to make it up to you."

The wiping stopped. Staring at the back of the cabinet, she said, "By keeping him as your friend after what he did to me?"

Duncan hesitated, eyeing her. When she finally continued stacking pans and platters on the shelf, he said, "I owe Kearney my life. When things went sideways that last time in the jungle, he was the one who plucked me out of that god-forsaken place. When I was in a PTSD-induced downward spiral, he kept me from hitting bottom. Without him, who knows what would have happened? He helped me get through the hairy times. He could help you, too, if you'd let him."

"He's done enough to me, thank you very much."

"You both are important to me, and this thing between you two puts me in the middle. It's awkward and sometimes downright scary."

She took one step down to start filling the second shelf of the cabinet. "Sure. Make this about you. It's always about you."

"I know I deserve this knothole of misery."

"Still about you."

"Let it go, baby. Let me bear the brunt of the pain. Just promise me you'll make an honest effort to get along with Kearney—for me." He pressed his lips together and exhaled loudly through his nose. "Are you going to look at me any time during this conversation?"

She turned and sat on the counter. While Duncan pulled two bottles of beer out of the refrigerator and opened them, she said, "You didn't see the look in his eyes."

"He always gets that glint in his eyes when he's in the zone. He loves it, but it wasn't personal. Trust me, it was business."

She shook her head and took a long pull on the cold, golden liquid. "He enjoyed it."

Duncan stepped between her legs. "Yes, baby, he enjoyed it, but not because it was you. Because it's what he does best. Because in that moment, he is in total control. Because—"

She pushed him back and stood up. "Hand me those cans of beans."

This whole line of conversation brought back too many bad memories, too much pain. They had discussed the topic, if not a zillion times, at least a dozen times, from as many angles. Talking about it with Duncan was getting nowhere. She took the cans one by one out of his hands and placed them on the shelf. Pressing her lips into a thin line, she groaned inwardly.

As hard as it was to admit, she had to have this conversation with Kearney. Though at times they seemed to get along, there was always an unspoken tension between them. They danced around each other. One misstep could release her animosity toward him. An animosity she kept in check out of respect for Duncan. But he wanted more from her.

The unfortunate bottom line was the fact that she had to find a way to forgive Kearney, get past that horrific event. She absently rubbed her chest where Kearney had skinned off her CDL tattoo.

She tucked away the idea of the uncomfortable dialogue with Kearney. She was getting good at compartmentalizing uncomfortable thoughts, and the back of her mind was getting jam-packed with them. If she opened up, they might tumble out and overwhelm her. Shut the vault, spin the dial, move on.

"Duncan, I need to ask you a couple questions."

"Ask away."

"Where does the money come from?"

"As the leader of the militia, all the money comes through my hands."

"That wasn't an answer. But I'm not talking about militia revenue. I'm talking about the wads of cash you bring back with you after you've been gone a few days. Where does that come from?"

He shook his head as he rubbed her calf with the back of his hand. "Next question, *nena*."

Nena. The endearment he used only when they made love. It sent a thrill down her spine. *Change the subject. There's still too much unpacking to do.* "Do you think I'm out of control?"

"Out of control? No, but you *could* learn a gentler way of dealing with problems. A little finesse can go a long way."

"It's not my style. You know me. I'm full speed ahead or stop. Break down the doors, guns blazing. Beat everyone into submission."

Duncan turned his wrist and slid his palm up her thigh, his hand fully under her shorts. He smiled. "Give it a try, if only because we're running out of space in the desert—you know—for the bodies." His voice was low, husky. His breathing elevated. His eyes dreamily, half-shut.

Again, she playfully slapped him away.

A heavy silence fell between them as she filled the bottom shelf with stacks of dishes he handed her. After the last dish was neatly put away, she wiped away the frown that had appeared on her face with the knuckle of her index finger.

Gentleness was long gone from her repertoire. And why did *she* have to change all of a sudden?

Finally, Duncan spoke up. "Jason's been off his stride lately, too. When I asked him about it, he said to ask you. So, I'm askin'. What's this tension between you two?"

"There's nothing between me and Jason. We're good."

After putting the last of the glassware onto the shelf, she stepped down, moved the stepstool to the last cabinet, and stepped up.

Keeping the incident with Wild Bill from Duncan was wrong. She knew that. Telling him could adversely affect future dealings with the Brotherhood. But he deserved to know. He needed to know. The air stilled between them. She felt him watching her and waiting. There would never be a good time to break the news to Duncan. The present was as good as any.

"There *is* something you should know." She turned sideways on the stepstool and faced him. "The day we checked out this place with the Demon Brotherhood, and you were dealing with the real estate agent, and I was in the basement, and—" She closed her eyes, "Wild Bill grabbed my wrist."

Nothing. No response. She opened her eyes. The only change was his mouth. It was tighter. The corners slightly turned down. With concentrated control, he quietly asked, "How did you handle it?"

"I knuckled him in the bicep so he'd let go. Then I warned him to never be alone with me ever again. It was just a grab. I made him let go, and we decided we wouldn't talk about it." There. It was out.

Duncan thoughtfully put down his beer. He reached for a wayward strand of her hair and tucked it behind her ear. His hand dropped to her upper arm and gave it a gentle shake. "See, there you go—finesse. Just what I was talking about." He smiled. "I have a confession to make, too, my angel. The first time I met you *I* wanted to grab you."

"No you didn't. The first time you met me, you thought I was a pain in the ass."

He slipped his hand up her leg. "That doesn't mean I didn't want to grab you."

She slapped him away.

He stepped away from her, picked up his beer, and leaned against the edge of the counter. "I just have more self-control, that's all."

"So then, you're not angry?"

"Not at you."

Yup. This guy's a keeper. She took a long look at him, as he casually peeled the label off a green bottle covered with beading condensation. A five-o'clock shadow framed his jaw and mouth. Shirtless, his well-developed chest glistened with sweat. His thick, muscular waist peeked out from the waistband of his jeans. The top button was unbuttoned. Damn, he was sexy.

He looked up at her and suddenly the kitchen was hot. Sweat broke out on her forehead and he reached up to wipe it away with his thumb. There was too much work left to do to get caught up in this.

She reflexively stepped back, and her foot slipped on the edge of the stepstool.

Duncan's strong hands grabbed her. Their eyes locked. He gently steadied her against his chest, and she slowly slid downward until her feet were on the floor.

"I'd never let you fall," he whispered, his mouth so close she could smell the beer on his breath. He kissed her lightly on the top of her ear and ended it with a little lick.

She wriggled to make room between them, break the spell. She really had too much unpacking to do to get distracted right now. Change the subject. "Am I getting hard?"

"No. But I am."

"I'm being serious, Duncan."

The smile disappeared. "Hard," he said as he tightened his grip and brought her tighter against him, his hand in the center of her back, "Yes, baby, you are getting hard."

Her body tensed, her head swam with questions. Her stomach clenched. Those were not the words she expected.

"I'm hard? When did I become hard? From the torture? Living as a fugitive? When I killed nine of the ten men who came after Miss Abigail and me? When Flora lost her baby? When?"

"All of those times. Not any one of those times," he said in a quiet tone as he gently rocked her. "It's a process. Rarely is there any one moment in time when one second you're normal, the next second your heart is covered with thorns." Duncan saw her knitted brow and whispered, "Personally, I think it's hot."

He thinks being hard is hot? Duncan could be weird at times. Another lick on her earlobe sent her blood coursing through her veins. Okay, weird wasn't necessarily a bad thing. She willed herself to resist until she got the answer she needed. "Do you do something illegal? For the money, I mean." Her voice was soft and breathy.

"That depends," he said between kisses on her neck.

"On what?"

He shook his head, leaned back and smiled. "Before you, I'd wave cash at strippers, and they came running to me. I wave money at you and it becomes a class-one interrogation. The only thing missing is the bright light in my eyes and being tied up in painful positions."

All resolve vaporized. Something about the words "tied up in painful positions" melted her into his arms. Not that tying each other up was part of their lovemaking. But it hinted at the hot, rough sex that opened the valve to his passion. And it was his passion that excited her. She softened, reached around his torso and dug her nails into his back.

She smiled. "Painful positions? Tell me about them."

He pulled her out of the kitchen, backing her around the boxes in the living room and down the hall toward the bedroom. "Marry me, *nena.*"

"No. Instead of ropes, can I use leather straps?"

With a boyish grin he said, "Leather? I like leather."

Between little kisses on his pecs, she asked, "What do—I get—to do—while you—are tied up?"

"You aren't going to hurt me, are you?" he asked in mock innocence as he reached the bedroom door.

She slowly shook her head. "I would *never* hurt you." She

added with a coy smile, "Unless you wanted me to."

A throaty chuckle escaped as he pulled her tee shirt over her head. Held tight against his rock-hard chest, she quivered as he backed her toward the edge of the unmade queen-size bed. "Marry me. Make me the happiest man in the world."

She bit him on his left nipple. "No."

Duncan grabbed a handful of her hair at the back of her head and pulled her head back. "Then someone's getting hurt tonight."

"I *know* you don't mean *me*," she teased.

"We'll see."

Her last words were, "Give it your best shot, tough guy," before his mouth covered hers.

After a long kiss that weakened her legs, he pushed her backward. As she fell, she wrapped her legs around his waist to pull him down on top of her. Braced on one elbow, he kept his full weight from pinning her to the bed as he kissed her. He stopped kissing long enough to lift her and move to the center of the bed. Then pressed his weight against her.

"Marry me, Iron Angel."

"No." She pushed him away. "Wait. I didn't make the bed. We can't make love on a bare mattress like animals."

"Too late, *nena*," he said, pulling off her shorts and unzipping his pants. "I guess you didn't get the memo. We *are* animals."

"I probably don't smell so good after working in the heat all day," she warned.

"You smell delicious," he said, after exaggerated sniffing. He kissed his way down her abdomen. Looking up at her through his lashes he added, "Let me see how you taste."

e/ɔe/ɔ

In the afterglow, Duncan held his Iron Angel to his chest as he lay on his back, staring at the ceiling, lost in thought. He absently stroked her back. With her head resting on his shoulder, she gently caressed his chest and stomach. The air conditioner in the window hummed. The light of day had yielded to the dusk of early evening.

It was a brief moment in time when the specters of ghosts from the past and the harsh reality of the present dared not intrude.

There was a brief ripple in the calm when Duncan reached to turn on the lamp on the bedside table. As he snuggled back into her arms, the yellow ring of light lit up the small bedroom. It was the only room in the house that, except for the bed linens, was completely put together.

To her it was the most important room: the first thing you saw when you opened your eyes in the morning and the last thing you saw before you went to sleep at night—or the last thing you saw as a free person if the SWAT team showed up at four in the morning.

He shifted to his side and pushed her onto her back. "Why won't you marry me?"

Lightly stroking the stubble on his jawline, she smiled up at him. "You haven't asked me."

"But I—"

She watched his eyes narrow as her words slowly worked their way through his brain.

His eyes lit up. He threw back his head and laughed. "You beautiful little shit." He tightened his embrace and looked her in the eyes. "God knows where I'd be if you hadn't come into my life. You brought with you a joy that brightened a life that was dark and empty and harsh. Everything I do, I do for you. To protect you, to support you, to love you. I can't promise we will grow old together, but every moment of freedom we have left, I want to spend with you. And if, through inescapable circumstances, we find ourselves physically separated, I know we'll always be spiritually close. Being separated from you would be a fate worse than death, and only you have the power to grant me what little contentment I could get from the situation—knowing I am your husband and you are my wife. Joan Bowman, will you honor me and our life together by marrying me?"

"Yes. I will marry you, Dennis Maurice Ar—" She went limp in his arms and continued, "—cher."

"You don't have cold feet *already*?"

"No. I just realized, my name will change from Bowman to Archer."

Duncan smiled down at his Life lying in his arms. "Pretty cool, huh?"

There were several light raps at the apartment door, a creak from the hinges as the door slowly opened, then the voice of one of the new militia members, "Duncan, you in here?"

"Go away," Duncan yelled the length of the apartment. "I'm busy." He looked back at Iron Angel and smiled.

The footsteps stopped. Message received. "Sorry to interrupt, but, there's a matter that needs your attention in the headquarters."

"Joe-Sam has full authority over the setup of the headquarters."

"Some of the other guys don't seem to know that," the voice called out from the kitchen.

"Then tell them!" Duncan bellowed.

Footsteps rushed across the kitchen floor. The door hinges creaked as the door closed behind them.

"Sorry, baby, I'd better go check this out," Duncan said, but before he could kiss her, she sat up and swung her legs over the side of the bed with her back to him.

"It's always going to be like this, isn't it?"

He snuggled up behind her and kissed the back of her neck. "Like what?"

"Our time will never be *our* time. The militia will always intrude."

"We'll get away. Soon. I promise. We'll go to Reno to get married. Spend a few days." He hesitated before adding, "Maybe in a couple weeks. We have that big raid planned for next weekend. So maybe after that."

She started dressing. "Yeah, maybe."

CHAPTER 17

Unpacking complete, the oasis of green grass lured Iron Angel to the park two blocks from the new headquarters. The delightful sounds of children playing enticed her to stay. She sat with both elbows perched on the bench back, head back, eyes closed, soaking in the sun. The heady aroma of the newly mown grass transported her to happier, more relaxed times. Birds sang to each other in the nearby trees.

Occasionally there was the *plop-plop-plop* of joggers' sneakers as they ran past, leaving behind little snippets of conversation.

She thought about her visit the previous day with Miss Abigail, who was confined to a wheelchair, unable to do many common tasks for herself and dependent on others for the simplest things—things others took for granted. Yet, she seemed happy and relaxed. She took charge of her household and kept it running smoothly. But forgiving Kearney wasn't the only forgiveness Joan had to work on—she had to forgive herself.

She frowned. "Forgive myself. How exactly am I supposed to do that?"

⌾⌾⌾

Little Al plopped down on the park bench beside Iron Angel, breaking her out of her reverie. "I don't recognize that verse," he said.

"What verse?" She was heavy-eyed and relaxed. "What are you doing here?"

"I'm waiting to pick up my little girl."

"You never told me you had another kid."

"She's from a different mama."

"O-o-o-h," Iron Angel murmured, still somewhat drowsy from the sunshine. "Oh," she said a little more forcefully when the meaning of his words sunk in. She opened her eyes and shifted her weight on the seat to face him. "And your wife—"

"She knows. It was rough for a while, but she eventually forgave me, and with God's help we got through it."

"I never would have taken you for the religious type."

"Nor I you—Psalm 119:11—the tat on your calf?"

She reflexively looked down at the red and blue winged-heart tattoo she'd forgotten when she threw on the pair of khaki Bermuda shorts that morning. She offhandedly cited the verse, "'I've written Your word on my heart that I—'" She sucked in a sharp breath, then continued softly, "'—might not sin against You.'" A lump formed in her throat. She swallowed hard.

An impish grin appeared between Little Al's mustache and beard. "Words catch in your throat, did they?"

"No, I just hadn't recited them in a while."

"They must have meant something to you at one time for you to ink 'em on your calf."

She resumed her relaxed posture on the bench. "It was a long time ago. Things were different then."

"Maybe not so much as you think. You are a good person." He gently touched her arm to keep her from disagreeing. "A good person, who lives in the midst of violence. Just remember, you don't start the fights, you finish them. It's not a sin to be a finisher."

She sat up and looked directly at him. "All right, Mr. Smart Guy, let me ask you something."

He nodded, his blue eyes sparkling above the beard.

"How do you forgive someone when the scars won't heal?"

Little Al thoughtfully ran his fingers through his beard. "You have to find a way to let the resentment go. And you should do it quickly. Sometimes people—and I'm not saying this is what's going on with you—they get invested in the negative emotions and it makes it even harder to let go. Let me tell you a story I heard a long time ago."

She nodded, placed her left arm on the back of the bench, and propped her head on her hand.

"A long time ago there were two Buddhist monks who had taken a vow of chastity and couldn't even touch a woman. They were walking along a path that followed alongside a river. It was springtime and the water was moving quite fast. After walking two miles, they heard a woman cry out to them, 'I must cross the river to attend to my ailing mother. Please help me.'

"The first monk tied the edge of his robe into a knot so the swirling water wouldn't wrap it around his legs, and stepped into the fast moving water. The second monk pleaded, 'Your vows! You cannot touch a woman. How are you going to help her across without touching her? Let us call for help and let someone else assist her.'

"The first monk said, 'We are here now. I will help the woman.' With that, he stepped into the water and waded across the river to the woman on the other side. When he reached the opposite bank, he told the woman to climb onto his back. Once she was securely in place, he waded back across the river.

"Once they had reached the bank, he set her down, climbed up the bank to the other monk, and they continued on their way. The second monk was so appalled and upset with the first monk that he didn't talk to him for thirty minutes. Finally, he could keep it to himself no longer and he said, 'I can't believe you went against your vows and carried that woman across the river.' To which the first monk replied, 'You are still carrying that woman? I put her down a half hour ago.'

"You, Miss Iron Angel, have to—" He poked her on the shoulder for emphasis. "Put. Your. Woman. Down."

"How did you get so wise?"

"Prison. It gives you plenty of thinking time."

"I heard you took the wrap to cover for Wild Bill. How do you *not* hate him for that?"

"It's history." He smiled and leaned in toward her as if to

tell a secret. "I put the woman down." He straightened up and looked away, down the path to his left.

The squeals of delight from the girls on the swings brought a rare smile to Iron Angel's face. Somewhere on the far side of the playground, beyond the teeter-totters, a small boy cried as his mother bandaged his boo-boo.

"Our God is a forgiving God," Little Al continued. "All you have to do is ask for his forgiveness. And, in turn, he asks us to forgive others—a kind of spiritual paying it forward." His eyes snapped to his left. "Gotta go, here comes my baby girl and her mama." As he unfolded his huge frame he said, "Think about what I said. It's never too late—unless you've taken your last breath." Fully upright and stretching, he added, "But don't wait too long to put the woman down."

Iron Angel watched a little girl with a bouncy blonde ponytail run from her mother's side into Little Al's huge arms. He lifted her high over his head and she giggled, knowing she was safe in his hands.

CHAPTER 18

L
ike a metronome, Duncan tapped his index finger on the
table that held the computer equipment. He stood with a
frown on his face, eyes fixed on the monitors, clenching
and unclenching his jaw muscles. Occasionally stealing a peek
over their shoulders at him, the twins, Joe-Sam, hunched over
their keypads and typed feverishly, hacking into every street
cam they could find, exhausting all efforts to find Iron Angel
and Kearney.

It was less than two weeks since he had asked Iron Angel to
marry him. Why hadn't he grabbed her and raced off to Reno
to tie the knot? Of course, that wouldn't change the current
situation, but it would ease the frustration that squeezed his
chest and burned his stomach. He'd lost sight of his priorities—again—and procrastinated on the one thing that meant so
much to him. There was no question of the priorities now.

The headquarters occupied a three-room apartment that
spanned the back of the building. The communications area
was set up in what would have been the bedroom. The only
light came from two desk lamps, their bent goosenecks shining
pools of light on the keyboards and the eight monitors. The
flickering light painted Duncan's face in eerie, changing patterns as he scrutinized each image that flickered onto the monitors.

Gunther sat in a wheeled desk chair and mindlessly pushed
it back and forth, then around in circles, than back and forth
again. The plastic rolling noise of the wheels and keyboard

clicks were the only sounds in the room. With arms crossed, Jason stood stock-still. His eyes shifted from the monitors to the back of Duncan's head. Back and forth—silently waiting for the command to act.

Duncan turned his thoughts from self-incrimination to analyzing the raid. It had gone well. An excellent team-building experience for his troops. No one got hurt except the bad guys. The War Spoil Gods had been very generous. The quantity of weapons and ammo was so substantial they loaded up one of *La Espada's* panel trucks to supplement the one they had brought with them. He had placed Iron Angel and Kearney in *La Espada's* truck, suggesting they use the time to work out their differences. A double slap on the driver's door, and the truck pulled out of the parking lot and disappeared down the street.

Gone.

If they had been stopped and arrested by the cops, it meant breaking everything down and going underground. The agreement of the Core Leadership was, once arrested, to hold out until the first time the cops offered a meal—usually four to six hours. After that, each was to make the best deal they could. Four to six hours. Not much time to break down, vanish, and set up someplace new and secure. To make matters worse, he didn't know where the safe house was. Only the security chief knew that, and he was with Iron Angel. Duncan smiled inwardly. Irony could be so damn...ironic.

Maybe the raid had gone too well. It could have been a set up. There could have been *La Espada* fighters they missed. There was a myriad of minor miscalculations or oversights— endless possibilities—any one of which could mean lethal consequences for his best friend and girlfriend—Duncan cleared his throat—his fiancée, who should now be his wife. His stomach tightened.

The tapping stopped while he rubbed his eyes with his thumb and index finger. What had been a simple, confidence-building mission had turned to shit soup.

If *La Espada* was responsible for this situation, the C-IA would hunt them down. One by one, their lives would suddenly be ugly and short. Duncan vowed he would not hold back.

Only one other person in the room knew the full savagery of his wrath, once unleashed. He looked over his shoulder at Gunther. The plastic rolling noise stopped.

Gunther's expression said it all. His face was frozen with tight lips and a tighter jawline—a fierce, primal predator waiting to be released. Gunther wasn't a surgical attacker. He'd kill everybody and let God sort them out.

"Think they got stopped by authorities, Gunny?"

"That's a possibility. Or Kearney finally pissed off Iron Angel and she's digging a shallow grave in the desert as we speak."

Duncan looked at Jason.

"I'm leaning toward the shallow grave theory," he said without hesitation or moving a muscle.

Duncan frowned at them. "Yeah, yuck it up, you two." The stomach acid spigot opened full force. He rubbed his stomach and scanned Jason's face.

Jason was patient and methodical. Detail conscious, *he* was a surgical predator. Duncan didn't know him as well as the others, but knew him well enough to be grateful he would be on the hunting party—if it came to that.

A glimpse at the clock reminded Duncan that things were getting worse. Too much time out of the net. Too little time left to efficiently move the headquarters. Damn it, where were they? His thoughts returned to *La Espada*. If any of them managed to live through the raid, they were the only people outside the room who knew their stolen weapons were being transported in their stolen truck by the people who stole them.

Then again, Iron Angel and Kearney could have been snagged in a routine traffic stop. Back to the police. *Where were they?*

After a loud exhale through his nose, Duncan said to Joe-Sam, "Give us the room."

∽∾∽

Iron Angel stopped peering through the dirt-smeared windshield into the darkness and glanced to the right. Kearney had a flashlight trained on a map opened across his knees. "Talk to me, Kearney."

She tightened her grip on the steering wheel just in time to hold it against a sideways thrust from a rut in the road that would have thrown them off the road onto soft dirt. Everything in the truck flew a couple inches into the air, then they hit the bottom of the rut hard. Teeth-rattling hard. Something clattered around in the back of the van.

"From what I can see on this map it's only two miles—" Kearney hesitated while he measured the distance on the map with his thumb. "—or so, until we reach this paved road, here." He pointed to somewhere on the map.

"Take this shortcut, you said," she sneered. "It'll cut off seven miles." She gunned the engine to push the heavily laden truck across a dry stream bed. "Where *are we,* Kearney?"

"We're good. Don't worry."

"Yeah? Then why don't I feel good? We might have crossed over into that Indian reservation, and a bunch of Indians might come up on us, strip the truck, and steal our weapons, then make us walk barefoot the rest of the way to the highway."

"Indians? Barefoot? Really? You watch too many movies."

As if on cue, the engine sputtered, then regained full power, then sputtered again. She pounded the dashboard with the heel of her palm. As if it were a lethal blow, the engine emitted a death rattle, shuddered, and gave up the ghost. It coasted to a stop in the middle of the dirt road. A deep blackness closed in around them.

Only the largest scrub brush and mesquite trees were visible, silhouetted by the light of the stars. And it was quiet. Disconcertingly quiet.

She looked at Kearney. "Desert Rule Number One—in the desert, anything that can go wrong will go wrong."

He grumbled something that was drowned out by the creak of the opening truck door. He headed to the front of the truck and, after a brief struggle, lifted the hood to check out the ancient engine inside.

"Try starting it."

She turned the ignition key. The engine made a half-hearted attempt to turn over, then nothing.

He used the edge of his tee shirt to wipe some dirt from one of the cables. "Try it again."

Nothing.

After turning the key to Accessory she said, "K, come here a minute." She waited while he walked around to the driver side window. "You dumbass, we're out of gas."

"No. No way," Kearney said, putting his head in through the window to look at the gauges himself. He turned to look at her, their noses only inches apart. "Didn't you think to check before we left?"

"Me?" She pushed him out of her way. "Who was in charge of the parking lot? Which means everything in it?"

"Oh, yeah? Who's the driver? The driver is responsible for the vehicle."

He pulled out his cell phone and started doing the reception dance. Holding it in the air. Twirling around trying to increase the bars. After climbing onto the front bumper and craning his neck to look up at the phone he held high above his head, he finally asked, "You have any reception?"

She got out of the truck checking her phone. "Nope. We're screwed. Gunther is gonna be pissed, and Duncan's gonna come unglued. Just remember whose idea it was to take a short cut."

"You were driving. You could have said 'no.'"

She slammed the door and looked around. "I've been at the wrong end of Duncan's anger, and it's not pretty. You are not pinning this on me."

The desert air was cool with a slight breeze. She thought about how quickly the temperature could change in the desert as she climbed onto the warm hood of the truck and leaned against the windshield. Kearney joined her, sliding his cell phone into the cargo pocket of his camouflage pants.

The breadth and depth of the night sky made everything else a mere pinprick in eternity. She soaked in the beauty of the distant mountain range silhouetted against the Milky Way. At home, in Pittsburgh, clear nights like this were a rarity. She relaxed and thought about their situation. Her irritation was with herself not Kearney. He was right. The driver was responsible for the vehicle. She leaned her head back against the windshield, closed her eyes, and sighed.

"We need to talk," he said.

"No we don't." She didn't want to spoil this peaceful interaction with Mother Nature.

"Yes, Iron Angel, we do."

It was going to be a while before help arrived. Duncan probably hadn't realized yet that she and Kearney were missing. He would search for them, but it would be even longer before they would be located. And his last, prophetic words were to use the time to talk things out. Well, they had the time. It was too quiet and peaceful, anyway.

She took the initiative. "Duncan says you can help me."

"Yes, I'm sure I can. But do you want my help?"

Iron Angel shrugged. Then she nodded without taking her eyes off the stars.

"Well, here it is—the CliffsNotes version. First and foremost, you have to forgive." He gently put a hand on her shoulder to stop her from interrupting. "Forgiveness is not for me. I have my own demons. Forgiveness is for *you*. 'For if you forgive men when they sin against you, your heavenly Father will also forgive you.' Matthew 6:14."

"*You* are quoting the Bible?"

Kearney shrugged. "My father was a Baptist minister. Look, forgiveness enables you to get past what's eating you up inside. To get past your anger, your hurt, and yes, your hate. Those negative emotions will affect the way you interact with others. It will infect your personal relationships. Damage you outlook. Degrade your self-esteem."

"I have plenty of self-esteem."

Kearney let the statement dangle in the air. He looked at the stars for a while then added, "Forgiveness will let your light shine through the shroud of darkness you've wrapped around yourself. And you have to shine that light where you stand. Where you stand, got it? Because the past jades the present. The future dilutes it. *Today* is all you have." He tapped the hood of the truck for emphasis. "Shine your light where you stand, Iron Angel. Live in each moment. Moments become hours, hours turn into days, days into weeks—until you have a lifetime filled with the fullness of life."

"But it's *hard* to let go. It's hard to get over what you did to me."

"I could tell you it wasn't personal. I could tell you it was just business. I could tell you I'm sorry. I could tell you a lot of things, but ultimately it's up to you to pick your own time and your own way to let go of the hate and resentment. And it isn't easy. If it were, it wouldn't be so important for your wellbeing."

Miss Abigail's words came back to her. How could everybody else know the key to getting her life back on track?

He eyed her before adding, "Let me ask you something. And take time to answer. Why is it so hard?"

"Because..." She pondered the question while she looked up at the stars. Why was it so hard to let go? There were the physical scars, the mental scars, the sense of having been powerless. All good reasons, but it was history. Unchangeable history that was trashing her present and undermining her future.

If her future was determined by her present actions, something had to change. She was in quicksand. Every move she made only sucked her down into a place where she would have no control. One wrong move and the peaceful, quiet future she wanted with Duncan would be banished to the realm of what could have been. Was her resentment toward Kearney the muck that doomed her to sinking into the murky depths where people like Gunther lived?

She shuddered and rolled her head on the truck's windshield to look at Kearney. "It's hard to let go of what you did to me because I've hated you for so long, I feel like it would have been for nothing if I let it go now."

"In other words, you're emotionally invested in your feelings."

"That's what Little Al said," she quietly said to the stars, "Fish or cut bait."

"What?"

"I was just thinking, if you're fishing for two hours in one spot and don't get any bites, do you continue to fish, or cut bait?"

"Good analogy. What would you do?"

"I'm goal-oriented. I'd cut bait."

Kearney gave a quick nod. "Lesson over."

"That's it?"

"It's all I've got. Oh yeah, payment for my very sage advice is one favor."

She squinted at him. "What kind of favor?"

"Pretend you forgive me. Make me and others believe you've gotten past it. You might find it helps you work through it." Kearney added with a crooked smile, "and it would make my life a whole lot easier."

"Play the game," she whispered.

"Yep. It worked to make you stronger."

She nudged him and winked. "Or am I just pretending?"

Headlights appeared in the distance to their left. They veered and headed straight for Iron Angel and Kearney.

"Do you think that's our rescue team?" he asked.

"Nope. They'd have flashed their lights or called on the radio to let us know it's them."

He rubbed his chin. "*La Espada*?"

"I don't think so. They couldn't possibly know where we are."

Four sets of headlights turn into six sets as trucks that had been hidden behind the first four fanned out. She groaned, not at the potential problem—they'd handle it whatever it turned into—but because she finally wanted to connect with Kearney, and these unknown newcomers were interfering at this pivotal moment in the contentious relationship between her and Kearney.

"I'm glad we had this talk." What else could she say? The situation was changing by the milli-second.

He patted her leg. "Yeah, I'm a walking self-help book."

"Time to go to work," she said as she slid off the hood of the truck.

She opened the driver's door. With one knee on the seat, she felt around behind the driver's seat and pulled out the Magpul FPG she had stolen from her attacker a couple months

before. She patted the cargo pockets of her pants. Two magazines of .45 ammo, one magazine of 5.56 for the FPG. Thirty-
eight rounds. A check of the magazine in her Colt .45 told her
she had eight more. Inhaling deeply through her nose and ex-
haling between tightened lips, she chambered a round and replaced the semi-automatic in the holster on her right thigh. She
slipped the sling of the FPG over her head so it rested diagonally across her chest.

As she joined Kearney at the front of the truck, she muttered, "Desert Rule Number Two—in the desert, things can go
to hell in a hurry."

He grunted in what she took to be agreement.

She leaned against the grill of the old panel truck. With her
arms casually draped over the FPG slung across her chest, she
was the picture of serenity, but her heart was already pounding
against the inside of her chest. Unable to outrun the trucks approaching at high speed, the only thing to do was stand and
face fate.

He must have read her mind. "Damn, I hate fighting in the
desert. In the jungle or a forest, there are trees, rocks—high
ground. The nearest high ground from here is a mile away, or
more. The desert is nice for a pleasant day on the trail, but I
have a bad feeling about this."

She nodded slowly. If they were Mexicans, she and
Kearney were dead. If they were Indians, they might get out of
this alive, but it wouldn't be pretty. This was going to be an
ugly day in the desert.

"Trouble is closing in fast and I'm stuck on the other side
of nowhere with you," she muttered. *You pussy.*

Without a word, he took off his billed cap, smoothed the
hair underneath, and replaced the hat on his head, taking extra
care to make sure it was centered and straight. "Who do you
think they are?" he asked.

She unwrapped a stick of gum and put it into her mouth.
After a couple chews she said, "Hell on wheels."

The oncoming trucks approached in an irregular line at a
slower pace. A huge lump formed in Iron Angel's throat, and
she glanced over at Kearney to see how he was coping. He

looked like he was gazing out over an ocean with a cool breeze in his face. Cool as a breeze. Maybe she had misjudged him. Maybe he did have a steel rod in his spine and wasn't a wuss, after all.

"Hey, I'm sorry I called you a pussy."

"You didn't call me a pussy, but I forgive you for thinking it." Kearney winked at her. "Honest communication— refreshing isn't it." He looked at the approaching headlights. "How far away do you think they are?"

"Hard to tell. In the desert, there's that Factor of Three. You know, where objects are always three times farther than they look."

"A football field, do you think?"

Joan snapped her gum and nodded. "Maybe."

After several agonizingly slow minutes, the trucks came to a synchronized stop. The dust from their tires continued the forward motion, and she resisted the urge to wave her hand in front of her face and cough. Kearney was not so disciplined and made a show of waving away the dust. She looked at him and shook her head.

There was a momentary silence while she shielded her eyes from the headlights, and the people on the other side of the headlights sized up the situation. The trucks were a little more than thirty yards from Iron Angel and Kearney's position. The outer corners of the line were farther away, but not by much.

A voice came from the other side of the headlights. "Drop your weapons."

Her blood stopped coursing through her veins. She stopped chewing in mid-chew. Her worst fears hit her smack in the face. The man had a Mexican accent—not a real Mexican accent with drawn out syllables. It was more like the unnatural accent adopted by Americans of Mexican descent. Shorter syllables. More American in lilt.

The man repeated the command. She resumed chewing and responded, "You first."

There was male laughter from the other side of the headlights. "Maybe you don't understand the difficult position you are in," the voice said.

"Oh, I think we understand," Kearney said. Out of the corner of his mouth he added, "These guys aren't cops. Cops would have identified themselves."

"Hey, gringos," the voice said, trying to get their attention. "No talking and drop your weapons."

Kearney said, without moving his lips, "Almost doesn't seem like a fair fight."

"What do you mean?" she asked, also not moving her lips.

"Say there's four guys in each truck. That makes twenty-four possibles."

"Yeah, that makes it twelve-to-one. Not very good odds."

Kearney raised his hands in submission, flashed his big white teeth, and nodded at the unseen threat beyond the blinding headlights. "For them."

"Do you think they know who they're up against?" She was feeling brave, or was she pretending to be brave? It didn't matter, brave was brave.

The voice again commanded them to drop their weapons. There was a new edge to the voice. This time he added, "You have to the count of five. One...two..."

CHAPTER 19

It quickly became clear that these guys were screwballs, just young, unruly men, raising hell, establishing their superiority by scaring others. They drove wildly, shooting handguns without aiming, doing doughnuts where the dirt was soft enough.

Crossing paths with Iron Angel and Kearney had been dumb, disastrous luck.

Great clouds of dirt swirled in the beams of crisscrossing headlights. After a few hair-raising dives out of their way, the dust was so thick that Kearney lost track of Iron Angel. As he skidded shoulder-first into a dry gulch not too far from the van, he saw the muzzle blast from her FPG. She was about twenty-five feet to his left. Good. Not in the line of fire. As a loud four-wheel drive roared straight toward him, he ducked and used the gulch for cover. Once the truck was past, he focused on shooting out the other darting headlights bouncing around the once quiet desert. Their lights ruined his night vision. They had to eliminated before he could concentrate on the jerks behind the wheels and bring this nonsense to a screeching halt.

When the last headlight was extinguished, Kearney aimed for the drivers. He was sure he had taken out two occupants of one of the trucks when everything went black.

かくの

While retracing the designated route Iron Angel and

Kearney should have taken, Duncan, Gunther, and Jason had stopped at the edge of the butte to the east and saw the bonfire in the desert. Knowing Iron Angel was attracted to trouble like a moth to light, Duncan had headed to this God-forsaken patch of real estate to check it out. It had paid off.

While Duncan and Gunther made their way toward the bonfire leapfrogging from scrub brush to scrub brush, Jason crept toward the stranded truck. As he neared the truck, he saw the exhilaration on the faces of the two young men standing between the open back doors. The men were feverishly loading magazines from an open box of ammo. He kept them in his sights, and listened for any other noise or indication of others nearby.

Somewhere farther out in the desert men excitedly yelled to each other. Later for them. Right now these guys might have the information he needed.

Stealing toward them, eyes down the sight of his silenced Walther 9 mm semi-automatic, placing each foot with care to avoid making any noise that might ruin his element of surprise, Jason closed the distance between himself and these two unknowns.

One of them slapped a loaded magazine into the M-16 he had lifted from the open crate in the back of the panel truck. Jason stepped from behind one of the back doors.

The gazes of the two men traveled up Jason's tattooed arms, to the red, white, and blue haskie, to the piercings, to the angry, unblinking eyes glaring back at them. Their smiles dropped from their faces when they realized this man was a stranger. They froze, mouths shaped in Os.

Looking down his sights at the man who had loaded the M-16, Jason said, "Where are the passengers of this van?"

The man's expression turned from surprise to condescension. "Fuck you."

Jason shot him in the forehead, and the man fell backward. Jason snapped the gun to the right and aimed at the other man's head. "Where are the passengers of this van?"

The other man raised his hands in submission. "Out in the desert somewhere."

His eyes nervously darted down to the dead man with a pool of blood under his head.

"Up here," Jason said to gain the man's full attention. "Are they together?"

The man pinned his gaze on the muzzle of the silencer. "I don't know."

"Those voices—out there—are they your friends?"

"I think so."

"You think so?"

"Yes. Yes, they're my friends."

"Are the two passengers out there with them?"

"I don't know." The man's eyes flicked to the subtle movement of Jason's finger tightening on the trigger. "I don't know. I don't know, really."

"What *do* you know?"

"Nothing. I don't know nothing. Please don't shoot me."

"Get on the ground, face down, hands behind your head." The man dropped to the ground. "Cross your ankles." No response. Jason kicked the man's ankle and repeated the command, then added, *"Do not move."* Jason activated his throat mike to tell Duncan what he learned—or didn't learn in this particular case. "Thunderbird, this is Blackbird, they are not near the van. Say again, *not* near the van. They are possibly with those voices. Over."

"Copy that," Duncan answered. "I heard from Songbird. She's near the location of the voices. I'm on my way to her. Bluebird is on his way to you. Thunderbird out."

"Roger, waiting on Bluebird. Blackbird out." One found, one to go. Kearney didn't jump on the radio. Maybe his radio broke, maybe he didn't have it on him, maybe worse.

"What are we doing with this guy?" Gunther asked as he walked around the corner of the van and shut the nearest rear door.

"He doesn't know anything," Jason responded, picking up the two M-16s and tossing them into the open crate in the back of the truck.

Gunther pointed his semi-automatic handgun at the back head of the man lying on the ground. "Then we don't need him anymore."

"Secure him until we see what Thunderbird wants to do with him."

Gunther hesitated. Jason knew it was taking all of Gunther's willpower to refrain from shooting the guy.

"Here," Jason said, shoving zip ties at Gunther.

With quick, efficient movements, Gunther secured the man's hands and ankles with plastic zip ties. He stood up. "Let's go. Thunderbird is going in close by Songbird. We're doing a wide sweep to check their six." He closed the other door and made sure it was latched shut. There was a burst of automatic gunfire. Then silence.

"Let's roll," Jason said, and they jogged off into the darkness in a crouch.

≈≈≈

Duncan closed in on Iron Angel. She was alive, and she said she had eyes on Kearney.

He found her holding her Malpug FPG on the band of delinquents, who were now face down on the ground. "What's going on here?"

"They knocked Kearney out, dragged him out here, and started a bonfire. Then they started loading magazines and the M-16s. When I confronted them and told them to get on the ground, they laughed at me and tried to shoot me." She smiled. "Evidently, they burned up all the rounds in their handguns in the beginning when they tried to scare me and Kearney. I guess these young know-it-alls didn't know there are no firing pins in the rifles."

Duncan chuckled and shook his head. "No one got shot?"

"Not us. They calmed down a lot after I sprayed bullets at their feet."

"You know," he said, "I was pissed as hell walking over here to you, but this has made my night. I'm proud of you."

"Why's that?" she asked.

His quiet tone was unnerving. She and Kearney had gotten lost, stuck in the desert, unable to communicate. Duncan should have been ranting and raving.

He smiled and slipped an arm around her waist. "You've had a breakthrough." After a light peck on the side of her head, he added, "You resolved a problem without killing everybody."

She smiled and joked, "Can I at least beat them up?"

"Not this time, my angel."

Jason and Gunther slipped past them and, with a hand under each of his arms, dragged the groggy Kearney toward Iron Angel and Duncan.

As they dropped him on the ground behind her, she said, "K, you really need to learn how to fight. I won't always be there to save your ass."

Duncan laughed out loud. At her quizzical look, he said, "That sounds like the words I said to you when you joined the Constitution Defense Legion." He shook his head and chuckled as he checked Kearney's eyes with a flashlight.

Headlights appeared to the west. There were three sets of them and they bounced and disappeared as they followed the rutted road Iron Angel and Kearney had driven in on. Everyone stilled.

Duncan looked through his monocular, lowered it, and waved his flashlight at the oncoming trucks. Headlights flicked on and off three times. "The cavalry," he said. He looked around at the stunned faces. "I called Jake Pennington and asked if he could help us find you. He brought along some help."

The trucks stopped ten feet from the C-IA fighters. The dust swirled forward into their faces and skipped-about in the headlights.

"I see you found your wayward soldiers," Jake said when he exited the truck.

Duncan shook hands with him. "Yeah, we found everybody. But thank you for coming out anyway."

"Need us for anything?" Lou Gomez said, nodding toward the prostrate men.

"We could use some gas," Iron Angel said.

"I have a gas can in the back of my truck," another rancher said. "Show me the way."

"Take Kearney with you," Duncan said. "As soon as you're gassed up, head back to headquarters."

Iron Angel draped Kearney's arm over her shoulder, reached around his waist, grabbed his belt, and headed toward the dead panel truck.

"Hey," Duncan said. When they stopped, he pointed in the direction the ranchers had come. "The road is that way. Use it."

Iron Angel waved compliance and she, Kearney, and the rancher disappeared into the darkness.

"What about these shitheads?" Jason asked, nodding toward the men face down on the ground.

"Collect our guns and ammo." He turned to the ranchers. "Do you mind cleaning up this mess?"

"It'd be our pleasure. I'm glad you found all your people in good shape." Jake nodded in the direction of the gasless panel truck. "Better keep a closer eye on your lady. She's a keeper. A loose cannon, but a keeper just the same."

Back at the truck, gas in the tank, engine running, Iron Angel made a U-turn in the road. "Remember when I said you weren't a wuss? I take that back."

"I think you used the word 'pussy.'"

She stopped short and glared across the dark cab of the truck. "I'm all riled up and no one to kill. Don't tempt me."

CHAPTER 20

Colors II was dark and cool, but smaller than the original. A few steins had been salvaged and, scrubbed clean of soot and smoke, they stood vigil over the new mirror behind the bar. Ruby, grouchy and coarse as ever, was tending bar, which gave the place a touch of homey familiarity in a biker sort of way.

"Hi, Little Al," Iron Angel said. She slid onto the stool next to him and waved to get Ruby's attention.

"Hey. I can't thank you enough for saving my son's life. I feel bad that I didn't mention it that day in the park. That doesn't mean I don't appreciate what you did."

She shrugged. "Samuel grabbed the gun. He didn't remember to take off the safety, but he reacted. That counts for something."

Little Al nodded and, after she ordered a tequila and coke, they sat in silence. The cool oak slab supported their elbows as she looked into the mirror and watched the scene behind her.

He twirled the beer glass in front of him, lost in thought. "How's that other thing going for ya?"

"Forgiveness? I'm working on it. I talked to Kearney about it when we were stuck in the desert last week, and he said pretty much the same things you did." After a brief pause, she said, "I joined the C-IA."

"So what does that mean for you?"

"I'm just one of the fighters. No leadership responsibilities." She took a sip of her tequila and coke before continuing.

"It didn't work out so well for me last time." She winced inwardly wishing she could bite her tongue. She took another sip of her drink.

"Last time?" he asked.

She pressed her lips together. She trusted Little Al, but if she told him about her past with the Constitution Defense Legion, it would implicate him or make him an accessory. Rather than drag him into the web of danger around her status as a fugitive, it was better to stay quiet about it.

Looking out of the corner of his eye, he smiled and said, "Do you mean when you were with the Legion?"

She sucked in a breath, rested her upper arm on the bar, supported her head with her hand, and leaned in close to him. "How do you know that?" she whispered. "How long have you known?"

"Don't worry. Your secret is safe with us. We all kind of knew you guys weren't a few jokers that blew in off the street. When Dee Dee—"

"How did Dee Dee find out? I never told her."

"I heard when she was part of the team to rescue you from the fire at the original Colors, she saw Jason's tattoo." Little Al raised his eyebrows twice. "Do you have one, too?"

"No." Iron Angel frowned. "Not anymore. It was taken from me."

"As in skinned off? I thought only bikers did that sort of thing. Who would do something like that to you?"

"It's not important." She had no intention of getting into the final interrogation by the Legion leadership. And how skinning the Legion tattoo off her chest was the group's way of saying it was over for her—permanently.

"Oh. I think I see." He turned on his stool to face her. "It's Kearney who you—"

"Forget about it. Whatever you think you know, you don't know anything."

She sat up straight and rolled the cool glass across her forehead. She vacantly looked into the mirror, and after a deep sigh, decided to tell Little Al her story.

Over a couple rounds of tequila shots, he listened intently

as she related her part in the Constitution Defense Legion. Her undercover work for them. Her rise to a leadership position in a little over a year. The paranoia. The leadership's cold-blooded descent into ruthlessness. Her betrayal and turning state's evidence. And if that hadn't been enough duplicity, how the CDL Task Force forced her to go back and get evidence on one of their agents who'd flipped and joined the Legion.

And, finally, after snitching and getting the majority of her former colleagues arrested, how Duncan had stayed loyal to her, taking her on the run with him.

When she finished the story with the trials of being a fugitive, she felt strangely calm and marveled at how she hadn't noticed the weight of her past until she unloaded it.

"That's quite a man you got there."

She nodded. "He can be weird and scary at times, but he sticks with me no matter what stupid-ass thing I do."

"So you're afraid you're gonna go down the same road, falling to pieces, and putting a monkey wrench in this new pow-wow."

"Yeah, wouldn't you?"

"You don't think your past has made you stronger and wiser?"

"I don't know. I don't feel wiser. The whole CDL-thing left me feeling weak and indecisive."

He searched her face—the line of her jaw, the crow's feet starting to show themselves at the corner of her eyes, the furrow between her brows. "You know what I think?" he finally said.

She shook her head.

"I think, deep down inside, somewhere in the murky recesses of your brain, you love this crap, and you're using your memories to keep from accepting your fate. That's what I think." He got Ruby's attention and made a circle with his finger for another round.

"You know what *I* think?" she countered. "I think you're twenty pounds of shit in a ten-pound sack. That's what *I* think."

"C'mon, think about it. There was nothing weak or indecisive about defending Abigail Pennington, or our guys in the desert, or those guys that were threatening my son, or last week rescuing Kearney from the jerks. And those are only the incidents I know about." He snorted, "Weak and indecisive, my big fat biker ass. *You're* the one full of shit, Iron Angel."

Her eyes softened. One corner of her mouth turned up. "I do like the adrenaline rush and the sense of invincibility when it's over and I survived."

"See what I mean?" he said, looking up as Ruby filled two fresh shot glasses. When she moved on to the other end of the bar, he continued, "Have you asked yourself why you are here in this place at this point in time with the skills that you have? It's either coincidence or divine intervention."

"Divine intervention? Hah! It's more like 'chance favors the prepared.'"

Little Al laughed and raised his shot glass. They clinked shot glasses and downed the liquor. She rasped through the burning in her throat, "But it's so hard and dangerous and...scary. Sometimes I wonder if it's all worth it."

"Look at it this way. You like the adrenaline rush, but you can't have it unless there's danger. You like the sense of invincibility, but you'll never feel that without a life-threatening situation. Iron Angel, there's no Easter without Good Friday, no adrenaline without fear, no glory without suffering."

"No guts, no glory," she mused.

"Amen to that, sister."

"But I'm not a glory seeker."

"You don't have to seek glory for yourself. The glory can be for your cause." He thought for a moment. "Know anything about falconry?"

She shook her head and wondered where this was going.

"The falcon is one of the world's fiercest predators, but when it's hooded it sits quietly on the falconer's arm. When there's prey close by, the falconer removes the hood. The falcon sees the prey, and its feral, predatory instinct takes over. It streaks toward the prey, kills it, then willingly returns to the security of the gloved arm. The hood is placed on it, and this savage predator again sits quietly in the dark, waiting for the light."

"Nice story, but I don't—"

"Under normal circumstances, you're a good person, leading a quiet life. But when you see prey to be taken down, you go right for it. You take care of business then willingly return to your quiet life." He took a sip of his beer. "You *are* a vicious predator, but you aren't all about the killing. You long for the security of the gloved arm and the quiet darkness."

"I don't know about the darkness. It hasn't been so good for me."

"I don't mean darkness in a negative sense. I mean you aren't distracted by every little event that could send you forever to the wild side."

She looked at the clock on the wall and slid off the stool. Duncan would be home soon for the meeting he had called. "Another great story, Little Al. You missed your calling as a teacher. I'd love to drink and talk with you, but I gotta go."

With a couple light, fraternal taps on the big man's shoulder, she headed to the back of the building. Climbing the back stairs to the third floor where the C-IA headquarters was set up, she thought about Little Al's words. Maybe being part of the Legion and now the C-IA was her destiny. She asked herself why she felt compelled to hone her fighting skills to the point of perfection. And why, of all the places in the United States she and Duncan could have settled down, they chose Arizona? It could be a coincidence, but she didn't believe in coincidences.

Everyone was assembled in the communications room of the headquarters. The men were playfully insulting each other while waiting for Duncan to arrive. Iron Angel got increasingly irritated as time ticked by. She could be downstairs drinking with Little Al, softening the serrated edges of her PTSD, listening to Little Al's sage advice.

Her cell phone rang.

She frowned at the Caller ID. Duncan was late for the meeting—the meeting he called. The meeting was supposed to have started at three—over an hour ago. *This better be good.*

She took a deep breath and answered the call. "Where have you been? I've been worried about you."

"I'm sorry, *chica*, something came up."

Her blood froze in her veins. Wishing she hadn't downed so many shots with Little Al that afternoon, she looked up at Jason, Kearney, and Gunther across the communications room. They were in the middle of some kind of joking, male bonding thing with Joe-Sam.

Eyes pinned on the unsuspecting men, she said, "Did you just call me *chica*?"

The joking stopped. All heads turned toward her. No one blinked. No one moved. No one breathed. *Chica* or *chico* used early in a conversation was code for making a call under duress. Joe-Sam remained seated, but the other three men crowded around her.

CHAPTER 21

Duncan glanced up at the face of one of his captors, presumably the leader. Seated on an old wooden desk chair, he found himself in a very tough spot in some abandoned building. Hands duct taped behind his back, he was bent forward and painfully held there by a rope wrapped around his neck then tied to each ankle.

The kidnapping had been brutal and his head pounded from the blows it took to bring him down. His left eye was half shut. There was the taste blood in his mouth. He was surrounded by eight wild-eyed, hate-filled Hispanic men. The leader poked him with the barrel of his own gun, and waved it to indicate to him to get the conversation moving.

"Hey, I found a great place that could work well as our arms depot, but I want you guys to see it and tell me what you think." Duncan looked up. The Hispanic man standing over him motioned to keep going.

"Who do you want me to bring with me?"

"Kearney, Gunther, Jason, you know, the leadership."

"So where is this place?"

He gave her the address, and she repeated it then asked, "Is Jason with you? All the calls are going directly to voicemail."

Duncan knew she was buying time, probing for information. Jason was probably standing right next to her. "No, Jason isn't with me. Try calling his girlfriend. You know what they say, if you find the woman, you find the man." His captor poked his temple with the barrel of the gun. Duncan winced as pain shot through his already pounding head. "How soon can you get here?"

"An hour, hour and a half, depending on how long it takes to find Jason."

The phone was pulled away. Duncan's captor grabbed his hair and yanked his head back sending lightning bolts of pain through his head and neck. Duncan groaned. The captor snarled, "You don't have that much time." And with a push, he let go. Pain zinged across Duncan's neck and shoulders.

"Look, baby," Duncan said when the phone was returned to his cheek, "the real estate agent is a busy man. Can't you get here sooner?"

"Well, it's going to take time to contact the guys. Then there's the traffic. Maybe an hour?"

"Hurry, baby."

The knot in her stomach tightened. "Can I bring you something to drink?"

"Water sounds great, but hurry up. Okay?"

ɛↄɛↄ

The line went dead in her hand.

Water was the code word for *La Espada*—at least she wasn't taking on the feds. She had heard the Spanish accent in the muffled voice of his captor. And Duncan's groan. Anger tensed her whole body. Her eyes narrowed. She gritted her teeth.

La Espada took Duncan.

He would have fought hard to prevent his capture. She pushed away thoughts of what they must have done to subdue him. She had to keep her head clear.

While she was on the phone with Duncan, Joseph had pulled up a Google satellite photo of the address she had repeated aloud. It filled the wall-mounted monitor over his head. Samuel had run from the room, but Jason and Gunther had taken up a position behind Joseph to pore over the image. Kearney remained by her side.

She approached the monitors. One had gone black. Trying

to get her anger under control, she asked as calmly as she could, "Where did Samuel go?"

"He went to release the drone."

Surprise stopped her anger in its tracks. "We have a drone?"

"No, Samuel and I have a drone," he corrected her. "This will be the first time we'll actually use it in a mission."

"Real-time test runs. Life doesn't get any better than that," she mumbled to no one in particular. She glanced over at Kearney. He lifted his chin in a quick nod of support.

"What can this drone do?" she asked.

"It has an infrared camera, a wall-penetrating thermal imaging camera, and a camera that can be changed from day to night vision. It has GPS so we can send it to a precise location." The black screen became a mass of rolling black and white snow. "It is now on its way to Duncan's location."

She shifted to the right to let Samuel pass. "Won't they be able to hear it?"

Samuel answered her as he slid into his seat. "It has a quiet electric motor with a battery life of six hours, and it can go as high as 2000 feet."

"Won't the images be useless at that height?"

"No," Joe-Sam said in unison.

Samuel typed commands to the drone and grasped a joy stick Iron Angel hadn't noticed before. The pixels worked their way into a clear image. A detailed picture came into view. Rooftops slowly passed into and out of frame.

"This will give us real-time information about the location."

Her anger flashed back, this time edged with impatience. She leapt into action. "Jason, you stay with the drone. Figure out a way into and out of the building. Joe-Sam, hack into their surveillance system."

"How do you know they have electronic surveillance?" Samuel asked.

"They'll have it. Gunther, contact Red Dog. Have him gather as many of the Brotherhood as he can. We'll need exterior security once we're inside the building, except have Red Dog and Dee Dee meet us here. I want them inside with us. If they can't get here fast enough, have them meet us two blocks south of the location." She leaned over Joseph and pointed to an alley on the Google satellite image. "Here. Kearney, stir up some of our new militia members and get them either here or have them meet us there."

He hesitated.

She bore into his eyes. "You have a problem with that?"

Kearney started dialing.

Pointing to Kearney and Gunther with the index and middle fingers of her right hand, she added, "Start gathering our weapons and ammo. Meet me at the van."

"Duncan has the van," Kearney said with his phone to his ear.

"I have an SUV." Samuel turned his chair, reaching in his pocket for the keys. He tossed them to her.

She snatched the keys out of the air and headed for the door. Before going through the doorway, she said over her shoulder, "We leave in ten. Joe-Sam, I'll be back to check on that inside feed before we leave."

She, Gunther, and Kearney disappeared through the door.

✂✄✂✄

Eight minutes later, Iron Angel's eyes were on the monitors, but her ears were concentrating on Jason's briefing.

"The drone has located a group of men on the third floor," Jason was saying. "We assume it's Duncan and his captors. It's where I would place a prisoner. Two stories below. Two stories above. There are six guards on the roof. There are several teams of two—"

Iron Angel put a finger up to stop Jason. "Joe-Sam, where's that inside video?"

"It has to be closed-circuit. We can't pick up any Wi-Fi in the area. We can't hack in. We can't jam it."

"Then one of you is coming with us."

Joe-Sam turned in their chairs to face her. "We don't work in the field."

"Samuel, you're going. You have more experience."

"But I only had the gun in my hand that one time, and I forgot to take off the safety."

"That gives you more experience than Joseph."

Red Dog and Dee Dee walked into the room. "Red Dog, go downstairs and tell Little Al to come with us."

"He isn't in the bar," Red Dog said.

"Contact him. Have him meet us there. Will you feel better if your dad is with you?" Iron Angel asked Samuel, but didn't wait for an answer. "Dee Dee, you and Red Dog will be Samuel's body guards until Little Al gets there, then you Red Dog will join the rest of us. Until Little Al gets there, you three will be joined at the hip. Got it?"

Samuel sputtered, trying to hide his fear. "But why do you need me? What am I supposed to do?"

"You will find and hack into their surveillance system. Since you can't do it remotely, you'll have to do it onsite. You have to blind them so we can get to Duncan safely. Gather up the equipment you'll need."

His mouth opened and tried to form words, but no sound came out.

"That would mean *now,* Samuel."

With shaky hands, he clumsily started throwing equipment and accessories into a backpack.

"Jason, give Samuel my revolver—no safety to forget." She unclipped her holster from her waistband shoved it into Jason's abdomen where he grabbed it. "Make sure he knows how it works."

"But if I'm with you guys, why do I need a gun?"

"We could get separated, we all could get—" She didn't have the time or the patience for this. "Just take it, Samuel."

She headed toward the door. "See everyone downstairs in two."

"Hey, what about me?" Everyone turned to Joseph, standing alone with his back to the computers and monitors.

"You're right," Iron Angel said. "This could be a diversion to take out our headquarters. Red Dog, get two or three of the Brotherhood up here to protect Joseph and the equipment."

Red Dog pulled out his phone and started dialing as he headed for the door.

Not realizing how anger had hardened her facial features, Iron Angel pointed and said, "Joseph."

Joseph's eyes widened and he backed into the desk. A pencil rolled and hit the floor.

"You are sharp. Good catch."

"What—" Joseph swallowed hard. His voice wavered, and his knuckles were white as he grasped the desk behind him. "What are you guys gonna do?"

She curled her lip and snarled, "Nuke 'em."

꽃꽃꽃

Iron Angel had told him she would be there in an hour. Duncan knew that was code for forty minutes. He hoped it would be sooner. He couldn't feel his hands anymore, and he knew some of his shoulder muscles were torn—his muscularity was working against him. His neck was cramped from looking up. And every time he looked up the rope squeezed his throat a little more.

He had put up a good fight during the kidnapping, but after the blow to the back of his head, his vision faded and his ability to fight had drained from his body. Now, his only hope was Iron Angel. She would save him or die trying—he knew that. What he couldn't know was if she would arrive in time.

His captors were foolishly celebrating their victory before the last lap. From what he could glean from the Spanish, they were proclaiming that they had the leader of the C-IA, and he had lured the remainder of the leadership into their trap. These were just dumb gringos. They would walk into their trap, and *La Espada* would cut off the head of the snake. Then they could concentrate on the authorities, without this small-time militia stinging them like gnats.

They were taunting him and, every now and then one of them would strike him. His other eye was now swollen, his nose was broken, and he was barely holding onto consciousness. His jaw was possibly broken. He couldn't be sure.

He noted they weren't watching their monitor, but he was. His vision was blurred, but he could see enough. He had no doubt that his captors would kill him as soon as they realized the rest of the C-IA leadership wasn't going to nonchalantly walk into their ambush. He just wanted to see Iron Angel once more before they took him out.

CHAPTER 22

Iron Angel accepted the piece of gum that Gunther offered her. They stood in middle of a litter-strewn alley surrounded by a ragtag group of fighters. Where the alley opened to the north, they could see a sliver of the building where Duncan was being held captive. Flying sentry over their heads, Joe-Sam's drone provided crisp images that downloaded to Samuel's i-Pad. She, Red Dog, and Dee Dee hovered over Samuel's shoulder.

"Dee Dee, Red Dog, you guys turn right at the end of the alley and walk like you're two lovers. Try to look casual," Iron Angel directed without looking up.

"How do we look casual with all these weapons?" Dee Dee asked.

She and Red Dog each had handguns in holsters at their waists and an H&K G36C across their chests. Thanks to the monetary support from the ranchers, the C-IA's armament was getting bigger and bolder. The H&K's were shortened rifles, but bigger than handguns. Much bigger. With 20-round magazines and pinpoint accuracy, the C-IA had become a force to be reckoned with.

"I said 'try.'" Iron Angel popped her gum. "There are two guards in a doorway, this side, halfway up the block." Jason put a hand on her right shoulder. "Oh, sorry, Jason, you're the tactics guy."

He squeezed her shoulder and leaned in to get a glimpse of the screen. "You're doing fine."

Iron Angel was wearing a black and tan shemagh and a black sleeveless tee shirt, which bared her bronzed, muscular arms. She bristled with weapons. Urban camouflage pants were tucked into calf-high brown boots that housed sheaths for her knives. There was a leather sack cinched at the top that hung from her belt. To those who asked, it was her talisman, but inside were her throwing stars. Her Colt .45 semi-automatic was in a holster strapped to her right thigh. Her precious Malpug FPG hung on a short sling that positioned the weapon across her chest.

"I see you didn't leave any weapon home," Jason commented with a half-smile.

"These? These aren't weapons, they're tools." She looked up at him. "I'm the weapon."

He smiled. "Roger that."

She thought through her plan and slowly chewed her gum.

"What about me?" Samuel pointed back and forth between himself and Red Dog. "Aren't we supposed to be joined at the hip, or something?" There was a tremor in his voice. He moved his i-Pad between hands as he wiped his sweaty palms on his pants.

"I'm getting to that. You will follow them about eight paces behind. Close enough for them to protect you, but not so close it looks like you're with them." His eyes widened and his mouth fell open. "Keep your eyes on your i-Pad. Pretend you're texting, like any young person today."

She looked over her shoulder at Jason, who had stepped back to be closer to the men who were part of his team. Standing behind him were three militia members, one of them still wearing his blue business suit. She briefly wondered where he came from to be with them. "You take your guys and go around to the fire escape on the far side of the building. Take out the guards on the roof. Work your way down to Duncan. We'll work our way up. We'll meet in the middle."

"Isn't Kearney the next in command?" a newbie standing beside Jason murmured. "I don't take orders from a woman."

Maybe it was the disrespect, maybe it was the fear of losing Duncan, maybe it was the frustration of leadership of an ill-prepared band of warriors, but something snapped. She spun around. With eyes narrowed and jaw set, she grabbed the front of his shirt with her left hand and pulled him in to her face. "I'm no *woman*. I'm Iron Angel."

"So?"

She looked at him from under the bill of her Arizona Suns cap. Through clenched teeth she warned, "You dumb fuck, if you say one more word, I'll knock you into tomorrow without moving any part of my body more than two inches." She pulled his shirt until his face was inches from hers. "Say something. Moan. Clear your throat. Anything. I beg you."

"Stop." Gunther jumped in, putting a hand on her right arm. "We need all the manpower we can get. Let's sort this out later."

In the middle of Gunther's sentence, the defiant militiaman swung his left hand in a wide haymaker toward her head. Before his hand made contact, she let go of her grip on the front of his shirt and executed a quick, powerful chin-jab. He flew backward three feet, smacking the back of his head on the ground.

Without taking her eyes off the groaning man on the ground, she said, "You're right, Gunther." She slid her gaze to her left. "Jason, he's on your team. If he expresses so much as a whisper of dissent, double-tap him."

Jason's eyes snapped up at her in shock. She wouldn't hesitate to kill someone in self-defense or the defense of others, but she had never ordered a hit before.

She winked. "Got it?"

"Roger. Double-tap," Jason said, hiding his relief. "You heard the lady. Get up," he said to the man on the ground.

Every militia member stood frozen in place around her. In turn, she looked each one in the eyes. "We are not men, we are not women, we are patriotic Americans. Anyone disagree?" She swept her gaze over the fighters gathered in the alley. No one wanted to be the first to speak, and an uncomfortable silence filled the alley. Turning back to Samuel's i-Pad, she said, "I'll take that as a 'no.'"

Kearney was the first to speak. "What's the plan, boss?"

She glanced over her shoulder at him. He was smiling, all

his front teeth gleaming in the shadow of the alley. Leave it to Kearney to break the ice with four well thought out words.

"I have a basic two-step plan. Step One, gain control the building." After a couple chews she added, "Step Two, go straight to Duncan."

"Anything more specific about gaining control of the building?" Gunther asked.

"Kill them all. If they're all dead, we control the building."

Gunther laughed, clapped his hands, and rubbed them together. "That's my girl."

"How much time do you need to get around to the fire escape on the other side of the building?" she asked Jason.

"Five...six minutes."

"Five it is." She looked into Jason's steady, dark eyes. They'd been together since her first day with the Legion. She was glad he was there when she needed a calm, reliable soldier. "Stay safe. Make every shot count. See you in the middle."

There were elbow bumps all around. Jason took charge of his squad, and Iron Angel chewed her gum as she watched them disappear out the opposite end of the alley.

She checked her watch and joined her crew at the mouth of the alley. "Where are the roof sentries, Samuel?"

"Uh, there are six of them. The one on this side is in the corner to our, uh, right," Samuel re-considered his position with the image on his i-Pad, "No, our left."

"Which is it?" she demanded sharply.

"Left." He bit his lower lip. "Left for sure."

After four minutes of silence, quiet checks of equipment, and words of support, she looked up at Red Dog and Dee Dee. "Try to take out the two guards as quickly and as quietly as possible. As soon as they're down, cross the street to the door diagonally across from them. We'll meet you there."

"See you across the street." Red Dog tugged on Samuel's tee shirt. "Let's go."

Before he reached the street, Samuel texted Joseph, *i'm in the wind*, using spy phraseology he had read in a book somewhere.

He sent the message and, without waiting for a reply he

typed, *if i don't make it, u can have my jazz collection.* He switched back to the video from the drone.

"Two-inch strike? Into tomorrow?" Gunther teased Iron Angel as he stood beside her and waited for her command to go.

In between chews, she said, "Okay, maybe it was four inches."

"How you doing today?" he asked, studying her set jaw and the intensity that radiated off her in waves. "Are you on the tracks?"

She slowly chewed her gum. "I'm tracking." Out of the corner of her eye she saw Gunther's familiar nod. He was on board. "Let's move out."

One step on the sidewalk and a gunshot echoed off the buildings. They all looked down the street and saw a struggle between the two guards and Red Dog and Dee Dee. Samuel was crouching next to the building, covering his head with one hand, and hugging his i-Pad to his chest with the other.

She smiled. She loved a functioning plan. "I'll get Samuel. You help Red Dog and Dee Dee. Rally across the street."

Gunther and Kearney raced past her as she stooped to help Samuel. Under protective fire cover by Gunther and Kearney, she grabbed Samuel's arm. He was petrified and welded to the spot. Several of the guards on the roof left their posts and moved to the edge, facing her and her team, and were leaning over the edge and firing. With one hand on Samuel's arm, one on his waistband, she muscled him to his feet and zigzagged him across the street. Bullets whistled past them, smacking the pavement to their left and right. In her rush to get him to safety, and adrenaline pumping up her power, she slammed Samuel against the side of the alcove to the door to the building. His knees buckled and he slid to a seated position with his back against the left side of the opening.

He looked at her with his mouth open, his shoulders hunched up to his ears. She had her eyes on the ledge above them. She looked down at Samuel and took a double-take. He sat still as a stone, not moving, not blinking, bottom jaw lax. "Breathe, Samuel." He didn't move. She leaned toward him and he flinched. She gently put a hand on his shoulder. "You're going to be all right. Just keep your eyes on your i-Pad. Don't worry about anything going on around you. You have the best body guards in the world."

"Who's that?" he squeaked out.

She blinked in disbelief. "Us." She leaned out of the doorway to check the ledge above them. "Keep me updated on who or what's around us." He didn't move. She leaned in again, inches from his face. "Samuel! I need you now. We. Need. You."

He looked down at his i-Pad, as if he didn't recognize it, then back up at her.

"Samuel, keep your eyes on Jason. Give me updates on his position."

Samuel nodded in little jerks then hunched over his i-Pad.

She stepped into the street. She looked down the barrel as she kept it pointed at the roof above them. A head appeared over the edge. She fired, but her round hit the ledge and blew a chunk of cement off. A shot was fired from across the street, and the man fell backward. Another head popped over the edge, firing his AK-47 in full automatic. She ducked back into the doorway. When the firing stopped, she ventured out. He was no longer on the edge.

"Where's Jason, Samuel?"

"He is on the fire escape—" He swallowed hard then continued, "—making his way up to the roof. It looks like he's on the third floor, heading toward the fourth."

Another head popped over the edge. Iron Angel fired and hit the target this time.

"Jason is heading to the fifth."

She motioned to Kearney and Gunther to cross the street and join her. "Get up. Let's go."

"Where?"

Kearney and Gunther darted into the shelter of the doorway. They were gasping for air. Their presence crowded the small alcove.

"Through that door," she said, nodding toward the door behind him.

"But isn't it—"

She reached around him and turned the knob.

"—locked?"

It was locked.

"Kearney."

"I'm on it," he said, pulling a lock pick gun from his left cargo pocket.

⌀⌀⌀

Duncan heard the gunfire like it was far away. Sweet blackness was closing in, but he fought it. The thought of seeing Iron Angel one more time gave him the inner strength to hang on. He repeated her name over and over to keep the darkness from overtaking him.

"It looks like your fellow militiamen just signed your death warrant," the leader said to Duncan.

"Wait! You need me alive."

"Yeah? Why is that?"

"My guys are all excellent shots. They'll kill off your guys before you take them all out. I can tell them to give up."

"What makes you think we aren't good shots, too?"

"I can tell by the sound of the gunfire which is your guys' and which are my guys'." It was all he had. It had to be enough to buy some time. "And it sounds like there are fewer shots fired by your guys now than a few minutes ago."

The leader motioned for two of his *compadres* in the room to go and check it out. He turned to check the monitor. Nobody but his men were in the hallways. There was some movement in the street, but his rooftop guards would take care of them.

⌀⌀⌀

Kearney pulled the trigger on his lock pick gun and, after a pop, reached up, and turned the knob. He looked over his shoulder at Iron Angel. "Are you ready? There could be explosives connected to the door."

"We've come this far. Might as well go for it," she said. "We can only hope they have less training than we have."

He remained on his knees while pushing the door inward. It opened into a large room with rusty iron stairs to the second floor along the left wall. A hail of gunfire greeted them. As soon as the barrage stopped, Iron Angel and Gunther had their rifles raised and ready for possible resistance. A man jumped up behind a rusty hulk of a machine, but they took him out before he could fire. The room went quiet—spine-tingling quiet.

The muffled popping of gunfire came from the roof. As they stepped through the doorway, Red Dog and Dee Dee raced across the street and joined them.

The abandoned building had the strong smell of urine. The paint peeling from the walls and ceiling gave the dark room an eerie, movie-set feeling. Iron Angel wrinkled her nose. Her head swiveling, her eyes and the short barrel of the FPG moved in unison. Ignoring the crunch of paint chips under their feet, they inched farther into the room. She tapped Gunther on the shoulder and pointed up the stairs. He took point.

"You three," Iron Angel whispered to Red Dog, Dee Dee, and Samuel. Before she could finish, they saw movement on the far side of the room. Iron Angel grabbed Samuel and threw him to the floor. Everyone else flattened themselves against the floor. A man ran out of a hallway and started firing.

Gunther, Kearney, and Iron Angel returned fire from the prone position. The man went down. Another man popped out, but he was cut down.

"Kearney, Gunther, go clear that hallway. Make sure we don't have any more surprises."

She asked if anyone was hit. Everyone shook their heads. Samuel looked a little shaken, but he busied himself checking to see if his i-pad still functioned. Several more pops came from the direction of Gunther and Kearney. Then nothing.

"Okay, you three, find the surveillance wiring. Hook into it. Blind them. Plug in so we can see the hallways."

Red Dog, Dee Dee, and Samuel headed along the wall beneath the iron stairs.

The downstairs rooms cleared, Kearney and Gunther rejoined Iron Angel. Gunther took point, followed by Kearney. Iron Angel took the six and they started the hair-raising ascent up the stairs. Stairwells were natural death funnels. No escape. The only way out is to fight your way out. Two-thirds up the flaking stairwell three heads popped over the railing above them. Kearney saw them first and fired. Gunther and Iron Angel joined in.

Bullets pinged off the iron stairs around them. When the shooting stopped, they raced up the remainder of the stairs until they could peek through the railing.

Like the floor below, the stairs opened into a large open room with a hallway on the opposite side that lead to more offices. The large room was clear and open. They remembered their lesson on the first floor, and Iron Angel motioned to clear the offices down that hallway, but there was no cover between them and the wall on each side of the doorway. The three C-IA fighters sped across the floor. Iron Angel ran backwards to protect their six. They rushed into the first office on the right.

"Dammit, I was hit," Gunther groused.

"Where?" Kearney asked, looking him up and down and not seeing any blood.

"I didn't realize it until I started to run."

"I don't see it. Where?"

"My ass. A piece of shrapnel must have ricocheted and hit me near to my heart."

When Kearney took off to clear the rest of the offices, Iron Angel used the time to put a field pressure bandage on Gunther's wound. She pulled one out of a pouch of her equipment vest and knelt beside Gunther's right thigh. While biting open the packaging, she said, "I love ya, Gunther, but I'm not going in there. Slide the ties of this bandage between your thigh and your testicles."

With the pressure bandage in place, she wound Gunther's shemagh around his hips and thigh. "Good thing you're skinny. This isn't pretty, but it'll have to do until we can get you some medical care."

Kearney returned from clearing the offices and watched the finishing touches of Gunther's patch up.

"A few inches to the front and the little senorita I'm seeing would be sorely disappointed," Gunther said. He winced when he took a step to see if the bandages would stay put.

"If she's dating you, she can't be any more disappointed," Kearney joked.

Gunther snorted then grimaced as he took another step. The bandage was secure. He nodded to Iron Angel that he was ready to drive on.

She shook her head, wondering how men could still taunt each other when the tension was so high. "Let's go."

They headed out across the floor, a little slower this time, moving at Gunther's pace. Since Gunther was now the slowest member, he took their six and Kearney took point.

"One more floor," she whispered when they reached the base of the metal stairs to the third floor. "Let's hope we can get to Duncan before we have any more casualties."

Before she could give the command to move out, they heard soft footfalls on the stairs, ascending from the first floor. She motioned for Kearney to check it out. He swung the barrel of his M-4 over the railing then just as quickly pulled it back. He whispered that it was Red Dog and Dee Dee and he motioned for them to hurry up the rest of the steps.

Samuel headed straight for Iron Angel. "I'm in," he whispered and held out the i-Pad so she could see it.

"What's with him?" Red Dog asked with a chin nod toward Gunther.

"He's got a bullet up his butt," Kearney said as he checked the stairway one more time.

"These are the hallways," Samuel explained about the images on his i-Pad. "This is us." He waved to demonstrate.

She pulled his hand down and glared at him. They were so close to Duncan and yet so far away. Time was running out.

He continued quickly, "I'll switch to the drone and its wall-penetrating thermal imager." An image of warm figures huddled together inside the building appeared. "This is us. I'll move the drone a little." After the drone was repositioned, he continued, "Here's them. In the middle of the floor upstairs along the west side of the building."

She gasped. One figure was hunched over and not moving.

Kearney leaned over the group to take a quick peek. "Don't worry, he's still warm. We'll get to him."

Their eyes locked. He gave her a quick nod of support then turned toward the stairway. More footsteps. Again Kearney pointed his M-4 over the railing then motioned for the newcomer to join them. Little Al's head appeared in the opening of the railing.

"Hi, Dad," Samuel said then, as if he'd been a field operative all his life, went back to business, "Here's Jason and his three guys clearing the fourth floor."

Iron Angel set up her new team. "Okay, Kearney, you take point. Then Red Dog and Gunther. You okay, Gunny?" A quick nod from Gunther, then she continued, "Then me, Little Al, and Samuel. Dee Dee, you take our six. Everyone good?"

Nods from everyone.

"Samuel, stairway clear?"

"Stairway clear," he responded.

"Go, Kearney," she commanded.

The third floor was all offices off a central corridor. Jason's team was in the middle, huddled against the right wall. Iron Angel's team headed toward him, quietly clearing each room as they got to it. Jason gestured to the room Duncan was in, and her team slipped into the office just before it.

Jason slowly peered around the doorjamb. Three captors were pointing their guns out the window, two were muttering and fiddling with their equipment and monitors that had gone black, and one had his attention on Duncan. Jason silently rolled across the opening and crept to the office where Iron Angel waited.

She squinted at his closed eyes and his finger rubbing the dot of hair beneath his lower lip. He was struggling to get his emotions under control.

After a few seconds, he said in a hoarse whisper, "I see six bad guys. Three on the right looking out the windows, facing away from the door; two on the left, one standing over Duncan. Iron Angel, you go in low and take out the guy standing over Duncan. As soon as you shoot him, cut Duncan loose. Don't worry about the other bad guys. Gunther, Kearney, you take out the three on the right. I'll take the two on the left. Little Al, you and Red Dog and Dee Dee keep your eyes on your end of the hallway. My guys will defend the other end."

He hesitated, leaned in to Iron Angel and whispered, "This is going to be hard for you."

"No, it's not," she said in a low tone, pulling a knife out of her boot, and putting it between her teeth.

"I don't mean shooting the guy," Jason whispered. "What's going to be hard for you is to not look at Duncan. Only look at your target. Got it?"

"Yeah, look at my target. What's so hard about that?" she asked through her teeth clenched on the blade of the knife.

"Do not look at Duncan," Jason emphasized.

"I got it."

"Angel, I'm serious. Look only at your target. You only have a split second. It's imperative that you only look at your target."

"I *got* it! Let's *go*."

Jason motioned for his ad-hoc team to follow him. They slinked along the wall and stopped just short of the target office. He raised an upward facing palm to Iron Angel. "Eyes up." He counted down with his fingers and, when the last finger disappeared, she bolted through the door and landed on one knee, the other three men right behind her.

She froze at the sight of the beaten, bloody man in the chair. The quick pops of gunfire around her sounded distant.

The man looked up. "What took you so long?"

The sound of Duncan's voice spurred her into action. She saw her target move behind Duncan and grab his hair with one hand, a large knife in the other. She sent a three-round burst from her FPG. The man flew backward from the impact of the rounds and landed against the back wall. He slowly slid to the floor. She continued to fire as she got up and walked over to the man. She shot at his head until he was unrecognizable.

"Hey, stop! What are you doing?" Kearney yelled, grabbing her arm.

She pulled the knife from between her teeth. "I'm communicating. It's what those Hezbies do. They mutilate the faces of our fallen soldiers. I'm telling them what goes around, comes around."

"You're lowering yourself to their level," Kearney said.

She spun around to face him and she sneered, "I'm *not* lowering myself to their level. I'm facilitating effective communication." She reached to cut Duncan loose.

"I think it's the Taliban that mutilates the faces of our fallen soldiers," Gunther said quietly.

She glared him into silence as she cut the duct tape securing Duncan's wrists behind his back. With one last slice of her knife, she freed Duncan's ankles.

"I can't move, baby." Duncan's voice was raspy.

Kearney stepped forward. "I got you, big guy. Let's slowly stand up," he said softly as he put an arm in Duncan's armpit.

Duncan winced. His hands trembled. "I don't have any feeling in my arms. I think my delts are torn."

"Can you walk?" Kearney asked as he helped Duncan stand erect.

"Yeah, I think so." Duncan tried to straighten up and groaned at the pain in his back. One leg gave out. "Give me a second or two to get the kinks out."

"I don't want to seem insensitive," Iron Angel said, grabbing his arm on the other side. "But, you're going to have to work out the kinks on the way. We have to get out of here." She turned to the newbie who had shown up in his blue business suit, now torn and bloody. "You, 'Suit,' take this side and help Kearney. Red Dog, you and Jason take point. Gunny, you're with me." With a long look at the militiaman who had been insubordinate in the alley, she continued, "You two guys cover our six." She gave a quick nod at the man who had been insubordinate, as if to say, "You with me?"

The man nodded back.

"Everyone else in the middle. Okay, move out."

Out of the corner of her eye, she saw Samuel raise his revolver. She dove for him but, before she could grab the gun, he aimed and fired down the hallway behind them. The other fighters turned and fired at a man, who staggered then raised his gun to fire again. Pops of gunfire echoed in the narrow passageway as Iron Angel and her other fighters dispatched bullets to the lone *La Espada* member. He went down. No farther movement.

She spun around and glared at the two new members. "You know what 'cover our six' means, right?"

They both took a step back. One of them said, "We didn't see him. He just jumped out of nowhere."

"You didn't see—" She wanted to tear them apart. Duncan could have been hit and hurt more than he already was. Or killed. She felt a firm hand on her arm and looked up into Little Al's eyes. He only shook his head, but it was enough to get her back on track. She took a deep, calming breath.

The C-IA fighters were congratulating Samuel for saving their lives. Pats on the back, meant to be congratulatory, almost gave him whiplash. He turned his attention to Iron Angel.

She nodded approval. A smile flashed across his face.

"Okay. Let's all stay alert." She had to get her fighters regrouped and headed out of this danger. "Enough atta boys. Fall into your positions. Heads on the swivel." As everyone got into position, she gave the order to move out.

Halfway down the hallway, a loud rumbling noise vibrated throughout the building. It rattled the few panes of glass that remained in the windows. Everyone froze.

"What the hell is that?" one of the new militia members asked, looking around at the walls and ceiling.

Gunther, Jason, and Iron Angel smiled at each other and said simultaneously, "Harley Davidsons."

"Our exterior security has arrived," Kearney announced with a flourish. He turned to Red Dog. "How many of the Brotherhood do you think came?"

Red Dog smiled broadly. "All of them."

They all rushed for the stairs.

Duncan looked up at Kearney as he struggled to keep up. "Thank you, buddy."

"Don't thank me. Thank your girlfriend. She took charge the second she knew you were in trouble."

"No one gave her a hard time?" Duncan asked.

"Would *you* have?"

With a raspy chuckle, Duncan shook his head. "Hey, Gunny, that's quite a girlfriend I got, huh?"

"Less talking, more walking," Iron Angel ordered from behind them. "We aren't out of this tight spot yet."

CHAPTER 23

The apprehension was overwhelming. To keep it under control, Iron Angel shouted orders at the group rushing down the stairs. Each step brought them closer to the rumbling Harley Davidsons outside and tightened the vise of anxiety on her insides. Duncan was slow and awkward, relying on Kearney and Suit too much. He didn't complain, but she knew he was in pain. *Keep your head in the mission. Get Duncan and the others out of here before the feds or national guard show up. Keep Moving.*

She tossed Samuel the keys to the SUV and told him to bring it around for the wounded. As he took off down the stairs ahead of the group, she grabbed Gunther's arm and yelled more orders.

It wasn't over yet. Exfiltration was one of the most dangerous parts of the mission. Partly because the adversaries knew where they were, but many times soldiers simply dropped their guard. They thought too far ahead—about getting home or back to base—and lost sight of the present moment. It only took a second to lose control of the situation, to miss the one flurry of movement that could mean failure at the end of a successful mission. They had luckily survived such an oversight just minutes before. She had to keep her team focused.

She blinked at the bright sunlight when she stepped out of the gloom of the building. As she squinted while her eyes adjusted to the light, two Harleys thundered past, carrying two of her fighters to safety. Half the Brotherhood shoved helmets into the hands of weary warriors—an attempt to hide their identities—got them on the backs of their bikes, and took off, taking them out of the area and back to their vehicles. The other half stood guard.

She looked to the right and stepped back when she saw the SUV hurtling toward her. The tires slid on the gravel as Samuel locked the brakes, coming to a halt just beyond where she stood. As Kearney rushed Duncan around the vehicle and helped him struggle into the front passenger seat, she opened the rear door on the driver's side for Gunther. With the wounded secured, she tossed her folded Malpug FPG into the cargo area and closed the hatch. Before she could get into the SUV, a firm grasp on her arm turned her away from the vehicle.

Wild Bill pulled her toward his bike. She resisted. She looked over her shoulder at the SUV pulling away.

"Don't worry," he said. "I'll get you to your old man."

She fixed hard, unflinching eyes on the President of the Demon Brotherhood. She didn't like being separated from Duncan, least of all by Wild Bill.

He must have seen the hardness in her eyes. "It's a Demon Brotherhood rule—leaders ride with leaders."

"Duncan's the leader of the C-IA." She looked over her shoulder at the SUV as it turned onto the service road that would take it to the highway.

"You led this operation," Wild Bill was saying. "As far as I'm concerned, you're the leader. You ride with me." The last motorcycle with one of her fighters rumbled by, blowing a strand of hair across her face.

She tucked the hair behind her ear and grabbed the helmet from Wild Bill. "My threat still stands."

Every nerve in her body screamed for her to turn down this ride. Catch another one. Walk. Anything but get on this bike. The guards had pulled back from their positions, started their bikes, and were waiting for their leader to pull out. She glanced at the bikers then studied Wild Bill. Maybe it was just the adrenaline draining from her system that was making her suspicious. Even *he* wouldn't pull something at a time like this.

The Harley Davidson in front of her roared to life. Wild Bill nodded for her to get onto the back. She hesitated, but sirens wailing in the distance caught her attention.

"Your choice," Wild Bill said. "The police, or me."

With the carnage inside the building, Wild Bill was the lesser of two evils—the emphasis on evil. She climbed onto the passenger seat behind him, and he sped off down the partially overgrown parking lot toward the pitted service road.

To the left she saw a white speck that was carrying Duncan as it headed down the highway, back to the headquarters and safety. She yelled into Wild Bill's ear to catch up to Duncan, and the bike lurched forward as he picked up speed. She relaxed.

At the end of the service road, Wild Bill leaned right, and steered the bike in the opposite direction of the SUV carrying Duncan. She pounded on his back. "Where the hell are you going? The headquarters is the other way."

He spoke over his left shoulder so the wind would carry his voice. "We want to break up the group so you're not all together when the cops come—harder target to nail down."

She looked behind her. "Well, evidently no one got the memo, because everyone else is going the other way."

The hair stood up on the back of her neck. Prickles coursed up and down her arms and legs. This was wrong. All wrong. She yelled into Wild Bill's ear, "Turn around *now*."

"I want to talk to you."

"This is not the time. Duncan is injured. I have to get to him."

"It'll just take a few minutes. Don't worry. I'll get you to your old man."

She pulled her .45 semi-automatic from the holster strapped to her thigh and jammed the muzzle into Wild Bill's back. "Turn this fucking bike around *now*."

Wild Bill chuckled.

You think this is funny, you bastard? The prickles turned into white-hot anger, and she ground the muzzle of her semi-automatic deeper into Wild Bill's kidney.

He yelled over his shoulder. "If you shoot me, how will

you explain the blowback to the police after we go down?"

She removed the gun from his back and holstered it. "You're right, Bill. Blow back would be messy." She slid her left hand over his shoulder and rested it just above his sternum and placed her right hand on his shoulder at the base of his neck. She leaned forward in a more intimate way. He relaxed in her embrace.

"Why don't we pull into that dirt road up ahead. It looks like it leads to a place where we can talk privately."

Wild Bill nodded and slowed the bike.

"You're also right about going down," she said in his ear as softly as she could and still be heard over the wind. She ran the fingers of her right hand through Wild Bill's sweaty, salt-and-pepper hair. "I'm not going to be able to stop you without laying down the bike. You got me there." As he downshifted, Wild Bill smiled and nodded.

Before the second nod, she grabbed the hair in her fingers and yanked his head to the right, simultaneously twisting his chin to the left. After a brief wobble, the bike went down on its right side. The sound of metal scraping the concrete pavement filled the desert air as the bike skidded away from the riders. She hit the unforgiving road with a thud. Wild Bill rolled away from her.

The hot pavement ground into her elbows as she rolled with the momentum. With every rotation, the pavement ripped out the knees of her pants. The holstered handgun pounded into the side of her thigh each time it hit the ground. Her butt was on fire, but, thanks to the helmet, she was alert and conscious.

When the rolling stopped, she lay in a heap on her left side. After curling her fingers and stretching them out, she wiggled her toes. Her elbows felt like they'd been sandblasted, and she winced as she eased herself onto her left elbow. A look down the length of her legs relieved her fears—no bones protruding from the pant legs. Her calf-high boots had spared her ankles and feet. Blood was soaking through her clothes at her knees. *Like they say—if you feel pain you're still alive.* A moan escaped her throat as she wobbled to her feet and realized she had wrenched her right knee.

After pulling off the helmet, she twisted to take a quick

look at the bloody road rash peeking through the shredded seat of her pants. The twisting motion sent a stabbing pain from the middle of her back down her left leg. From neck to knees, she hurt like hell—on a pain meter of one-to-ten, this was an eleven-point-five—but she had more important things to think about than her injuries.

Suddenly overcome by a bout of nausea from the pain, she rested her hands on her knees, swallowed hard, and looked around for the bike. She saw Wild Bill lying motionless fifteen feet from her, braced against a mile marker. *Screw him. Where's the bike?* She spied it ten feet beyond the unconscious biker. She gulped down the bile in the back of her throat and raced to the bike in a half-limp, half-run.

Unless you were an Olympic weight lifter, there was only one way to get eight-hundred-eighty-some pounds of an Ultra Glide Classic Harley from its side to its tires. Iron Angel turned her back toward the bike. She took several deep breaths, reached with her hands behind her, grabbed the seat, and lifted with her legs. A long grunt forced its way through her gritted teeth as she lifted the massive hunk of metal. Just short of vertical, she turned and grabbed the handlebars. The sudden twist intensified the pain in her back.

To block out the pain, she set about assessing the damage. A quick once over of the controls revealed the handlebars were a little bent, but the cables were intact and working. There weren't any liquids leaking onto the pavement—at least not any more than was normal for a Harley Davidson. Satisfied that the bike remained in good working order, she straddled it and pushed the ignition button.

Twice the engine struggled to start. *Show me some love*, she urged the machine. On the third try, the throaty rumble of the engine answered her plea. She commanded her right knee to hold the bike, ignored the shot of pain when she raised her left leg to put it into gear, pulled in the clutch lever, and nursed the throttle. It stalled. After wiping the dirt-soaked sweat off the side of her face with her arm, she hit the ignition button again. The engine came to life. This time she was more assertive with the controls and the motorcycle lurched forward.

She executed a U-turn on the highway and stopped next to Wild Bill. Her first impulse was to kill him, but that would jeopardize the alliance between the two groups. Instead, she pulled her cell phone out of a pouch in her equipment vest and dialed a familiar number. After speaking a few words, she replaced the phone in the pouch, then raced the powerful machine through the gears, and headed toward the headquarters—and Duncan.

∽∽∽∽

"Where's Iron Angel?" Duncan's voice was raspy.

He pressed his lips into white bands. Kearney and Jason supported his weight as he sank into the recliner in his living room.

"I don't know." Kearney handed Duncan a prescription bottle. "She was a couple bikes behind us, I think, with Wild Bill."

Duncan frowned as he popped the bottle open with his thumb. "Get him up here. I want to know where she is." He held the bottle as if he was drinking water. Three capsules slid into his mouth. He placed the open bottle onto the end table.

Vibrations and the roar of motorcycle engines filled the room. Gunther peered between two slats of the window blinds and watched a dozen or more Harley Davidsons accelerate away from Colors II, disregarding honking horns and screeching tires of the street traffic. When the vibrations faded, the room fell deathly still.

"There's something you should know, Duncan," Jason said. "Wild Bill grabbed Iron Angel in the basement once. She said—"

"I know. She told me."

Jason ran his fingers over his hair down to his ponytail. "I would have said something, but she swore me and Bill to silence."

"I know that, too." With a smile that was more of a grimace, Duncan said, "We don't have many secrets."

The three men turned their heads in unison as Red Dog burst into the room. "Little Al got a call that Wild Bill was in an accident." He looked from one C-IA member to the other, eventually settling his gaze on Duncan. "If they received a phone call, it must mean Iron Angel is okay, right? I mean, somebody had to make that call." His voice trailed off when Duncan's head flopped back onto the headrest on the recliner.

Duncan looked at the ceiling. "Did anyone say it was Iron Angel who called?"

"No, but—"

Duncan rolled his head toward Red Dog. "Go. Catch up to your brother bikers. Find out what happened and get back to me ay-sap."

"I'll go with you," Jason said, and the two men ran out of the apartment.

Five minutes later, Duncan turned his head to take in the ripped clothing, the blood, the limp as Iron Angel entered their living room.

She had raced toward the headquarters, quickly leaving Wild Bill behind as the road flew by under the tires of the bike. When she had seen the line of Harleys coming toward her, first dread then relief had washed over her—dread that they would recognize Wild Bill's bike and chase her down, relief because none of them did.

Joe-Sam rushed into the room with wet washcloths and an ice pack. Duncan waited while Iron Angel took the items from the two brothers and started patting at the blood on her knees. He motioned for Joe-Sam to leave the room.

When they were gone, Duncan said, "I heard you were in an accident. Are you okay?"

She stopped blotting the blood from her wounds and set her jaw. "It was no accident." She patted her elbows with the bloody, wet cloth.

"What does that mean?"

Without looking up, she said, "Just what I said."

"You have to get right to the point. I took some pain meds. What do you mean, it wasn't an accident?"

With the washcloth in mid-blot, she looked straight at Duncan. "He was taking me away from you, so I made him lay down the bike."

"You asked him to turn around first, right?"

"Well, sort of." She flinched as she blotted her butt that looked like red scrambled eggs. "It was really more of a demand. I don't know what he was up to, but—"

"Do you think it had anything to do with the incident in the basement?"

"I didn't ask why he was taking me out to the desert. And, frankly, I don't care." She looked around for some place to put down the damp, bloody washcloths. Kearney took them from her and she continued, "I just wanted to get back to you. And he wouldn't turn the bike around."

"Please tell me he's not dead."

"I don't know. He wasn't moving when I left him."

"Did you at least check before leaving him lying in the hot sun?" Kearney asked.

"For all I knew, the man was kidnapping me. I wasn't going to render first aid to the no-good piece of shit."

"Kidnapping is a little strong." Duncan winced as he changed position. Once resettled, he sighed in relief. "This will strain our alliance with the Brotherhood."

Applying ice to her knee, Iron Angel replied absently, "They'll understand that I wanted to get back here to you."

"Not likely," Duncan said weakly. His eyes were getting heavy.

"I'll take care of it. You just get some rest," she said.

Duncan's eyes opened wide for a second then fluttered to half-mast. The pain and the medication was draining his energy. "No. I know how you take care of things. Kearney takes the lead on this." She opened her mouth to protest, but Duncan put up a finger to stop her. "You left their president lying on the side of the road. In the middle of the desert. In the hot sun. And rode away on *his* bike. He better be alive. If he's dead, there won't be anything I can do."

CHAPTER 24

Cars raised clouds of dust as they pulled into the vegetable-slash-taco stand on Route 10 eight miles west of Phoenix. It was a small, family-owned business, and as far as the tacos were concerned, it was a terrific roadside stopover. Off to the side were picnic tables for travelers who wanted to eat their tacos before getting back onto the highway. Wearing dark sunglasses and an Arizona Suns baseball cap, Iron Angel sat at one of the tables next to her dark red Honda.

As she took another bite of her taco, she watched two kids, oblivious of potential danger, pile out of a dusty Chevy. Parents rushed to herd them out of the pathway of cars pulling in and backing out.

After loud admonishments by the parents and sulky responses by the kids, they disappeared behind a long table loaded high with cabbages and ears of corn.

The unmistakable rumble of an approaching Harley Davidson caught her attention. She pushed the last of the taco into her mouth and wiped her fingers on a napkin. Dust billowed from the tires of Little Al's bike as he pulled into the parking lot and parked his big Harley beside her Honda. With exaggerated purpose, he heeled-down the kickstand and leaned the Harley over. Assured the ground would hold the weight of the bike, he dismounted and walked around the Honda to where she was sitting.

"Do you want to talk here, or go somewhere else," he asked.

"Here's fine, if it's okay with you."

"I'll get something to eat. Want me to take that?" he asked, indicating the empty red-and-white cardboard "boat" that had held her taco and fries.

She handed it over. As she sipped sweet tea, she watched Little Al bend over to talk to the server inside the taco stand. It was interesting to watch people move away from the hulking biker. He looked formidable, but he was here on a mission of mercy. At least, that's what she hoped. Duncan had chosen the Let-Iron-Angel-Squirm leadership method, similar to the way he had dealt with her following her arrest in Cleveland a couple years before.

She knew it was to get her to think about her actions and to make her stronger and more independent. Meanwhile relations between the C-IA and the Brotherhood grew tense, bordering on explosive.

In desperation, she had texted Little Al, asking him to meet her at this neutral meeting site. The two groups occupied the same building and what had seemed like a good idea a month or so ago, had become a living nightmare.

The potential for violence was enormous, and the only thing keeping an armed confrontation at bay was the pending apology Wild Bill demanded from Iron Angel—an odd way for a motorcycle club to work out a solution, but the president was the undisputed leader. What he decided was law.

With the weight of the outcome falling on her shoulders alone instead of the leadership of both groups, a lot was riding on her attitude and choice of words. Attitude and verbal communication—not her two best qualities. She waited as Little Al ate. He downed a taco in two bites. After stuffing a dozen French fries into his mouth, he took a long drag on his soda. He wiped his beard and moustache with a paper napkin, belched, and opened the conversation.

"I hear you're going to meet with the Brotherhood leadership tonight. Any idea what you're going to say?"

She crossed her arms on the picnic table and leaned on them. "Any suggestions?"

"I know how I would do it, but you are going to have to walk a fine line. Too bold, and you'll set them off. Too soft, and they'll think they can steamroll right over you. I wouldn't want to be in your shoes."

The apology scheduled for that night had been weighing on her mind. She was not sorry for what she did to Wild Bill. He deserved what he got—and more. The C-IA faction supported her and offered moral s

But the bikers questioned whether she should have shown more restraint. She *did* exercise restraint. He was alive, wasn't he?

Kearney's words had echoed in her head for days. "Sometimes you have to play the game." She curled her ponytail around her finger trying to figure out what the game was. Stepping into Wild Bill's arena made it *his* game. Exactly what game would he play?

Men claimed to be simple creatures, but she felt testosterone made them unpredictable. How should she play the game of testosterone? She didn't have any, didn't want any, and surely didn't understand how it affected the actions and thoughts of men.

Men were strange creatures at best.

Little Al finished his second taco—in three bites this time.

She took a long sip and slurped that last of her iced tea. "Tact isn't one of my stronger points. I thought I'd just say what was on my mind and hope it's good enough."

"Think again," he said with the last of the French fries stuffed in his mouth. With the help of some soda, he swallowed the fries and continued. "There's a lot riding on these two minutes, or however long it takes to say what you're gonna say. Think of the first moon landing—few words, historic impact."

"Okay." She took the top off the Styrofoam cup and slid the ice toward her mouth. She snagged an iced cube and, between crunches on it, said, "How about 'Be grateful you're alive. Now let's get back to business as usual'?"

"That's wonderful, that's perfect—if you have a death wish." A silence fell between them. After a couple minutes, he broke the silence. "You're lucky he likes you. Otherwise, we wouldn't be having this conversation, if you catch my drift."

She dropped her head into her hands. "Yeah, I kinda picked up on that. Why me?"

"You're an alpha female. None of his old ladies had that sense of leadership. You stood up to him—presented a challenge—and Wild Bill *loves* a challenge."

"It was a rhetorical question, Little Al." She lifted her head. "Wait, old ladies, as in plural?"

The big biker chuckled. "He goes through 'em like a buzz saw."

She moaned. "Maybe I should give this apology more thought."

"Yeah, maybe." He removed the top from his Styrofoam cup and guzzled the rest of his soda.

When he was down to just ice in his cup, he thoughtfully swirled the ice cubes around for a moment then offered some words of advice. "I read a devotion once that talked about not letting past failures haunt you. Even though you make mistakes, refuse to keep going over and over them. Admit to them. Make plans to correct them. And move on. You made a mistake. Express your regret and promise to do better. Wild Bill isn't a heathen. He remembers that you saved the lives of two of the Brotherhood when you could have walked away." He added with a wink and a slow nod, "And remember, he *likes* you."

She ignored the dig. "You're right. When you make a mistake, pick yourself up, and dust yourself off. It was just a mistake. And mistakes aren't fatal, right?"

"Right. Mistakes aren't fatal, except if you make a mistake during the apology. *That* just might be the exception to the rule. No pressure or anything."

"Did you come here to help me? If so, you're not doing so good."

He chuckled. "Don't worry. Act sincere and apologetic. Throw him a bone. Help him save face. You have to remember, he got knocked out and his bike stolen by a *girl*. Let him be the man in the room, if you know what I mean."

"Let him be the man," she repeated, considering the idea out loud. "Like I let Duncan be the man in our relationship."

"You *let* Duncan be the man? I thought he *was* the man." Little Al's blue eyes sparkled with amusement.

"He's gonna be 'the man with a dead girlfriend,' if I don't get this right."

CHAPTER 25

They were on their way home from a day at the Renaissance Fair. A sizzling, sunny day filled with comedy acts, craft kiosks, and great food—to say nothing about a crowd of people and no surveillance cameras—had transported them into a fantasy-filled world that was light years from their everyday lives. The fair wasn't Duncan's idea of fun. His enjoyment came from watching Iron Angel decompress and unwind as the hours passed.

Little Al drove while Duncan sat in the back seat with one arm draped around her as she nestled against him. The position made his slowly-recovering shoulder muscles ache but he refused to move his arm. Two weeks ago this woman put her life on the line to save his. Pain be damned, he wasn't letting go of her. He leaned his head forward and smiled at the relaxed expression on her face.

He caressed the sunburn line on her shoulder. The skin that had been protected by her sleeveless shirt was golden, but it stopped abruptly where the sun had done its damage. He marveled at how such a tough woman was so vulnerable in so many ways and tightened his embrace.

He thought back over the covert meeting he had had with Wild Bill and his VP, Blackie. He apologized for Iron Angel's lack of judgment and mended fences with the Demon Brotherhood. They had made a secret pact that Bill would accept Iron Angel's apology, but not until after making her squirm a little. Duncan didn't ask that of Bill to be mean, but he wanted to impress upon her that actions had consequences, and he wouldn't always be there to protect her—although in this case he was there, behind the scenes, smoothing everything out.

Most importantly, he wanted her to have some experience dealing with leaders of other groups. If something happened to him, she was the most logical person to take over the militia. She had leadership abilities, but she had to develop tact and a sense of compromise.

After a tense, potentially explosive week, Iron Angel's apology marked a turnaround in the hostilities between the Demon Brotherhood and his Counter-Insurgency Army. During the weeks following the apology, tensions eased and reconciliation began. But the laughter was too loud, the slap on the back too hard, the friendly one-ups-man-ship a little too sharp.

Duncan hoped time together in a neutral setting would level things out. He had suggested this outing to rebuild trust and friendships between the two groups—and to keep a close eye on the interactions between them.

He glanced over his shoulder out the back window. Behind them Joe-Sam were enjoying Samuel's new Camaro. Kearney's van followed. With him was a new female militia member he was dating. Gunther was in the back seat with his lady friend. Somewhere behind them, several Brotherhood members and their old ladies were enjoying the ride on their motorcycles. Jason and Flora rode with them. Duncan faced forward, hoping Flora's recovery from the loss of her baby was a positive sign for the future.

After a few miles, the bikers roared passed the cars and disappeared in the rippling heat waves rising from the pavement. It left the three vehicles of militia members driving on the straight, flat highway, heading back to Phoenix.

Iron Angel stirred. Duncan stroked her hair and eased his embrace. She relaxed, gave out a little sigh, and settled back under his arm. He smiled. For the last several months, she had circled the rim like a basketball. Instead of spinning off out of bounds, she seemed to have dropped through the net.

He was pleased and, for the first time, hopeful that she was back on track—or at least headed in the right direction. He looked through the heavily tinted side window at the barren landscape as it flew past. Since the kidnapping, his sense of invincibility was shaken. It was a foreign and uncomfortable sensation. He had seen this same thing happen to other mercenaries over the years, but never thought it would happen to him. Iron Angel's appeal for the peaceful life under the radar was more alluring now than ever. He shook his head at his self-absorbed attitude. A quiet life was all she had ever wanted from him. When she had gone missing, he had vowed to put her first, and when *La Espada* was defeated it would be all about her. He couldn't quit now, but it would be over soon. Soon he would marry her and settle down.

His phone vibrated, and he pulled it out of his pocket. "Talk to me."

"I think we're being followed," Kearney said.

Duncan glanced down at Iron Angel, not wanting this tranquil interlude to slip away. "What makes you say that?"

"He pulled out of the fair parking lot right after us. We slowed down to get him to pass, and he didn't. He slowed down, too."

"Turn-offs are few and far between. Maybe they're just going the same way." She eased out of Duncan's embrace. "Keep me posted," he said, before cutting the connection. "I didn't mean to wake you up. Why don't you put your head back on my shoulder and relax?"

She stretched and inhaled to expand her lungs. Through the exhale she said, "Ask him if there are three females in the car and if they're wearing pink ball caps."

"How did you—"

"I could hear his voice."

Duncan speed dialed Kearney and asked him about the women and caps. He got his answer and disconnected the call.

"He says there's a man driving and a woman and two little girls, and the females all have pink caps. Are you psychic now?" He couldn't resist the urge to turn and look, even though he knew he couldn't possibly see the tail, if that's what it was.

"No." She grabbed a water bottle out of the cup holder,

opened it and took a swig of the cool water. "Remember when we were all sitting at the picnic tables eating ice cream, and I told you I felt like we were being watched? And you told me to turn off my instincts and relax? Well, I looked around, anyway, and to our left there was a guy taking a picture of his family."

"A guy taking a picture of his family got your spidey-senses revved up?"

"It wasn't so much a dad taking a picture of his kids as much as what seemed out of place." She took another swig of water.

"Which was?"

She screwed the cap onto the bottle and looked at him through the corner of her eye. "All your Special Forces training and you didn't notice it?"

"Notice what?"

"Damn, it's a good thing you have me."

Duncan frowned. He was getting sloppy and distracted. It *was* a good thing he had her.

She got right to the point. "This wonderful dad put his kids right in the middle of the gravel area to take the picture. No minstrel player, no jester, no Renaissance backdrop, no mom. Just his kids in the middle of nowhere with guess what in the background—" She didn't wait for his answer. "Us."

∽∾∾

Agent Ramirez was trying to act relaxed and normal, but he knew he wasn't fooling his wife. She had been staring at him off and on since they left the fair parking lot. Her mood gained in intensity as the miles drifted by.

After turning on the DVD player and inserting a disc for the movie *Despicable Me* to keep the girls occupied, his wife turned in her seat to face him. "Okay, what's going on?"

A smile appeared under his dark mustache. "Nothing. What makes you say that?"

She glared back at him. He couldn't hide anything from his wife of fifteen years.

Friday afternoon, the Phoenix fusion center had received an anonymous tip that a woman who might be a former member of the Constitution Defense Legion was in the Phoenix area. Agent Ramirez had immediately downloaded all the information and photos in the case. This afternoon, he thought he recognized the woman and two of the men whose photos had been part of the download. It was a stroke of luck that he could not overlook.

He was being very careful about following them, and was reasonably sure he was still undetected. If he could find out where they were headed, it would be something to go on when he got into the office. He knew it wasn't right to tail fugitives with his family in the car. He was a federal agent 24-7, but his family was not. He would have to cut this off soon.

Before leaving the fair, he uploaded his photos to the number at the Pittsburgh fusion center. It might be a false alarm, but he didn't want to take the chance of losing fugitives who had been on the run for over a year. The case file said the trail had gone cold at the Texas border with Mexico. After months of dead ends and no new leads, the task force had been disbanded. The open case was the sole responsibility of one man, Special Agent Woyzeck.

൚൚൚

While Agent Ramirez was following suspected criminals in Arizona, Special Agent Woyzeck was winching his fifteen-foot sailboat onto its trailer. He had spent the afternoon and early evening on the lake at Moraine State Park in western Pennsylvania, enjoying the fresh air and sailing with his family. His phone chirped, indicating an incoming text.

His wife shook her head in disgust. He knew she wanted to get through one day without work interrupting their family time. As he watched his family loading the trunk of the car with coolers and other equipment, he checked the photos the Arizona agent uploaded to his phone.

The world around Special Agent Woyzeck froze in time. His heart stopped then started beating furiously. In the middle of the first photograph was Joan Bowman. She was wearing sunglasses and an Arizona Suns baseball cap, but he'd recognize that face anywhere. The man to her right was Dennis Archer, aka Duncan, and the man standing at the end of the table looking at the female to his left was Kearney, whose real name had never been determined—it was as if he never existed. Woyzeck didn't recognize any of the other faces, but once he got into the office, it would be only a matter of time. He texted a reply confirming the identities of the three suspects and reminded Agent Ramirez this group was armed and dangerous. He pocketed his phone and finished securing the boat with slow, deliberate movements, trying to hide his exhilaration from his wife.

The case had become personal to Agent Woyzeck, and he worked an angle of it almost daily. He'd put his well-deserved retirement on hold until Bowman and Archer were behind bars. He had been a part of deposing Bowman when she gave state's evidence and had been instrumental in working out the deal. Even worse, she had been kidnapped out of his car en route to prison. He felt both responsible for losing her under his watch and betrayed. Betrayed because he had made the best deal he could for her and he had saved her from certain death at the hands of the Legion. Yet, she willingly returned to the same toxic subculture. He shook his head, checked the hitch, and headed toward the driver's door.

As he slid into the driver's seat next to his scowling wife, he knew his life was about to go from slow motion to mach-one.

He had to get to Arizona.

CHAPTER 26

Duncan formulated steps to determine if they were being followed. "Little Al, call your sons and tell them to head east at the next intersection and go directly to Rally Point A, unless they're being followed. If they're followed, tell 'em to keep driving to give the rest of us time to catch up to them and get them off the hook."

Little Al immediately dialed Joe-Sam.

Duncan phoned Kearney. "We're gonna do some evasive actions to see if we're being tailed. Joe-Sam will take the next exit and head east. We're going to head west at the same intersection. You guys continue straight ahead."

While Duncan filled Kearney in on the details, Iron Angel unclicked her seatbelt and leaned forward. "What's the next intersection, Little Al?"

"Route 202."

She leaned back and put a hand on Duncan's thigh. "Bad news. If we get off and go west, we'll be in a direct path to the rally point. I don't think you want that, right?"

Duncan shook his head while he texted Jason. "See what else we can do."

She leaned forward, stared at the GPS on the dashboard, and touched Little Al's wife on the shoulder. "I'm sorry to get you involved in this. It might be nothing, but we have to be sure. They probably don't realize the boys are with us. They'll let them go and follow the rest of us."

The mother nodded and looked away.

After studying the GPS, Joan said, "Little Al, turn west at the next opportunity past Route 202."

They rode in silence for two miles. Iron Angel leaned on the backs of the two front seats, concentrating on the road ahead. At the exit ramp, Joe-Sam peeled off as ordered, and their mother's head turned to follow the car as it made the wide sweep onto Route 202. The concerned mother watched until her sons were out of sight.

Duncan's phone beeped as Iron Angel put a hand on the loving mother's shoulder. "They'll be all right. They're smart kids."

Joe-Sam's mom glanced over her shoulder at Iron Angel, nodded, and faced forward.

"Gunther says the tail is still behind them," Duncan said.

She patted Joe-Sam's mother's shoulder again and glanced back at Duncan. She did a double-take when she saw him studying her. She kept her eyes on him but asked Little Al, "How far to the next exit?"

He glanced at the GPS screen. "One-point-three miles."

She peeled her eyes from Duncan and studied the GPS screen again. After a couple seconds, she leaned back in the seat and reached for Duncan's hand. "If we take Route 60 East, it parallels Route 202, and eventually intersects with it," she whispered. "If we aren't followed, we could catch up to Joe-Sam."

Without hesitation Duncan said, "Little Al, go east on 60 instead of west." He looked back at her, smiled, and nuzzled her ear. "Aren't you the caring little she-bear all of a sudden?"

She elbowed him in the ribs. A few miles later, Little Al turned onto the gently sloping exit ramp onto Route 60 East, Kearney stayed on the highway as planned. Duncan frowned when Little Al told him the possible tail was behind them. A knot tightened in Iron Angel's stomach. They were approaching the southern city limits of Phoenix. If they were going to do something, they'd have to do it soon.

"Get off at the next exit and onto the city streets," Duncan said. "If he follows, do what you have to do to get him someplace where we can take care of this."

"There are kids in the car," she reminded him.

Duncan released her hand. "*I'm* not the one putting his kids in danger." He must have seen the concern on her face, because he looked deeply into her eyes and put a gentle hand on the side of her face. "It'll be okay, my angel. I don't hurt children. We'll do everything we can to make sure they don't get hurt—or their mom."

She exhaled when the car did not follow them off the ramp. She hadn't realized she'd been holding her breath, hoping a beautiful day with Duncan wouldn't be ruined. Violence seemed to follow them like smoke from a campfire—no matter where they stood, it blew toward them. She leaned back and took a long, cool drink of water.

Little Al looked in the rear view mirror. "What do you want to do?"

"Call Joe-Sam. Tell them it was a false alarm and go ahead home."

Duncan dialed Kearney. "Meet up back at headquarters. If we go to the rally point, we can't use it again."

ოოო

The meeting was held in the middle room of the three-room apartment used as the militia's headquarters. Joan was fussing over Flora, and Kearney was passing out bottles of beer when Duncan asked everyone to take a seat so they could bring Jason up to speed on the events.

Jason kissed Flora, who made her exit. Iron Angel turned to follow her.

"You stay." Duncan nodded toward the chair in front of Iron Angel. "You've earned your place at this table."

She looked around the table at the men seated there. She wasn't a member of the leadership but, when there were no objections, she pulled out the chair and sat down.

After listening to the description of the events on the ride home, Jason said, "I can see a few possibilities. First, we're all on edge and blowing some small inconsistency out of proportion. Or it was some law enforcement guy out with his family who recognized one or more of us and followed us briefly. Or they are onto us, and we have to go into full protection mode."

"Let's think this through," Duncan said. "We don't want to ramp up and waste a lot of energy and resources only to find out it was just some guy going in the same direction as us."

"Iron Angel noticed unusual behavior at the fair," Kearney said. "And these very same people left the grounds right behind us and got off on at the same exit as the leader of our group. I don't like this at all."

"How many exits are on that highway? Very few. It could be just a coincidence," Duncan insisted.

Gunther casually draped his arm over the back of his chair. "I don't believe in coincidences."

"Me, either," Jason agreed.

Iron Angel crossed her arms. "My instincts have never let us down."

"Then there's that," Kearney said. "My money's on Iron Angel."

Her gaze snapped to Kearney's eyes. The ordeal in the desert had formed a fledgling bond between them. It was weak, but tenable, and time would tell how it would play out. It was comforting to know he supported her.

He gave her a chin nod before taking a swig of beer.

Duncan leaned his forearms on the table and scraped his chair in closer. "We don't know exactly what this was, but we have to consider the possibility that there might be something to it. So what can we do that won't put a kink in our operations, but still protect us?"

"I have some ideas, but I don't want to step on your toes," Iron Angel said to Kearney.

"I have the feeling you're going to, anyway," he responded. When she didn't say anything in response, he said, "Go ahead."

She sat up straight. "There are some things we can do to tighten security without going overboard. We can start using throw-away phones for business dealings. If we're going to assume we're being followed, we have to assume the phones are tapped. If not now, they will be soon." She looked around the room but couldn't read the faces of the men she'd come to know so well. "It's never too early to get in the habit of good communication discipline," she continued. "We can establish challenge and passwords. Set up code words for situations we can foresee." She stopped when she realized Kearney had not been serious about letting her jump into a security actions summary. She leaned back in her chair. "Just to name a few." She looked from Kearney to Duncan and back to Kearney. Duncan was scowling, so she added, "I'm sorry, Duncan, I thought he gave me the okay to go ahead."

Duncan zeroed in on Kearney. "You are head of security. Why didn't you think of these things?"

"I was going to bring them up, but she jumped in before I could stop her."

"Don't insult my intelligence." Duncan's eyes pierced through Kearney. His hands gripped the edge of the table. The room fell silent and everyone stilled. "I sat here and heard you give her permission to speak about security issues. Now I have to decide if you are incompetent or lazy."

She tapped him on the arm.

He pushed her hand away without taking his eyes off Kearney. "Or are you overworked and can't handle all that I've dropped into your lap. Give us the room."

With the last four words, everyone jumped out of their chairs and scrambled into the hallway, leaving Kearney alone with Duncan's growing anger.

As soon as the door closed behind them, Gunther poked his finger in Iron Angel's sternum. "Damn you. You and Kearney were starting to get along. Now he's really going to be out to get you."

"Don't you poke your finger at me." She grabbed his hand and leaned into him so their noses were inches apart. "I took Kearney out once when we were in the Legion, and I can take him out again. And I can take out you, too, you gray-haired old goat."

They glared at each other for a couple seconds. The change started in the corners of Gunther's eyes. He pressed his lips together, then suppressed laughter squeeze between his lips with a "Pffft."

They both started snickering.

"That's the best you could do? Gray-haired old goat?" Gunther asked between fits of laughter.

She gave him a friendly shove.

Duncan yelled Iron Angel's name from the room they'd just left. She hesitated at the edge in his voice, but Jason pushed her toward the door.

The door opened to Duncan looming in the opening. "Dammit, get in here."

She rushed past Duncan and slid into the nearest chair, opposite the grinning Kearney. Her gut twisted into a knot.

Duncan gave her a hard stare. "You are taking over security and operations."

She shot up to her feet and leaned on the table. "I made it clear, I don't want any responsibilities. I'll help out with the missions. I'll train people in hand-to-hand combat, anything except a leadership position, especially after how things turned out with the Legion."

"It was not an offer or a suggestion. This is not up for discussion."

"Or what? You'll kick me out of the group? Or make me eat spinach?"

"I'm not in the mood for your sarcasm, and I don't have the luxury of time to deal with it." Duncan's unblinking eyes and set of his jaw silenced her. "Security and operations is what you do best—better than anyone I know. We need to discuss security and we need to do it now."

She leaned on her elbows, before hunching into her seat. She stared at the table. Just the thought of what lay ahead was exhausting. The old paranoia and dread engulfed her. She could decline, but flinching at responsibility wasn't part of her nature. Her stomach soured. *Damn Duncan.* She glared at Kearney. *And double-damn Kearney.*

Duncan looked at Kearney. "Tell her what you just told me."

"Well—" Kearney started.

It wasn't fast enough for Duncan. "Kearney hasn't done any security work. No vetting. No setting up of safe houses. Nothing."

"By no vetting, I'm assuming you mean of new militia members?"

Duncan nodded.

She opened her mouth several times to speak, but couldn't find the words to express her shock, her disbelief, her fear. She finally found her voice. "Any number of these new members could be undercover agents or moles for *La Espada* or have records that could sink the group. How could you be so stupid? How could you be so careless?" She set her jaw and said through clenched teeth, "You put us all at risk."

"Maybe you haven't noticed," Kearney said, "but I've been busy with arms procurement and combat firing training while you played around with your martial arts and sat around—"

"Played around? *Sat* around?"

Her face turned red with rage. She raced around the table at Kearney. He jumped up from his chair and backed up until he stood in front of the window that opened onto the small back-yard.

Duncan moved to block her path. "What's done is done."

"You mean what hasn't been done, *hasn't* been done."

Duncan grabbed her shoulders. "Calm down. We can't change what has been done or not done, we can only move forward from here."

"Yeah, with me doing Kearney's job." She leaned to her left and looked past Duncan. "The job he should have been doing these past four months." She pointed her finger at Kearney. "If you couldn't do the job, you should have said something *before* we got into this situation. I was beginning to think I had been wrong about you. That you just might have some redeeming quality, but you're the same lazy-ass, worthless piece of shit I always thought you were. You—"

"Put a lid on it," Duncan interjected. "Name-calling isn't going to get us back on track. Let's sit down and calmly discuss where we go from here."

No one made a move.

"Seats. *Now.*"

She and Kearney slid into the nearest chairs, bumping shoulders as they wound up sitting next to each other.

CHAPTER 27

The past week had been long days checking police records, longer nights tailing borderline members to check out their lifestyles, even longer hours hunting for the perfect safe house. Caffeine lost its effect somewhere around the fifth day, which left cursing Kearney as the only stimulant to keep Iron Angel awake.

She crossed her arms on the conference table and put her head down. The headquarters was quiet. The meeting wouldn't start for another five minutes. She could use that time for a rejuvenating power nap. She tried to relax and let sleep overtake her. *Just five minutes. I'll be good for another four hours. Just...five...minutes...*

Her breathing slowed, but her body resisted letting go.

"You're here already?" Kearney asked as he entered the room.

She raised her head and squinted at him over the dark circles under her eyes. "That's it. You're dead. You just don't know it, yet."

Kearney stopped with his hand on the back of a chair. "Whoa, what'd I do?"

"What haven't you done?"

He slid into the chair at the end of the table to her right. "Hey, I went out with you at night, tailing guys. I tried to make it up to you."

"Yeah, except for those nights you were bone dancing with that new female member, what's her name?"

"Misha."

"That's not her real name."

"I know. It's Doris, but the name Misha is hotter than Doris. Exotic, like her."

"I need to talk to you about her."

"She's okay. Actually, she's better than okay—"

"Stop. You're private life does *not* interest me. But she does. She's on my short list."

"Jealous?" Kearney asked with a double lift of both eyebrows.

"Just don't tell her anything until I'm sure. Okay?"

Kearney shrugged.

She put her head back down on her arms. "Can you sit quietly for five minutes and let me get some sleep?"

It was hard to relax with Kearney in the room. He was probably staring at her. And the information she had dug up over the last several days swirled around her head. Out of fifteen new members, only two were iffy. Doris, exotically known as Misha, and the newest member, some guy whose name she couldn't recall in her sleep-deprived state.

Her thoughts turned to the safe house. She had found the ideal set up in the little overlooked town of Salome. Nestled in the mountains west of Phoenix, it was far enough to be out of the way, yet close enough to get to in a pinch. Just off Route 10, the standalone, unused storefront was perfect. Rear access from an alley opened into a small backroom with an ancient, musty-smelling kitchenette. Off the kitchenette was a grungy bathroom with only a toilet and a once-white porcelain sink. *Better Homes and Gardens* it was not.

"Anybody know what this meeting is about?" Jason asked as he pulled out a chair next to Kearney, who gestured to be quiet and jerked his head toward Iron Angel.

Jason lifted his chin and, with an impish smile, said loudly, "Hey, Iron Angel, you're not going to get any work done with your head on your arms."

Before she could tell him what dark hellish place to go to, Gunther strode into the room, held the door for Duncan, then took a seat opposite her.

Pulling out his chair to her left, Duncan started the meeting without hesitation. "We have some important things to cover, so let's get started."

She plopped against the chair back in resignation and looked at Duncan. She felt him taking in the disheveled hair, dark circles under her eyes, newly added lines around her mouth.

"You okay?" he asked.

They hadn't seen much of each other the last few days.

"Yeah. I'm fine." Her gaze remained on Duncan, choosing to ignore her tormenters to her right.

After another couple seconds of scrutiny, Duncan told Kearney to share the latest information.

"We are low on ammo and guns."

Short and sweet. Kearney could be depended on to neatly sum up the problem. *Meeting's over. My bed is calling me.* But her mouth betrayed her. "How can we be low after that great haul a month ago?"

"We've been doing some intensive firearms training, which burned up a lot of the rounds, and with the ghosting of guns policy, and the small sorties we've had, the arsenal is getting low. If we didn't ghost the guns and held onto them—"

Duncan cut him off. "The ghosting policy stays. It keeps the authorities busy trying to find out who's taking out the *La Espada* fighters." He looked pointedly at Iron Angel. "Ghosting will save us from being nailed down by ballistics."

She knew he was referring to her FPG, but it was a rare, expensive, and irreplaceable rifle. Rather than stand up to his stare, she closed her eyes and rubbed her face with both hands. It was too exhausting to think about giving it up. She had killed to get it. She would kill to keep it. Or she would if she wasn't so damn tired.

"One of our regular suppliers turned us on to this group that's promised a boatload of rifles, handguns, ammo, everything we need," Kearney said.

She stopped rubbing her face and looked at him as if to say, "So then why are we here?"

Noting her look, he continued, "There's a catch. They want to meet the boss."

She dropped her hands and looked at Duncan. She leaned toward him, shaking her head. "No. Oh, no. No one meets the boss. No respectable arms dealer asks to meet the boss. No." She looked at Kearney. "No." She looked at Gunther and Jason. "No."

"They won't transact a deal this size without meeting the boss," Kearney said.

"Then we go somewhere else."

"There isn't anyone else who can deal in these numbers."

"Then we do several smaller deals with our regulars."

Kearney leaned forward. "Don't you think we tried? They can't scare up enough. Their suppliers are dry."

The hair stood up on the back of her neck. "Dry. What does that mean? They don't have any arms or they aren't dealing?"

"They wouldn't say."

She matched Kearney's abrupt tone with her own. "Or you didn't ask."

The room went silent to give the security chief time to digest the news. She finally asked, "What happens if we don't take this shipment?"

"We can't continue."

"Then we suspend ops until we're resupplied and fully ready to fight." She turned to Duncan. His face was unreadable which told her to work this out with Kearney. She rubbed small circles on her temples. "Okay, let's think this through. Maybe I'm overreacting. If our regular suppliers can't *get* supplies, it could mean there's a kink in the supply chain. Could be anything. Could be the ATF. If it's the ATF, we might be insulated from investigation for a while. If they are *refusing* to deal with us after all the business we've thrown their way, it only means one thing—someone got to them. Someone with deeper pockets than our rancher buddies."

She looked at each of the men around the table. They were watching her, waiting for her assessment of the problem. "They won't—or can't—deal with us. That funnels us to this brand-new group that magically appeared out of nowhere, who can miraculously get everything we want and need. The only thing that's missing is the pretty little bow."

"You're jumping to conclusions," Duncan said.

"Am I? The way I see it, the feds—or someone—is involved and most likely trying to sink us. We need to bump up security another notch. And that means treading carefully in uncharted waters." She waited for someone to come to her defense, but their silence told her she was on her own on this one. "Look, Duncan, I know you want to win this battle. I do, too, but we can't win it from behind bars or from the grave. A little caution is all I'm asking for."

"We need these weapons and ammo," he said.

Even through the dull ache of fatigue, every nerve ending in her body prickled. "This stinks. Before we do *anything*, we need to figure out what's really going on, and who is involved."

"We don't have the time to spare." Duncan looked to his left. "Gunther?"

"We can't let up now. *La Espada* is almost whipped. This reminds me of the Tet Offensive in Nam. The Viet Cong put everything they had into that and we beat 'em. If only we'd continued the fight. If only we'd kept up the pressure, we would have won that war." He looked at each of the people around the table. "I don't know about anyone else, but I'm not an 'If-Only' kinda guy."

Duncan looked across the table. "Jason?"

He rubbed the dot of hair under his lower lip with his index finger, leaned his tattooed arms on the table, and cleared his throat. "We're sitting ducks without an arsenal and sufficient ammo. Choose the right place. I can get us in and out."

"You're a tactics guru, Jason, but what if it turns out to be the *feds*?" she asked.

"A motivated force will always prevail. We're nothing if not motivated. And tactics is what I do."

She tried to glower at Jason, but was sure it only came across as a sleepy, blank stare. Damn she needed sleep.

"And we don't know for a fact that it's anything other than a new, well-connected arms dealer," Jason continued.

She looked at Duncan. "All the more reason to step back. Check it out first. It could be *La Espada*. It could even be a back-stab by the bikers. It's too iffy."

"Then do your job, Iron Angel. Do it fast. Do it well. It's a Go." He stood up.

She raised her hands palms up. "When did this become a democracy?" but she was talking to his back. Helpless, she watched him leave the room.

Nothing about this mission was promising. Too many unknowns. Too many weak links. Too many red flags. And too damn neat. She could see it through her sleep-deprived haze, why couldn't anyone else see it?

She leaned toward Jason and glared into his eyes, tapping the table with her index finger for emphasis. "You better plan this as if we were going up against Navy SEALs."

"We don't know that this is a sting," Jason said.

She stood up and pointed at him. "Navy SEALs."

She left the room. Maybe it wasn't too late to talk some sense into Duncan.

CHAPTER 28

The sun had already sunk below the horizon, but its rays still illuminated the sky with bright orange mixed with shades of yellow and pink. Facing south and crouched with her back to a cinder block building, Iron Angel soaked in the last light of day.

A freight train rumbled past as she pulled a laminated Google satellite map from a pocket of her black equipment vest. It was already imprinted in her memory, but she hoped the situation had improved since the last time she looked at it—two minutes ago.

"How many times are you gonna look at that map?" Duncan asked. He squatted to her left, closest to the corner of the building.

Without a word, she refolded the map, stuffed it into her right upper pocket of the vest, and secured the flap. She had failed to talk him out of this arms deal, so he wasn't her favorite person right now.

Ignoring his comment, she looked to her right and asked, "Everybody ready?"

Nods all around. Directly on her right was Dee Dee. To her right was the man Iron Angel had nicknamed Suit—this time dressed for combat. Three other militia members formed the team. They all had their game faces on. They were ready.

She mentally reviewed the satellite image. In the center were two long buildings that ran east-west. The one at her back was designated as Building One. The mirror-image building to the north was Building Two. Between the two buildings was an open paved area used predominantly for backing tractor-trailers up to the loading docks of Building Two. That's where the deal was going to go down.

On either side of these long buildings stood thirteen other commercial buildings—some occupied, most vacant. Two access roads bookended the primary long buildings in the center and connected the complex to the public road that bordered the industrial complex on the north.

Her thoughts turned to the mission. Yesterday, their contacts texted they had everything Kearney had ordered, but warned they needed to meet the C-IA leader before they would complete the deal. She didn't trust them. She couldn't find any reliable information about them. The arms dealers who had referred the C-IA to them weren't talking. In two words: This stunk.

As she had told Duncan a gut-wrenching three days ago, these unknowns didn't need to meet him. No reputable arms dealer would ask to meet the leader of the buyers. All they needed was to see the money. Money talked. If money had lost its powerful voice, it was news to her.

But she did manage to secure a compromise. Duncan agreed to initially stay back. Maybe once this new group was onsite and saw the money, they'd overlook their demand to meet him.

Well, anything's possible. She activated her throat mike. "Mamabird, this is Songbird, over."

"Go, Songbird," Joe-Sam responded.

"Where's Freebird?" she asked, using the call sign for the drone.

"Two blocks south of your location." There was a pause. "Railroad tracks are in view. I see you, now."

She looked up and saw a dark object silently moving across the darkening sky. "Mamabird, what do you see?"

Her nerves were on fire. Security and operations was her forte, but Duncan had steamrolled over her assessment and recommendations. The lack of intel meant they were basically blind. They could be walking into anything. A three-day planning period intensified her dread. She rubbed her burning stomach and glanced at Duncan.

Two rescue teams—the word rescue told her Jason didn't have any faith in this mission either—were established to save and extract Kearney, Red Dog, and their guards if the buy slid into a shitty place. Duncan was the leader of the team she was on. The other team headed by Jason and Gunther, aka Blackbird and Bluebird, was waiting on the western perimeter of the commercial complex. They had a straight-in route, but they were farther away. She and Duncan were only the width of a building away, but they had to go between the building at their back and another, smaller building to the east. A death funnel—no cover, limited entrance and egress points.

She closed her eyes and shook her head. *This just gets better and better.*

Although the temperature had dropped ten degrees since sunset, a bead of sweat formed on her forehead and trickled over her temple. She wiped it away with her bare upper arm. The uneasiness increased to a black, heavy sensation as if her blood had stopped circulating. Yet her heart was pounding. She rested her head on the building.

Joe-Sam's voice came over the radio. "Songbird, Mamabird, over.

"Go, Mamabird," Iron Angel answered.

"There are two men on top of Buildings One and Two," Joe-Sam said. "One guard is stationary on each building, watching the docking area. The other guard on each building is roving."

"Mamabird, those are our sentries."

"I don't think so."

The heaviness increased, and her heart sent the pounding to her head. Couldn't anything be easy? "Why do you say that?"

"We're all in black. I see green camouflage clothing. Could be anybody."

She looked over at Duncan who could hear what she heard through his ear buds. His chin was tucked to his chest. His eyes were pressed together, causing a scrunching at their corners.

Say something, Duncan.

Surprisingly, with all the battles the C-IA had been in, this was the first time she and Duncan would fight side-by-side—if it came to that. Duncan was a hands-off leader and always remained at the headquarters while the field teams took care of business. If this was his pre-fight preparation, she didn't want to interfere.

She eyed the new lines at the corners of his eyes. It occurred to her that he was paying a price for his leadership. This was harder on him than it was on her. She should have been more supportive. Did he understand the gravity of the demanding tasks he had given her? She groaned silently. When had their interactions, that had always kept them connected, stop?

The voice in her earbuds took her attention from away Duncan and their relationship. Joe-Sam was talking to the guys on the roof as if they could hear him. 'C'mon, c'mon, somebody look up." One must have looked up because he said, "Thank you. Doing facial recognition." Their facial recognition database was small, so it only took fifteen seconds to exhaust all data.

"Roof guy is a bogey, I say again, bogey. I'll try to get another—wait, cars." A spike of tension edged Joe-Sam's voice. "Two approaching from the east at high speed along the road on the north perimeter. One turned into the east service road at your end of the building. The other one is heading toward the west entry." There was a brief pause before Joe-Sam continued, "Guns. They're piling out of the cars heavily armed. They look like gang members."

She touched Duncan's arm. "It's a trap."

He was already standing up and warned Kearney. "Firebird, abort, abort, abort! Get out of there. Watch your backs." Then he set Jason and Gunther's team in motion. "Blackbird, Bluebird, go, go, go."

Duncan looked into Iron Angel's eyes for a fleeting second before giving the hand signal to move out. One by one, they filed around the corner of the building, hugging the wall, guns raised and ready.

They crossed the width of the building in silence, maintaining a safe tactical distance between them.

Gunshots echoed off the buildings.

❧❧❧

At Duncan's command, Jason and Gunther began their part of Kearney's rescue. Swiftly crossing the open area between their staging area and the west end of Building Two, a car screeched to a halt behind them and men on top of the buildings in front of them. Bullets whished past their heads. Other rounds kicked up chunks of pavement.

The team members dove for cover in doorways as Mamabird relayed the locations of the attackers, trying to help Jason and Gunther's team as best they could.

It was not enough.

By the time Jason and Gunther's team had knocked out the other shooters, hustled diagonally across the driveway, and broken through a glass door to make entry into Building Two, four C-IA members lay dead on the pavement. All the gang members and the guards on top of Building Two were dead.

"Through the building. Get to Kearney. Go!" Jason commanded.

"Jason, I won't be going with you."

He spun around to see Gunther hunched over, leaning on the wall just inside the door. He pulled his hand from his side. It was covered in blood.

Jason helped Gunther across the space toward the reception counter. "You're gonna be all right. Hang in there, buddy. I'll help you."

"I'm having trouble breathing. It clipped my lung. You go. I'll cover this door so they don't come up behind you."

"No!" Jason looked toward the door that led to the warehouse—and Kearney—then back at Gunther. He grabbed Gunther's vest and slowed his slide down the front of the reception counter to the floor.

"Go, Jason, before it's too late. Get Kearney."

Jason hesitated.

"Go!"

He tore open the flap holding Gunther's first aid supplies. His combat first-aid training kicked in as he applied a pressure bandages to the entrance and exit wounds on Gunther's chest and back. He found two more entry wounds and field dressed them, looking into Gunther's unfocused eyes.

Jason gave Gunther's shoulder a gentle shake to get his eyes to focus. "See you in five."

"You do that." Gunther coughed and winced. A trickle of blood appeared at the corner of his mouth. "And Jason, tell Iron Angel she's one of the best warriors I—"

"You'll tell her yourself, because she'll be with us when we come back." Jason stood up and grabbed his rifle. "In five, buddy."

Gunther looked up at him. "I ain't goin' nowhere."

With one last look at Gunther, Jason took off through the doorway into the warehouse to find the last two members of his team.

ɔɔ

Four blocks away at the ATF staging area, Agent Woyzeck's head snapped toward the sound of the gunshots. "That's our cue, Zapper" he said, using the nickname of the leader of the ATF team assembled for the sting operation.

"They're early," he said.

"Yeah, and now we're late."

"Mount up," Zapper ordered his team.

He climbed into the back of the black, unmarked ATF truck and sat near the front. He leaned toward the agent who was in touch with the men on the rooftops of the buildings.

Agent Woyzeck plopped down next to the team leader. "Sir, Beta Team says two cars of party crashers pulled up and started firing on the militia members. Most of the crashers are dead. Several of the militia members are down. Alpha Team on the north building is down."

The ATF team leader frowned. "Who are the crashers?"

"Not sure. He thinks maybe *La Espada*."

"Dammit," Agent Woyzeck said. "Nothing goes right when it comes to getting this group."

"Don't worry," Zapper said. "We'll get your fugitives."

"Don't underestimate them. Catching these two is like picking up mercury with your fingers." Before the gunshots rang

out, Agent Woyzeck could almost taste the sweetness of victory. Now, as he heard the command to go hot, all he had was a
sour taste in his mouth. He smacked the charging hammer of
his ATF-issued M-16 and thumbed the safety lever off safe.
He was hot.

ೞ౩ೞ౩

At the sound of gunshots, Iron Angel motioned to the militiaman behind her to break through the side door into the
building. Suit joined in smashing the door and, with one mon-
strous push with the bottom of his boot, the tempered glass
cracked and fell inward in one piece. Their team flew into the
office space. Duncan ordered the man nearest the rear of the
office to scout out a way to the central area between Buildings
One and Two. He pointed to a second man to go with the first.

He turned to face Iron Angel. No words were necessary.
They both were thinking the same thing. Jason and Gunther's
team was taking the heat.

She activated her mike. "Mamabird, come in."

"Mamabird, go." Joe-Sam's voice had a hint of shakiness.

"What's the status of Blackbird's team?"

"They took out all of the guys who came in the cars and
both guys on the roof of Building Two. Four of the team made
it into the building."

She stared at Duncan and asked Joe-Sam, "Do you know
who made it?"

"I saw Blackbird for sure. Not sure who the other three
were."

"How many fighters came out of the cars at our end of the
building?"

"I'm not sure. Three, maybe four. I was watching the action
at the west end."

"Copy, three or four. Songbird out."

She rolled her head to loosen her neck muscles and adjusted the sling of her FPG. All her fears were coming to life
around her. She looked into Duncan's eyes. If this was the end,
at least they would go out together. The scouts returned and

motioned for the rest of the team to follow them. The team maneuvered through the maze of hallways in single file, surrounded by the muffled rattle of the equipment of war. The building was bigger than it looked from the outside, and it took an excruciating lifetime of seconds to get to the door that opened onto the central area between the two long buildings.

Iron Angel inched along the wall in the small foyer toward the glass entry doors that opened onto a six-foot wide grassy area bordered by a sidewalk. Beyond that a paved open area stretched to the loading docks at the back of the other building that mirrored the one they were in. Kearney's van was where he had parked it. The doors hung open. The van was empty, waiting for its cargo that would never come. Kearney, Red Dog, and their two guards were nowhere to be seen.

She stared at the macadam just beyond the grassy area and sidewalk. It was only thirty yards to the other building, but it might as well have been a mile.

დ

A Hertz twenty-foot truck backed into the access road on the east side of the complex. The driver spotted the black ATF truck speeding toward him. When the ATF truck was ten feet away, the agent behind the wheel emphatically motioned for the driver of the rental truck to get out of the way. The Hertz truck driver motioned okay, but the engine stalled. When he looked up, he saw the agent in the passenger seat motion for his driver to use the other entrance. The ATF truck whipped in reverse to the road then sped toward the west entrance.

The driver abandoned the Hertz truck in the middle of the road and headed for his motorcycle hidden behind a pair of dumpsters.

At the western entrance, Wild Bill and Blackie hustled away from the gate they had just locked and rushed around the nearby building that housed a bunch of small businesses. They had to catch up to the militia before the ATF agents gained entry and ruined their plans.

Wild Bill was the first inside the door. Gunther raised his 9 mm semi-automatic, but his arm was slow and weak, and his hand was shaky. His eyes were dull and unfocused. Red foam oozed from the corner of his mouth. He pulled the trigger. It clicked. He was out of ammunition.

"What do you want to do with him?" asked Blackie.

"He's as good as dead. Leave him. We have to help Red Dog with his part of the plan," Wild Bill said as he tugged on Blackie's leather vest and headed toward the warehouse.

Quick pops from automatic weapons came from the warehouse behind Gunther as he struggled to activate his throat mike.

CHAPTER 29

"Bluebird, say again?" Iron Angel pressed on the ear bud in her left ear.

Gunther's words were garbled.

She looked at Duncan. "Did he say not to trust the Brotherhood? Something about a plan?"

Everyone turned their heads to stare at Dee Dee. She took one step backward. The other team members stepped forward, blocking her escape.

In one motion, Iron Angel grabbed the front of Dee Dee's shirt and slammed her against the wall, pressing her forearm against the helpless woman's throat. With her face mere inches from Dee Dee's face, she said through clenched teeth, "What's the plan?"

Dee Dee wiggled to try to free herself. "I don't know of any plan."

Iron Angel's power and body weight prevented escape and the increased the pressure against the base of Dee Dee's throat partially closed her airway.

Her eyes widened and she forced out, "I only know what you guys know." Her eyes darted back and forth between Iron Angel's eyes and Duncan's. "If there's anything else, I don't know anything about it."

Duncan's face was red, his eyes hard, his jawline harder. He leaned toward Dee Dee. "So you're saying you don't know anything about this?"

Dee Dee shook her head in quick jerks. A sweat broke out on her forehead.

"That's bullshit." Duncan motioned to Iron Angel. "Get her to talk."

She pulled a Ka-Bar Fighting knife out of its sheath and pressed the unsharpened edge of the blade against Dee Dee's throat. Cool steel could be a powerful inducement to speak up.

"Honest," Dee Dee rasped in a weak voice. "If the Brotherhood has anything planned, they didn't tell me or Red Dog."

Iron Angel increased the pressure on the knife.

"Stop! I don't know anything." Dee Dee's eyes pleaded to Iron Angel. "Think about it, they know we're friends. If they were up to something, they know I would tell you." She swallowed hard. "And I would. I'd tell you if I knew they were up to something."

Iron Angel turned her wrist and pressed the point of the blade against the soft tissue under Dee Dee's chin. "Not if they're holding something over your head. What do they have on you, Dee Dee?"

"Nothing. They don't have anything on me or Red Dog." Her words tumbled over each other. "There's no plan. You gotta believe me."

Iron Angel increased the pressure on the point of the blade just enough to pierce the skin. Just enough for Dee Dee to feel blood trickle down her neck.

Dee Dee panicked and flailed her arms. "*Stop*, Iron Angel, I'm begging you, don't kill me! I don't know anything. *Please.*"

Iron Angel kneed Dee Dee in the stomach and hit her with a hammer fist, sending the hilt end of the knife hard against the tender area behind her left ear. She wilted and dropped to the floor. Iron Angel looked down at one of the few female friends she had, trying to put a finger on the feeling that filled her chest, momentarily pushing aside her tension.

Regret. She regretted that their friendship had come to this.

She looked up to see Duncan's scrutiny. "Most people will talk with a knife to their throat," she said as she sheathed her knife. "She might be telling the truth. But I sure don't want to spend the next half hour or so looking over my shoulder."

Duncan pointed past her. "You, Suit, watch Dee Dee—joined-at-the-hip type watchin'. Got it? One wrong move, take her out. One hint that she's part of a conspiracy against us, take her out. Anything suspicious—"

"Take her out. Yes, sir," Suit responded as he stepped toward Dee Dee, who was now stirring and moaning. He snatched the back of her shirt and yanked her to her feet.

Iron Angel turned her attention to the mission. "It's over thirty yards to the next building, Duncan. You should stay here until we get everything under control."

He put his hands on her shoulders. "You aren't going anywhere without me," he said in a lowered voice. "We're a team."

"They want you. Stay here until it's safe."

Duncan increased the pressure on her shoulders. "Or we can stick to the plan."

Security and Operations Chief was a powerful position. She had the power to pull the plug. She could insist that he stay where he was—away from the Demon Brotherhood, away from the arms dealers, away from the action. But something in his eyes told her his mind was made up. And damn it to hell, Boss trumps Security Chief.

"Okay," she said. "What's your plan for getting across the space to Building Two?"

"We'll send three guys back to the south side to create a diversion. We'll cross over then provide cover for them to join us."

"Let's do it." She hoped she sounded more convincing than she felt.

Three militia members took off down the hallway. A silence fell over Iron Angel, Duncan, Suit, and Dee Dee while they waited for the gunfire to indicate it was safe to cross over to the other building. Iron Angel eyed Dee Dee, who looked a little wobbly, but was tough. She'd make it across the parking lot.

Duncan led the group to the foyer. After motioning everyone to hug the walls, he reached for the latch to unlock the deadbolt on the glass doors.

Iron Angel tried to raise Joe-Sam on the radio, but all she got was static. *Now what?* Only ten minutes into this mission, and it turned into a trap, commo was on the blink and they had possible traitors in their ranks. She laid her head against the wall behind her, took a deep breath, and waited. No sarcasm to cut the tension. No witty remark to get everyone to relax.

The diversionary gunfire started. It was game time.

Duncan flung open the door and went through first, Iron Angel second, with Dee Dee and Suit right behind them. They raced toward the shelter of the loading docks on the opposite side of the open area. Three-quarters of the way across the parking lot, bullets dug chunks out of the pavement around them.

Dee Dee shouted she was hit. Duncan staggered forward putting out his hand to break his fall. Before he hit the ground, Iron Angel grabbed him under the armpit. With the assistance of momentum, she half-carried him to the safety of the over-hang of the docking area. She propped him against the loading dock. Suit did the same with Dee Dee.

Iron Angel whipped the sling of her rifle over her head, leaned it against the loading dock, and broke out first aid supplies from Duncan's equipment vest. She ripped open his vest. Blood oozed through his tee shirt. *Oh, God!*

"Turn me over. Find the entrance wound," Duncan said through a wince. "Damn, this hurts."

She pushed his shoulder to turn him. He grimaced as he wiggled his shoulder to off the equipment vest. She pulled it off the rest of the way and raised his tee shirt.

Before she finished securing the field dressing, blood seeped through the thick wad of gauze. The blood made her fingers sticky. The coppery, raw-meat smell of blood filled her nostrils. She fought the corners of her mouth as they tried to turn down.

"I think this is serious. I might not make it," Duncan whispered.

"Don't talk like that." Her voice was on the edge of a scream. She leaned Duncan back against the dock. Nodding her head in hopes of encouraging him, she cleared her throat and said with surprising calmness, "You're going to be okay. We're all getting out of here together."

Duncan clutched her arm. "I—" He moaned and writhed from the pain. "I have to know. Did you kill Rosemary?"

Every muscle in Iron Angel tensed. "Not now. Let's talk about it later."

With a fierce yank, she opened another field dressing and busied herself with plugging the exit wound on Duncan's chest.

"There may not be a 'later.' I have to know."

"You're shot. Dee Dee's shot. Kearney is in danger. Everything is going to shit around us. And you're asking about *her*?" She ripped the tape with her teeth then pressed the strip against the bandage. "I can't believe this, Duncan."

"I'm not asking because I care about her, *nena*. I'm asking because I care about *you*."

She tugged the edges his equipment vest together to maintain his body heat. "I can't believe you are asking about *her. Now.*"

Duncan took a deep, rattling breath. "I'm worried that if you killed her, it would mean something changed in you. You always—" Duncan coughed and continued more weakly than before. "—killed only in self-defense. Killing—" Duncan stirred and grimaced. "Killing Rosemary would be murder. And that's not you."

Iron Angel thumbed away a trickle of sweat from the side of his face. "I was out of control for a while, but I'm good now. Don't worry about me. Everything is going to be okay."

"I won't be there to—"

"Hey, you aren't going anywhere, tough guy. You're not going anywhere without me. We're a team, remember?"

"*I* killed Rosemary." Dee Dee's words pierced the air.

Iron Angel's eyes snapped up to Dee Dee's eyes. "Dee Dee, you don't have to do this."

Continuing to stare at Iron Angel, Dee Dee repeated, "I killed Rosemary. Me and Gunther—we did it. The bitch was screwing around with my old man. She deserved everything she got."

One corner of Duncan's mouth curled upward. He extended

a shaking hand to touch Iron Angel's cheek. "I knew it. I knew you wouldn't—"

As soon as she grasped his hand and brought it to her lips, he went limp.

"No!" she yelled, no longer trying to hide her anguish. "Duncan. No, no, no—stay with me." She wanted to throw herself across his body. Protect him from death—from life—from whatever would hurt him. Hang on and never let go. Instead, she checked for a pulse—five desperate times. Finally. There it was. It was weak, but it was a pulse. She leaned down to speak into his ear.

"You hang on, baby. Suit and I will be back before you know it." She thought she saw his eyelids flutter. "Wait for me. Don't you go anywhere without me, okay?"

Suit appeared at her side. She looked up at him.

"We gotta go." He was looking down the length of his rifle barrel, scanning, checking, analyzing.

"Don't worry," Dee Dee said. "I'll stand guard until you guys get back."

Gunther's warning played in Iron Angel's head. She stood up and walked toward Dee Dee until she stood looking down at her. "If anything happens to Duncan—" She knelt on one knee, leaned in and lowered her voice. "But threats aren't necessary. I know you'll do the right thing because, well, you know me."

Dee Dee flashed a weak, knowing smile at Iron Angel. "Don't worry. I'll protect Duncan with my life. I'm not part of any plan."

Iron Angel's eyes bored into Dee Dee's, trying to read them. She relaxed. Touching her forehead to Dee Dee's temple, she whispered, "Thank you." She caressed Dee Dee's head one more time.

Dee Dee's eyes followed Iron Angel as she stood up.

Suit paced in quick, short steps. "We're in a shitty place. Those other guys should be back by now. I don't think they made it. We gotta go. We gotta go now."

Iron Angel knelt next to Duncan and kissed him lightly on his unresponsive lips. Staring at the ground, she activated her throat mike and called Joe-Sam, "Mamabird, Songbird, come in."

"Go, Songbird," Joe-Sam replied, barely audible over the static.

Iron Angel stood up, slipped the sling of her rifle over her head, and adjusted it. "What are the rooftop guys doing?"

"The guards on top of Building Two are down. The ones on Building One are all facing your location." That meant there were no guards on the rooftop above them. It wasn't much, but it offered wiggle room.

Suit jumped onto the dock and offered her a hand up. "We gotta go. Time's running out."

Iron Angel looked at her World lying on the ground at her feet. In the few minutes it took to care for Duncan's and Dee Dee's wounds, darkness had fallen and swallowed up everything in sight.

All she could make out in the darkness was a dark, solitary lump next to its body guard.

She contacted headquarters. "Mamabird, where are the three guys we sent to the south side of Building One?"

"They're down."

She rubbed her forehead. "Why is the transmission so bad?"

"We're transmitting directly. I shut down the radio transmitter on Freebird." The transmitter on the drone amplified their radio signals and extended their range.

"Why?"

"Someone was trying to hack into it."

"We have to move." Suit's growing anxiety was palpable.

Thoughts of someone hacking the drone filled Iron Angel's head as she took his offered hand and leapt onto the loading dock. She swallowed the last of her saliva. All her gastric juices turned to hot tar.

Freebird's technology was well protected—its firewalls had firewalls. There was only one group with the ability to hack a well-protected drone. One group with the resources. The only ones who could possibly know about the drone—or care.

The ATF team leader was incredulous as he talked into his mike. "They have a *drone*? How can they...You hacked into it? Maybe we can hear what they're saying and see what they're seeing."

Agent Woyzeck waited in Building Two, near the entrance on the west end. He could only hear one side of the conversation, but he heard enough to know that Joan and Duncan had moved into the twenty-first century. The Rules of Engagement established by the United Nations prohibited the United States from using drones, as well as helicopters and satellites, to track the insurgents. And the administration in Washington was happy to accommodate the UN these days. The good guys couldn't have drones, but these fugitives could use drones to evade the authorities. Agent Woyzeck shook his head. The world had turned upside down.

In a matter of minutes, this simple sting operation had escalated into a multi-headed snake. Local uniformed police, maintaining the perimeter, reported sighting members of the Demon Brotherhood in the area. Not only were they facing the militia and *La Espada*, but also outlaw bikers.

Special Agent Woyzeck listened patiently to Zapper's claims that hacking into the militia's drone was a positive development, and it far outweighed the negatives. As he tagged after the ATF agents starting the slow process of clearing the building, Agent Woyzeck wasn't so sure.

◌◌◌

With the feds in the picture, everything took on a heightened sense of urgency. The mission had changed from a weapons deal to getting Kearney, and everyone else, out safely. They had to move fast. Get in. Get out. It wouldn't be long before Duncan would be too weak to move. An ominous voice in Iron Angel's head warned her that getting Duncan to safety grew more unlikely by the second. She stifled it. Wetness built up on the inside of her lower eyelids and blurred her vision. Her nose stung.

She motioned for Suit to go into the building. As she followed him, she said, "Mamabird, terminate Freebird."

"Songbird, did you say 'terminate?'"

The full realization of her circumstances flooded into Iron Angel's mind, bringing with it thumping heaviness. Her arms and legs felt like lead. "Affirmative. Terminate Freebird. How copy?"

"Only the person in command can issue that order," Joe-Sam countered.

"Thunderbird is—" The words caught on a squelched sob in her throat. She pinched her tingling nose. "Thunderbird is down. Terminate Freebird. Do it now."

"I have to ask why. Over."

As she followed Suit through the maze of pallets, she decided to overlook the insubordination. She understood what the drone meant to Joe-Sam. It was their baby. Killing it would be genocide. It was as hard for her to issue the order as it was for Joe-Sam to carry it out.

"The feds are hacking the drone. They can hear all our transmissions," she explained.

"But I shut down the radio transmitter."

"They're *in the net.* They can trace it back to you. Terminate Freebird and—break—" She hesitated to give the next command. If she was wrong, they would lose all outside assistance unnecessarily. But she had to protect Joe-Sam. They were too young to spend the rest of their lives paying for some cock-eyed militia leader's mistake.

Suit stopped and looked over his shoulder at Iron Angel. She gestured for him to move on.

"Mamabird, fry the chicken. I say again, fry the chicken. How copy?"

Fry the chicken meant erase the drives, destroy all evidence. Wipe the room clean of fingerprints. Bug out. The headquarters and all assistance they offered would be gone. In seconds, the militia members would be in the wind.

She tightened her jaw and repeated, "How copy?"

"Terminate Freebird and fry the chicken. Over."

She leaned against a support beam as a flash of anger blasted her. Duncan had dropped the command of this group into her lap. The situation was unraveling—the very situation she had dreaded and had tried to convince him to avoid. This was *Duncan's* mission. This was *his* screw up. If he had listened to her, they would be at home clinking shot glasses. Or better yet, in bed, slick with sweat, locked in each other's arms. He had always been there to motivate her, save her, and love her. The vision of the motionless figure she had left behind popped into her head. Her World was helpless and now depending on her. The anger dissipated. A single tear trickled down her right cheek.

She brushed away the tear with the back of her hand. It was time to wrest what she could from the jaws of failure. "Mamabird, do it *now*. You have *no* time. *No* time! How copy?"

"No time. Copy that," Mamabird said. "Frying the chicken as we speak. It's been real and it's been fun. Over and out."

She mentally finished the line, *but it hasn't been real fun.* One corner of her mouth tightened. Leave it to Joe-Sam to inject a bit of humor when things were going to hell.

She signed off, not knowing if the radio at headquarters had already been destroyed. When she turned her attention to the man at her side, the expression on his face told her he understood what had just happened.

She motioned for him to move forward. After a quick check over her shoulder to check their six, she said, "Well, Suit, we're in the hand basket."

"Firebird, for Songbird." Kearney's voice was barely audible over the static.

"Did you hear the last transmission?" she asked.

"Affirmative, Songbird. You have command."

"All operatives, work your way to Rally Point Zulu. How copy?"

Rally Point Zulu was a pre-arranged position in a building at the east end of the complex. Once there, they would regroup and plan their next move to break through the perimeter, spread out and vanish into unsuspecting America.

"Firebird copies Rally Point Zulu."

"Blackbird copies Rally Point Zulu," Jason responded.

There was a long silence.

"Bluebird, how copy?" she asked.

"Bluebird is down." It was a simple statement with a tone of resignation, sent by an unidentified operative.

Overcome with two great losses, Iron Angel pressed her eyelids together. After wiping her face with the crook of her right arm, she closed down her emotions. "Consider the local net compromised. Radio silence until further notice. See you at RPZ. Be safe. Songbird, over and out."

CHAPTER 30

Rally Point Zulu was at the eastern edge of the complex, not far from where they stood. After rescuing Kearney and getting back to Duncan and Dee Dee, it would be skipping distance to RPZ. With any luck, they'd cross paths with Jason, and he could help move Duncan.

Suit turned left and headed toward Kearney's probable location. Iron Angel grabbed his arm and shook her head. "The feds are here somewhere. If we go down the center of the building, we can't help but bump into them. We'll go straight back, then turn left along the far wall."

That would make it harder to flank them. If they needed to escape, they would be nearer to the exterior doors.

Suit nodded and headed toward the back of the building. She followed closely behind him, looking down the barrel of the FPG.

Before reaching the back wall, several popping sounds in quick succession came from their left. They froze.

Suit whispered, "AK-47 and small arms."

"Red Dog had an AK."

The sound of someone running in soft-soled boots stopped them in their tracks. The footsteps went past them then stopped.

Suit pointed to his ear then straight ahead to signal he heard voices.

Iron Angel nodded.

Suit changed direction. The deep rumble of male voices became louder and clearer as he honed in on their location. He stopped at the edge of a plastic-wrapped stack of pallets loaded with bags of dog food. Flattening himself against the stack of pallets, he inched toward the corner of the stack. After a brief glance back at Iron Angel, he slowly peeked around the corner. He took a two-second peek then motioned for her to move away so he could tell her what he saw.

"Two bikers are holding Kearney at gunpoint," Suit whispered.

Her brow tightened. "But Kearney was with me when we saved the two Brotherhood bikers in the desert. Why would they threaten *him*?"

"I heard one of them ask about you."

"Damn. This must be about the Wild Bill thing. I don't have time for their testosterone bullshit now."

"Wild Bill thing?" Suit asked.

"I wrenched Wild Bill's neck, stole his bike, and left him on the side of the road in the middle of the desert."

"Oh, *that* Wild Bill thing," Suit whispered. "I thought you apologized and everything was okay."

"Me, too."

"So what do we do?"

"Well, there are feds and *La Espada* in the building, so we'll have to be quiet."

"You don't do 'quiet.' Remember when you rescued Duncan from the kidnappers?"

With a wry smile, she brushed past Suit and pulled her .45 caliber semi-automatic from its holster. Looking down the sights of the .45 cal, she stepped into the standoff. She didn't have to look down the sights to shoot accurately. It was a more intimidating posture, than a simple point and shoot. But intimidation could go a long way toward 'quiet.'

She heard Suit click off the safety of his 9 mm semi-automatic and step forward to her right.

With her handgun pointed at Wild Bill's head, she motioned for Kearney to come to her. "C'mon, Kearney. We have to get Duncan and get out of here."

"No one's going anywhere until I get my pound of flesh," Wild Bill said.

"There's a bigger picture here, Bill. The feds and *La Espada* are in the building. We have to move."

"Like I said, no one's going anywhere until you pay for leaving me in the desert to die."

"You take out Kearney and I'll take out the other guy," Blackie said. "We'll grab the bitch and take care of business someplace else." He pointed his handgun at Suit.

Suit pulled the trigger of his 9 mm.

Blackie fell backward with a red spot in the middle of his forehead.

"Everybody stay calm," Iron Angel said. "No one else has to get hurt. Wild Bill, let's take this up some other time. Kearney, let's—"

"Hey, gringos, where are the weapons?"

She spun around and leveled her gun at one of the four Hispanic men who had just stepped into the opening between the mountains of pallets. *Well, isn't this cozy? Let's roast some marshmallows.*

Wild Bill and Suit spun and aimed their guns at the new-comers. Kearney lunged for his 9 mm semi-automatic on the floor. She nodded at him. He nodded back. She dropped to one knee and they fired simultaneously. Bullets flew everywhere from both sides, but the party crashers didn't get more than a half dozen, poorly-aimed shots off.

When the shooting stopped, she offered a hand to Kearney to help him to his feet. "Anyone hit?"

Everyone patted themselves and shook their heads.

"Good." She looked at Wild Bill. "Those shots are going to bring the feds running. Let's part company and take this up another time."

He pointed a finger at her. "This isn't over." He headed toward the back door of the building.

The pop of automatic gunfire erupted, from the center of the building.

"Blackbird come in." The gunfire possibly came from Jason's position. Iron Angel wanted to know Jason's status.

"I'm taking fire," Jason said. "I think it's the feds."

"We'll be right there to help you."

"No," Jason said. "I'll hold these guys off. You head to RP Zulu." There was another barrage of gunfire. "I'm right behind you."

"Roger that. Songbird out."

Iron Angel, Kearney, and Suit headed toward the loading docks. They moved single file. Looking everywhere. Expecting a surprise around each corner.

While on the move, she whispered to Kearney, "Where's Red Dog and the others?"

"Red Dog pulled a gun on me. I didn't know who was on what side, so I took everybody out."

Her blood turned to ice. "Oh, no." She raced past Kearney. "We have to hurry. I left Dee Dee watching Duncan."

ℰↃℰↃ

Three shots rang out in front of them, followed by rapid popping of automatic gunfire. Two dozen shots. Maybe three dozen.

They were too fast to count.

Iron Angel clenched her teeth and raced toward the gunshots. There wasn't much time. Dee Dee knew there'd be a price to pay, and she wouldn't hang around for long. Iron Angel wanted to get her before she got away. Make her pay.

Suit tackled her before she took three steps. When she hit the floor, the FPG jammed into her solar plexus, knocking the wind out of her. She scrambled to her knees willing her lungs to expand.

Suit grabbed her arm and yanked her to her feet. "That was the feds. We have to get out of here."

Kearney grabbed her other arm and, together, he and Suit propelled her in the opposite direction of the gunshots.

She stumbled after them, impaired by her inability to breathe.

Air. Oxygen at last. Iron Angel took a huge breath then balked. She braced her legs to change directions. To go back to the loading docks. And Duncan.

Both men muscled her in the opposite direction. Toward safety and escape.

When they reached the exit door, she wrestled out of their hands. "Okay, *okay.*" She clamped her lips between her teeth. Pressed her fingers against her eyes. "I get it. Duncan's—" The words caught in her throat. When she was sure her voice wouldn't crack, she said, "I get it. We can't go back."

With a fierce tug, she adjusted her equipment vest, set her jaw, straightened her shoulders. After a couple deep breaths, she nodded her head toward the exit door. "We're going to head for that building directly across that parking lot. Then we're going to leapfrog from building to building to get to Rally Point Zulu. Ready?"

Without waiting for a reply, she bolted out the door and across the open area. If she couldn't get to Duncan, she needed to get as far away as she could. As quickly as possible. Before everything caught up to her. Tears blurred her vision as she plowed through the door and into the other building.

While wiping her tears, she glanced around the room. This was the front office of a chemical company. Typical office papers and files cluttered the desks, and sticky-notes framed the monitors. Indications of normal office life. A pang stopped her. There was that word again. Normal. Like the normal life she would never have with Duncan. She locked the tears behind her stinging eyelids and swallowed hard.

Kearney touched her arm so lightly that she almost didn't feel it. When he spoke, his voice was as soft as his touch. "Let's keep moving. We have to clear these rooms."

She nodded and followed the two men.

Clearing the rooms gave her focus, purpose, clarity. The distraction helped her ignore the emptiness deepening inside her.

Satisfied they had the building to themselves, Iron Angel peered through the small six-inch-by-nine-inch window in the exit door. There was a storage yard between their location and the next building en route to Rally Point Zulu. The storage yard was about forty-five yards across.

To the right were fifty-gallon drums that would conceal their movement toward a storage shed that stood halfway to the next building. Iffy, but doable. She pressed her right cheek against the glass and looked to the left. The same distance to the north was West Washington Street, the northern boundary of the commercial complex. It represented freedom—and a heavily guarded perimeter. There was no doubt in her mind the feds wouldn't let them mosey on out of there without opposition.

The proximity of freedom was tantalizing, but her command had been to get to the rally point. At the rally point everyone could be accounted for. They could all get out together. Well, not *all*. Her eyes clouded over.

Pull the plug. That's what she'd wanted to do a half hour ago. Or eons ago. Time had taken on a surreal quality. The past was distorted as it stretched like an elastic band that extended backwards. The future was out-of-focus by its proximity, as if her nose was pressed against a movie screen.

Pull the plug. But Duncan's words *stick to the plan* rang in her head. Pull the plug—Stick to the plan. She bit her lip and looked at Kearney and Suit. They were waiting for the next order from their leader, for their next move. It was up to her.

She broke radio silence. "Blackbird, this is Songbird. Over." If Jason was at the rally point, the decision would be made for her. They'd work their way to Jason. But with each unanswered call out to him, her spirits dropped. Her shoulders sagged. A part of her wished the feds would barge into the building and end this fiasco. Put her in irons and drag her away. She didn't want to do this anymore. Duncan was gone. The prospect of life without him was unbearable.

After the fourth attempt to reach Jason, Kearney put his arm around her shoulders. "It's just us," he said in a voice barely above a whisper.

She pressed her lips together and inhaled deeply through her nostrils that were starting to sting again. With the exhale, she said, "We're getting out of this hell. We're going through the perimeter."

"Let's do it," Kearney said.

Suit nodded. "Let's rock and roll."

CHAPTER 31

As Iron Angel regained consciousness, the first thing she noticed was the pounding in her head as if Brain Indians were on the warpath. It felt like a hot, metal band was squeezing her skull. The Indians in her head pounded on their war drums, rebelling against the pressure. As her vision cleared, she realized she was on her stomach on the floor of a very small room. The cool, blood-stained mini-tiles under her cheek told her she was in a bathroom. She reached to hold her head, but her hands were handcuffed behind her. She tried to remember how she got here—wherever *here* was. The last thing she recalled was crouching to sneak through the perimeter. After that, nothing.

Pain shot down her neck as she looked around for Kearney and Suit. She was alone—they must be in another room. She rested her head on the floor as she blocked out the thought that they might be dead.

She ran her tongue over her teeth. All there. But her mouth was filled with blood. Her tongue examined her lips and felt a split in her upper lip. The stinging made her eyes water. Her nose ached. Pain gnawed at her whole body.

When she twisted to get on her right hip, her feet wouldn't move. She looked down and blinked, trying to make sense of what she saw. Her boots were duct taped to a forty-eight-inch long metal bar—one of those metal reinforcing rods used to strengthen cement.

She searched the room to find something useful. Her

equipment vest was gone. The holsters on her thighs were empty. Her FPG—gone. *Bastards.*

Deep voices rumbled through the door, and she quieted her breathing to hear what they were saying. They got louder as the men approached the bathroom. The doorknob turned, but stopped as the men paused to finish their conversation. They droned on, no distinguishable words. The voices stopped and the door inched open. A head popped around the door. A deputy. There was something familiar about him, but her head was still too foggy to put her finger on it.

"You're alert. Good," he said. He had tape across his nose and a swollen left eye. Spattered blood covered the front of his uniform. He stepped into the bathroom, and as he sidestepped around the bar bound to her boots, he motioned for someone in the hallway to follow him.

A Hispanic man stepped into the bathroom, shut the door, and crossed his arms as he leaned against it. He didn't look like law enforcement—his haskie suggested he was *La Espada.* His frown made a perfect upside down U. His brown eyes were dark. Angry. Malevolent.

"Where are my friends?" she asked.

The deputy reached over the tub and unwrapped a chain from the cold water tap. At the end dangled a rubber drain stopper. He plugged the drain and turned on the water full force.

Her heart quickened. Being restrained near pooling water was never a good thing.

The Brain Indians picked up the beat, drumming an urgent message: *Get the hell out of here! Vamoose!*

"You know who this is?" the deputy asked, gesturing toward the Hispanic man at her feet.

She glanced over her shoulder, shook her head, and looked back up at the deputy.

"Well, darlin', let me introduce you to Tito Orrozco. He's the brother of the man you choked to death at the Pennington Ranch."

Iron Angel's eyes snapped to Tito and took in the prison tattoos on his face and arms. "What do you want from me? Where's Kearney?" she croaked.

It was difficult to enunciate with a split lip and a mouth full of dried blood.

"Now you see, Lisa Brown, or do you prefer to be called Iron Angel? We kind of like that handle. Don't we, Tito? Iron Angel. We're not sure about the angel part, but 'iron' says a lot about you. You're a hard woman to kill." He smirked as he glanced at the Hispanic man then back to her. "This might be a good time to explain the protocol to you. You see, the bind-*ee* doesn't ask questions. Only the bind-*ers* get to ask the questions. *Comprende*?"

Lisa. That's it! The only person who knew the name on her false ID was the deputy who responded to the Pennington Ranch home invasion. She looked up into the young face of the deputy. Questions stirred in her mind, but they were slow and disconnected, as if her head was filled with hair gel.

She swallowed hard and licked her lips. Tito grabbed her hair and pulled her head back. She winced and a groan escaped her throat.

He sneered and said with a heavy Mexican accent, "The man ast you a question, *mija*. Now. You answer."

When she didn't answer right away, he tugged her hair harder, sending a lightning bolt of pain down her back, across her shoulder blades, and through her midsection.

The throbbing in her head intensified. "Yes. Yes, I understand," she gasped through the pain.

The deputy braced his hands on his knees as he bent over to talk to her. "We need some answers from you." He looked up at Tito and nodded. Tito picked up the bar bound to her boots, and the deputy grabbed her under her armpits.

The realization of what they were about to do sent a wave of panic through her. "Oh, no. No. *No*." She thrashed to break their grips. She wriggled her hips and pushed her feet at Tito. She struggled and twisted to try to break free. It was useless. She was powerless to save herself. *She—Iron Angel* was powerless.

Tito placed the bar across the top of the tub, and the deputy let go of her armpits. She plunged face first into the shallow water.

The deputy grabbed her hair and jerked her head out of the water. "You are going to answer our questions. Understand?"

She nodded.

"I didn't hear your answer."

"Yes."

As soon as the words were out of her mouth, the deputy plunged her head into the water. No time to take in more oxygen. Her ears filled with the sound of the water streaming from the faucet near her head.

With her feet higher than her head, braced on the edge of the tub by the metal bar, it was impossible to arch her back enough to get her mouth to the surface of the water—her nose was plugged with dried blood. She fought her panic. Was this how she was going to die? Bound hand and foot at the hands of two wannabe interrogators. Drowned in a few inches of water. When she thought her lungs were going to burst, her head was yanked upward. A wide, arcing splash of water spattered the tiles on the wall.

"Where are the bodies of the five men who came to your house to kill you?"

"I don't—" Her head was dunked again. The water bubbled pink as the clotted blood liquefied in the water.

The deputy jerked her head out of the water. Water sloshed. She inhaled one long gasp.

"Try again. Where are they?"

"I swear—" She sucked in a lungful of precious air. "I don't know what you're talking about."

"Tito, this lady has a death wish."

The deputy let go of her. Her head plunged into the swirling pink water. Bubbles gurgled around her. Her lungs burned. She fought to get her head above water. Air. She *had* to breathe.

The deputy lifted her head again. She desperately gasped for air, but before she could fill her lungs, the deputy pushed her head against the bottom of the tub and held her there. Water went up her nose. She squelched her choking reflex.

This time she was underwater longer. She thought she heard Tito telling the deputy to stop screwing around. Kill her and get it over with.

Just as she was about to gulp in water, the deputy pulled her head up. She gasped for air, as he said, "Okay, maybe we're being a little rough on you. Here's an easier question— where are the bodies of the two men who came to your house after that?"

She shook her head and got a lungful of air before being submerged again. She heard the muffled sounds of an altercation in the small bathroom. Forgotten, face down, helpless, she heard garbled yelling. Out of the corner of her eye, she saw the blurred image of a large man fighting with the deputy and Tito. Then she heard what sounded like gunshots. Just as she was accepting her fate, a strong hand grabbed the back of her shirt, and pulled her upward. He unplugged the drain, and the water eddied out of the tub.

"Detective Ramos!" She coughed and sputtered. "Thank God you're—"

Before he could get her free from the tub, Tito fired his gun at Detective Ramos. The detective fired back. He released his hold on the back of her shirt and dropped to the floor. With a heavy splash, she plunged face-first into the water. Back to square one. But the water was less deep than before. And she had a lungful of air.

She cast a look out of the corner of her eye. She listened. The room was quiet. Clearly, she had to get herself out of this predicament. Rocking the re-bar back and forth, she finally slid it over the side of the tub. With one final Herculean effort, she twisted her body around until she was kneeling on the outside of the tub. For several minutes, she leaned across the edge of the tub coughing out water that lingered in her air passages and gulping air into her screaming lungs. In time, her heart rate slowed. The coughing stopped. Her head cleared.

Exhausted and racked with pain, she scooted backward on her butt until her hands felt the coin pocket in Detective Ramos's jeans. The handcuff key was there. Working by feel, she slipped the key out of the pocket and groped around until it slid into the cuff keyhole. And after several agonizing, fumble-filled minutes, a moan of relief escaped her throat as one cuff released.

One more second and the other wrist was free. She rubbed her wrists. They were already turning purple from the metal cuffs. Boots next. She searched Detective Ramos's pockets, found a knife, and a minute later the duct tape was cut and pulled from her boots. She was free.

She steeled herself, but she wasn't prepared for the throbbing agony that filled her body when she stood up. Every nerve ending from her head to her feet was on fire. Purple welts covered her arms and hands. The pain rocked her to the right. She stumbled over the deputy's leg and fell shoulder-first against the wall with a moan. She leaned her head against the wall and inhaled deeply until the pain subsided.

Using the wall for support, she reached forward to grab the edge of the sink and splash some cold water on her face. She eyed her swollen, bloodied nose and a puffed-up split lip. Her left eye socket was black-and-blue, but her eye was open. While working her jaw to loosen it up, she gingerly touched the back of her head and flinched. Under her blood-matted hair was a lemon-sized lump.

She wrung out her hair and clothes. The dunking had washed away the majority of the superficial blood. All that remained were the clots and the caked blood in her nose. It would have to wait. Escape was the number one priority.

She picked up Detective Ramos's revolver and slid it into the holster on her right thigh. She grabbed his full moon clip with extra rounds for his gun and stuffed his key ring in her pants pocket. But Tito's body blocked the door. She gritted her teeth against the pain and pulled his hips and legs far enough to allow her to squeeze through the doorway.

The door opened into a small, vacant apartment. The only furniture was a round table against the right wall with a couple white resin chairs. Styrofoam cups and takeout boxes littered the table and floor. A first aid kit lay open on the kitchen counter surrounded by paper bandage wrappings. She popped three naproxen tablets into her mouth and washed them down with a handful of water from the sink.

She located her equipment vest with spare magazines still in the ammo pouches, but no guns. No knives. No sign of Kearney and Suit. Ignoring the pain as she slid her arms through the armholes of her equipment vest, she wrestled it into position across her lower back. Her shoulders ached and were stiff, but with one painful shrug she got it on. When she removed Detective Ramos's key ring from her pants pocket to put it in a pouch of the equipment vest, she noticed the Nissan keyless entry button. Maybe he drove his own car to this site. The idea of an escape vehicle gave her a jolt of energy.

She heard footsteps behind her and spun around.

Tito was leaning against the doorjamb to the bathroom with a semi-automatic gun in his hand. "*Buenas noches*, Super-woman."

Her heart stopped. As she stared at the bleary-eyed man pointing a gun at her, she thought of the one small mistake she had made. She should have taken all the guns and knives from the dead men in the bathroom before she left. But who would have guessed one of them would regain consciousness and threaten her, like Tito was doing now.

"I'm not a superwoman," she said, taking a small step toward him. "I'm just a normal human being trying to make sense of the world."

He waved the gun in an uneven arc. "No, *chica*, you are special." His slurred speech made his accent difficult to understand. "You go around killing anyone you want to."

"I only kill people who threaten me." She looked around for something to use as a weapon. If she tried to pull Detective Ramos's revolver out of her holster, it would take longer to draw and shoot Tito before he pulled the trigger. He was unsteady, but she had come too far to risk him getting off a lucky shot. She'd have to wait for him to make a mistake of his own.

"No, uh-uh, *chica*." Tito made a futile attempt at a smile. "You and me, we take what we want. So what if someone has to die to make it so?"

"I don't kill people to get what I want, only if they threaten me."

"You killed my brother from behind." He pushed off the doorjamb and shuffled toward her. His mouth took on a shape somewhere between a grimace and a sneer. His left arm hung useless at his side. "You choked him to death."

Good. Come to me. Keep talking. Keep wasting what time you have left.

"From behind," Tito repeated with another wave of the gun. He tucked his chin. It looked like he was having trouble focusing. "He wasn't threatening you."

"He was threatening a helpless invalid."

Tito stopped and teetered in place. "She was living on *our* land." He pointed the barrel of the gun in a general indication of his chest. "Our land. The land that belongs to May-hico."

"For that you decided she should die?"

"Yes. All white people must die." He took another small step. "It is called ethnic cleansing. You know of this ethnic cleansing?"

"Ethnic cleansing is reprehensible. It never has been, and never will be, acceptable." She took another step toward him. "As far as who the land belongs to, that's a political issue. It's the government's job to deal with it."

"Governments." Tito spit on the floor. "They are filled with money grabbers who only do what big money tells them to do." He shuffled a few more steps toward her.

She eyed the bloody saliva on the floor between them.

"It is up to people like us," Tito continued, waving the gun in a wobbly back and forth motion. "People like you and me cannot stand still and watch the world go down the toilet. We have to act."

"No, we don't."

"The hottest places in hell are saved for the people who do not act when they are faced with a moral *problema...*" He thought for a moment. "Or so'thin' like that."

He's quoting Dante? She eased two steps toward Tito. He didn't seem to notice. "You're assuming we're all going to hell."

He chuckled. It turned into a coughing fit. She debated jumping him but thought better of it. He was fading fast—the right moment was near. It would present itself in time.

When the coughing stopped, he continued, "Do not thin' you are...what is the word...exempt from going to hell, *mija*. Oh, yes, I will see you there, but you and me, we will not be in the hottest places because we did so'thin'."

She took one more step.

"Stop right there. Do not come any closer." He waved the gun in erratic circles. "You are a sneaky one. I knew I had to keep my eyes on you." He groaned and fell to one knee. The barrel of the gun hit the floor.

She dove for him shoulder first and knocked him over. She struggled through her pain to get to her knees. Tito flailed his good arm that held the gun. She blocked that arm and, at the same time, smashed an elbow into the side of his neck. He fell backward, forgetting about the gun. She took it from him without any trouble.

In a slow, agonizing movement, she struggled to her feet and pointed the gun at him.

He lay motionless at her feet, his eyes open and unfocused. After three labored breaths, his head rolled away from her. She waited for more breaths but none came.

As she tucked his semi-automatic into the waistband at the small of her back, she said to the lifeless man, "If you're going to shoot, shoot. Talking doesn't get the job done, at least not when you're dealing with me."

Like a robot, she turned toward the door and zeroed in on making an escape. But every step across the small room was measured torture.

She opened the door a sliver and peered out. It was clear, but unfamiliar. The sound of a passing train faintly rumbled through the walls. Another jolt of energy zipped through her body—she was still in the commercial complex. The odd-looking doors in the hallway were storage units. She knew exactly where she was—in the vacant caretaker's apartment in the southwest corner of Building One.

An exit sign beckoned to her from the far end of the hallway, and she sidled stiffly toward it. After cautiously opening the door to the stairwell, her one good eye squinted and blinked at the brightness of the light reflecting off the white walls. After shuffling down the stairs, using the railing for support, she grabbed the knob to open the door to the first floor. And froze. Someone was whistling as he approached from the other side. She hobbled quietly down the stairs then through a door marked "Basement" in block letters.

Thinking there may be another exit, she crept down the dim, dank hallway. The makeshift walls were made up of heavy-duty chain link fencing that sectioned off storage areas to her left and right. She used it to steady herself as she worked her way toward the other end of the building. Huge pipes loomed overhead. The sound of tiny, scurrying feet of rats scratched out of the shadows. A faint odor of rat urine filled her nose.

Someone moaned in the darkness. After a quick glance over her shoulder, she headed toward the sound. In one of the storage areas, Kearney was strung-up by his wrists over an overhead pipe. The balls of his feet skimmed the floor. His chin rested on his chest.

She pulled out Detective Ramos's knife and rushed to cut the plastic zip ties securing Kearney's wrists. "Kearney! Wake up."

His eyelids looked heavy when he opened his eyes, then they widened in recognition. "I thought you were dead."

"Almost. They tried to drown me in a cock-eyed version of water torture."

The plastic gave way to the blade, and he collapsed onto the floor. She broke his fall as best she could and tumbled down beside him. She vigorously rubbed his arms to encourage the return of circulation.

"You, lady, put up a fight to end all fights. You had 'em goin' for a while."

"I don't remember any of it."

"Too bad. You would have loved it. It took three of them to take you down. And a taser. And a blow to the back of the head. That's what put out your lights."

"That explains the goose egg and this splitting headache. We have to get out of here. Do you know where Suit is?"

"Dead. They shot him point blank in the head."

"Damn these people. Why didn't they kill you?"

"And I'm glad *you* made it out alive, too," Kearney said, flexing and extending his fingers.

She frowned as she kneaded his shoulders. "You know what I meant."

"Maybe they thought I was more useful to them alive. I don't know. A deputy started to beat the crap out of me, asking a bunch of questions. Real amateurs. But when some Hispanic guy showed up, they left. We have to hurry. They might come back any minute."

"They won't be coming back."

Kearney shook his head. His big, white teeth flashed in the gloom. "Even when you're at the losing end of a battle, you win."

"I didn't kill them. They kinda killed each other. The deputy must have volunteered to clear this building," she mused, taking a minute to regain some strength. "That's why the feds didn't find us. Detective Ramos must have come looking for his deputy." She grimaced as she stood up. "But that doesn't mean we aren't on a timetable. Can you stand?"

"I think so." Kearney groaned as he tried to get up. It took two tries, but finally he was on his feet, limping and favoring one leg.

She put an arm around his waist to support him. "Let's go."

Kearney's face contorted in pain when he put weight on his right leg. "O-o-ow, my knee. I'm going to slow you down. You go ahead. I'll be right behind you."

"I'm getting out of here, and you're going with me. All we have now is each other."

It was slow going. Each step sent a new round of pain through her, but she was getting out of this mess, and she wasn't leaving anybody behind—again. The memory of Duncan lying motionless and alone flashed before her eyes, but she buried it. There would be time later to work through what happened. Right now, with her mental processes slow and pain draining energy with every step, concentration and fortitude had to be foremost in her mind.

By the time they reached the first floor, both of them were exhausted. She steered Kearney toward the ladies' room.

"Freshening up are we?" he asked.

She pushed on the door to the ladies' room. "Want to rest in the men's room where a security guard may go to take a piss?"

Kearney moaned when she helped him to the floor and

braced him against the tile wall. His head flopped back against the wall, and he sat there, mouth open, looking up at her.

She plopped down to his right and felt the coolness of the tiles on her back and butt. She folded her arms across her bent knees and pressed her forehead on her arms. *If only this pounding in my head would stop.*

Without looking up she said, "The bastards took my FPG."

Kearney rolled his head to look at her. "You lost your old man, you lost friends, got the shit beaten out of you. You were tased, almost drowned during an interrogation, you're in excruciating pain—"

She opened her one good eye to look at him.

"You think I couldn't tell how painful it was for you to carry my sorry ass up those stairs?" His Adam's apple went up and down as he swallowed. "And on top of all that, the only team member left is the person you hate most in the world."

"I'm hurtin' here, Kearney. If you have a point, get to it." She closed her eye and returned to trying to ease the pain in her head.

"All that serious shit, and the only thing you can think about is that damn Magpul FPG."

"I really liked that gun," she said, without looking up.

Kearney rolled his head to face forward and looked across the narrow room at the chrome plumbing under the sinks. "Yeah. That *was* a sweet piece."

Five minutes later, Iron Angel froze with a hand on the bar that would unlatch the door to exit the building. On the other side of that door was escape. Freedom. The right to pursue happiness. On this side was the security guard who had just yelled for her to stop. His words echoed in her pounding head.

"Turn around slowly," he said.

Head bowed in an attempt to look submissive, she turned with hands open and in front of her. The guard raised his radio and told someone at the other end he had a battered woman, covered in blood, trying to exit the building. *Shit. Now I'm going to have to fight two of them.*

The guard was armed, but the fear and indecision in his eyes, the fact that he backed up, all indications he would not shoot—at least not purposefully. If she reached for Detective

Ramos's gun, he'd definitely pull the trigger. She smiled and looked directly into his eyes. She knew that she didn't have to be faster than a bullet. She only had to be faster than his decision to shoot her.

She walked slowly toward the security guard, hands still open and in front of her. Three more steps, and she would be too close for him to have sufficient time to decide to shoot and pull the trigger. She took a step. It sent lightning bolts of pain up her neck and into her head. She pinned her eyes on the security guard's eyes. Another step.

The guard told her to stop, stay back, get on the ground— all useless orders. Orders she was not going to obey.

Another step.

Too late. I'm too close.

∽∾∽∾

Iron Angel leaned on the bar to open the door to the eerily vacant docking area. She took two shuffling steps forward and let the door close behind her. The two fights took a lot out of her. The security guards had had some martial arts training— not a lot, or at least not good training. But it had been enough to be a pain in the ass. If she had been stronger, the fights would have been shorter. Instead, the fights drained what little energy she had and added a swollen left cheekbone to her list of injuries.

Reeling from fatigue and blows to the head, she scuffled to the edge of the sidewalk where it abutted the asphalt docking area. Her weary eyes, squinting from the pain, scanned the steamy pavement between the two buildings.

The pavement was wet, as if it had rained sometime during the night. The dampness absorbed the security lighting in some areas and reflected it in others, producing a mosaic of light-and-dark patterns, but her attention kept returning to the pavement. It was wet but other objects in the area were not. She rubbed her forehead trying to make sense of it all.

It hit her like a powerful punch to the sternum. Her breath caught in her lungs. She reflexively stumbled backward and collided with the building. The pavement had been hosed down to wash away the blood—Duncan's blood.

Her legs gave out, but she refused to sit on the ground. She stood erect and pushed herself off the wall. This was no time to be squeamish. Too much depended on her. Kearney was waiting in the ladies' room with Tito's gun, but he couldn't stay there. Sooner or later a security guard would come upon him. She had to find Detective Ramos's car and get them out of there.

She stepped forward. Her arms swayed back and forth with each step as if lead weights hung from her wrists. Both legs quivered as if they were made of jelly. She commanded them to keep her upright and keep going. After two more steps forward, she staggered to the left and stopped. Swaying like a reed in the wind, she fought the urge to return to the wall and rest. It wasn't just about her. Kearney was depending on her to get them out of there. She took another shuffle forward. Another sidestep for balance.

She hit the Unlock button on Detective Ramos's key remote. Nothing. His car had to be there somewhere. Three more steps forward. A step backward for balance. Her body begged for rest. Dispirited, beaten, and depleted, she gave into her body's demand. A short rest couldn't hurt.

With a dragging gait, she lurched toward a stack of wooden pallets. Her legs buckled. She sank into the dark shadow of the pallets where the wet pavement absorbed all the light. With her back against the wall, her deadened arms fell to the pavement on either side of her. Her chin dropped to her chest as if her neck could no longer support her pounding head.

Visions of Duncan smiling and saying, "*Joi d'vivre*" taunted her. The words, "Marry me, *nena,*" echoed from the depths of her memory. His validation of her place in the militia warmed her. "You've earned your place at this table."…"Marry me, *nena.*"

She recalled her words to him, "Are you angry?" and his loving response, "Not at you." She longed for his muscular arms around her to love her, comfort her, strengthen her.

"Marry me, *nena.*"

Dennis Maurice Archer, I will marry you. Come back to

me. Tears left salty tracks on her throbbing, swollen cheeks as she cried big, shuddering sobs. She raised her leaden arms, flopped them across her bent knees, and laid her head on them. With Duncan's words, "You're not going anywhere without me," ringing in her ears, she emptied her soul in the dimly-lit, deserted loading area—where this catastrophe began. Where her life with Duncan ended. *Come back to me, mi corozón.*

She didn't know how long she sat there, alone with her memories of Duncan, when a motorcycle started up somewhere to her left. Startled, she raised her head to see a single headlight at the opposite end of the docking area. The short rest gave her beat-up, exhausted body the energy to stand. Her arms were freed from their imaginary weights. Her legs were still rubbery, but standing was easier than it had been when she exited the building.

The driver revved the motorcycle engine.

She looked around and picked up a discarded two-by-four. Perfect. She wobbled four steps forward, one back. She locked her knees and braced herself.

The Japanese motorcycle whined toward her. With the two-by-four held along the outside of her leg, she waited for the right moment. One shot, that's all she would have. She tried to calculate the speed of the bike and the speed of her swing, taking into consideration how fast, or slow in this case, it would be. In the end, she let her instincts rule.

The motorcycle was thirty feet away. Twenty feet. She raised the two-by-four. Ten feet. She swung the board and clotheslined the driver.

The rider flew backward and hit the pavement. The bike continued forward. On its own, without a rider to keep it upright, it swayed first one way then another, and finally crashed onto its side, engine racing.

She walked toward the bike, scuffing the heels of her boots, unable to lift her feet. This was it. This was hers and Kearney's ticket out of this place. She heard the motorcyclist moaning. She didn't care.

She had set her course. Get the bike. Get Kearney. Get out of there.

The motorcyclist spoke. "Joan, wait."

She spun around. Hot blood raced through her veins as she lumbered toward the man on the ground. She reached him as he was pulling off his helmet.

"You were going to leave without me," she said through clenched teeth.

"No. I was going to hide the bike then try to find you," Kearney said as he struggled to his knees. He sat back on his heels and held his head in his hands.

"You were going too fast. You were going to fly right by me. You were *leaving*." Standing over Kearney with clenched fists, she looked up at the star-filled sky and said, "I am such a fool!" She turned her attention back to Kearney and kicked him in the ribs which sent him sprawling onto his side, groaning.

"I could have gotten out of here a long time ago." She leaned over him and pointed her finger for emphasis, even though he wasn't looking at her. "But everything I did, every move I made, was to save us *both*. But when *you* get wheels, you're only thinking of yourself. Screw Joan, right?"

"You took so long getting back to me, I thought you were captured or arrested or dead. I didn't know what to do."

"You didn't see me standing there?"

"No, really, I—"

"Okay. It's dark and you're a dumbass. So let's say you *didn't* see me. So then, which is it Kearney? You were going to hide the bike and look for me, or you thought I was compromised?"

"Both. Joan, believe me, I wasn't leaving you."

Kearney flinched when she raised her leg to kick him again. "You are the most despicable man on the planet." She thought twice about it, lowered her leg, and plodded toward the sound of the screaming motorcycle engine. No backward steps now. Her anger propelled her toward the bike and escape.

"I wouldn't leave you," he called after her.

Her slow but steady pace toward the bike never faltered.

"Wait. You're all I have left of Duncan."

She stopped and turned slowly. "What? What did you say?"

"You're all I have that connects me to Duncan," Kearney

cried openly, making no attempt to hide his tears.

Forgetting her fatigue and her pain, she stomped back to Kearney. "How dare you *mention* Duncan's name?"

"I'm sorry. The loss must be hard for you."

"*Me*? This isn't about me. You are so loathsome, so abhorrent that Duncan's name merely crossing your lips disgraces him. He had more honor in his pinky nail than you have in...than you've had in your whole life."

Kearney flinched, thinking she was going to strike him again. Instead, she raised her hand and shook her head, dismissing him and everything about him. She turned on her heel and walked away.

Still kneeling, he called out to her again, "Joan."

She kept walking.

"Wait, I have a message for you from Duncan."

When she continued walking away without acknowledging him, he sat back on his heels, pressed his fingers into his eyes, and hung his head.

After pushing the bike up onto its wheels, she climbed on, and gunned the engine. She spun the tires into a U-turn, and sped out of the parking lot.

She stopped at the chain link fence where the Demon Brotherhood had blocked the ATF's entry with a rental truck hours before. Leaving Kearney didn't seem right. All she had gone through, all she had sacrificed to save him, she couldn't leave him behind now. The mission wouldn't be complete. *Leave him. He was going to leave you. Let the feds find him. Better yet, call them and tell them where he is.*

She engaged the clutch, turned the throttle, and sped toward the main road. But she couldn't shake the feeling that she was leaving Duncan behind. Joan pressed her lips into a thin line. She *did* leave Duncan behind. And now she was leaving someone else behind. She locked the wheels. The bike skidded to a stop. The engine puttered beneath her.

Kearney said he had a message from Duncan. A message? From Duncan? *It's a Kearney mind game. Leave him. Do not look back. Go. Now.* She raced toward the main road and stopped where the service road intersected with it.

Her curiosity got the best of her. She turned the bike around and headed back to the docking area where she found Kearney still on his knees, his head in hands, just as she had left him. She squelched a pang of sympathy. *He doesn't deserve anything from you.* The bike was fifteen feet from Kearney before he looked up.

"So I'm the only connection you have to Duncan?" she said over the puttering engine.

Kearney nodded.

"And, why should I care if I'm *your* only connection to Duncan?"

He looked up and said, "Because he would want you to."

She read his lips as much as heard his voice over the motorcycle engine. "And how do you have a message for me from Duncan? He was all but dead when I left him."

"It's from before. A month or so ago, he made me memorize a phone number and a name. He said if something happened to him, to tell you to call the number."

"What's the number and name?

Kearney rattled off the number. "You have to ask for Jack Daniels and—"

Joan pulled out Detective Ramos's gun and pointed it at Kearney. "You think this is a time for jokes? You are one fucked up bastard." She thumbed back the hammer on the revolver. "That's it. I'm not dealing with you anymore."

Kearney flinched and covered his head with his hands. "It's not a joke. I swear. Don't shoot me."

"And what's preventing you from making the call?"

"You have to give him the code name he gave you."

"What name? Duncan never gave me a code name."

"He told me he did. He said he told you the name you should use to identify yourself."

"What name?" she asked no one in particular. The hand holding the gun slowly dropped to her thigh. "What name?"

Kearney shrugged.

She thought back to the day Duncan had come to her in the basement of the house they had shared. She was working out after she and Kearney had saved the two Demon Brotherhood bikers in the desert. At the time, she thought he was comparing her to Rosemary when he said, "Your name should be Rose."

The words were so clear, she twisted on the bike, expecting to see Duncan standing behind her, arms folded across his chest, smiling at her. She snapped her head around the other way. Except for Kearney, she was alone in the docking area. The voice had been so clear, so—real.

Joan tucked her chin to her chest and took several deep breaths. To stop the quivering spreading across her chin, she covered her mouth with the back of the hand holding the gun. *I left Duncan behind.* She carefully placed the hammer against the cartridge and holstered the gun.

She drove the bike in two circles around Kearney then stopped in front of him. "I want to run you over and leave you here to die. You know that, right?"

Kearney didn't answer.

After a long pause, she said, "You despicable piece of shit, I should have my head examined for doing this." She nodded her head toward the seat behind her. "Get on."

CHAPTER 32

T he safe house was just as Joan had left it—grungy, dark, and uncompromised. As morning light chased away the shadows of the night, she and Kearney manhandled the bike into the small kitchen area in the back of the vacant store. After making two cups of instant coffee on the propane camping stove, they stood in the light of a Coleman lantern looking at each other. Both of their faces were swollen and purple, unrecognizable. But they knew who and what each other was.

She broke the silence first. "I stocked the place with all kinds of camping stuff so we wouldn't leave a utility paper trail."

Kearney nodded and took a sip of coffee. His eyes were fixed on hers.

"There's a first aid kit under the sink and towels and soap and stuff in the bathroom." Her eyes darted around the room—not wanting to rest on any one thing. Especially not Kearney. She struggled with the downturned corners of her mouth.

He watched her eyes and took another sip of coffee.

She cleared her throat. "There are bunches of sweat suits in a pile in the front store area. I bought them at—" Her façade crumbled. Her voice cracked. "—Good Will."

Kearney set down his coffee, approached her, and enfolded her in his arms.

She allowed him to hold her while she let the tears flow. Her body shook as loud sobs escaped her throat. Her legs weakened, but he didn't let go. After several long minutes of clinging desperation, her sobbing slowed. She looked up at him and saw the agony on his face and the tears in his eyes.

"You're crying, you big wuss." Her heart dropped. How could she have been so self-centered? "Kearney, I'm sorr—"

Duncan had been his best and only friend in the world. His sense of loss had to be as great as hers.

"It's okay," he said, pulling her into his arms again. "We both loved him. We'll get through this together."

Her voice was muffled against his chest. "That doesn't mean you're any less of a wuss."

"Wuss is my middle name."

Realizing she really didn't know anything about Kearney, she asked, "What *is* your real name?"

"You don't want to know." He gave her a little squeeze, released her, and reached under the kitchen sink for the first aid supplies.

ひゑひゑ

After cleaning up and rendering first aid to each other—with lots of admonishments to stop whining—they dressed in the sweat suits from Good Will. Kearney rolled out two sleeping bags in the front area that used to be a Ma and Pa candy store.

Standing in the middle of the dimly lit room, morning light filtering through the brown paper over the front windows, Joan stared through watery eyes at the remaining sleeping bags. She wished Duncan was there to claim one of them.

"Joan," Kearney said and, when she looked at him, he patted the sleeping bag on his right.

She plopped down with her back against the dusty, yellow wall and slid her feet into the bag. Leaning forward, she hugged her knees.

"Let's try to get some sleep," he said.

Without a word, she slid into her sleeping bag and turned onto her right side, facing away from him. She stared at the brown paper on the windows and heard him slip into his sleeping bag.

Praying for sleep and the resulting release from the ache that filled her body and her mind, she felt what was left of her tears slide down her face.

She said aloud to herself, "Maybe he's not dead."

Soft words answered her. "False hope is worse than dealing with the truth."

Joan twisted to look over her shoulder at Kearney. "I mean, he wasn't dead when I left him. Maybe Dee Dee didn't shoot him. Maybe those gunshots were something else. Maybe someone got him some medical attention—" A sob caught in her throat. *Someone other than me.*

"That's a lot of maybes."

"I left him *behind*, Kearney." Fresh tears streamed down her swollen face.

"You did what you thought was right at the time."

"My last words to him were that I would come back for him. I didn't." She rolled onto her right side. "I didn't go back."

"You couldn't."

"He would have come back for me."

"Maybe."

She spun to a sitting position. "What do you mean *maybe*? He would have come back for me."

"I've known him for a long time through every struggle imaginable. Believe me, if the roles had been reversed, he would have done *exactly* what you did. Ex-act-ly."

She threw herself onto her side, facing away from Kearney again. "He would have come back for me."

She tasted the blood as she bit her lip in anger. Damn Kearney. *Duncan would have come back for me. He would have found a way. And I should have found a way, too.* She thought through the whole evening, beginning to end. Nit-picking her actions. Rewriting the scenarios to create a way to get back to Duncan. They all crumbled under scrutiny. She should have gone back to him, but she had been overcome by rapid-fire circumstances. In the end, she came to the bitter conclusion that *should have* wasn't the same as *could have*.

She swallowed hard and twisted to look over her shoulder at Kearney again. He was sitting with knees bent, elbows on his knees, head in his hands. When she stood up, he looked up at her with glassy, red-rimmed eyes. She slid her sleeping bag over so that it touched his. After sitting down next to him, she pulled his right arm around her shoulders.

Laying her head against his shoulder, she said, "Tomorrow we'll make plans for our getaway, but right now, tell me something about Duncan from before I met him."

ᕠᕠᕠ

Duncan looked around the hospital room, rested his eyes on the needle in his arm, then followed the tubes upward to the IV bags. In the hallway, a woman was telling someone that the repositioning of the chest tube and the insertion of a second tube had been successful. While the woman reported there was no injury to the aorta or pulmonary vasculature and babbled other medicalese, Duncan looked under the sheet and fingered the tape around the tubes that drained excess body fluids from his chest. The woman in the hall went on to say that the post-operative CT scan showed extensive pulmonary contusion, but the bullet had not severed any major veins or arteries.

Duncan relaxed. *In other words, I'll live.*

Whoever the woman was talking to was granted a few minutes to talk to him.

He turned his head to his right and, when he did, a well-built man swaggered through the door. The man flashed a badge.

"You may not remember me," the man said.

"Special Agent Woyzeck of the CDL Task Force, Pittsburgh Office," Duncan rattled off. *The man I beat the shit out of a couple years ago for hurting Joan,* he wanted to add, but thought better of it. This man might have some important information. No sense pissing him off from the get go.

The federal agent smiled. "You have an excellent memory." He flipped shut the billfold that held his badge and put it into his front jacket pocket. "You gave us a run for our money, that's for sure. I have to talk fast before the nurse comes in and tells me to leave."

"Dee Dee. How is she?" Duncan asked.

Special Agent Woyzeck frowned and shook his head. "She shot at us. We had no choice."

Duncan groaned inside. He had been alert when the ATF agents came upon them. He gave up, but Dee Dee didn't. She died defending him—just like Joan had asked her to do. Afraid of the answer he might receive, he asked, "And Joan?"

"That's what I need to talk to you about."

Duncan clamped his eyes shut and groaned aloud. He made it through alive—for what? To live, knowing he was alone on the Earth? Though physically separated, knowing she was alive would have made his wretched future worth living—even behind bars. He clamped his throat around the lump that threatened to halt his breathing, resisting the urge to rip out the IV needle and the chest tubes and try to make an escape. Maybe the agents would end his life so the pain would stop. His hand gripped the bedrail.

"The carnage in those buildings was substantial," Special Agent Woyzeck was saying. "Tito Orrozco is dead—looks like your girlfriend's handiwork—we won't know until we get the ballistics report back. With the head of the snake severed, the rest of the group has scattered, given up the fight. We're still trying to piece together the chronology of the events, but Joan was not among the dead."

Duncan's eyes flew open. He scanned Agent Woyzeck's face for misdirection or cruelty.

"You can make it easier on her if you tell me where she is," Special Agent Woyzeck said. "She's considered armed and dangerous, so I can't vouch for her safety if she's found by other law enforcement officers. If you tell me where she's hiding out, I guarantee you I will bring her in unharmed. You want to help Joan, right?"

Duncan nodded.

"Do you think she and Kearney would be together?"

Duncan closed his eyes and smiled inwardly. A warmth surged through his body as if the sun had broken out from behind dark-gray storm clouds. In those few words, he'd learned a wealth of knowledge.

Joan was alive, and she was free. He'd taught her everything he knew about disappearing in plain sight. If they found her, it would be pure luck. Kearney was free, too. And the feds had no idea where either of them was.

"I don't know where she is," Duncan said.

"C'mon, you two must have talked about what you would do if things went south."

"She's probably at a safe house."

"Tell me where it is and I'll go get her. You have my word, she won't get hurt."

"Only the security chief knows where the safe house is," Duncan said.

"Who's that?"

Duncan smiled. "Joan."

"You never discussed its location?" Agent Woyzeck leaned in toward Duncan and raised his eyebrows as if they were two buddies drinking at the local bar. "No pillow talk?"

"She was professional twenty-four-seven."

"Do you think she and Kearney are together?"

"Nah. Those two are like a mongoose and a cobra. I'd bet the ranch they went separate ways."

If they *were* together, the feds would never find them. Although Kearney could be creepy, CIA operatives weren't called spooks because they liked to scare people. If they didn't want to be found, they ceased to exist. Gone. Untraceable. Not even a breath in the wind.

"Look, Archer, by the time you're well enough to travel, the extradition papers will be signed and you'll be on your way back to Pennsylvania. You'll do all twenty years you racked up before coming to sunny Arizona. And once they complete their investigation here, you'll be looking at another twenty years, maybe more. Considering your age, that's almost a life sentence."

"Tack 'em on. I'm not gonna help you find Joan."

A nurse came in and headed toward the IV bags to check them. "You'll have to leave now. Mr. Archer needs his rest."

Duncan did a double-take then pinned his eyes on Agent Woyzeck. Duncan knew this nurse, but he didn't want the federal agent getting suspicious. Things were looking up.

If the agent noticed anything, he didn't act like it. "Think about what I said, Archer," Special Agent Woyzeck said. "Joan's life is in your hands."

Damn right, her life is in my hands. She left me behind. She has a lot of explaining to do. Duncan watched the agent's back as he left the room. While Special Agent Woyzeck stood in the doorway for a few minutes and talked to two fresh-faced agents, presumably assigned to guard him and prevent his escape, Duncan turned his attention to the nurse. It was Joe-Sam's mother.

"Joe-Sam. Are they okay?" he asked.

She ignored him and fiddled with the drip regulator in the tube. He touched the edge of her blue scrub shirt with his pinkie finger.

She looked down at him with a hard stare. "They're fine—no thanks to you."

Duncan winced as if her words were a punch in the face. This wasn't what he expected, but he had to get out of the hospital.

She was his only hope. It was too late for niceties, so he jumped right into his request. After a glance at the door, Duncan whispered, "Can you help me get out of here? I have to get to Joan."

The nurse resumed fiddling with the tubes. She didn't look down at Duncan. "What makes you think I'd risk my job to help you?" she hissed.

Duncan licked his parched lips. "You don't have any reason to help me. I'm just appealing to you as a friend."

"Friend? Hah!" After a check over her shoulder to see if the guards at the door had heard her, she pulled the pillow from behind his head and fluffed it. She continued in a lowered voice, "I spent all my energy keeping my boys out of the motorcycle club. For what? So you and Al could drag them into your vile underworld. Because of you, they are in hiding. I have to steal time to see my sons." She slipped the pillow back behind Duncan's head. "I should report to the agent outside the door that you asked for help to escape."

Duncan didn't say anything. She was right. She was the last person in the world who would help him.

He had to think fast. If she reported him to the agent, they'd bump up security and he'd never get away.

The nurse poured water from a plastic carafe into a plastic cup. "Because of you Joseph and Samuel have to be in hiding—probably for the rest of their lives," she said in a hoarse whisper as she removed the paper covering from the straw and put the straw into the cup. She leaned in and brought the straw to Duncan's lips. "But because of Iron Angel they are in hiding and not locked up in some jail with hardened criminals. She shut down the headquarters in time for them to evade the authorities. I know that act left her without the support they were giving her. She was selfless. I don't owe you shit, Duncan, but I do owe her. And she loves you, although only the Lord knows why."

Duncan looked into her eyes. "So you'll help me get to her?"

The nurse raised her voice so the agent outside the door could hear her. "You'll have to ask the agents if you are free to walk the halls, Mr. Archer." She straightened the light-weight blanket and tucked it under his ribs. "Against my better judgment, Al has a plan." She glanced over her shoulder. "He wants to do it soon, maybe as early as the day after tomorrow."

❧❧❧

Duncan waited for the elevator doors to close. The IV needle was only taped to his arm to make it look like it was inserted into his vein. Slumped in the wheelchair, he looked like a tired, beaten man on his way to physical therapy. As soon as the doors slid shut, he jumped up and punched the federal agent in the abdomen. The physical therapist hit the agent in the throat with the aluminum case containing Duncan's patient records—only he wasn't a physical therapist, he was one of the Demon Brotherhood. The biker bound the hands of the agent with plastic ties and removed the agent's Glock 19 semi-automatic handgun from the holster at his waist.

After grabbing the small .38 cal handgun from the agent's ankle holster, he inserted a barrel key, compliments of Joe-

Sam's mother, into its slot on the elevator panel. They had full control of the elevator car. Duncan stopped its descent and changed direction. He pressed the button next to the number five, the top floor. Washed out from the minor scuffle, he leaned against the wall of the elevator car to the left of the door.

When the doors opened on the fifth floor, the biker peered into the deserted hallway—this floor had been closed down and vacant for over a year. He hooked an arm under Duncan's armpit and guided him around the moaning federal agent.

On the way out of the elevator, Duncan pushed the L button. "This will go directly to the Lobby so you'll be near the ER," he said to the agent before the doors closed.

He didn't have anything against the agent. The man was doing a job and just wanted to go home to his family at the end of his shift. Like Duncan wanted to get to Joan.

He and the biker hurried down the empty hallway. Their footsteps were the only sounds as they headed toward the stairs to the roof. With each step, Duncan's energy drained from his body. He dug down deep inside for the grit and fortitude to get to the roof, although he wasn't looking forward to what awaited him there.

They reached the steps. After a brief stumble, when Duncan caught his toe on the edge of a step, they pushed on the door that opened to the roof and the cool darkness of an autumn desert evening. There was a slight breeze, and the fresh air revitalized him as the biker steered him to the left. He didn't see it until he was right on top of the apparatus. Waiting for him, resting on the gravel rooftop, was an olive-colored sling. The three-foot-by-six-foot piece of vinyl looked barely strong enough to hold his weight.

"You okay?" the biker asked.

"I've been better." Duncan looked down at the sling with apprehension. "Let's get this over with."

"Lay down on the sling. I'll strap you in, and when I motion to our buddies on the other rooftop, you'll zip line over to them."

Duncan lay down on his back, feet toward the edge of the roof and watched as the biker tightened and buckled the straps

across his legs and chest. Good thing he had pants on underneath the hospital gown.

"Ready?"

Duncan gave him a thumbs up.

"Keep your arms inside the sling. As soon as you hit the
other rooftop, I'll be right behind you, so no screwing around
over there. Okay?"

Duncan nodded and, a second later, he was hurtling across
the gap between the two buildings, completely at the mercy of
the people working the zip line. He liked calling the shots and
had never liked putting himself in the hands of others, but he
had to get to Joan. He would have jumped across the chasm to
get to her—whatever it took, including getting strapped to a
flimsy piece of vinyl and flying into the darkness.

The wind took his breath away as the sling picked up
speed. And just as quickly as it had begun, waiting hands captured the sling and stopped his forward momentum. Like a
NASCAR pit crew, the unidentifiable strangers—wearing
black haskies—unbuckled him, threw the straps aside, and
pulled him from the sling. Just like the biker had warned, he
zipped into the disembarking area as Duncan stepped clear of
it. In seconds, the biker was free and they were headed to the
southwest corner of the roof.

The pain in Duncan's side turned from a dull ache to full
blown, rib-racking pain, but it wasn't enough to stop him, or
even slow him down. The escape wasn't over. He still had to
get off this roof and onto the wonderful, hard-packed earth that
beckoned to him from below. One more dangerous leg, and it
would turn into a cat and mouse game—on the ground.

A haskie-wearing woman pulled off the hospital gown and
rolled down the pant legs of Duncan's camouflage-colored
pants that he had concealed underneath it. He took a sweatshirt
from another person's hands and slipped it over his head. A
black windbreaker followed. He slid his feet into combat boots
without taking the time to lace them.

"Duncan, over here."

Duncan looked up to see a young man with slicked-back
brown hair and a goatee. A great disguise, but he recognized

Joseph—or Samuel. He never could tell them apart. He opened his arms and winced as the younger man hugged him for all he was worth.

"Good to see you again, Duncan," the twin said. After three pats on the back, he broke away from Duncan. "We gotta go, so climb aboard."

Duncan looked at the metal bracing that supported a black, delta-shaped vinyl wing inches above his head. He eyed a motor that looked like it belonged on a lawnmower rather than a flying machine. "Won't this make too much noise?"

Joseph smiled—Duncan decided to think of him as Joseph until he knew for sure which of the twins he was. "We made some modifications," the kid said. "This is a *stealth* ultra-light. It won't make any more noise than an electric toothbrush. Listen." Joseph pushed up the sleeves of his hoodie, reached toward the control panel, and pushed the ignition button. The motor started the first time and whirred in the darkness. "Climb in. Get comfortable."

With the biker's assistance, Duncan slid into the rear seat of the contraption. He was surprised at how comfortable it was. After locating the foot supports, he leaned back against the custom-leather bucket seat between the pilot seat in front and the muffled, whining motor behind him. The biker handed him the strap for the shoulder harness and lap belt.

As soon as he was buckled in, Duncan looked up at Joseph. "Let's fly this toothbrush."

Joseph flashed a smile, climbed into the front seat, and secured himself to the ultra-light.

The biker leaned over and pressed the side of the agent's Glock into Duncan's chest. "You're the gunner. Good luck." After heavy clap on Duncan's shoulder, he turned toward the pit crew on the roof, making small circles in the air with his hand. "Let's go. Everybody off the roof. Disperse. Disperse. Disperse."

As the ultra-light slowly picked up speed, Duncan did a quick check of the Glock's magazine. When he looked up, a wave of dread flooded over him as the two-foot high lip on the edge of the roof sped toward them, but at the last minute, Joseph had them airborne. When he looked back at the rooftop, it was empty. The zip-line apparatus was disassembled and gone, as were his aiders and abettors. The ultra-light hummed along steady and sure. He was in good hands. He relaxed, settled into his pain, and thought of Joan. When he closed his eyes, he could feel her arms around him, holding him tight, saving him from his past.

Like birds in flight, they whisked through the air above the flashing lights of police and emergency vehicles racing in the opposite direction. Joseph banked left and the flashing lights were no longer in their field of vision. A short eight-minutes later, after a hard bounce, the ultra-light landed in an open area of a cemetery east of the Phoenix city limits. They slowed to a snail's pace and crept toward a black hearse.

Before they came to a complete stop, shadowy figures appeared out of the darkness and raced toward the newly arrived aviators. Through a mental fog from the pain and exhaustion, Duncan watched as the haskie-wearing men and women grabbed the metal frame and released the latch on the shoulder harness that held him secure in the bucket seat. Suddenly, Grisly Adams in a black suit, white shirt, and somber gray tie elbowed his way through the crowd of people and offered his hand.

"Welcome, Duncan," Little Al said. "I'm your next leg. I don't fly well, so we'll be staying on the ground from here on out."

Duncan smiled a thin, weak smile and grasped the meaty hand offered to him. "I didn't know they made suits that big."

The big biker chuckled and lifted Duncan to his feet. Little Al slid his beefy arm around Duncan's back. When his legs wobbled and gave out, the biker supported him as they walked toward the back of the waiting hearse. "Hope you don't have claustrophobia," Little Al said as he opened the back of the big black car.

Duncan settled into the coffin—lid open until it needed to be closed. Little Al squeezed into the driver's seat and turned the ignition key. He looked at Duncan through the rearview mirror. "What's your final destination?" He gave a quick snort, evidently amused at his wordplay.

"Yonkers, New York," Duncan said without hesitation. "Where's the other twin?"

"A friend of an uncle's cousin's brother-in-law has a hunting cabin in the Ozarks, and Samuel went ahead of us to get it ready. We're going to stop off there until you're strong enough to make the rest of the trip. Are you up for that?"

"Roger that. At least we're headed in the right direction." Duncan ducked his head to peer through the heavily tinted windows. He pulled back a gold brocade curtain with shimmering tassels across the bottom. "Who were all those people back there? I thought I recognized some of them, but the others—"

"Bikers. Ranchers. Patriots—"

"Patriots?" Duncan winced as he shifted his weight in the coffin. He squinted to see through the tinted windows that only reflected his unshaved, tired-looking face back at him. "Where were they when we were in the thick of things with *La Espada*?"

"Not everyone is a soldier, Duncan." Little Al looked both ways then drove the big hearse onto the street. "It seems everyone now wants to help. Flip-off the authorities. Change the direction of local politics." He glanced in the rearview mirror at Duncan. "You and Iron Angel are folk heroes."

Duncan snorted and relaxed back into the coffin.

EPILOGUE

As Joan entered an office in downtown Yonkers, a tanned man placed both hands on the desk and pushed himself to his six-foot-one-inch height. The man had light-brown hair with flecks of gray, neatly combed straight back from his face. He was about Duncan's age. And like Duncan, he had a stocky, muscular physique that showed through his pinstriped shirt. He wore a rose-colored tie, and she wondered if it was in deference to her code name, or if he was simply comfortable with his masculinity. The loosened tie at the neck, with the top button unbuttoned, gave him a casual, approachable appearance. The brown eyes were direct, and she felt them soaking in every detail of her as she crossed the short distance between the door and his desk. He held out his hand.

Kearney skimmed past her, barely missing bumping into her. He had his hand extended in front of him. "Durham, you old dog, how long has it been?"

"Hey, Milton. Too long," the man behind the desk said as he took Kearney's hand and glanced back at Joan.

It was obvious the two men knew each other well, but the smile of the man behind the desk now looked forced and his tone was not as enthusiastic as Kearney's. He glanced past Kearney at her a few times as if he really wanted to talk to her.

Something tugged at her memory, but indifferent about talking to either man, Joan turned her attention to her surroundings. Framed photographs covered the walls. Upon closer examination, she recognized them as typical soldier photos. A couple men kneeling in front, a few more men standing in the back. Some of them smiling. Most wearing sunglasses. All had automatic rifles slung at angles across their chests. One photograph of four soldiers standing shoulder to shoulder caught her eye. It hung at the end of a line of photos, closest to the desk. Joan wandered toward it.

The man standing second from the right, smiling broadly, was Duncan. Younger eyes, thinner build, bushier hair. It was him. She leaned forward to get a better look. As she reached to touch the spot on the photo that was an image of her late lover, the man behind the desk addressed her. Before turning, she closed her eyes and pressed her fingers on her lower lids to stop the stinging and to keep the moisture from overflowing.

"That's us when we were young and wild. We were invincible." The man moved from behind the desk, and she noticed he had a slight limp. "At least we thought we were invincible. I stopped soldiering when I got injured, but Archer, he couldn't stop. It was in his blood."

"I know," Joan said in a quiet voice.

If only they could be together again, she would support him. Support any and all of his endeavors. They would fight side-by-side. She'd have his back and he'd have hers. *If only...*

She pinned her eyes on Duncan's image. The room around her receded into the background. She choked on her next breath—she didn't have any photos of her and Duncan together. Tears welled up in her eyes. Her nose stung.

The man was now behind her, slightly to her right. "You can have this photo, if you like." He reached over her right shoulder and removed the framed photo from the wall.

"Oh, I couldn't," she said, but when it was offered to her, she took it. She stared at Duncan's young, smiling face. A tear escaped and plopped onto the glass at his feet.

"By the way," the man said, "I'm Jeb Durham."

Joan wiped the tear from her cheek, juggled the picture, then accepted his offered hand. His handshake was firm, and she felt the warmth of his hand in hers. They locked eyes.

Two days earlier, when she had finally made the call, fully expecting it to be a practical joke, she heard the secretary announce the company, Durham Security. And when she had asked for Jack Daniels, there was no surprise, no accusation of a prank call.

Her code name, Rose, seemed to expedite the transfer of her call to Mr. Durham.

Something that had been niggling at the back of her mind hit her full blast. She turned on Kearney. "Your name is Milton?"

He had been rolling up the sleeves of his shirt. He stopped mid-fold, eyes on Joan. "Yes."

"Former CIA interrogator. Fugitive. You—" She pointed her finger at him. "You're Milton Probst, *The Magician.*" She squinted her eyes, as if she were seeing him for the first time. "You were nicknamed the magician because so many prisoners suspiciously disappeared after you were assigned to interrogate them. As in poof—gone. *That* Milton Probst, right?"

Kearney stilled. "Yes."

She sucked in a breath and shook her head. "So that time in the Constitution Defense Legion, when you interrogated me— I'm lucky to be alive."

He crossed the room and reached out to her, to stroke her arms. Make contact. "No. It wasn't like that."

She brushed him aside with a sweep of her arm and changed the subject. Waving a finger back and forth between Jeb and Kearney, she said, "You two *know* each other?"

"We were in Angola together with Duncan. The 'Three Blind Mice' the locals called us," Kearney said.

Joan turned her scrutiny to Jeb. "And you, what's with all the spy versus spy crap?"

Jeb ignored the question and waved her toward one of the comfortable, padded leather chairs that faced his desk. "Please, Joan, have a seat. We have to discuss the disbursement of Archer's estate. He left you two-thirds, and one-third to you, Kearney."

Joan sank her fingers into the back of the brown leather chair. "Two-thirds of what? Duncan didn't have a pot to piss in."

Jeb smiled, flashing a charming dimple to the left of his

mouth. "If that's what you think, you are going to be pleasantly surprised. *Very* pleasantly surprised."

Joan slid into the chair as her body went numb.

❧❧❧

Jeb watched Joan as she disappeared down the hallway to the ladies' room in the Chinese restaurant he'd suggested for lunch. He rubbed his upper lip with the side of his right index finger as he contemplated the story Kearney told about the final battle in Phoenix. The slight tilt of her head and squint in her eyes during parts of the story suggested either Kearney was embellishing or out-and-out lying. But Joan had not corrected him. She was a class act.

He turned his attention to Kearney. It was obvious he was interviewing for a job with Durham Security—not the legal, storefront portion of the business. Security and loss prevention was merely a front for the kind of security Jeb really did. The covert part of Durham Security made its money by correcting the wrongs the judicial system was too inadequate, convoluted, or corrupt to get right—a modern version of the Samurai or Knights Templar.

Jeb was more interested in the kind of woman Joan was. It was simply a matter of juxta-posing Kearney's account of the events in Phoenix with what Archer had told him about the woman in his life.

"So that's the woman who breeched Archer's defenses," Jeb said. He leaned toward Kearney on his right. "How did she do it?"

"She didn't do anything. The first time Duncan met her he recognized something of himself in her. At least that's what he told me."

Jeb glanced down the hallway that was now empty. "So what's her deal?"

"What do you mean 'deal'?"

"She hates you, yet she tolerates you."

Kearney fingered the salt and pepper shakers. "She doesn't hate me, exactly."

"No, she *exactly* hates you," Jeb corrected. "Why is that, Milton? Or do you prefer Kearney?"

"Call me Kearney," he said. "As for her dislike of me, well, a couple years ago—" He leaned forward, placing his elbows on the table, still fingering the salt and pepper shakers. "—I may have interrogated her a little too...uh...rigorously."

Jeb resumed rubbing his upper lip with his index finger. "Is that right?"

"And she may be under the impression I was going to leave her behind, you know, at the end."

"Yet she saved your ass."

"She didn't actually save me. The bad guys were dead. They weren't coming back."

"Is that right?" Jeb continued to rub his index finger on his upper lip as he scanned Kearney's face—every angle, crease, and blemish.

"All she did was cut me loose. I would have gotten free in time."

"You haven't changed a bit from the lying CIA puke I knew a decade ago. You, my friend, give honorable operatives a bad name." Jeb leaned back in his chair as he crunched thoughtfully on some fried noodles before continuing. "If she hates you so much, why didn't she just leave you there? Why didn't she just take off and save herself?"

Kearney shrugged his shoulders. "The mission of the extraction teams was to get me out if everything went into the weeds. Things went into the weeds. She got me out."

"In other words, in spite of her antipathy for you, and in spite of the whole team being wiped out, she completed the mission?" He popped another fried noodle dipped in hot mustard sauce into his mouth. *Is that right?*

He reached for the stainless steel teapot and poured tea first in Kearney's cup then his own. He picked up the cup in Joan's empty place and filled it. Before continuing his inquiry, he smoothed out a wrinkle in the white table cloth then set down the teapot. "It must be difficult hanging around with someone who openly hates your guts. Why bother? I mean, why put up with it?"

"Duncan would want me to stay with her. You know, help her get over the PTSD. She would be a mental mess if I didn't help her through the rough spots."

There it was—the tell. The minute flinch in the corner of Kearney's mouth. The extra blink. He was lying. *Mental mess, my ass,* Jeb thought as he turned his attention to the fried noodles and dipped a fingerful of them in hot sauce.

"Or is it because she was going to get Duncan's money?" Jeb watched Kearney's face as he popped the fried noodles into him mouth.

"I didn't know there was any money," Kearney said truthfully. "All Duncan said was, if something happened to him, give Joan the phone number with the instructions to wait two weeks, use the code name he gave her, and ask for Jack Daniels. That's all I knew."

"What did you think it was about?"

Kearney shrugged. "Assistance in disappearing. Fake passports. I don't know."

Jeb sipped his tea, watching Kearney over the rim of the white cup that looked tiny in his large tan hand. A slow, crooked smile crept across his mouth. "You old dog, you don't want to live alone." Kearney started to protest, but Jeb continued before he could say anything. "Why doesn't she tell you to get lost? If what Archer said about her is true, she wouldn't need a mook like you hanging around."

"She says I'm her only connection to Duncan. As long as I'm around, she can feel his presence. It's loony, I know, but Duncan's death hit her pretty hard. Once the reality of his death sank in, she went off the deep end, and she's been out of it ever since. She wouldn't have gotten through these last couple weeks without me."

There it was again, the micro-tightening of the corner of Kearney's mouth. The tell.

"Off the deep end. Is that right?" Jeb sipped the green tea in his cup. *And yet, the three blocks over here, she studied every pedestrian, every car, every rooftop. Off the deep end, in a pig's ass.* Some jobs required a woman's touch. He could use a woman like her.

"I know what you're thinking," Kearney said. "You want to

put her to work on one of your teams. Forget about it. She's turned over a new leaf. No more killing. Now me, I've got some skills…" His voice trailed off as he followed Jeb's gaze.

Joan appeared at the far end of the dining room. A waiter struggled with the folding stand to hold the large, serving tray he held over his shoulder. She opened the stand for the waiter, flashed a smile at him, then headed toward the table where Jeb and Kearney sat.

"Warrior Imperative Number One—help the troubled, the adrift, and those in need of assistance," Jeb recited to no one in particular. He watched Joan saunter toward him in her graceful, leonine way. While rubbing his right index finger along his upper lip, he leaned back in his chair. "Turned over a new leaf. Is that right?"

About the Author

After 22 years in the Army, Janet McClintock exhaled and settled down in Pittsburgh. She has completed two novels of her four-part *Iron Angel* action series, the first of which, *Worst of All Evils*, was released by Black Opal Books on November 8, 2014. She is in the process of writing the third book in the series.

Action comes easy to McClintock. Over the years, she has owned motorcycles and horses and driven a tractor trailer across the country. She has trained in various martial arts over the past 38 years and is currently training in Kali and Jeet Kun Do. She is also a certified Edged Weapons Combatives Instructor.

If you liked *Hottest Places in Hell*, please take a minute to go to Amazon.com and leave a review. Reviews to an author are like tips to a waitress.

You may contact the author by leaving a message at her website: janetmcclintock.com or on Twitter: @JanetMcClintock.